THE BURIED CIRCLE

Also by Jenni Mills

Crow Stone

THE BURIED CIRCLE

Jenni Mills

Harper
Press

HarperPress
An imprint of HarperCollinsPublishers
77–85 Fulham Palace Road
Hammersmith, London W6 8JB
www.harpercollins.co.uk

Love this book? www.bookarmy.com

First published by HarperPress in 2009
1

HB ISBN 978-0-00-725122-3
TPB ISBN 978-0-00-729267-7

Typeset in Minion with Photina MT display by
Palimpsest Book Production Limited, Grangemouth, Stirlingshire

Printed and bound in Great Britain by Clays Ltd, St Ives plc

Mixed Sources
Product group from well-managed
forests and other controlled sources
www.fsc.org Cert no. SW-COC-1806
FSC © 1996 Forest Stewardship Council

FSC is a non-profit international organisation established to promote the
responsible management of the world's forests. Products carrying the FSC
label are independently certified to assure consumers that they come
from forests that are managed to meet the social, economic
and ecological needs of present or future generations.

Find out more about HarperCollins and the environment at
www.harpercollins.co.uk/green

I sought for ghosts and sped
Through many a listening chamber, cave and ruin,
And starlight wood, with fearful steps pursuing
Hopes of high talk with the departed dead.

Percy Bysshe Shelley,
Hymn To Intellectual Beauty

Time wounds all heels.

Groucho Marx, John Lennon,
and others, including Margaret Robinson

In memory of my father, Robert Mills, who flew
1916–78

and my mother, Sheila Mills, who danced
1921–2007

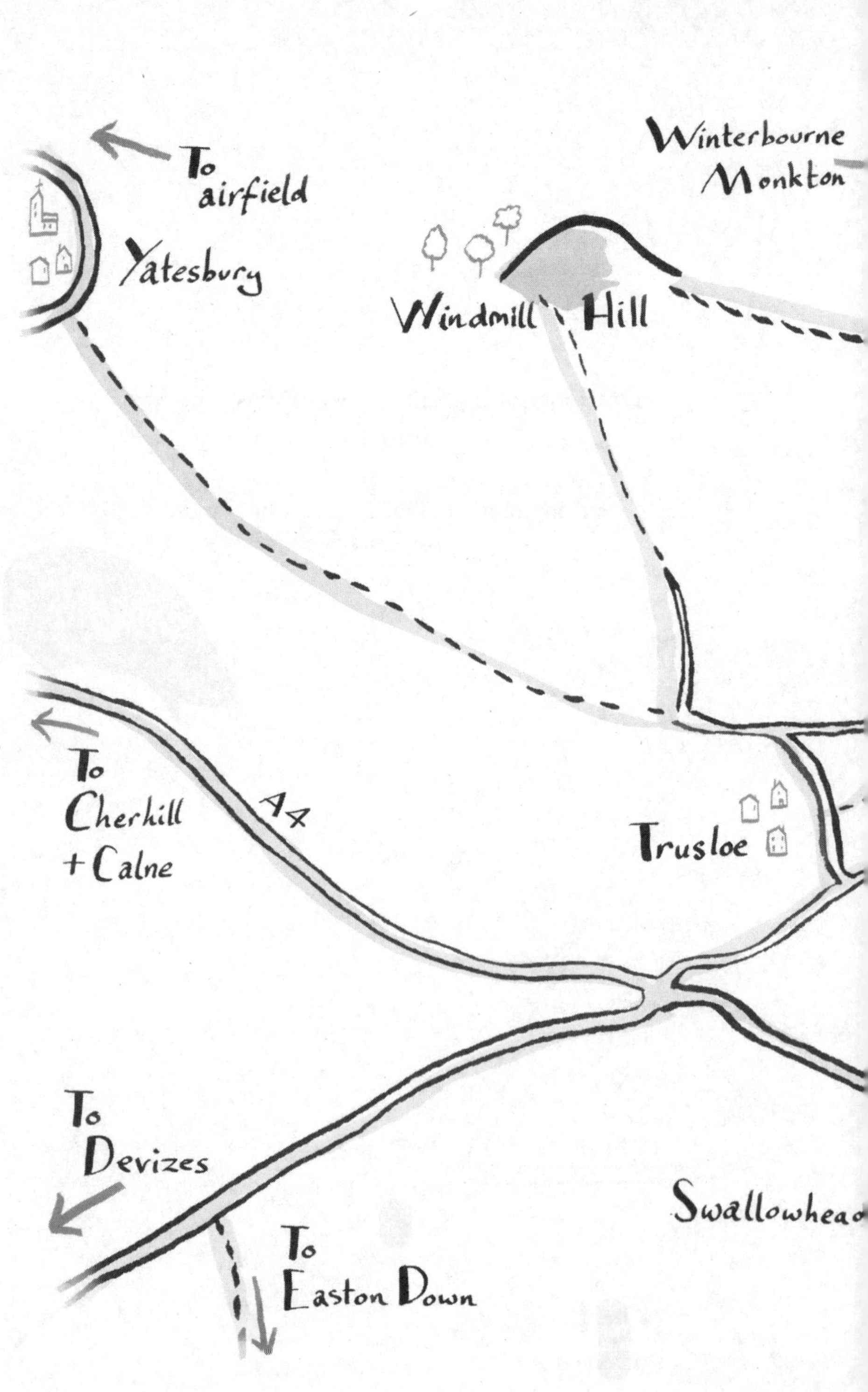

To airfield
Yatesbury
Winterbourne Monkton
Windmill Hill
To Cherhill + Calne
A4
Trusloe
To Devizes
Swallowhead
To Easton Down

PART ONE

Memory Crystals

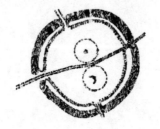

'History, archaeology, it's all moonshine, really. We're only guessing.'

Dr Martin Ekwall,
interviewed on BBC Wiltshire Sound

1942

'Don't be afraid,' he says. The Insect King. 'It's only a mask.'

Eyes like a fly, elephant's trunk that's long, rubbery . . .

'It's only a mask,' he says again.

'I know it's a mask,' I says, braver than I feel. But there's masks and masks. I've seen masks. I've seen what happens in the moonlight in the Manor gardens.

'Frannie . . .' It's only a whisper, so I'm not sure if it came out of his mouth or out of my head. He's at me now, pressing himself against me, and I'm feeling all the bits of him, long gropy fingers and the hard poky bits. There's a glow in the sky, something burning near the railway yards, searchlights over Swindon, the banshee howl of the warning, and the anti-aircraft batteries have started up.

'Take it off,' he says.

'The mask?'

'Your fucking robe.' At least, I think he says robe.

'Coat.'

'Whichever.'

'A bit nippy for that.' I'm trying to keep it calm, trying to be funny, pretend I'm in control, because this isn't what I meant to happen. He gives me a push, quite hard, and I'm up against the stone. It's cold against my back, like moonlight, and scratching at me like fingers through the thin material of my coat. There's really nowhere to go now.

I would be afraid, but I won't let myself. You can't let them have everything. You can't let them have your fear. You got to keep a bit of yourself. I'm going to put my bit where it's safe, a long way away from here.

Beech trees, black against a silver sky. Somewhere else the real moonlight is pouring down. Bombers' moon. A killing moon. Planes like fat blowflies trekking high above the Marlborough Downs. I take myself away, as far as I can, trying not to feel the burning down there, fingers, hands, other things, feels like there's lots of them all at once, wanting a piece.

A voice whispering again, *Frannie, Frannie.* It's terrible dark. There's a smell of rubber, thick and choking. Hard to breathe. An awful slick, oily smell of rubber . . .

CHAPTER 1

Lammas, 2005

'I don't want to do it,' I said. 'It's too dangerous.'

'Don't be ridiculous. The shots will be fantastic. You'll love it. Unless you'd like us to use someone else on the series?'

The usual blackmail. If you're experienced enough to do the job, you can say no. If you're not quite twenty-five, and desperate to claw a foothold in television, you'll do anything. I made one last pathetic attempt to get him to change his mind. 'Seriously, Steve, I've never filmed like this before. I'm not properly trained. If this was the BBC, the hazard-assessment form would have it flagged up as a major risk.'

'There's a harness, Indy. You'll be strapped in.'

'My legs'll be dangling.'

'What's happened to your balls?'

'My balls, if I had any, would be dangling too.'

So, my legs *are* dangling. My non-existent testicles are dangling. My bum, perched on the edge of the open helicopter door, has gone entirely numb. Below me is – well, if I were a proper cameraman I'd be better at judging these things, but I'd say a good six or seven hundred feet of nothing. Below that is hard Wiltshire chalk, with a skimpy dressing of ripening barley. The helicopter's shadow races across it, a tiny black insect dwarfed by the bigger shadows of the clouds.

Steve, crouched behind me, taps me on the shoulder. I turn my head towards him, very, very carefully, in case even this simple move-ment unbalances me and I go tumbling out to become another shadow on the chalk. He's saying something, but the wind and the noise of the rotors snatch his voice away. He makes cupping motions with his hands by his ears.

He wants me to put the earphones on so I can hear him – he's wearing a set with a microphone attached. Like I have, too, only mine are round my neck and not on my ears yet, and to put them on I'm going to have to let go of my death-grip on the door frame.

With *both* hands.

I send a signal from brain to fingers to unprise themselves. Nothing happens. Fingers know better than brain what's sensible. They're going to stay firmly locked onto something solid, thank you very much, until someone hauls me back safely into the interior of the helicopter and there's no more of this dangling.

Steve taps me on the shoulder again. Maybe if I try just one hand at a time?

My left thumb, fractionally more adventurous than the rest of my hand, comes free. Right. That wasn't so bad, was it? Clear proof it *is* possible to move and not fall out of the helicopter. In fact, now my thumb's no longer involved, the fingers are really not doing that much to secure me, so I might manage to let go altogether that side . . .

Very good, Indy, but one hand doesn't seem to be much help getting the headset onto my ears. All I've achieved is to get my hair into my eyes. Should have tied it back more securely. The headset has knocked the pins outs. I can't see. Perfect moment for the helicopter to bank and drop down towards Pewsey Vale.

Oh, God, I'm going to fall out . . .

Steve's hands gripping my ribs, hot breath in my ear. 'Let GO!' he yells, practically rupturing my eardrum. The shock loosens the other hand. 'I've GOT you.' His arm snakes round my waist. 'Now put the fucking headset on.'

'OK.' Not that he can hear me until I do. I could spout a stream of hangover-distilled vitriol and the wind would whip it straight out of my mouth into nowhere. 'I hate you, you spotty little toilet-mouth. I despise the fact you walked straight out of a media-studies degree and into a job as a producer just because your father was a foreign correspondent for ITN, while I've had to spend two years hoovering the coke off the edit-suite floor. I loathe that you get to tell me what to do, although I'm the more experienced of the two of us and you're far and away the biggest twerp I've yet met in my admittedly not extensive media career. In fact, right now, because you made me do this horrible, scary thing, I'd be delighted if you leaned over too far and tipped yourself out of the bloody aircraft.'

Of course, I never would say it, don't really mean it (not *all* of it, anyway), but imagining it has made me feel a whole lot better. I fumble the headset off my neck and onto my ears, using it as a kind of Alice band to keep my hair off my face.

'Everything OK back there?' Ed, the pilot, his voice tinny through the earphones.

'Marvellous.'

'Fine.' Steve and I speak at the same time, both of us lying through our gritted teeth. He wants Ed to think we bear some resemblance to a professional TV crew; I want the man I slept with last night not to notice I'm a gibbering wreck.

Steve – the man I *didn't* sleep with – retracts his arm. 'Comfortable now?'

Comfortable doesn't seem to be in it, but I feel more secure, and can admit it would be pretty difficult to fall out. Tough webbing straps are digging into my shoulders. They join in a deep V at the waist, meeting the belt that circles my middle and the strap that comes up from the groin. I'm very glad indeed, now I come to think of it, that I don't have testicles, though to be truthful, life would be less painful without breasts. Wrapped in layers against the wind chill, even though it's August – a duvet jacket I borrowed from Ed over two fleeces, and thermal long johns under my jeans – I could still use more padding under the chafing straps.

'Ready for the camera?' asks Steve.

'No.'

'Look, you'd feel more balanced if you rested a foot on the strut. That's what most cameramen do.'

'Steve, I'm not most camera*men*. I'm not six foot three. I'd have to be leaning right out of the helicopter for my leg to reach. You saw me try when we were still on the ground.' I'm taller than scrawny little Steve, but that's not enough – though it might have something to do with why we haven't hit it off on this series. The main trouble is that Steve considers himself an expert. He's been aerial filming more often than I have – which means he's been out exactly once, and that must have been with a cameraman who had legs long enough to span the Severn Crossing.

'Well, whatever.' His real concern is how steady the shot will be. We both know we should have hired a footrest to screw to the helicopter's landing skids, but it would have cost too much. 'Now, can we please get a bloody move on? The budget only runs to two hours' filming up here.'

Budget is, as usual, to blame for everything. The only job my limited experience (and lack of famous father – *any* father, for that matter) qualifies me for is assistant producer/researcher/camera/dogsbody at Cheapskate Productions, a.k.a. Mannix TV, who are making an entire series (working title: *The Call of the Weird*) on the televisual equivalent of about two and a half p. Today we are filming episode four, 'Signs in the Fields', which is about Wiltshire's world-famous crop circles, after Stonehenge the county's main tourist attraction. In fact, one year a farmer with crop circles in his field took more money from visitors than the ticket office at Stonehenge.

It took some doing to screw enough money for aerial filming out of the digital channel that commissioned the series, but crop circles can't be fully appreciated from ground level. As it is, most of the programme will be made up of interviews in the back bar of the Barge Inn, on the Kennet and Avon canal and right in the heart of crop-circle country, with avid cerealogists, as crop-circle investigators are called. They will tell us (I know because as the series' researcher I've already spent several hours listening to their theories) that only aliens could be responsible for such intricate and portentous patterns. It is simply not possible that such a primitive civilization as our own could have produced them. How *could* they have been made by humans? they ask, plaintively and rhetorically.

Well, I know the answer to that too. You need a thirty-foot surveyor's tape, a smallish wooden plank, and a plastic lawn roller, obtainable from any good garden centre. I watched John do it, one moonlit May night in 1998, with a group of his friends who call themselves the Barley Collective. I was supposed to be the lookout but I was laughing so much that an alien mothership could have landed behind and I wouldn't have noticed. The bizarre thing is that since people like John came out in the 1990s to admit they trample out the crop circles – gigantic art installations, the way John sees them – more people than ever have become convinced they can't possibly be man-made. Apparently there's a sociological term for it, John says, something to do with disconfirmation leading to strength-ened belief, an idea that also lies at the heart of most religion. I gently put it to one of the cerealogists at the Barge that I'd seen it done, and he almost punched me.

Our time aloft this afternoon is limited, thank God, so limited I doubt we'll achieve half of what Steve plans. He can't afford to hire a proper cameraman – or a proper camera-mount, for that matter. Any minute now he's going to thrust into my unwilling hands a DVC – digital video cam – secured only by a cat's cradle of bungee cords. Financial constraints also dictated the choice of aircraft. We're crammed into the back of a helicopter operated by 4XC, the CropCircleCruiseCompany, proprietor a wild Canadian called Luke, chief pilot his best friend Ed, with whom I made the enormous mistake of getting off with last night. Also in the helicopter are five paying passengers, three Americans and a Dutch couple, enjoying one of the aforementioned CropCircleCruises over Mystic Wiltshire. That way Steve hired flying time at a cheaper rate.

If I live, I'll light a candle to the Goddess.

'Crop circle coming up at two o'clock.' Ed's voice in the headphones. The helicopter lurches as three blond heads, a black ponytail and a bald spot all lean to the right to get a good look.

'Jesus Christ, will you take the fucking camera off me, or we'll miss it,' snaps Steve, pushing the DVC in its sagging net towards me.

'Relax,' says Ed. 'We'll catch it on the way back.' Almost as crazy as his friend Luke, who was drinking tequila shots last night in the pub, but fortunately more sober, and he seems to know what he's doing. More than I can say for my esteemed director. For a moment I can feel sorry for Steve, trying to live up to his father, the famous name a curse tied to his inexperienced neck. I caught his expression while Ed and Luke were strapping me in, back on the ground. He looked like a little boy splashing in the bay, suddenly realizing that's a big grey fin circling the lilo. Under other circumstances, this should have been fun, but he's terrified we'll fail to come back with any usable footage.

'The best circles aren't here, anyway, they're at Alton Barnes,' adds Ed, levelling the chopper. All I can see of him, if I twist in my harness, is the back of his neck, dark brown hair sticking out under his headset and over his collar. Hair into which I laced my fingers last night. I close my eyes with the embarrassment of it: what was I thinking? And if I'd known he was married . . . 'I'm going to head north first, to fly over Avebury for these guys.'

My stomach lurches, my gut contracting with the scary falling feeling of coming home.

Avebury: state of mind as much as a landscape. The place my family came from, where my grandmother was born and brought up – until the old serpent entered Eden, as Frannie used to say. A place I never lived in, apart from a few weeks one long-ago summer, but entering the high banks that enclose stone circle and village has always felt, in some strange way, like coming home.

Below us, the summer fields are gold, ochre, tawny, separated by knotty threads of green hedgerow. I'm getting used to the dangling now; it's almost – but only almost – exhilarating. We fly over the Kennet and Avon canal, a brown ribbon winding away into the after-noon heat haze, little matchbox barges meandering along it, while the helicopter gains height to rise over the escarpment. I can see the long, double-ridged scar of the Wansdyke, an ancient Saxon boundary, bisecting the Downs, then the land folds and drops away and already there's the ridiculous pudding that is Silbury Hill jutting out of the fog in the distance, so unmistakably not a natural feature that you can understand why CropCircleCruiseCompany makes money out of people convinced it was plonked there by aliens.

I bring the camera viewfinder up to my eye, and Steve's hand grips my shoulder, helping to steady me while I get used to the weight.

'Looks fabulous on the monitor,' comes his tinny voice, breathless with relief. 'We couldn't be luckier with the weather, could we? Shame about the haze – makes the horizon a bit murky.'

'Can you give me a white balance?' I say, and he leans over me, inhumanly unworried by the yawning void, holding a piece of white paper in front of the lens. I make a quick adjustment, set the focus to infinity, and film the ground like a gold and green carpet being pulled away beneath us. Slowly tilt up to reveal Silbury and the whole damn distant shebang, humps, bumps, ridges and secrets you can only see from above, fading into a wash of pale umber that then shades into an overhead blue so intense it hums. Through the lens, height, motion and scariness are pared down to beautiful. OK, I'm a bit ropy still on the technicals (did I remember to set the toggle switch to daylight?) but *this* is what I'm good at, composing a picture: colour, angle, geometry.

Euphoria unexpectedly fills me, and I can even admit the sex last night was good; not to be repeated, but maybe forgivable. Guilt sneaks back with the memory of his fingers strapping me into the harness, and I enjoyed that too – why do I get myself into these scrapes? I should have made it clear before breakfast: I don't do married men, full stop, after a nasty experience with a tutor at college – but there wasn't time for conversation.

The helicopter loses height as we fly towards West Kennet Long Barrow – 'Just like a big vulva,' says one of the passengers, the American woman, as I tilt down so it fills the frame – and then banks to the

11

right, so my lovely shot ends abruptly in the clouds. I can hear the gnashing of Steve's teeth because we've missed a close-up. We cross the A4 – 'The old Roman road,' calls Ed – and come over the green shoulder of the hill. A sigh comes out of me. There, at last, the first white tooth of the Avenue. I hadn't even noticed I was holding my breath. The rotors are saying it: home, home, home. The image in the viewfinder is blurry, the wind pricking water into my eyes. England's full of little exiles, and one of them happened at Avebury, for my grandmother, sixty-something years ago. One of them happened there for me, too, in 1989, so both of us were, in our own way, expelled from Eden.

Get in the van, Indy. Now

As far as blood relations go, Frannie is all I have. Grandfather, mystery man: not only did I never know him but neither did his daughter, born at the end of the Second World War after he was killed in action. Mother: well, best not to go there, but let's just say she died, abroad, when I was in my early teens, having left me with my grandmother when I was eight. Father: itinerant Icelandic hippie my mother met in a backpacker's hostel in Delhi, and never saw again. That was how I came to be called India. Could have been worse – Mum had been doing the world trip and I might have ended up with any name from Azerbaijan to Zanzibar.

We're almost there, following the Avenue as it marches up the hillside. From above, the double row of stones looks tiny, but at ground level most are taller than a person. A single figure is walking between them, a dog racing ahead, then wheeling back to jump at the legs of its owner.

'This must be the way they would pro-cess,' comes a Dutch accent, female, in my headphones, separating the syllables. 'Up from the Romans' road, led by their priestess . . .'

Only a few thousand years out, not to mention one or two other errors, like there were no roads, unless you count the Ridgeway. And as for priestesses – well, I wouldn't mind betting the boys were in charge back then, with the Neolithic equivalent of Steve leading the party. I swing the camera round – 'Great shot,' breathes Steve, watching the image on the monitor wedged behind the seats – and pan along the course of the reconstructed Avenue, as we approach the village.

If Silbury Hill is an upturned pudding through the camera lens, Avebury is a bowl, an almost perfect circle of grassy banks and a deep ditch, surrounding a vast incomplete ring of stones. Five thousand years or so ago, those banks would have been gleaming white chalk, enclosing an outer circle of more than a hundred megaliths, with two separate inner circles, north and south, and more scattered sarsens within. Half the stones are missing now, like rotted teeth, some replaced with concrete stumps. Two roads meet near the middle, cutting the circle into quarters, and the village straggles along the east–west axis, a scatter of cottages half in and half out of the circle.

'This is Avebury,' calls Ed, moving up a notch into archaeological-tour-guide mode. He told me, last night, he's doing a part-time MA in landscape archaeology with a view to getting into aerial survey. 'Similar age to Stonehenge, but bigger – biggest stone circle in Europe.'

'It's like a giant crop circle, isn't it?' says one of the Americans. 'D'ya think it coulda been, like, a signal to the aliens?'

Ed grunts in a way that could be roughly translated as *For Chrissake, beam me up, Scotty.* Down below, dots of colour between the stones mushroom into people as the camera zooms in. There's a gathering over by Stone 78 – the Bonking Stone, so-called because it's conveniently flat – probably a handfasting. Someone is beating a small drum, arms moving rhythmically and flamboyantly, the sound inaudible above the noise of the rotors. I zoom in further, but it isn't John.

'We'll make a couple of circuits,' says Ed. 'I'll go in as low as I can but the National Trust run the place and they don't like us doing this. Ready? Hang onto your hats.' The helicopter suddenly banks steeply, throwing me forward. The camera tries to tear itself out of my hands and I feel like I'm about to be diced by the webbing straps. There's a dizzy glimpse of wheeling megaliths between my legs.

No. No. 'Hold on. We can't do this.'

'Won't take long, Indy. The Trust won't have time to identify us.

Tell 'em you bought the footage in. You and Steve can slo-mo the film
and it'll look gorgeous . . .'

I don't care about the Trust or the fact we're filming without a
permit. We're going round the circle widdershins. Anti-clockwise. The
bad way.

*Always respect the stones, girl. Sunwise, that's the way you goes round
the circle.*

'Can we go the other way?'

'What?'

'The other direction, I mean. Clockwise.'

'Don't be ridiculous,' says Steve, witheringly. 'You're on the left
side of the 'copter. We have to go anti-clockwise, or you'll be pointing
the camera at the fucking sky.'

He's right, of course. And if I press the point Ed will think I've
gone barmy. The passengers don't seem to be concerned that we're
going widdershins. And they're all probably right – what does it matter
if we go the wrong way round?

Except – I never have.

Call me superstitious, but it's the way I was brought up. *Respect the
stones, girl, they go sunwise, so should you . . .*

But, as with everything on this production, it seems I have no
choice. Widdershins it is. I point the camera away from my dangling
feet, and hit the record button.

The helicopter banks away as a dark green Land Rover with the
National Trust's acorn-and-oak-leaves logo on the side comes tearing
up the Manor driveway. We managed three circuits and some great
pictures, though I say it myself. Hard to go wrong, really, on a day
like this – aerial shots always look fab and Ed takes the helicopter
round at perfect height and speed.

'Can we head back over Silbury again?' asks Steve.

'No way,' says Ed, gaining height so rapidly that I'm becoming dizzy.
'They'd follow along the road, and I don't want them to identify the
helicopter. Some of our work comes from the Trust and English

Heritage. You've only got about fifty minutes left for the crop circles, anyway, unless you want to pay for another hour?'

'Fifty minutes?' squawks Steve. 'We've been filming less than half an hour and I paid up front for two.'

'Factor in fly-back and landing. Every minute we're in the air counts.'

'Oh, great. Now he tells me.'

You have to feel sorry for him. Under all that effing and blinding, Steve hasn't a clue how the real world turns. He thinks people ought to feel honoured and privileged to be part of his amazing ground-breaking (ha ha) TV production. I ignore the bickering in my headset, and crane my head to look back at Avebury, disappearing behind us.

You're like the rest of us, our kid, said John to me once, in his flat Brummie voice. Yo-yos. Once Avebury has hold of your string, you have to keep coming back. He'll be in his cottage on the A4 below, smiling that twisted smile, crushing his roll-up in the ashtray. Look at Frannie. He's right. After decades of exile, my grandmother sold up the terraced house in Chippenham, where I'd grown up with her, and moved back to Avebury. I thought she was mad. Not how John sees it. He knows why I do my damnedest to resist the pull of Avebury. Her life, Indy. Don't fret. You need a massage. Or a healing. Drop in and I'll do your feet.

The Marlborough Downs slide by beneath, a golden landscape sliced by chalky white trackways and dark green hedgerows. Pale grey sarsen stones lie in drifts like grubby sheep. High as we are, the camera lens makes the ground look close enough to tap with a toe. I imagine myself tossing the camera to Steve, jumping down, hiking back to Avebury . . . It doesn't help that I feel guilty about Frannie because, in spite of what John says, I haven't been back, not since Christmas, and I was away again to London on Boxing Day. Could you stay another night? she said, her eyes full of hope. I couldn't.

Television's full of wannabes jostling to fill any vacancy. The job at Mannix represents the first time I've had anything more long-term than a three-month contract, apart from a set of rip-off merchants

15

in Leeds who took me on for twelve months' work experience, paying expenses only. (Not much in the way of those while I slept on people's floors and once or twice in the back of the cameraman's car.) No wonder I have to grit my teeth, listening to Wonderboy Steve wrangle over how much it will cost to charter the 'copter for an extra hour. I told him last week we ought to have three hours in the air, not two. But he has the senior job and the mansion flat in Hammersmith, while I've the commute from Hades every morning, sharing a bedroom in SW17 with two Australian girls doing the London leg of their round-the-world tour . . .

'Indy!' *Mein Führer* is about to issue his orders, now he's told the pilot what's what. 'Is that OK with you?'

'Is what OK with me?'

'Weren't you listening?'

'Of course I was. What I meant was, you're the director. I do what you ask me.'

'Fine. Then do it.'

Mmm. Maybe I should have been listening. Never mind, I can wing it.

The 'copter is banking again steeply. 'It's an *ankh*,' says one of the American men, pointing at something below. 'These guys built the Pyramids, you know.'

Really?

The crop circle is lovely, intricate, a series of different-sized circles centred on a long, stave-like axis – nothing like an *ankh*, as it happens. Inside each big circle are little circles of standing barley. It looks like a radial lay, the crop flattened from the inside of the circle outwards, which some cerealogists will tell you can only be produced by the down-thrust of a hovering UFO's engine. We're coming in fast towards it, the helicopter dropping down and down. Damn, the light's changed. And I'm going to get flare off the sun – but I suppose that's what Steve wants. Makes it look nuclear-spooky.

The sun goes behind a cloud.

'Shit,' explodes my headset. 'Pull out. Ed, you'll have to go again.'

I told you, Steve, but you wouldn't listen, would you? Filming always takes longer than you think.

The helicopter rises in a stomach-emptying corkscrew. 'You still want the run into the sun, Steve?' asks Ed. 'It'll be out again in a second.' Even through the headphones, his voice is a turn-on. There's something unbearably attractive about men and machines and competence. He told me last night that piloting a plane is a technical exercise, but flying a helicopter's an art form. I grit my teeth and remind myself that he's married; I don't do married men.

'Fine,' says Steve. 'But lower, this time, right? I want to feel we're just above the barley.'

'Can't go in too low at this speed or we could get yaw.'

None of this means anything. I should have been listening earlier. 'Don't we need a shot from higher up?' I ask.

'I told you, we'll do the low shots first. Low as you possibly can, Ed.'

The 'copter starts its run-in again, skimming the tops of some trees and dipping down towards the barley. 'Wooo!' yells one of the Americans. 'I *love* the smell of napalm in the morning!'

It is a great shot, though, because it feels like we're in the UFO coming in to land. The crop circle unrolls around us, immense, foreboding, the sun winking at the edge of inflated cumulus clouds as we lift again.

'There,' I say, pretty pleased with myself, if I'm honest. That looked professional.

'We have to do it again,' says Steve.

'You're joking. What was wrong with that?'

'Too high.'

'Oh, come on. Any lower and my foot'll be scraping the ground.'

'The shot will only work if we're really low. Let's go for another approach.'

'Steve, I'm not happy about going much lower.' Ed sounds uncertain. 'You can get some tricky air currents round these fields at low level, not always predictable.'

'Aw, come on,' says the *Apocalypse Now* junkie. 'Let's do it. We ain't scared, are we, guys?' There's an embarrassed silence. One of the women shifts a little in her seat. 'Just a couple of feet lower,' wheedles Steve. 'I want that *Gladiator* shot, skimming the ears of corn. You can do it. I've directed moves like this before, and it's always been fine with other pilots.' I'm sure this is an out-and-out lie: Steve's a shameless bullshitter and, if you ask me, they didn't use a helicopter for the *Gladiator* shot.

'O-*kaaay*.' Never let it be said that Ed is afraid to rise to a challenge, as I remember all too well from last night. He swings the helicopter round, and we start to drop towards the crop circle.

The shot is not so good, whatever Steve thinks. We're so close to the ground on this pass that we're losing all sense of the shape we're flying over. The viewfinder makes it appear we're travelling much faster. I tilt up to get the flare effect on the sun again, but this time the exposure's wrong and it looks like an explosion.

'Slow down!' yells Steve. 'You're fucking it up.'

For once someone else is getting the blame instead of me. But, suddenly, we *are* going slower, in a horrible, stuttery kind of motion that doesn't feel right at all. It feels like the tail of the helicopter is trying to pull away, and we're zigzagging over the flattened barley, coming closer and closer to the ground.

Nobody apart from me seems to think anything's wrong. The Americans are whooping, and Steve's yelling: 'Keep it STEADY, for Christ's sake!' But there's no way I can keep this shot steady, the bungee cords bouncing and the hiccuping motion threatening to pull the camera out of my arms altogether. I take my eye from the viewfinder, and twist round in the webbing straps to tell him so. Behind me, Steve is shaking his head furiously, staring at the monitor, oblivious to everything but the picture. I twist the other way, towards the front. Ed's shoulders are knotted and writhing under his T-shirt. I remember the feel of those shoulders moving under my fingers, but this time it's different. He's fighting the controls. Shit, something *is* wrong. The note of the engine is rising to a howl. The tail seems to be trying to wrench itself right off. The helicopter is slewing sideways over the barley like a dragonfly with a torn wing. We're going to crash.

'Going to be bumpy,' yells Ed. 'Brace!'

Now we're starting to spin. The rotors seem to be getting louder in my head – thoom, *thhooom*, THHHOOMMM, until everything else is drowned in the noise of beating air and beating blood and vibrating metal. God, the camera. If that comes loose when we crash it'll bounce around in here like a lethal beachball. I wrap my arms round it, and try to fold myself and it into a foetal curl but the straps won't let me and everything is shaking so much, the spin dizzying, like being sucked into a whirlpool. How long is this going to take, how high off the ground are we can only be a matter of five or ten feet at most we're still going too fast what happens when we come down will it blow like in the films the helicopter always explodes in a fireball I don't want to—

The helicopter hits the ground, bounces, metal tearing with an awful howl, my stomach tries to jump out through my throat, then we hit earth again and the whole thing rolls over and I'm being tumbled backwards, the camera flying out of my arms OW its whipping lead catching me on the ear and I feel sick with pain, someone's shouting FUCK FUCK FUCK in an American accent and there's so much noise, grinding, shrieking, smashing glass—

and the sledgehammer shatters the windscreen, my mother calling no no no, blood between my fingers—

All my fault. We shouldn't have flown widdershins round Avebury. I should have made them take out the right-hand door, and we would have flown sunwise—

And I'd have been underneath the helicopter now, as we grind over the crushed barley and the hard dry chalk, and the metal skin on the right-hand side crumples like paper—

And we stop.

Silence. Blessed silence. Nothing. It's all stopped, apart from a humming note that must be my ears, and the odd creak and sigh and tick of settling metal. I wait for the sound of running feet through the barley, of some sign there's someone else alive somewhere, but nothing happens, as I hang in my straps, the helicopter suspended between worlds. I'm holding my breath waiting for the real one to rush back in.

'Goddamn.' It's one of the Americans, his voice a croak. 'You OK, Ruth?' Then Ruth starts sobbing and the world is back with a bang, the others going Jeez that was close Didya see how we got caught in like a vortex? and Was it the forcefield of the crop circle that brought us down? and Ed's voice saying Is everyone all right, take it easy, we're on our side, be careful how you unbuckle and there's a groan of shifting metal and everything sways sickeningly and something falls off outside and he shouts I said be careful you fat fuck stop panicking you'll all be able to climb out through the side door there's plenty of time it's only in the movies that they blow up we came in really slowly hit the ground with hardly any force

Steve is uncharacteristically quiet.

He wasn't belted in, crouched at the back of the helicopter behind me, watching the shots unroll on the monitor. I twist in my webbing straps to see if he's OK.

He's lying on his back staring up at me, on the stoved-in wall of the helicopter. It looks like he's reaching out one hand to catch the camera, which has landed beside him, its eye pointed towards him and the red light still winking, the black plastic rim of the lens smeared with thick red. Colour, angle, geometry: all fit perfectly, all come together to centre the shot on the ugly dent in the side of his forehead.

CHAPTER 2

Autumn Equinox

'India! Been a fair old time since you phoned. Orright? Did you get my birthday card?'

'Sorry, John. Should've been in touch sooner.'

I can picture him in the kitchen of his cottage at West Overton, his feet up on the scarred pine table, setting September sun refracting through the quartz crystals that dangle at the window, making a dappled pattern of light. It's late enough in the afternoon for his lovely ladies, the middle-aged country wives who drive over in their 4×4s for reflexology and a shag, to have gone home. He'll be rolling a spliff one-handed. There'll be a home-baked loaf on the breadboard, and maybe even a rabbit suspended by its feet from the hook on the back of the kitchen door, waiting for him to skin and stew it. John grew up in suburban Sutton Coldfield, but he embraced rural life with a vengeance when he moved to Wiltshire after my mother left him. He's good at it too, maybe because he was once in the army.

'So, how's life in the big city? You running the BBC yet?'

'Not exactly. Um, John, I'm ringing because . . .'

'You OK, our kid?'

'Yeah, fine, just – wanted to ask if you think it's a good idea to come to Avebury.'

When I tell people I've known John for ever, he'll give me that look that says, *Yeah, really for ever, baby girl*, because he's a shaman and into reincarnation and all those books about how life is a spiritual journey and you'll meet up with the same group of significant people every time round. John believes the three Rs get you through life: reflexology, *reiki*, and rebirthing. He and my mother were a lopsided kind of item for about five years, though even an eight-year-old could tell the devotion was one way: all his to her. Mum wasn't the most faithful of partners. Or the best of mothers, when it comes down to it.

When John does my feet, kneading and probing and smoothing with his long reflexologist's fingers, he says he can feel two big hard knots of anger just back from my toes. I walk on my fury.

'Why shouldn't you come back?' he says. 'Love to see you. There's a band Sunday night at the pub in Devizes, if you don't have to drive back early.'

'Not just the weekend. I mean for the foreseeable future.'

'Right.' There's a pause, John holding the idea up to the light at his end, turning it carefully this way and that, as he always does. 'I thought you were involved with some big ghost-watching series for ITV.'

'UFOs, actually, and it was for a digital channel. That's been – cancelled.'

'Bad luck.'

'Yeah.'

Another pause. I can hear John taking a long, deep drag on his rollie. 'This wouldn't have anything to do with a fatal helicopter crash over Alton Barnes way last month, would it? Bunch of Americans and a camera crew, overloaded chopper?'

The tears have started rolling down my face. 'Oh, John, I've fucked up again, I've really fucked up this time . . .' Voice all choked and clotted. I'm beginning to shudder.

'Hey, hold on. Way I heard it, the pilot crashed the helicopter, not you. He'll probably lose his licence.'

'Yes, but—'

'No but. Listen, darling girl, you haven't fucked up. Not then, not now. Believe me, I'm a world expert in fuck-ups. Blame Wyrd, if you like, web of fate, will of God, karma, whatever else carries us through the night, but it was *not your fault.*'

'You don't understand. I *killed* someone. I should have held on to the camera but I didn't and it killed him, there was this *hole* in

22

his head, it was awful – I'll never get another job in television.'
I've thought this through. I ponder it every night, sweating when
police helicopters fly over the block of flats, while the Australian
girls heave and struggle with their lovers on the other side of the
thin wall. 'Who'd want me? I'm bad luck. And, oh, God, John, he's
dead, and I didn't like him very much but I so wish he wasn't dead,
he was twenty-three, his parents . . .' I keep remembering his mother's
stricken face when they came to the office to collect his stuff. Soon
as I realized who she was I went and locked myself into the loo.
'There was this piece about him in *Broadcast*, saying how talented
he was and stuff . . .'

'Hey hey hey. You been sitting on this for a month, mithering, all
by yourself in London?'

Can't manage even a yes. John takes gulping silence for confirmation. 'Listen to me. Get on the train. Don't even think about driving.
Come straight down. I'll pick you up at Swindon. We can fetch your
car some other time. Don't go to Frannie's, come to me, for tonight
at least. Then tomorrow I'll drive you back to London, load up your
stuff, and . . . maybe it's time you came home.'

There it is. The H word. A shudder goes through me, relief this
time, though mixed with something darker. Avebury tugging at my
string, reeling me back in.

Get in the van, Indy

'Do you good to hang out at Fran's as long as it takes.' John's gone
into fatherly mode, he being the nearest thing I have to a dad, Lars
(or whatever the Icelandic backpacker's name was – I've never known)
being blissfully unaware of my existence. 'She always keeps the bed
made up, she'd love to see you – there's more room there than in that
shithole of yours in London.' The voice coming down the phone line
is like the water of a hot bath. I can feel myself relaxing, letting the
warmth slip over my tense skin. 'Find a job, nothing demanding.
They're always looking for people in the café or the shop.' Easing it
all away. I can almost smell the scented steam. 'Give yourself time.
Frannie could do with some help.'

An unexpected drip from the cold tap. 'What do you mean?'

'Only that she's over eighty. Not as spry as she was. And she sold the car a couple of months ago, said she was too old to drive.'

'She told me she still walks a couple of miles every day.'

'Oh, yeah, she's up and down that path from Trusloe to the post office at Big Avebury, rain or shine. But you might see a change.' Another long draw on the roll-up. 'Anyway, that's not the point. You get your arse down here and we'll talk everything through.'

I can feel myself getting tearful again. 'John, I don't know...' Because I'm bad luck. I'm widdershins. I'm not safe to be near.

'None of us know, Indy. That's bleedin' life. Stop thinking so hard, and live it.'

A dusty golden harvest moon is hanging low on the horizon as I drive my rust-nibbled red Peugeot past the art-deco garage on the road into Avebury, two days later. Alban Elfid, the autumn equinox: strictly speaking, still a few days away, but who cares with a moon like that casting its magic?

Alban Elfid, said John in London this morning, as we loaded the back of his pickup for him to drive ahead with my stuff. Harvest home. Whatever you like to call it. A time for reflection and healing. I know you don't believe any of it, Indy, but doesn't matter, I believe it for you. You couldn't be coming back at a better time.

The road bends, passing a high bank and an enormous diamond-shaped stone, and I'm inside the Avebury circle. It gives me a jolt every time: the stones gleaming like big scary teeth in a smile that sweeps towards the church tower rising out of the trees. My route takes me through the old cottages and the circle, and out again towards Avebury Trusloe, with its grid of twentieth-century former council houses. Poor old Frannie – she'd have loved to live in a thatched cottage in Big Avebury but, buy or let, they're way beyond reach of her pension. So she's in Little Avebury, as Avebury Trusloe is known locally, with the rest of the exiles.

Past the cricket field, past the National Trust car park, off the main

24

road, and a bit of a wiggle takes me into the cul-de-sac where Frannie bought Bella Vista, a red-brick semi, after I left home four years ago. Whoever named it was incurably optimistic. It has a view mostly of identical red-brick semis and bungalows, although from the bedroom window, if someone held your ankles, you might glimpse an awe-inspiring panorama of waterlogged fields and the odd telegraph pole. Frannie adores it.

When I climb out of the car, she's already opened the front door, standing there with a beaming smile bunching the smoker's wrinkles that seam her cheeks. Suddenly I can't think why I stayed away.

'Hello, stranger,' she says, in her gravelly voice – such a big voice, I always thought, for such a small person. 'Your bed's made up. Beans and bacon for tea.'

Our ritual every year when the home-grown runners were ready in the garden at Chippenham. It was the first meal she made me when Social Services left me with her in 1989, the year she took over my upbringing. I'm vegetarian, I said to her. Bollocks, she said. Eight years old? Too young to be vegetarian. You ever tried bacon? 'Tidn' really meat.

I give her a hug, feeling the boniness of her back through her lumpy hand-knitted cardigan. I'd swear she's shrunk: I have to stoop. Her hair's cut badly – why do hairdressers always hack old people's hair as if they won't mind the shape so long as it's short? – but still the colour of sweet sherry. She seems to think I don't realize she dyes it; that I never noticed her locking herself in the bathroom every six weeks, leaving clots of purplish foam clinging to the back of the tap after she'd wiped the basin and let herself out.

'You OK?' I say to her.

'I'm OK. What about you?'

'I'm OK.' And I am, now I'm home.

I follow her along the hallway to the kitchen. Not quite so spry, maybe, but still a bounce in her step. She *is* OK.

Then I see the tin on the table.

'Not fresh beans, then?' Trying to make it casual, uneasy all the

25

same. Fran never serves tinned vegetables she could grow herself or buy fresh.

'Lor' sake, India,' she says. 'Don't you know there's a war on?'

While Frannie wields the tin opener, humming ballads from the Blitz, I go upstairs to check where John's put my things. Mostly, it seems, in the front bedroom, where the bed's made up for me. 'Fran! Mind if I shift some of my things down into the dining room?'

A clatter, a muffled 'Oh, buggeration,' from the kitchen. That sounds like the old Frannie. She comes out into the hall. 'You can't, India, I'm sleeping in there.'

'You *what*?' I lean over the banisters. She's standing at the foot of the stairs with her hands on her hips.

'John moved my bed downstairs in the summer.'

'What's the matter with upstairs?' A worm twists in my gut. I can hear myself sounding like a social worker jollying her along. 'Don't tell me you're too old to climb stairs. John said you were down the post office showing them how to hokey-cokey the other week. Left leg in, left leg out, shaking it all about like a spring lamb.'

'Lights,' she says. 'Bloody lights, can't sleep at night because of 'em.'

'Your room's at the *back*. No lights out there, apart from the people in the bungalows, and far as I remember their average age is ninety-two. Anyway, you could've moved into the other bedroom. I don't mind swapping.'

There's a guilty but defiant look on her face. 'Buggerin' lights. Keep me awake. Rather be down here.'

'What brought you back?' she asks over supper.

'Bored with London.' Steve's staring eyes, which a part of me never stops seeing, accuse me of cowardice, as well as murder, but I can't burden her with the truth. 'And to be honest, Fran, I don't think I'm getting anywhere in television. You need connections, or luck, or mega-talent, preferably all three, and I haven't any of those.'

'Don't be silly,' she says briskly, the way she always does. 'You're a clever girl, India. Don't know where you got it from, but you are. Anyway, you stay here long as you want. John said you needed a good rest.'

'I'll find a job.' I take hold of her hand as she reaches for her glass of water. Her knobbly fingers are cold between my warm ones. 'Can't ask you to support me.'

'You've no idea what money I got.' She's grinning.

'Millions, probably, all under the mattress. I don't care. I'm not going to sponge off you.'

'Well, that's a relief. Can I drink my glass of water now?'

I let go of her hand reluctantly. Millions under the mattress wouldn't compensate if I lost Fran. Then something comes to me out of nowhere.

'I've been meaning to ask,' I say.

Frannie pauses with the glass halfway to her lips. There's a wary expression in her eyes. 'Yes?'

'Grandad.'

The story I've been told is that Grandad's plane fell out of the sky a few months before my mother was born. But Fran has never talked about him, and the impression grew, during childhood, that it was better not to ask: the briefest of answers would escape through tight lips. Now I'm all too conscious that one day the opportunity to find out more will be gone for ever.

'Which one?' Her eyes have slid away from mine, and she's put down the water glass to fiddle with a bean that has escaped onto the tablecloth. Have I upset her? Surely not, he died more than sixty years ago. Then the weirdness of her response hits me.

'What d'you mean, which one? You never met my father, let alone his family.'

'Course I didn't. No bloody idea about his lot. Could all've bin in Reykjavik prison far as I'd know. Your mother had terrible taste in men. Family trait, mind.'

I take this to be a reference to my unfortunate affair with the tutor at uni, which ended in an abrupt return to Chippenham and floods of tears. Although it brought the near implosion of my degree,

Fran was amazingly non-judgemental. I wondered if she'd been through something similar when she was young, though I never liked to ask. She'd have told me not to be nosy, same as she always did if I asked anything that struck her as invasive. Personal information, in Fran's book, is something to be offered, if you're lucky, rather than extracted.

'I mean *your* husband,' I say, knowing I'm crossing a boundary from the uneasy look on her face. 'What was his name? David?' I'd seen his photograph once, when I was a kid and nosing through the drawers of Fran's dressing-table. It was in a polished rosewood box, Fran's name engraved on the lid, that must once have contained a watercolour set, though its pans were empty and scrubbed clean. Now it held only a faded watercolour sketch of the stone circle, seen through the window of one of the cottages, an early sun lengthening the shadows of the stones, and Grandad's picture. Even with the ageing parted-and-slicked-back hairstyle men affected in the 1940s, he seemed hardly more than a boy: a Brylcreemed cowlick falling over his forehead, wide, heavy-lidded eyes, and a cheeky grin. When I'd asked whose photo it was, Fran had been surprisingly curt.

Lovely chap. Navigator in the RAF. Hardly trained, then he was killed. Long time ago, though.

Killed on a bombing raid?

A flicker of impatience around her mouth. On a mission, she said firmly. Her lips pursed.

So . . .

So that was it. Sad, but it happened a lot in the war. Had to get used to it. Frannie had eyes like knives. That's why I don't talk about 'im, easier not to, see?

Her eyes have that same steely flash now. 'Davey,' she says. 'That was his name.'

'Where's he buried? You never—'

'He in't buried. He's with what was left of his aeroplane, ashes mostly. There's a headstone to him in Yatesbury churchyard.'

This is so much more than I've gleaned previously that it almost drives the gruesome picture of Grandad's cindered remains out of my head. 'Yatesbury? That's—'

'Coupla miles away, yes.'

'So . . .'

'India,' she says, 'not tonight. I'm bone tired. Don't mind if I crawl off to bed, do you?' Her supper is only half finished.

'Didn't mean to upset you.' I take her hand again.

'You didn't. All a long time ago. But I don't like digging them days up, bad time for everyone.' She pulls her fingers out of my grasp, and stands up, leaning on the table to balance herself. 'Can I leave you with the washing-up?'

The line of light under Frannie's door winks out as I sit at the kitchen table after supper, the washing-up done, turning the stem of my wine-glass between my fingers, seeing how the overhead light slides inside it and sparkles. My mother had a bag of polished stones she took every-where, arranging them some nights in a circle on the fold-down table in our travellers' van. My memory crystals, she'd say. The clear oily one with a rainbow in its heart is a Herkimer diamond. It can remember things for you: you pour thoughts into it and retrieve them later. That milky pink-banded crystal – agate – is layered, like your mind: it helps you tease out memories that are laid underneath each other. The blue *boji* stone is for healing hurtful ones. This is phantom quartz – see how there's another crystal inside it, a ghost crystal? It reveals what you've forgotten. And that black one's onyx, a stone for secrets. It will soak up your memories, the dark ones you want to hide.

I've managed to forget almost everything that led up to the moment of the crash. What time we took off, how long we were up there, what I filmed, Steve's instructions in my headset. I hardly even remember the last part, the moment when the helicopter started to spin, the sounds of grinding and tearing as it skidded on its side over the barley field. But I do remember that we spun widdershins. And Steve's eyes. I don't think I'll ever succeed in blanking out Steve's dead eyes.

Through the party wall comes the *thud thud thud* of the neighbours' stereo. It's chilly: the central heating must have gone off, though it's not yet ten. The kitchen's never warm: draughts sneak through its seams from the wind-raked fields. The previous owners were into a fatal pairing of acronyms, DIY and MFI, and the cupboards look very nice, cream Shaker style with big brown doorknobs, but close up, everything's crooked. The extractor fan in the cooker hood hasn't worked since the year zero, and if you turn on the grill, smoke pours out of the oven. Frannie hasn't done a thing to the place in the four years she's been here.

By my elbow, my mobile phone trills once. A text:

U ever going 2 call me back?

No. My thumbs work furiously. Please leave me alone.

As I come out of the bathroom after cleaning my teeth, the strangeness of Fran's reluctance to sleep upstairs strikes me. In her old room at the back the bed is stripped, the dressing-table layered with dust, nothing on the floor except my own boxes of stuff. The wardrobe is empty, apart from a cardboard poster tube leaning against the back. I shut the mirrored door again quickly. I know what's in there: my bloody mother, making an exhibition of herself.

All that can be seen in the blackness of the uncurtained window is my own reflection, backlit by a dingy forty-watt bulb on the landing. I press my nose right up to the glass. *Lights, buggerin' lights.* What was that all about? The bungalows behind are already dark. The light from our bathroom falls on the square of mole-riddled lawn that passes for Frannie's garden, neglected in a way she would never have tolerated only a year or so ago. In the distance, towards Windmill Hill, there's a single fuzzy gleam that must be one of the Bray Street cottages. Otherwise the night is a creepy sort of void.

The emptiness of Steve's stare comes back to me. Slowly, the picture that's burnt into the back of my head is changing. Now one eye's fixed on me, the other off beam and staring towards the front of the helicopter. His pupils are huge, both as bleak and black and empty as the night.

CHAPTER 3

Next morning everything seems brighter. Frannie has her hat on, ready to stump off to church with a sunny grin on her face, carrying two cans of carrot soup as her harvest offering.

'Off to do good works?'

'Being good in't what takes a body to church. You don't want to come?' Dying to show me off to her friends. My granddaughter, works in telly . . .

'I'd prefer to get straight first. Unpack, maybe go for a walk. Tell you what, I'll stroll with you to Big Avebury.'

It's glorious weather: deep blue sky, and the beech leaves shivering in a gentle wind, the first loving nip of autumn. The stones have already snagged the day's first minibus-load of visiting hippies, who are wandering through the inner circle behind the Methodist chapel-cum-tourist office. Another half-dozen people are marching fat-tyred pushchairs round the top of the banks. Frannie meets one of her friends in the high street, and the pair of them totter through the churchyard together to St James's. I sit on the bench by the lich-gate, to check the map for the route of my walk. A ragged 'We plough the fields and scatter . . .' floats from the church as I set off.

It takes me nearly half an hour from Avebury at a brisk clip. The fields either side of the broad, level track are indeed ploughed, greyish-white flint scattered across the brown earth. I'm ever hopeful that one day I'll spot a prehistoric stone arrowhead, a perfect leaf shape, lying on the surface, and every so often something catches my eye – disappointingly, when I stoop to check, always a leaf.

Yatesbury boasted an airfield used during the First and Second

World Wars, mostly for training. The RAF closed the base some years ago, and microlights fly out of there now. The church, crouched like a grey rabbit among trees, is silent; Sunday services must rotate from parish to parish. Ancient yews shade the path to its door. An old box tomb leans at an angle defying the laws of geometry. The grass between the graves hasn't been cut for a while, and the hems of my trousers are soon soaked.

It isn't difficult to find Grandad's memorial. At the far end of the churchyard there are several rows of white stones with RAF insignia. Young men's graves, blank tablets of unlived lives. Like Steve's. For a moment, I have a creepy sensation of him here too, behind me, sitting with his back against the box tomb watching me as I walk slowly along the ranks of headstones.

Grandad is about halfway along the third row – at least, I assume this is Grandad, because he's the only Davey or David among the Second World War graves. David Fergusson. Stupidly, I'd been expecting his surname to be Robinson, even though I knew that was Fran's family name. Either she'd reverted to her maiden name or maybe she's coy about him because they were never married. No big deal now, but I suppose she'd have wanted to keep it quiet then.

Blackbirds chirp and commute from yew trees to hedge. Autumn sunlight glints on dewy cobwebs slung between the headstones. Davey's is simple: his name, his age – twenty-four, making him, when he died, a year younger than I am – the date of his death, the words *In loving memory*. How little there is left to know of a person, then: not even his birth date. I didn't bring flowers, and I'm sorry for that now. My eyes fill as I imagine what it must have been like for Fran, already pregnant, hearing the news that her baby's father had been killed, somewhere over England, or France, or Germany. Not even a body to bring home and bury. Then years of coping alone, a widow in her early twenties (or pretending to be), never marrying, earning a living as a clerical assistant in a meat-processing plant, struggling to bring up a wild-child daughter who'd never known her dad . . .

The daughter. A smoky crystal twists, turns to the light, revealing a pale ghost of itself inside. Something I'd almost forgotten.

My mother's birth date. Margaret was born in October 1945.

Davey Fergusson was killed in August 1942.

CHAPTER 4

Coming out of St James's, Carrie Harper asks me if I want to have a bite of lunch with her and her sister. They always have a roast on Sundays. No, I say, my granddaughter's home now. She works for the telly, you know.

We stand there gossiping, where Percy Lawes used to set up his cine-camera back in the thirties and film us coming out of church, the women showing off their new babies and everybody wearing a hat, even us young girls. A nippy little wind gets up, rattling the dead flowers that need to be cleared from the headstones. It's a while since I took some to Mam's grave. Thinking of her, suddenly I'm in that place where all the pathways of time meet and cross and twist round on each other, like the moonlit paths between the box hedges in the Manor garden. My mouth stops working in the middle of whatever it was saying.

'You all right, Fran?' asks Carrie.

I give myself a good shake. 'Goose walked over.'

'You're a long way from the boneyard yet, Frances Robinson,' says Carrie.

But I don't know about that. Seems to me I never left the bone-yard from that day over in Yatesbury when I found him leaning on the box tomb. Seems to me there's secrets under stones: near half the circle still buried, and better it should stay that way, especially where India's concerned. But now there's people nosing round digging where they shouldn't. Them lights on Windmill Hill – there's someone up there, searching, night after night. They in't found nothing yet, but it's only a matter of time.

Sometimes I think I knows exactly who it is up there. It's him, come back again, looking for what's his.

Wherever you go, Heartbreaker, he said, you take me with you.

PART TWO

Imbolc

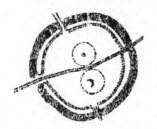

Like all prehistoric landscapes, Avebury is as remarkable for what you can't see as what you can. Apart from what Alexander Keiller started to reconstruct in the 1930s – a stone circle originally comprising about a hundred megaliths, some further stone settings within, the whole enclosed within a bank and a ditch, and the West Kennet avenue sweeping southwards from it – a number of other features in the landscape hint at what must have been a vast complex of monuments in the Neolithic period and the Bronze Age: long barrows, round barrows, and parch marks suggestive of other stone or timber circles, palisades and enclosures. A second avenue winds westwards, towards Beckhampton. A causewayed enclosure, one of the earliest types of Neolithic earthworks, sits atop Windmill Hill.

The past is a story we tell ourselves. There can be no certainties, only surmise. At the start of February, new-age pagans gather in the henge to celebrate the old Celtic festival of Imbolc. In the Middle Ages, people would have met in the village's Anglo-Saxon church, St James's, on the same date, and called it Candlemas. Both are festivals of light, of new beginnings: for Christians, Jesus lighting a candle in a dark world; for the pagan Celts a celebration of the first signs of spring penetrating the barren land, the first snowdrop, the first fat lamb suckling at its mother's teat. Do the origins of such festivals go right back to the first farmers who built the stone circle?

Dr Martin Ekwall, *A Turning Circle:*
The Ritual Year at Avebury, Hackpen Press

CHAPTER 5

Candlemas

There's a funny thing about Avebury: can't rely on mobile phones working here. But it doesn't stop me trying, faith in technology against all the odds. Coming back down the high street from the post office, I thumb out a text to John to tell him I'd like my feet done this afternoon. On the edge of the stone circle, along from the shop that sells crystals and crop-circle books, you can sometimes pick up a ghost of a signal, but today the message won't go. There are no bars at all on the display and the little blue screen says *searching*. Top marks to Nokia for encapsulating the human condition.

The closed sign is still in place on the door of the café in the court-yard between the barns. As I shake the rain off my umbrella, Corey comes bustling out of the kitchen, looking like she's been shrink-wrapped in her National Trust T-shirt, apron wound double over Barbie-doll hips.

'They want to see you in the office. Right away.'

Ouch. Am I up to this? Was sure I didn't drink that much last night, but my eyeballs seem to have been sanded, then glued into place.

'What about?'

'How should I know?' She glances at the clock on the wall. The shine off the countertop makes my head hurt. 'You look a bit rough. And, for God's sake, pin your hair up properly before we have customers in. That red's, er . . . unusual.' The nozzles of the espresso machine are already gleaming because I cleaned them yesterday after-noon when we closed up, but Corey makes a big thing of wiping and polishing each one, while I pull up the hood of my jacket again to stop the sparkle searing my eyes.

'When you come back, better tackle the toilets.'

'I did them yesterday.'

'So do them again.'

'There's a limit to how much Toilet Duck a girl can sniff.'

'Go.' She stares at my hair again. 'What do they call that colour? Blood Orange?'

A gust of freezing rain hits me in the face as I open the door again. The puddles are pitted like beaten metal, reflecting a leaden February sky. A couple of Druids are hanging around outside the Keiller museum, wearing donkey jackets over their white robes, cheeks purple with cold above their greying beards. Deep in conversation about some druidy business, they don't give me a second glance. Under racing clouds, the limes in the long avenue are threshing wildly as I walk up to the National Trust offices. Everything today is restless movement, and I'm twitching too, nervy as the snowdrops that shiver and ripple in the wind under the trees, hoping this could be about my application for the temporary job of assistant estate warden.

The offices are housed in what was once the Manor's indoor racquets court, with a mellow but utterly fake Georgian façade. Inside, a row of damp boots stands on the mat by the door. At the notice board, two volunteers, gender indeterminate, mummy-wrapped in layers of woollies and waterproofs and multi-coloured knitted hippie hats, waist-length hair on both, are scrutinizing the rota for checking the public conveniences on the high street.

At your average National Trust property, gentle old ladies and garrulous retired gentlemen volunteer as room stewards. At Avebury, an army of local pagans has been co-opted and given bin-bags, sweatshirts and a suitably spiritual title – the Guardians. They police the activities of their fellow pagans, who persist in leaving offerings around the stone circle. Next to the toilet rota is pinned a phases-of-the-moon chart. There *is* a connection: pagan festivals linked to the moon mean the lavvies get more use.

'*Told* you Cernunnos protected us.' One of the volunteers examines its partner's Gore-Texed shoulder while I'm wrestling with my wellies.

'Your coat's *bone dry*. It was tipping down while we crossed the circle, but not a drop landed on us.' A waft of mandarin essential oil (for alertness) hits my nose as I pad past them on stockinged feet into the main office.

The estate wardens' desks are a wasteland of empty coffee mugs and neglected paperwork. On the far side of the room, Lilian's head is down, stabbing fingers telling her keyboard what's what. She looks up and gives me a quick nod. 'He's expecting you.' The property administrator's door is open.

Michael's at his desk, immaculately turned out in a tweedy country-gent-ish sort of way, jacket, shirt collar peeping over the crew neck of a bobble-free cashmere sweater, which he must shave along with his chin every morning. Everybody else pads about indoors in socks, but he's in leather brogues, a spare pair he keeps at the office to avoid muddying them, polished to military brilliance. Photos of wife, children and a grinning black Labrador are aligned just so on the desktop. The distance between them, determined by some golden architectural mean, hasn't varied so much as a nanometre since I first came in September to ask for a job.

He's on the phone. It must be to Head Office, because his voice is perfectly polite but his face is all screwed up. 'First-aid kits, right,' he's saying. 'Of course we check them. Yes, regularly. But, come on, it's February. There isn't much call for Wasp-Eze in February.' He waves to me to sit down. I haul a chair over and park it on the opposite side of the vast desk. His paperwork isn't as organized as his photos. The filing trays threaten to avalanche, and the area around the phone is littered with yellow Post-it notes. One of them probably refers to me, but it's hard to read upside-down.

'I take your point,' Michael continues. 'Yes, it's windy here too. I agree, we don't want any accidents. I'll get a warden onto it right away. Though Graham's up to his eyes. Have you looked at the possibility of cover to replace Morag? . . . Right. See you at the meeting next week.' He puts the phone down, not gently, and rubs his eyes. 'Bloody-Health-and-Safety.' In Michael's mouth it has contemptuous capitals and hyphens. 'It gets more ridiculous every day. I'm an architectural historian. Checking first-aid kits every six months is a waste of my . . .' Finally, he works out who I am. 'India. Of course. Yes, I asked you to come over, didn't I?'

'Corey said . . .'

'Corey? Oh, yes, at the café . . .' He stares out of the window, brown eyes unfocused. 'You didn't see any strange Druids hanging about by the museum, did you? Strange, that is, in the sense of not the local ones we know and love.'

'There were a couple of men in frocks, looking cold.'

'Damn.' He lifts a couple of piles of paper. 'Damn, damn. Got a letter here somewhere from some bloody Reclaim-the-Ancient-Dead group. They want us to give our skeletons back to the Druids. Not that they came from them in the first place, said skeletons being five thousand years old and modern druidism going back roughly two hundred, at a generous estimate.'

'They wouldn't say that.'

He stops quarrying the paper mountain, and gives me a surprised look. 'You're not a pagan, are you?' I shake my head, and he resumes the search. 'Thank God. Bane of my bloody life. Give me a nice quiet Palladian mansion for my next job, where all I've got to worry about is room stewards dropping dead of old age. You didn't hear that, by the way. I hugely respect our Druid brethren, but that doesn't mean I'm going to hand over our skeletons. Hang on a minute . . .' He reaches for a pair of half-moon glasses. 'Mustn't forget the tree survey. Oh, Lordy, supposed to be done by next Friday. Bloody nightmare being short a warden . . .' He gets up and strides over to the door. 'Lilian! Tree survey! Get Graham onto it, will you? And when did we last check the first-aid kits?' Lilian's reply is inaudible. 'What do you mean, not in living memory? Fix it, woman.'

He sits down behind the desk again and stares. 'Now, India. Am I right in remembering you used to make television programmes?'

'Well . . .' Can't help it, I drop my eyes. There's a hole in the toe of my sock. I cover it quickly with the other foot while Michael's gleaming brogues accuse me of fudge, if not an outright fib: perhaps I was a little liberal with the facts on my CV. I conquer the urge to wriggle and force myself to meet his eye.

'"Well" meaning what exactly?'

'I was mostly only a runner and a researcher.'

'That'll do. Bloody hell, where's the bit of paper? I've had a request from a TV company about filming – here it is. They've unearthed some old cine footage of the excavations in the thirties, and want to do a programme about Alexander Keiller.'

'The ones who are holding a meeting at the Red Lion next week? I saw the notice outside the post office. "Were you in Avebury in 1938?"'

'Your grandmother was here then, wasn't she?' asks Michael. 'How is she, by the way?'

'Not too bad.' I really mean not too weird, but it's complicated to explain.

'Anyway, this media rabble wants access to the archive. I cast an eye over what we have, and it needs a tidy, in my opinion. I'm reluctant to let TV people loose in there. Would you mind sorting the box files at some point, instead of beating the bounds with Graham?'

This is a blow, because I've only recently managed to talk Michael into letting me do the odd day helping the estate wardens, who are soon to become even more short-handed when one of them disappears on maternity leave. Four months' working part-time in the café and I'm bored rigid. I'm determined to prove I'm wasted wiping tables but, alas, my BA in creative studies (described on the CV as an upper second, not altogether accurately) doesn't seem to impress. On the other hand, with the weather so bad, browsing in a cosy archive trumps litter-picking soggy plastic bags any day, not to mention the pervasive odour of Graham's socks. So I muster a grateful smile. 'Be delighted.'

'Rightio.' Michael stands up, anxious to usher me out before I start plaguing him again for a full-time job. 'Thought it'd be up your street. And ask your gran what she remembers of AK. They don't make archaeologists like him today. Shame he never finished what he started.'

As things are still quiet in the café, Corey sends me to exercise my toilet-cleaning expertise in the education-centre lavatories behind the Barn Museum. We've been visited this morning by a party of schoolkids from Salisbury. Half of them forgot to pull the chain, and one was sick in the Gents.

Still, snowdrops under lime trees. Life returns to the frozen land. I can't help my heart beating a little faster at the thought of a TV crew turning up. It sets ideas buzzing in my head. On the way to fetch a fresh bottle of disinfectant, I check out the display in the Barn Museum on Alexander Keiller's life, and help myself to a couple of leaflets to refresh my memory of the story every Avebury resident knows: how the Marmalade King bought himself a village and a stone circle.

Mop into bucket, wring it on the squeezer, shake it aloft like a ritual staff, and go cantering sunwise round the Gents bestowing my blessed droplets of disinfectant on the tiles.

Corey cashes up early. The café has been virtually empty the whole afternoon, the weather deterring all but the hardiest stone-huggers. But the day has saved its best till last. The rain has blown over and the Downs are washed in clear light. Setting out for John's, I clip the iPod on my belt, and Dreadzone's 'Little Britain' crashes into my ears.

A gust of wind conjures a vortex of dead leaves. A couple of sheep grazing among the stones lift their heads and stare at me, amazed as sheep always are at the sight of humans: life, Jim, but not as we know it. On the high street a few raw-fingered tourists are trying to capture the gap-toothed grin of the circle on their mobiles. There's said to be a stone buried under the metalled road where I'm walking. Whenever I pass over it, I feel a little shiver, crossing a boundary.

Better respect the stones, girl . . .

Frannie would tell me stories about growing up in Avebury, playing among the stones. Overgrown, then, hidden among trees and bushes. Loved them stones, we did, but we didn't think they was anything special, not until . . . She brought me here to show me where her parents' guesthouse had been, now an empty green space. Pointing down the high street. Baker's there. Butcher's further on, used to slaughter 'is own meat. That white cottage was the forge. Blacksmith was called Mr Paradise. Sam Pratt, he were the saddler . . . Wouldn' believe it today, would you? Nothin' but a post office, everythin' else for bloomin' tourists. Eyes narrowed against the smoke from her cigarette, searching for the lost village, wishing it back. Could imagine 'em coming along the high street now, 'cept they never comes back, do they? Nineteen twenties, thirties, when I were a little girl – I tell 'ee, India, thic there times was magic. Frannie tried to speak what she called 'nicely', but Wiltshire dialect crept in whenever she talked about the past. No, they never comes back, that's for sure. Not the ones you want to, anyway.

She took me to the museum, and showed me the skeleton of the little boy that had been dug up at Windmill Hill, in the 1920s, with his big, misshapen skull. She patted the top of his glass case, and said, You'm still here, then, Charlie. There was a funny smile on her face, the muscles around her mouth twitching, her jaw grinding and wobbling as if her false teeth had worked loose.

Keiller, though . . . did she ever talk about Keiller? She must have mentioned him – you couldn't talk about the village in the 1930s without reference to what he did to it, but I don't remember her banging on about him the way everyone does here, with that mixture of admiration and loathing usually reserved for figures such as Oliver Cromwell, Margaret Thatcher and Bill Gates.

I cross the main road on the bend by the Red Lion and follow Green Street through the stones, past the gap in the houses where Frannie's old home stood. The lane continues beyond the circle, eventually petering out to become a white scar on the flank of the hill: the old coach road from London to Bath, now a chalky, rutted bridleway, known as the Herepath. Thousands of years ago, it might have been another ceremonial route into Avebury. Some people think that since there were stone avenues to south and west of the circle, perhaps rows of stones ran east and northwards too. John swears that by dowsing in the fields he's found evidence of buried megaliths beside the main road to Swindon.

The skyline is dotted with spiny beech hangers – the Hedgehogs, Wiltshire people call them – planted over ancient round barrows. The Ridgeway, a track even older, runs along the top of the Downs. When dusk gathers, it can feel like the loneliest place in the world up there, peopled only by ghosts.

A small red car with European plates is parked on the verge at Tolemac – the stretch of the lane I like least. The neat, wedge-shaped plantation of pine, ash, wild cherry and beech holds a particular set of memories from my own childhood and still gives me the jitters, all these years later. Bare twigs scrape against each other like dry, bony fingers. This afternoon woodsmoke is in the air: someone's camping under the trees.

woodsmoke overlaid with the acrid smell of burning plastic, a van on fire, branches above it catching light. A cut on my hand, blood beginning to ooze between my small fingers . . .

Most of my itinerant childhood is a blur: odd moments caught in the memory crystals. My mother Margaret – Meg to her friends, but always Margaret to me – never had a job, unless you count dancing on stage with Angelfeather at free festivals. In winter we lived on benefits in Bristol, but in summer we followed the band from festival to festival in her decommissioned ambulance, painted purple. Stonehenge, Glastonbury, Deeply Vale, Inglestone Common; we wandered through Wales and stayed in tepees, we joined the women at Greenham and slept under plastic benders. And in 1989, the year they call the Second Summer of Love, we camped in Tolemac: our last summer together. I was eight. That year the ambulance had been replaced by a British Telecom van with windows hacked out of its sides and a door at the back. Because John hadn't sealed the glass properly, everything leaked if it rained.

The first thing Margaret always did when we arrived at a new place was collect up her crystals, which always fell off wherever she'd put them and rolled around when we were travelling, and arrange them in their proper places. Black tourmaline outside the door, for protection and geopathic stress, in case she'd accidentally parked on a dodgy ley-line. Citrine in the money corner, behind the passenger seat, to dispel negativity and in the hope we might actually make some dosh that summer. Rose quartz behind the driver's seat, in the equally vain hope that Margaret would find love. The irony was that she could have had love, if only she could have brought herself to accept it, from John. He'd done her van for her but she wouldn't let him sleep in it with us: he was camping twenty yards away under his old green army poncho, like a faithful dog forced to sleep outside in its kennel. Then Margaret would go out and gather wild flowers to stick in a glass of water on the fold-down table. They'd be shrivelled and wilting by nightfall, but she always convinced herself they'd survive.

'There,' she'd say, every time when she finished these rituals. 'Home.'

Behind me the red car starts up, its engine sounding like an old sewing-machine. I step off the road to give them room to pass, but it slows to a halt and the driver, a girl with hair chopped in a lank brown bob, winds down the window. She's wearing an expensive mohair sweater. Not one of the campers, then. 'Excuse me. This road takes us to Marlborough?' Her accent is Germanic.

'I'm afraid not. It ends up ahead.'

'It goes to the Ridgeway, no? It shows it on our map.'

'You can't drive the Ridgeway. It's not allowed. Anyway, you'd never make it without a four-wheel-drive. There's a farmyard further on where you can turn.'

Her thin olive-skinned face settles into petulant disappointment as she slams the car into gear. The Road Less Travelled turns out to be a No Through Road. Isn't it always the way? I get a fleeting memory of Margaret's face the day Social Services took me to

Frannie's. The odd thing is, I remember there being tears in her eyes. Perhaps I'm imagining it, because I've always assumed it was a relief to her to be rid of me.

You're too hard on her, Indy, says John.

The red car comes chugging back with part of the hedgerow attached to its bumpers. I send Margaret's crocodile tears away with it, *pffft,* evaporating into the exhaust gases that hang on the frosty air, then wish I could call them back, make the tears real, make her real too. Sometimes I find it hard to recall what she even looked like.

High on the Herepath, the air is exhilarating. Everything is still crisp and clear, a last flush of brilliance before night, though light will already be fading in the fields below. The sun's dropping fast, an egg-yolk stain seeping up from behind Waden Hill to meet it. I sit down on a sarsen. This one, bum-freezingly cold through my jeans, lives up to its geological past: a stone shaped and tumbled by ice sheets. Sheep baa somewhere below, as a farmer drives the flock into another field. Sound carries weirdly up here, especially on frosty air. John says there are places on the Ridgeway where you can hear voices from within the stone circle itself: Neolithic landscaping was about sound as well as space.

Some way off something splashes, startling me: a boot, maybe, in one of the water-filled ruts on the old chalk track. The gate at the top of the Herepath clicks as someone comes off the Ridgeway. There's a whistle, and a dog comes racing across the field, like Whip used to when I called him.

He was my dog when I was small, but I lost him at the Battle of the Beanfield. Another of the iconic moments of Alternative History: 1985. I don't really remember it. It's a story I've been told, caught in crystal. We were among a convoy of a hundred and forty travellers' vans on the way to Stonehenge, but the police put up a roadblock. Margaret drove after some of the other vans crashing through the hedge into a beanfield. And then it was like some Hieronymus Bosch nightmare, says John, smoke and rage and contorted faces, people slipping in mud and blood, Whip and the other travellers' dogs barking, screams, moans. Somebody with dreadlocks making a weird ululating noise. Overhead, the dogged *whump whump whump* of helicopter rotors. John says Margaret was holding me in her arms, but still the police kept on coming, truncheons raised, still they hit her on the shoulder as she turned away to protect me. There's a picture of John, which was in the newspaper, looking ridiculously young, blood running out of his hair and down his face into his beard, being led away by policemen in riot helmets, made faceless by sunlight reflecting off their Perspex masks. I never saw Whip again. The travellers' dogs were taken away by the police and put down.

I turn round in time to see the walker bending to pat his dog, then he strides off again down the hill towards me, the animal running ahead at full stretch, leaping the puddles. It's some sort of small hunting dog, more solidly built than Whip was, with a shaggier coat. It stops a metre short of me, and stares, panting, mouth half open like it's never seen a girl sitting on a sarsen before.

'Here, boy.' I rub my fingers together. It takes a step forward, quivering with curiosity, as its owner follows it towards me.

A dark woollen trilby jammed over light brown corkscrew curls, a long grey scarf wrapped round his neck, a blush of cold on the smooth-skinned cheeks: it makes him look hardly more than a boy, though he's probably early- to mid-twenties. The cool eyes, half hidden under the tangled fringe, hold mine for a moment, then slide away, gone before I can get out a 'good evening'. He carries on down the hill towards Avebury. Strong shoulders, hands tucked into the pockets of a brown fleece jacket, legs in mud-spattered skinny jeans. He takes a hand out of his pocket – no gloves – and snaps his fingers. The dog swivels its head after its master, looks back at me, blinks, then races off to follow him.

Reluctantly, I clamber to my feet and start to walk up to the Ridgeway, turning to catch a last glimpse of the twilight walker before he disappears below the curve of the slope. He's taking the steep, slippy bit fast, with a polka-ish sideways gait like he's scree-running. Perfect balance. Perfect arse. You have to admire.

John's home below Overton Hill is not pretty by Wiltshire-cottage standards: instead of thatch and sarsen, it's square-built of plain red brick, with a tiled roof. Living room downstairs, with a kitchen at the back, like an afterthought; two small bedrooms and a minuscule bathroom upstairs. Seventy years ago, when Fran was a girl, a farm worker and his wife would have brought up half a dozen children here.

I'm half expecting John not to be in, but the door opens almost immediately when I knock. In the living room, the stool he uses for reflexology sessions is drawn up to the sofa, and there's a green silk scarf on the floor. 'You haven't got company?'

John bends down to pick it up. 'She does that every time. Leaves something so she's an excuse to pop in and collect it.'

'Thinking she might catch you at it with one of your other clients?'

He grins. 'Does make me nervous. Sit down, kettle's on the stove.' He disappears into the kitchen, and I settle myself in front of a cheerful fire, checking first that no other female client has left a memento, like a pair of knickers stuffed behind the sofa cushions. In the corner of the room, leather-skinned drums are stacked on top of each other, next to a shelf full of drumming cassettes and books with beefy, muscular titles like *The Way of the Shaman*, *Recognizing Your Power Animal*, and *Psychic Self-Defence*.

'How's Frannie?' he calls from the kitchen.

'Still refusing to utter another word about Grandad.'

Every time I've tried to raise the subject, her eyes fill with tears and her mouth turns down. When I questioned her after seeing the date on Davey Fergusson's headstone, last autumn, her response was to suggest I'd found the wrong grave marker. Then she told me I'd misremembered Margaret's birthday. Your mother was always coy about her age, she said.

This was true, but there's coy and there's eye-wateringly unbelievable. Margaret liked people to think she was still in her thirties long after she'd hit the big four-oh, but I'm certain I've seen 1945 written down. I'd had her passport, once, with a whole parcel of other stuff that had been returned to us after she died in Goa, when I was thirteen – a stupid accident, falling off the side of a stage. That was so Margaret it can make me smile now: she was graceful when she danced, but clumsy in every other setting. I burned everything on a ceremonial pyre. Now I wish I hadn't.

John returns with mugs of tea. 'You should stop nagging her. Frannie'll tell you in her own time – if there's anything to tell. She OK otherwise?'

'Fine, I think. Except . . .' I stir mine vigorously, then remember I promised myself I'd cut out sugar this week. 'Except she keeps having air-hostess moments.'

'Having *what*?' John, in the middle of stoking the fire with another log, stops and turns round. 'Air hostess?'

'Calm, polite, smiling, but sort of empty.' I'm groping for words to describe the indescribable, but deep down, very deep down, worrying that it *is* describable, with some horrible medical term like dementia. 'I'm not sure if it's to stop me pestering her about the past, or her way of trying to conceal when she gets confused. You know how air hostesses delete part of their personality. "Please fasten your seatbelts, ladies and gentlemen, a little turbulence is not any cause for concern."'

'Know what I think?' John kicks the reflexology stool into place between us as makeshift coffee-table, and settles himself in the armchair. 'Could be TIA.'

'That some sort of airline?'

'A mini-stroke. When I was nursing, we used to come across it all the time.' After he left the army, with a bad case of combat stress, one of John's jobs was in a geriatric nursing home in Bristol. 'You find them on the floor, all in a tizz, can't remember what happened, how long they've been there. No paralysis, none of the obvious symptoms of stroke, but it wipes part of their memory. Very common.'

'You think that has anything to do with not wanting to talk about my grandfather? Like she really *can't* remember?' Relief is sluicing through me. At least John didn't suggest Alzheimer's. Maybe it won't become any worse.

'Who knows? I'm no expert.'

I hate it when he talks about Frannie as if she's ill. Makes me want to shout: You're supposed to be a bloody shamanic healer. Can't you do something? But he'd only tell me there's no healing old age. Instead I say: 'Maybe I should take her to the GP?'

John, not the greatest fan of the NHS having worked on the inside, pulls a face. 'Half the time what's wrong with people is the last set of pills the doc prescribed.' He pulls out his tobacco pouch and papers. 'Not much can be done about TIA, anyway, apart from putting her on blood-pressure medication, and she's already on that.'

'I wish she was closer to the doctor. Why'd she have to move out here, miles from all the stuff old people need?'

John's faded blue eyes meet mine, telling me I know the answer. She came back to end where she began. Where her mother and father are buried, in the churchyard at St James's. A neat little roll-up starts taking shape between his fingers. 'And how are *you*?' he says.

'Hey, you know. Same old.'

The busy fingers pause. He cocks his head on one side. 'Different hair. Red for danger, is it, this week?'

'Think it works?'

'Honestly?' He pulls a couple of errant strands of tobacco from the end of the roll-up, and stands up to light it from the candle burning on the mantelpiece. Imbolc, of course: I'd forgotten. John always lights a white candle for Imbolc. 'No. Prefer you brunette. Remember when you did it blue? Though even that was marginally preferable to the raven-black interlude.'

'That was my sad Goth phase. I was thirteen. This'll fade when I wash it.'

John settles back in his chair. The ever-changing colours of my hair, which he maintains are an indicator of the state of my psyche, and I insist are no more than fun, has long been a bone of contention between us. 'How's your new-year resolution going?'

'John. I'm hardly Feckless Young Ladette Binge Drinker of the Decade.'

'You were putting away a fair bit before Christmas.'

'You're not used to what media people drink in London. I was . . . winding down.'

He shakes his head. 'Looked more like depression to me. I was worried the helicopter crash had brought back . . . other stuff.'

'*No.*' I push down hard on a surfacing memory of my mother under the trees in Tolemac, a look of panic on her face. *Get in the van, Indy* . . . John, as usual, is spot on the button. 'Well, perhaps when I first came back . . . But no. Everything's cool.'

He grimaces. 'God, you're like your grandmother. Never willingly admit anything. I remember seeing you surrounded by cardboard boxes in that miserable flat in London and I thought, How come our India's ended up like Nobby No-Mates?'

This is really not fair. 'I had plenty of friends—'

John is a master of the single eyebrow-raise.

'It's just that in London . . . it's harder.'

'Yeah.'

I glare at him. 'I still have a lot of friends in television.'

'Those would be the ones you keep telling me you're never going to see again, then?'

'You're a complete bastard, you know that, don't you?'

We sit in silence for a while, watching the log on the fire catch, John puffing his roll-up.

'Is that pilot bloke still texting you?' he asks eventually.

'Not since I told him to piss off.'

'Right.'

'I know it hasn't got anything to do with what happened but it feels like another thing that was wrong about that day.'

'Indy, people make dubious decisions all the time without the universe throwing a moral tantrum. Forget your bad experience at uni. Sleeping with a married man doesn't always unleash the Four Horsemen of the Apocalypse.' He stands up again to relight his roll-up from the candle. 'Not that I'm recommending it, you understand.'

I glance pointedly at the green scarf. 'You shag married women.'

'I've learned to manage their expectations.' John chucks his dog end into the fire, lifts the mugs off the reflexology stool and pulls it into position. 'Can't be bothered with the couch. Get your shoes off.'

'Anyway,' I attempt to muster some dignity as I haul off my socks, 'I think I might be ready to resurrect my career in television, after all. Did you see the notice at the post office? Bloody hell, that hurts.'

'Stress always collects in the soles of the feet.'

'Fran!' I call, as I open the glazed front door into the hallway. Usually at this time of day she's in the living room watching one of those TV programmes that, by some miracle of demography, unite both elderly people and kids. Instead she's in front of the hall mirror trying on a hat like a hairy raspberry.

'Does this make me look like an old lady?'

'It makes you look mad.'

'It'll do, then.' She grins, then frowns. 'What time is it? I'm sure Carrie Harper said she'd drive me to Devizes to do a supermarket shop. Or have I got muddled again?'

Fran has a relentless social life that revolves around people from church – every one at least twenty years her junior. I check the calendar on the back of the kitchen door. Under today's date, in her shaky writing, it says, '6 p.m. Broad Hinton W.I. '.

I'm snapping on rubber gloves and plugging in the vacuum cleaner before she has her coat out of the cupboard. Never enthusiastic about housework, Fran has recently decided it's not worth the effort at all, so I grab every opportunity to clean unhindered.

'What got into you? In't you the girl I could never get to keep her bedroom tidy?'

'Sorry. Once I start . . .'

'Well, I wish you'd stop. I feel exhausted watching. You in't thinking you'll go fiddling in my room? Because don't. Can look after it meself.'

'I wouldn't dare.' There's little point in fiddling in her room, as I discovered when I tried a few months ago to find Margaret's birth certificate there. An immense old-fashioned bureau in one corner holds Fran's bank statements, chequebooks and personal detritus, and it is locked. The key is probably under her pillow, but Fran knows I'd never steal it. What a person chooses to lock away is private: that's our rule, drawn up in the years when I kept a teenage diary. 'Anyway, when was the last time *you* dusted in there?'

But I'm saying it to her back. The doorbell rings: her lift to W.I. She jams the hairy raspberry on her head, and stumps out of the front door: fully-functional Fran, because it wouldn't do to be daffy in front of her friends.

The letter is jammed down the side of her armchair in the living room, the high one she finds more comfortable than the others. Could have been there a day, a week, months, years even, creased, with a strange greasy feel that makes me think it's been handled over and over again. My fingers snagged the corner of it while I was plumping the cushions. I smooth out the paper – pale grey, torn off a pad, a curl of gum still attached to the top. Impossible to know whether it slipped down accidentally, or was pushed there deliberately, to hide it.

You have a nerve, it says. Typed, on an old-fashioned typewriter, not a computer. No address, no 'Dear Mrs Robinson' or 'Dear Frances', no punctuation.

```
Saw you in Church You have a nerve coming back
after all these yrs not even bothring to pretend
you married There are people here whom remember
why you went away to Swindon no better than you
ought to be Your dear mother would be turning in
her grave good job she didnt live to see it But
anyone with eyes in their head at the Manor knew
what was going on the Devil was at work there I
saw you call him in the garden with your five
```

```
point star and your mask You should burn up
wher you stand.
```

One final, vicious full stop.

I turn over the envelope again, pale grey to match, a brown teacup ring on the corner. No postmark, hand-delivered. It's addressed to **MISS** – capital letters and underlined – `Frances Robinson`.

I fold the letter back into the envelope and put it on the coffee-table with this week's *Bella* and the *Radio Times*. Then something – embarrassment? Fear? – makes me slide it back down the side of the chair where it came from.

CHAPTER 6

1938

'What time do you call this for going out?' my mam said.

There was a big old moon through the kitchen window, sending down splashes of silvery light like someone was chucking paint about. The wireless was playing dance-band music, Ambrose and His Orchestra, 'There's A Small Hotel', bit of a laugh really since they was playing at the Savoy. Mam was doing the drying-up, dancing round the kitchen flicking the tea-towel in time with the music, marcel wave bobbing. Da, da, diddly dit, doo. Gliding with her arms held stiffly round nothing, pretending she was dancing the foxtrot with Fred Astaire. She loved that tune.

I hung my white apron on the hook behind the door and took off the white cuffs Mam made me wash out by hand every night because we only did a proper boil wash for the towels and sheets on Mondays.

'Scrub them cuffs, mind,' she said automatically.

'I'll do them later.'

'Now, Frances.'

'I'll put them in soak.'

Mam narrowed her eyes but gave up for once. She was in a good mood because the guesthouse was full with friends of Mr Keiller, posh gents and ladies from London who were all having dinner at the Manor tonight in their evening dress, even though they was having to pay us full board. My dad insisted on that. If you want come-as-you-please, he told people, you'd be better off at the pub. But Mr Keiller's friends were rich enough not to care what they paid, and we'd had an easy time serving supper, only a man walking the Ridgeway, and a couple of mad old biddies staying with us the weekend, who held hands under the table.

'Where do you think you're off to anyway?' Mam said to me, as she hung up the tea-towel to dry by the range. A small-boned woman, she was, like me, inclined to be plump, though lately she'd slimmed down a bit. 'You're going nowhere till we've put the leavings away.' There was a twinkle in her eye.

I said nothing, and played for time by twiddling the dangly bits on the doily as I hung it over the cut-glass bowl of trifle. We had the only Frigidaire in the village, apart from Mr Keiller's up at the Manor, but Mam didn't trust it because it made a noise, and preferred to keep things in the larder. It was more hygienic, she said. Closed space like the fridge, running with water, stood to reason germs would breed. Besides, though Mr Rawlins's big Crossley generator supplied us with the electric, the wind often brought down the power lines he'd rigged from tree to tree through the village, and then we was all back to oil lamps.

'Are you meeting someone?' Mam slapped a net cover over the ham joint like she was nailing down a butterfly.

As usual, her curiosity made me want to wriggle. She couldn't wait for me to get a proper feller and bring him home. Only left school last summer, but Mam'd have me married off the minute I showed the slightest interest in a lad. She'd wed at seventeen. She'd been in service, living away from home since she was thirteen, and that was where she met Dad, though he was more than a dozen years older.

Me, I'd rather have died than bring Davey back for Sunday tea to be quizzed over tinned-salmon sandwiches. So where do you come from, Davey? Stevenage? A pause while they tried to work out where that was. Further off than Hungerford, is it? Town boy, then? Eyebrows would lift, oh, yes, they would. And your dad? *Scottish?* Oh . . .

'None of your busies,' I said. Might as well have said, yes, Mam, clear a space on the calendar to get them banns read out in church. She winked.

*   *   *

There was a bit of a tired old wind batting at the beech trees, nothing much but enough to bite, as I slipped out of the back door and through the tall rows of bean sticks, which Dad had never bothered to take down last year. The ground was soft and claggy but not too wet underfoot: it'd been a mild January and there was no frost. I unlatched the garden gate into Green Street. Dad didn't like us using the front door: he said it was for the guests, and my job to wash the tiles in the hallway every morning.

There was a light on in Tommy's cottage, him that'd been a drummer boy in the Boer War. No electric there – Tommy didn't want it or couldn't afford to pay Mr Rawlins for it, so the soft yellow glow of an oil lamp spilled out of his top window. Funny place, that cottage, damp as all-get-out, and cold even on a sunny day. There's places like that in the village and I always walked faster past them. Still do. Some nights, too, you'd think you heard drums coming from the north of the circle, but Dad said that was only the wind in the trees, or Mr Rawlins's generator.

I made my way along Green Street towards the middle of the village. There was a lot of noise coming from the Red Lion: Mr Keiller's men. They gathered there of an evening and some was staying there too, the archaeologists who ran the digs. Mr Keiller would book all the bedrooms for the season while they was digging, which was usually June to September; but Mr Young and Mr Piggott had carried on sorting the finds all through the winter. This year it would be a long season, I'd heard, because they wouldn't stop until they had the western half of the stone circle complete.

That was Mr Keiller's mad dream, you see: to put up all them stones the way they'd been. Don't ask me how he could've known what Avebury was like five thousand years ago, but he reckoned he had the measure of it. Good luck to him, I used to think, though there was plenty of people in the village thought it all a load of old tosh and *bad* luck, too, to mess with what was long gone. When I was small, you'd be hard pressed to say you could see them stones forming any sort of circle whatsoever. Until last year there'd bin trees growing that hid the banks, and most of the stones was laying down like dead soldiers, hidden among bushes and trees and in people's gardens. Folk in times gone by had knocked down stones and buried them and broke them up and now half the village *is* the stones, walls and whole cottages built out of them.

I'm going off at a whatsit. A tangerine, as my mam used to say. That night, Davey was waiting for me at the crossroads under the trees. He gives me a kiss on the cheek, and then because he's getting bolder by the day, one on the lips, even though anyone could have seen us in the light from the lamp on the outside of the Red Lion. Then he steps back, and looks meaningful towards the dark field.

I shook my head. That was a step too far. In the part of the circle Mr Keiller hadn't turned his hand to yet, which is to say most of it, the wild part where the cottage gardens ended and the trees and bushes still grew tangled, the darkness would have been full of whispers. There'd've been some out there doing their courting even in winter. People like to give themselves a good shiver under a big old haunted moon. Tell you summat else'd surprise you. We used to hug them stones, same as they hippies do today. They was warm, see, even on a cold day. Don't ask me why. They held summer's heat all winter under veils of grey-green lichen. That's why courting couples used to go there, not just for privacy, or whatever magic was left in them – for warmth, too. That's what it all comes down to, in't it, needing a bit of warmth?

But I wasn't ready for any of that with Davey. He was my first beau, three or four years older than me. He'd been working at the stables over Beckhampton when I first saw him, on top of a big bay in a string of racehorses walking out up Green Street headed for the Gallops, but now he had a job with Mr Keiller at the Manor, looking after his cars, and sometimes he even drove Mr K about, though there was a proper chauffeur who was Davey's boss. From horses to horsepower, Davey said. He preferred motors because they didn't kick.

I'd first talked to him at a village cricket match last summer, ever so clean in his whites. Not very tall, but he was sturdy at the wicket, a big hitter and he could run like blazes. Clever, too, in his bowling. He coached the younger boys on Saturdays, if he wasn't busy with his chammy leather cleaning the cars.

His dad had been a bookie who bullied his son into an apprenticeship at a racing stable in the hope he'd pass on useful tips. Too late: Davey were hardly started when Mr Fergusson miscalculated the odds at Brighton, couldn't pay out, and hanged hisself with a halter under the stands. Davey'd stuck out the job at Beckhampton for two more miserable years – everyone knew the trainer took his fists to the boys when the temper was on him. But then he met Mr Keiller and somehow he wangled a job. A Scottish surname maybe helped.

We linked arms under the trees, and he pretended to lay his head on my shoulder like he was too tired to hold it up, as we walked down the track that leads to the back of the barns and the duckpond, glimmering under the moon. He had a typical stable-lad's build with narrow hips and strong arms; shame he hated the horses so much because he'd have been perfect for a jockey. But Mr Keiller owned racing cars, and was involved with the speedway course near Wroughton, so Davey had his taste of speed working for him.

The great dark shape of the church loomed above the trees. Our footsteps rang on the frosty cobblestones Colonel Jenner had laid between his barns, which belonged to Mr Keiller now. In the colonel's day there'd been Jersey cows, and pale creamy butter made at the Manor twice a week, which you could buy for a shilling a pound. Wasn't many in the village could afford it, but we bought it for the guests. The livestock had all gone now. Mr Keiller didn't bother with cattle and horses and hay. He'd decided to convert the building where the colonel stabled his polo ponies into a museum, to keep skellingtons and bits of old pot, and he parked his cars in the barns, where the bats did their doings on them if Davey didn't cover them over with tarpaulins.

In Colonel Jenner's day we'd never have walked in the dark through the stableyard, and I didn't feel right doing it now. But Davey had heard something special was happening at the Manor, some sort of party that was more than a few posh people coming for dinner.

'What kind of a party?' I asked.

'There's a spiritualist down from London. Mrs Oliver.'

'Hoping to catch sight of the White Lady, is she? She'd do better hanging round the Red Lion looking for Florrie.'

'Florrie only comes out for men with beards.'

They was our local ghosts. Florrie got thrown into the well at the pub when her husband caught her with her Cavalier lover. There was some likewise tale about the White Lady, and a powerful scent of roses wafting along with her, but don't tell me *they* come back because I never seen anything like them, nor expect anyone else would if they hadn't downed a few pints of Mr Lawes's best beer.

'They've never got one of those ouija whatsits?'

'It's not ghosts they're after. Miss Chapman says Mrs Oliver wants to help them find buried stones. Mr Keiller thinks there's some under the ground that was never broken up.'

How educated people can be so outright stupid is beyond me. Mr Keiller was as clever as they come, but he'd invite an old phoney in a floaty dress to sit at his dinner-table. Or maybe she wasn't so old. There was rumours Miss Doris Chapman, his official artist, was going to be the third Mrs K, but that wouldn't have stopped him giving the eye to another good-looking woman.

'They in't looking for stones tonight? In the pitch dark?'

'How would I know?'

We came round the corner of the stable block to the wrought-iron gate of the Manor garden. All the downstairs windows of the house was lit up, and we could hear music. Not one of Mam's dance bands but heavy thudding like I imagined jungle drums would sound.

'That's Stravinsky.' Davey surprised me. How come he knew who was making that racket? 'Mr Keiller likes modern music.'

'Call that modern?' I said. 'Voodoo music, more like. Modern's Jack Hylton or Billy Cotton. How do *you* know what Mr Keiller likes, anyway?'

But he never replied because at that moment the front door of the Manor opened and light splashed down the gravel path between the lavender beds. There was laughter mixed in with the music, then some shushing, and in the doorway was Mr Keiller himself.

'Bloody hellfire,' says Davey. His hand squeezed my arm and hurt, though I don't think he meant to. 'What *is* he carrying?'

Mr Keiller was in his tails, white tie and all. Sometimes at night he'd wear his kilt, but tonight it was trousers and the real film-star look. They always dressed formal for dinner at the Manor. He was a tall man who filled the doorway bottom to top; no mistaking him, with his long elegant legs. There was a lamp over the door, but his face was in shadow because he had stopped under the lintel, waiting for everybody else to catch up. The light fell instead on the thing in his hands. He was holding it carefully, as if it was fragile, his arms held away from his body so the bottom of the thing was level with his chest and the top maybe an inch or two below his chin. Davey started to laugh, quietly in case they heard us, and I could feel his hands digging into my arms as he stood behind me, peering over the wall, his chin parting the back of my hair. I was glad it was dark because I could feel myself going red: oh, I knew what Mr Keiller was carrying, all right. Davey's breath was hot on my ear, and he was awful close behind me, and I could feel the same kind of thing that Mr Keiller had in his hands butting at my back through our clothes.

Mr Keiller steps forward, and the light falls on his high shiny forehead and his handsome rich man's face that's tanned but not weathered. He's got a long, straight nose and a strong, wide mouth and a full head of hair, never mind that he's in his forties. The thing falls into shadow and I'm happy about that – what would Mam think? – though something makes me want to see it again, something to do with Davey's breath that's a bit faster than it ought to be when we're standing still.

Out of the door behind Mr Keiller come a couple of ladies, carrying cocktail glasses, so maybe they hadn't even started dinner yet, never mind it was gone half past nine. Miss Chapman was one of them, in a long silky dress with a wrap the same pale shade round her shoulders. Moonlight had stolen all the colours. As she walked under the lamp she was trying to look serious, like him, but I could see she wanted to giggle. The other was a middle-aged lady in flouncy stuff and a white fur stole, who could've been Mrs Oliver. Her face was a mask under too much powder. Behind them were three or four men, and two more ladies. One stumbled as she stepped onto the path, and the other shouted, 'Alec, darling, your cocktails have malicious potency!' I recognized them as the people staying at our guesthouse, and all of them carried candles, long white tapers that sent flickering light along the gravel path. They milled about under the trees, waiting for Mr Keiller to take the lead. He stood a little apart, the white thing cradled in the crook of one arm. One of the other ladies came up to him, and as they chatted, I saw his free hand steal casual like round her back, where Miss Chapman and the other guests couldn't see, and rub her bottom.

We'd been watchers all our short lives, Davey and I: people who waited on tables and polished cars and cleared up after rich people. But when it came down to it, the only difference was they had more money. In the moonlight, drunk, they acted silly as any fool. That younger man at the back, with hair that flopped over his eyes and a cigarette in his hand, sauntering about like he owned the place, he was one of the archaeologists – I'd seen him in the fields with a notebook and a measuring tape. I wanted to be following them, a pale ghost in my own silky dress. All you had to do was believe you deserved to be among them, and act ridickerlus as they did.

The heavy Manor door shut with a thud and coming out of the porch was Mrs Sorel-Taylour, the short, buxom lady that was Mr Keiller's secretary, keeping her distance to make sure nobody thought she was so daft as the rest. She was carrying a torch instead of a candle.

Mr Keiller raised the gurt white pizzle up high – had to call it that, didn't know any other word for it, then, and right enough it was near as big as a bull's or a stallion's. Moonlight poured down on it, making it look like bewitched silver. Everybody bowed to it. Davey pulled me back into the shadow of the stable wall, in case they came our way, but there was no need because Mr K led them instead round the corner of the house into the more private bit of the garden where we couldn't see what they was up to.

'Whew,' said Davey softly. 'What do you think they're going to do there?'

I didn't want to think about it, but I did think about it, and Davey's fingers on my arms. And Mr Keiller's face too, solemn like it was carved out of stone, holding up the thing made of glimmering chalk like the high Downs. For all that what we'd seen was silly, it stirred something else in me, something I couldn't explain. Magic, some of it to do with floaty dresses and film stars, but some of it the old sort of magic. The sort that makes me feel cold now, makes me need to feel warm again, but there in't no fire that'll warm that kind of cold once you have it in your bones.

'Mad as hares,' I said. 'Maybe that medium lady's going to raise the dead to ask 'em where they put them stones.'

'More'n the dead they've raised,' said Davey, sliding himself against my back, all accidental-like. 'We in't going to see any more tonight.'

'Don't think that means you'll get a cuddle,' I said. But something had stirred in me, too, and I didn't understand what it was.

CHAPTER 7

As the sun starts to sink towards the dykes on Wednesday afternoon, the car park of the Red Lion is already filling, several cars displaying blue disabled badges. Wednesday is biker's night at the pub, but the Harleys and Beamers won't roar into the village until later. The public meeting to show the 1938 cine footage has been timed to lure out older people before dark, but Frannie showed no enthusiasm for coming along, though it was filmed during the years she grew up in Avebury. Despite my best efforts to persuade her, I left her at home in her slippers, settled in front of the TV with a pot of tea and a packet of gingernuts.

The letter I found down the side of her armchair has been bothering me all week. It looked like it'd been there a long, long time – possibly since right after she moved back to Avebury, four years ago. I don't know how to raise the subject with her: she'll accuse me of prying again, and maybe get upset, the way she did when I was trying to find out more about Davey Fergusson.

Close to the door of the pub, a black 4×4 has drawn up, an orange and white logo on the side: Overview TV. My heartbeat begins to quicken. A woman in a maroon suede jacket and a black polo-neck is unloading a cardboard box from the tailgate, and I follow her in.

Every time I come into the Red Lion, breathing in a comforting smell of beer and cigs and chips, I remind myself that this is where it all began, the renaissance of Avebury, in the inn at the heart of the circle. It's 1934 or thereabouts. The Marmalade King has, as usual, booked every room in the pub for his staff, and is digging the West Kennet Avenue. Late one night Stuart Piggott is woken by AK hammering on the door of his room. He bursts in like a force of nature. I know what I have to do, he announces – it's always a *have to* with AK, always an announcement – I'm going to buy up the whole village. I imagine him lighting a cigarette, pacing up and down Piggott's room, ignoring the startled archaeologist in the bed and staring through the walls to the dark landscape beyond. Yes, he says, I'll buy up as much of the place as I can and devote my life to the study of Avebury.

This afternoon the tables in the snug have been rearranged, with chairs facing a screen set up on the far wall. Almost every seat is filled, and the curtains have been drawn, though it's not yet dark. A young man with deep-set, intense eyes is standing behind a TV camera on a tall tripod, panning round the room and filming people at the tables. They nudge each other and whisper every time they catch the lens pointing their way – no doubt why the cameraman's jaw is clenched with frustration.

At the back of the room is a long table with a reserved sign. The woman in the suede jacket has set down the cardboard box and is laying out DVDs in neat piles. She glances at me and smiles, as if she knows me, but it's the professional smile of the TV person, warm and inclusive and utterly meaningless.

'Hello, girl,' says a voice beside me, and there's John, at a table by himself, with a pint at his elbow and the usual scrawny roll-up smouldering in the ashtray. 'Orright? Come and park yourself with me.'

I sit down, checking to make sure I won't obstruct anyone's view of the screen, since I'm half a head taller than most women in the room. 'Didn't think you'd be here.'

'Couldn't miss a chance to appear on the telly.'

'They aren't going to be interested in you,' I say, watching where the dark-eyed young man is pointing his camera. 'They want people like the Rawlins brothers, who are in the film. You going to spin them your idea about a northern avenue?' Not that I believe for a second that John's enthusiasm for dowsing is likely to reveal the archaeological discovery of the decade.

67

He shakes his head. 'Get your mates at the National Trust to take the idea seriously and do a full geophysical survey.'

'On the say-so of a mad old hippie with a pair of bent coat-hangers?'

'You'll be laughing the other side of your face when I make the cover of *British Archaeology*.' He takes a mouthful of his pint, and tucks back a strand of greying hair that has escaped his ponytail. In 1982 he had short hair and a rifle that killed an Argentinian in the Falklands. 'No point, though, in pitching it to this TV crew. They're only interested in Keiller.'

'You don't know that.'

'Don't be naïve, Indy – you used to work in the business. Telly people get an idea in their heads, that's the programme they make, never mind the truth. They'll turn him into a bloody archaeological saint.'

'Well, he was, wasn't he, as far as Avebury's concerned?'

John snorts. 'Archaeological Satan, more like. He's the reason you didn't grow up in a posh house in the village.'

'You make it sound like it was personal,' I say. 'He was only . . .'

'Trying to achieve a vision? So was Hitler, round about the same time.'

The camera fixes its cold fishy eye on us, but only for a moment. The cameraman has decided we're the wrong age to be interesting tonight. Instead the lens settles on Carrie Harper, chair-to-the-parish-council (all said quickly on one breath so you won't mistake her for something that can be bought in Ikea), resplendent in orange cable knit and a pair of flared jersey trousers that probably date from her heyday in the seventies. But the rustles and whispers have reached a pitch: a man with white hair strides to the front, by the big plasma screen that's usually for the football. He waves the remote control at us, like a conductor's baton, and the room falls silent.

'Welcome,' he says. 'We're going to show you a film. I could tell you what it's about, but I think most of you know far better than I do.' The oldies laugh; go on, Mister, flatter us, we like that. 'It was found at the back of a wardrobe, six months ago, and eventually ended up at my production company for cleaning and transfer to DVD.' He looks round, taking in their rapt faces, and smiles, a broad grin, directed at them but also at the camera with its pulsing red light. 'It's rather special, because it's a record of the way this village was in the late 1930s. Some of you are in it, and that would be interesting enough in itself. But, more importantly, it opens a window on a critical year for archaeology.'

John turns and winks at me.

'Nineteen thirty-eight. A year in which Avebury was transformed by the man we'll see on this footage. We're going to film *you* as you watch it, as part of a documentary we're hoping to sell to Channel 4 or the BBC. Everyone happy?' Nods and grunts, presumably enough to count for assent. 'Right. Let's run it.' He raises the remote and presses play.

White scratchy lines flicker over a black background. A square of light appears, not quite filling the screen. I've been expecting one of those countdowns you see on old cine film, 5–4–3–2–1, or at least a clock with a sweeping second hand, but the picture's there immediately, and Percy Lawes himself swaggers up to the camera, Jack-the-lad puffing on his cigarette with a knowing smile, enjoying his Hitchcock moment. Frannie remembers him: he figures in her stories of the old days. He was the son of the landlord of the Red Lion, thought himself a bit smarter than the rest, with his little hat and his cine-camera. He went off to Calne or Chippenham or somewhere like that to be a piano teacher, then died a bachelor, and his films would have died with him, except his nephew was curious about the contents of the battered film cans he discovered while clearing his uncle's effects. On the screen Percy doffs his hat, as if he knows we're going to be watching in his dad's old pub nearly seventy years later.

The picture jumps and there's the village street, not the same as today but recognizable. A dozen or so kids come running up the lane, right up to the camera, laughing. All the people in the audience break out talking and nudging each other, all these old people who are seeing themselves suddenly as they were *then*. There's one old lady crying, and in the flickering TV light I can make out in the audience's faces some of the same features that show on the screen, blurred now with age, plump rosy cheeks that have slipped like melting Christmas candles down their faces, eyes that are clear in *then* milky now with cataracts.

It's the little kids who are crowding close to Percy's camera, but behind them a few older ones hang back, giggling. Could that be Frannie, her hand over her mouth to hide her grin, with a bobbed hairstyle like the Queen wore when she was a princess? Too late, the scene's changed, racehorses being walked out along the high street to the Gallops, long-gone Classic winners whose bones now moulder under the downland.

Now heavy horses, pulling the haywains, and men in cloth caps pitchforking hay onto the ricks. It's in black-and-white, but Percy Lawes was good with that cine-camera, knew how to use the light. No sound, but you can see the men laughing and joking with one another, easy with their work even though they were being filmed. Suddenly that's gone too, and we're inside the stone circle, watching a massive stone with ropes and pulleys wrapped round it, and men with crowbars heaving and tugging to get it upright.

And there he is, sitting on a camp stool, sketching or writing up his notes, it's hard to make out which. The man himself. AK, Alexander Keiller, who moved into the Manor House in 1937 to reshape Avebury. He's wearing a Panama hat and a blazer, all long elegant legs and knees and elbows on the tiny stool, working on his pad, not bothering to acknowledge the camera, as arrogant and insouciant as an old-time squire. The smile lifting the corners of his mouth – he knows he's being filmed – is familiar. Where the hell have I seen those features and that expression before?

No. It can't be. But it is: the smile on the poster at the back of Frannie's wardrobe, the smile Margaret used to wear when she knew someone was photographing her. She was tall and beautiful and kind of arrogant as well, with her strong nose and high forehead. At Greenham, journalists made a beeline for her, and when she danced naked on top of the trilithons at Stonehenge, one midsummer dawn, tossing her long thick hair and with that exact same smile on her mouth, someone snapped it and turned it into a poster. *They never comes back, that's for sure.*

But maybe that smile did. The thought explodes like a firework in my head, though it isn't so much a revelation as the confirmation of an idea that's been quietly creeping up on me over the last few days.

It explains the letter tucked down the side of Frannie's armchair. Might even be the reason she didn't want to come this evening. Most crucially, it makes sense of the date on my so-called grandfather's headstone, of Frannie's reluctance to talk about him. Because if David Fergusson wasn't my grandfather, who was?

Next to me, John leans across and stubs out his rollie, and the sweet tarry scent of grass comes bursting up from the ashtray.

I touch his arm and whisper so no one else will hear.

John frowns and shakes his head. 'You have to be wrong, Indy,' he whispers back. 'That's never in a million years your grandad.'

After the film, the white-haired man tells us to have a break and more drinks before they start the discussion proper. Everyone in the room is a bit red-eyed, including John, only in his case it's the weed. Even the TV woman blows her nose. The camera sweeps the room, relentlessly prying into *then*, all the weepy conversations that have broken out as people remember their childhood and how England used to be before supermarkets and television and tractors.

'I'm going,' says John, unexpectedly, picking up his lighter and tobacco pouch.

'Won't you stay?' I was fizzing, but now I've gone flat. He's probably right. It's impossible Keiller and Frannie had any relationship. Or, if not impossible, highly unlikely: wrong age, wrong class. I've let myself be carried away by some old biddy's poison-pen letter, hinting at scandal, but what was going on at the Manor could mean anything. It might not even relate to the time Keiller lived there.

'You don't want me cramping your style when you chat up telly people.' John stands up, squeezes my shoulder. 'You need a massage.'

And he's gone, limping through the tables, his narrow bony back the full stop it's always been at the end of our conversations.

I take a sip of his unfinished pint, glancing round the pub again. There will be people here who knew Fran when she was a girl. Unfortunately, most of them were probably too young to have picked up the gossip of the day. Still, someone sent that letter, and he or she could be in this room. Although I know John's right, really, there's no way Keiller could have been my grandfather, I can't help spinning the idea round. That smile . . . so exactly Margaret's, I'm amazed John couldn't see it. I cremated all my photographs of my mother – part of my sad Goth phase again – but Fran has a little one, in her bedroom, of Margaret in her teens, with white lipstick and three layers of false eyelashes. Maybe she keeps others, too, locked away in the bureau.

You know, Ind, one day you might regret that, said Fran on the day I burned my mother's things. Never get 'em back, that's for sure. Then she stumped away to the garden shed to fetch the rake, and spread the ashes of the bonfire across the flowerbed.

I'm heading for the loo, admiring the dark-eyed cameraman's profile as he tips back his head to swallow the last of his lager, when the TV woman and I nearly collide in the doorway.

'Sorry,' she says.

'My fault, not looking where I'm going.' We both stand back to let the other through first, then, when neither moves, step forward simultaneously.

'You first.'

'No, you. There's more than one cubicle in there, anyway.'

Of course, when we go in, they're both occupied. A sickly manufactured scent of rose pot-pourri hangs in the air, and a volley of old-lady farts comes from behind one of the doors. We exchange smiles.

There's never going to be a better moment.

'This programme you're doing . . .'

'*If* it gets commissioned. Not always a given, these days.'

'Would you be interested in an idea for it?'

This look comes over her face, the one that says she's had a million people offer her ideas and only two and a half have ever been remotely any good. It's replaced immediately by a polite, bland mask. 'Try me.'

'Next spring's the seventieth anniversary of Keiller starting work in the circle.' I'm gabbling to spew it all out fast before one of the toilet doors opens. 'I understand about commissioning, I've worked for Mannix and other TV companies –' (go on, India, tell a really big lie about your qualifications to keep her listening, and hope your nose doesn't grow to give it away) ' – and I did a master's at Bristol University in archaeology and media, with my thesis on Keiller's work. Only he never finished – you'll know this. He never managed to reconstruct the whole circle.'

'Uh-huh.' She's interested now, I can tell – in fact I've a feeling she could be way ahead of me.

'So I thought . . .'

'You want to finish the job for him and put up the rest of the stones.'

'Well, no, not actually *all* the stones.' I'm explaining now in the bar. My bladder aches because I never did get round to that pee. The TV woman marched me straight out and collared the white-haired man, who was talking to Carrie Harper over by the windows.

'Daniel, you've got to hear this.'

'Ibby, I'm talking to someone.' Rude to her, though he was schmoozing Carrie like she was lady of the Manor.

'Seriously, it's a really good idea.'

His eyes went hard, and for a moment I thought he was going to cut her down to size in front of Carrie and me, but instead he said smoothly, 'Would you excuse us a moment, Mrs Harper?' I could tell he'd already sussed that Carrie wasn't going to be as much use to him as she'd like to think, since she only arrived in Avebury ten years ago. Now she's hanging onto the edge of the conversation, as I explain my Big Idea. I've pulled open the curtains to show them. There's a fine view, across the darkening roadway, of the space where Frannie's parents' guesthouse stood.

'Doesn't matter which stone. The Second World War interrupted Keiller's excavations, so nearly half the outer circle hasn't been touched – there could be twenty or more buried stones in the north-east quadrant alone. The point is to do something that would get press coverage and set people talking about Avebury and Keiller again.' And secure me a job on this production.

'India's family have lived in the village for generations,' says Ibby. Weird name. Maybe she was conceived on Ibiza. 'She works with the National Trust.' In the café, but they don't need to know that. Lucky that Michael isn't here to put them straight. I raise my eyebrows at Carrie in the hope she'll keep her mouth shut.

'So you could get us permission to film?' says White Hair. His name is Daniel Porteus.

'Well, that would be up to someone higher than me. But I'm sure . . .'

He doesn't seem to have noticed that I'm making most of this up as I go along. 'It's bloody brilliant. I like it already. Can I get you a glass of wine?' He shoots a triumphant smile at Ibby. 'Get us a bottle, Ib. Merlot, if they have it. All right for you, um, India? So what exactly is it you do for the Trust?'

'Sorry,' Carrie butts in. 'India, don't want to interrupt or anything, but I think I saw your gran out the window. She could break a leg, you know, walking round the dykes in the dark.'

There's still enough light in the sky to outline the small figure making its uneven way along the top of the bank, near a clump of beech trees.

'Fran!'

She stops, turns and waits, thank goodness. A waxing moon is coming up over the horizon, and as I dash through the stones, there's a disconcerting glimpse of it, like a tilted D, between Frannie's bandy elastic-stockinged legs.

The grass is slippery with frost. My ankle goes over with a sickening twist. Daren't stop, so I go hobbling on, terrified that Frannie will start slithering down the bank into the darkness of the ditch and her ankle will go too, pitching her over and snapping her leg like the dry old twig it is. At her age, broken bones can kill.

'Stop right there. I'll come and get you.' A risky strategy: out of sheer cussedness she might do the exact opposite. Panic's making me breathless.

She sits down, plonk, on a big tree root curving out of the hard, chalky slope. The wind rattles the bare beeches. A smile cracks her face, as if this is a game. She must know it's going to be hard to get her up again. She's not even wearing a coat, for God's sake. Her feet are in slippers, soaked.

My breath scrapes in my chest from the climb up the bank, and the fear. 'What are you doing?' I puff.

Frannie lifts a hand and brushes her fringe off her forehead, a 1940s starlet posing for the camera, the rising moon backlighting her hair and turning it silver. She stares straight ahead over the stone circle, gaze lasering between the pair of massive entrance stones. Something in the inner circle has caught her attention. There's movement down there, someone in a long dark coat, a bluish light that could be torch or camera-phone. Frannie shakes her head, chewing over some possibility that apparently she regrets having to reject.

Then she says, like she'd heard me thinking the exact same words earlier this evening in the pub: 'They never comes back, that's for sure.'

CHAPTER 8

1938

They never comes back and goodness only knows the place they've gone to. But sometimes I think they're out there in the moonlight, and I have to go to see.

Our mam used to say that the two roads that cross in the middle of Avebury – the main Swindon road running north–south, and Green Street that was the old Saxon way going east–west – were like big blood vessels carrying time through the village. Because they was so old now the walls had gone thin, and time sometimes bled out one way or t'other. Mam'd reach out her hand to me in the hospital and I'd see the bruises, the places where her blood leaked out under the skin because, after all the injections, her veins were too wore out to hold it in any more. I see the same bruises on my arms now, old-lady bruises, and I think that's how time has become for me, now I'm eighty-whatsit. The past leaks into the present, and who's to say the present doesn't leak into the past?

If I'd been a bit bolder and let Davey take me into the stones that night, instead of watching what happened in the Manor gardens, would we have come through? There'd've been a kiss and a cuddle and a warming of the hands inside his coat. Then, all in good time, maybe our mam would've had her way, tinned-salmon sandwiches and banns read out, and two of us beside the old font with the snake carved on it when the vicar dips his fingers to wet the babby's head.

There's a photo of Davey in the back of the drawer in the dressing-table, in the box where I keep all me bits and pieces. It was taken later, in the war, after he'd enlisted with the Raff. He's grinning at the camera with his forage cap at a jaunty angle; somewhere out of view there'll be a cigarette between his fingers, because he smoked something terrible after he joined up, but they had them for free, or near as, at the NAAFI. Perks of the job. Blowing smoke rings into the face of Death, hoping she'd squint her eyes and not see him. It's black-and-white, so you can't see them golden-green eyes of his that never seemed to match right with his thick brown hair. That hair stood up like a lavatory brush if he didn't cut it every couple of weeks, but after he joined the air force he Brylcreemed it flat, with a little finger-wave at the front, curly as Mam's marcel. It used to creep forward over his eye when he was hot and bothered. Me wayward tendril, he called it.

He's grinning at the camera in that photograph, but what I sees now is the hurt in his face. *Frannie*, he says to me, *what did you want to go and do that for?*

Yes, I say, but you wasn't exactly whiter than whatsit, was you? Didn't understand then, but I reckon you had your secrets too, up on Windmill Hill on that motorbike. How was it you caught Mr Keiller's eye so he give you a job? But no good asking: he and Mr K never come back, for all I go looking in the moonlight.

Percy Lawes had set up his movie camera on the bit of green opposite the Red Lion when I got off the Swindon bus coming home after my Thursday-afternoon shorthand class. There was a group of kids hanging round him as usual.

'Back down the high street,' he was saying to Heather Peak-Garland and her pals. 'Go on. You were too quick for me last time. I didn't get you all in the picture.'

They trooped down the road towards the shop.

'Further.'

Back they went again, almost to the school.

'Further.'

I left them to it and crossed the road. I had decisions to make, about what I was going to do with my life – didn't intend spending it all being a skivvy for Mam and Dad – and the best place to think was in among the stones. There was a big old lad fallen on his side that I liked to curl up on when I needed time and space to myself. The Rawlins boys used him as a sliding stone, tobogganing down his polished flank to land with a splash in the puddle at the bottom, then clambering back on over and over till they near wore out the seat of their pants. But today they were dancing round Percy having their pictures took on that camera of his, so I had the stone to myself.

Except no sooner had I settled myself, pulling up the collar of my wool coat and shoving my hands in my pockets, than the breeze blew the sound of voices my way.

It was two of the archaeologists that worked for Mr Keiller. You could tell they was archaeologists because one was carrying a tall measuring pole painted black-and-white, and the other had some sort of survey equipment on folding legs. They were over by one of the few stones that was still standing in this part of the field. One had his back to me, bending over his tripod. The other, holding the pole, was the same tall, languid fellow with sloping shoulders and floppy hair I'd seen in the Manor gardens. They'd either not seen me or thought me not worth the noticing.

'Keep the flaming pole steady, Cromley,' shouted the shorter one. He had darker, wavy hair, and a thick tweed jacket. 'You're waggling it about like a wog with an *assegai*.'

'It's too bloody cold to stand still,' yelled the other. 'This'll have to be the last one. The light'll be going soon.'

They were both young men, in their twenties, with carrying voices, like they didn't care who heard 'em say what. I wondered what made them want to spend their lives digging up old stones, but maybe it wasn't that brought them here: maybe it was Mr Keiller. You could imagine him marching up to some smart young lad, coming all inno-cent out of a college gateway in Oxford or Cambridge, and saying, *Follow me*. And they would.

'There,' said the tall one called Cromley, lowering the pole. The rays of the low sun caught his soft little moustache, the colour of Demerara sugar above fine, sculpted lips. 'That's where there should be a stone buried, if the spacing's constant. And another . . .' He moved along the rim of the ditch, sweeping the pole over the grass, then stopping and jabbing the ground with it. 'The next here.' Finally he speared the striped stick into a molehill, and took out his cigarette case to light up. The match flared and fizzed.

The dark-haired chap ignored him, dipping a long pointed nose towards his notebook. He took his time writing something, then folded the legs of the tripod.

'You know, Piggott...' The taller man was using the pole like a hiker's staff as they walked back in my direction, his cigarette trailing from the fingers of his other hand. 'AK's driven off to London again with the Brushwood Boy. Don't you think someone ought to enlighten Doris?'

'You don't know what you're talking about,' said Piggott, revealing a glimpse of big, flat teeth. There was irritation in his voice, and he looked quite red in the face, though that was maybe the cold.

I didn't hear any more, because I felt suddenly shy and thought they might laugh at me for being a gurt grown girl climbing on the stones like the children did. Besides, the light was fading, and the moon coming up already, and Mam would be wondering where I'd got to. I slid off the stone, tugged my skirt down, and ran off between the trees, before they reached where I'd been sitting.

Running back the way I'd come, running widdershins. First time I didn't think to follow the light round the circle, like my mam always told me.

CHAPTER 9

The hobble across the circle seems to take for ever, Fran's hand on my arm tightening every time her soaked slippers skid on the frosty grass.

'I'm going to take you into the pub,' I say.

No response. Frannie glares straight ahead, brows knitting in concentration. We cross the road, and as we approach the light on the outside of the Red Lion, she lifts her eyes up and stares at it as we pass underneath, like she's never seen it before.

Although the snug is still packed with reminiscing villagers, the main bar is almost empty. My grandmother settles herself in the corner, sees Carrie coming out of the Ladies and waves. But weather conditions haven't entirely returned to normal on Planet Fran: still cloudy, with patches of freezing fog.

'Where are my cigarettes?' She pats her cardigan pockets. 'You got one on you, Meg?'

'I'm India, and you know I don't. I'll bring you a packet with the drinks.' Which would be better: whisky or hot coffee? I order both, scribble my mobile number on a scrap of paper for the TV people, and ask Carrie to look after Frannie while I fetch the car.

The shortest way home is through the field, but after several days' rain, the Winterbourne's nearly as high as the bridge. Moonlight glimmers on water round the foot of Silbury Hill, and without a doubt the meadow will be one big sucky bog. The path's never been tarmacked: locals claim that's another of the ways Keiller and the National

Trust exiled ordinary folk from Avebury. Better to take the longer, dryer way: along the lane, past the outlying cottages with their thatch and Range Rovers.

At night I don't much like either route, my townie instincts not yet comfortable in the darkness of the countryside. Something's made me more than usually twitchy this evening. The tiniest whisper of wind in dead beech leaves. I could swear that was a footstep behind.

Nobody. I know there's nobody there.

All the same, I cast an uneasy glance over my shoulder as I take the fork for Trusloe. In the far distance there's a light, moving slowly in the darkness across the slopes of Windmill Hill. Telling myself it can only be a late dogwalker, I sprint along the last stretch of lane towards the streetlight.

Frannie becomes suspiciously quiet once I persuade her into the passenger seat of the Peugeot.

'You're sure you'll be OK?' asks Carrie, as I close the car door. 'I don't mind coming along if you need a hand. She seems fine, now, but . . .' Neither of us can define what *but* is.

'Did she say anything to you about what she was doing there?'

'Not a word.'

'Come over for supper next week,' says Carrie. 'Both of you. You're not getting out enough, India. What do you do in the evenings? We've hardly seen you since Christmas.'

What do I do? I watch television with my grandmother. I know every twist of the plotline of *EastEnders* and *Holby City*. After she's gone to bed, I open a bottle of wine – bugger the new-year resolution – and play Free Cell on the computer. Can only manage the card games, these days; too much blood and destruction in anything else.

'Oh, I don't mind a quiet life,' I say. 'After London – you know . . .' Too late I realize that the wave accompanying this, meant to convey I'm weary of the shallow pleasures of the metropolis, makes it look as if I'm rudely batting away Carrie's invitation. 'I'd *love* to come to supper some time,' I add. 'If Frannie's . . . up to it.'

All through the conversation, my grandmother sits in the front seat with a puzzled, shut-up-don't-interrupt-me expression on her face, like she's working out a difficult sum in her head.

On a cold February night, Trusloe seems bleaker than ever, looming out of the windy darkness under rags of cloud backlit by the glow of Swindon to the north. There are not enough streetlamps, and most windows are unlit. On our road everyone, apart from the couple next door who make amateur porn films in their living room, apparently heads for bed straight after supper. Either that or they still use blackout material for curtains.

'You OK?' I haul on the handbrake outside Bella Vista.

Frannie stares straight ahead, brows knitted.

'I said, are you OK?'

'What have you brought me here for?'

'So you can go to bed.'

'I don't want to go to bed.' There's a petulant droop to her mouth. 'Too buggerin' early.'

'Come on, let's get you out of the car.'

'India, I'm not a bloomin' parcel. I'm perfectly capable of getting myself out.' She's adopted that posh tone she puts on when she wants to be bloody-minded.

'Please yourself.'

'I will.' Frannie waggles the catch on the car door. 'Won't open.'

'That's not the way. Stop messing about. Use the handle.'

'Locked.'

'It's not locked.'

Now she's wrestling with the seatbelt. 'I'm *trapped.*'

Just for a second, a feeling of utter panic seizes me. I'm close to tears: frustration, grief, despair, the sheer bloody unfairness of having to watch the person you love most in the world start to lose it, all vying for the honour of making me bawl.

But I won't give way.

Pressing my nails hard into my palm to stop myself screaming, I reach across and press the button to release her.

While I'm boiling the kettle for her hot-water bottle, Frannie comes into the kitchen wearing her nightie inside out, one strap slipping off a bony, stooped shoulder.

'You'll catch your death. Get into bed, or put your dressing-gown on. And your other slippers.' Her feet are purple. Have I noticed before how scrawny her arms have become, flesh hanging in loose, empty pouches?

She reaches out a swollen-knuckled paw and touches my face. 'Sorry. Don't mean to be a trouble.'

'You're not a trouble.' I catch her hand before she withdraws it. It feels like a piece of raw chicken out of the fridge. I squeeze it help-lessly, not knowing what else to do. 'You're no trouble at all, you old bat.'

She smiles up at me, her eyes showing a ghost of their familiar twinkle. Then she turns and shuffles out of the kitchen. The glow of the lamp in her bedroom backlights her, turning her into a bent shadowy thing crossing the hallway.

Suddenly I recognize what's been bothering me. Frannie, silhou-etted against the sky, stumping along the top of the bank. Going widdershins round the circle, anti-clockwise. She never goes widder-shins. *Always sunwise, girl. You follows the light. Bad luck else.*

Steve's open eyes . . .

I will *not* think about that.

Keiller's papers are kept in the curator's old room, tucked under the eaves above the stableyard museum, in a series of box files. Eventually all the Keiller material will be moved to the main offices, but the curator, a world expert on obscure bits of Neolithic pottery that look like digestive biscuit to me, is too busy cataloguing finds from a dig at Stonehenge.

'There you are,' says Michael, wheeling a library stool into place. 'I wasn't expecting you to be *this* keen.'

'Sorry,' I say. 'Thought I should start soonest.' It's the morning after the film show, ten minutes short of nine, and my first opportunity to tackle the job of ordering the archive since I'm not on shift in the café today. The sun is already bright outside the window at the end, but its leaching light doesn't penetrate the room. Even with the radiators on, the attic office is freezing.

'Top shelf, photo albums,' explains Michael. 'Organized, possibly, by AK himself.' Bound in brown morocco, the year in gold lettering on their spines. 'Next shelf down, correspondence – letters received and flimsy copies of letters he sent. Not so organized, I'm afraid, and certainly not complete. His executors threw away anything they didn't consider strictly relevant to the archaeology.'

'So nothing juicy in there?'

'One or two hints, maybe. Haven't read them all.' Michael scoops up an armful of files and descends with them. 'The really spicy stuff went on the bonfire. Legend has it that W. E. V. Young – the museum's first curator – scattered the ashes on the Thames.'

'Makes it sound like there was something frightfully scandalous.'

'Well, there were four wives and God knows how many mistresses. He put it about a bit, did old AK. But the big secret – not very well kept, obviously, or we wouldn't know about it – is supposed to be correspondence relating to what may or may not have been ritual sex magic.'

'I *beg* your pardon?'

Michael grins wickedly as he steps onto the library stool again. 'Put it another way, he was a bit kinky. According to the diary of a reputable lady novelist, he asked her to step into a large wicker basket wearing nothing but a rubber mackintosh so he could prod her with an umbrella through the gaps.'

'The old goat. Did she oblige?'

Michael shakes his head, dumping another armful of box files on the table. Suddenly this is starting to look like a harder task than I'd expected. 'Which box is which? They don't seem to be labelled.'

'Told you they needed organizing.'

I open a box at random. It's stuffed to the brim with flimsy blue sheets of paper.

'Those are copies of the letters he wrote. After dinner he'd retire with a brandy snifter and dictate into the small hours. He was a prolific correspondent, employed several secretaries to transcribe. You never know, you might be looking at something your grandmother typed.'

'Sorry?'

'Your grandmother worked at the Manor.'

I stare at him. 'Where on earth did you get that from?'

'She must have told you,' says Michael, reprovingly, as if holding me to account for all the neglectful young people who never listen to what their elders tell them. He leans over my shoulder and opens one of the photo albums. 'Lilian reminded me last week, after you'd left the office. There's hardly anyone left alive who knew him, so we're keen to get memories on tape. She's in here somewhere . . .'

As he turns the pages, separated by leaves of tissue paper, there are glimpses of men in Panama hats and plus-fours, lean women in droopy skirts. 'We had a Memories of Avebury day last spring, and I invited the old dears who'd lived in the village all their lives to come and talk about it. Where is the bloody thing? We blew up copies of some of the pictures in the albums . . . *There* . . .' he lays the album in front of me '. . . and asked people if they could tell us who was in them. Your grandmother didn't come, but one of the other old ladies identified her . . .' He points to a group photograph that takes up most of the page. 'She told us that was Frances Robinson, who'd done secretarial work at the Manor, and that she'd come back recently to live in Trusloe. Lilian went to see your gran, but couldn't get a useful word out of her, unfortunately – bless the poor old love, Lilian thought she seemed confused by all the questions. If there's any chance of you getting her to talk . . .'

Confused? Or simply being Frannie, keeping her mouth shut?

In the picture three women, seated on wooden crates, flank a man who is leaning forward and smiling at the camera. Behind, there is a line of men, standing, most in waistcoats and cloth caps, but the younger ones at the end of the row are in sports jackets.

'Nineteen thirty-eight,' says Michael. 'They're excavating the south-western quadrant of the stone circle. Keiller in the middle, of course, with Doris Chapman on his right, soon to become the third Mrs K. Piggott and Cromley at either end of the back row, both cutting their teeth as archaeologists with him. Piggott, as you know, went on to excavate at Avebury long after Keiller was gone – pity about Cromley, though, great loss to archaeology. Keiller thought a lot of his abilities.'

These are people I'm not interested in. Impatient, I pull the album towards me to see better. 'So which . . .?'

Michael's manicured fingernail moves along the photo to the slight figure at the end of the front row, shielding her eyes against the sun. 'Would you say that was your grandmother?'

She looks shy, younger than the other two women. Although there's a smile on her face, she seems more solemn than the rest. 'I don't know,' I say slowly, disguising my mounting excitement. 'Might be Frannie . . .' The age looks right, the set of her mouth. 'To be honest, Michael, couldn't say one way or the other. Who was it reckoned her to be my gran?'

'I forget her name. Used to live in a bungalow in Berwick Bassett.' He lays the tissue paper carefully over the photo, and shuts the album. 'She worked for Keiller too. Not one of the women in the picture. She was a housemaid.'

After Michael has gone downstairs, I open the brown leather album again and leaf through it, looking for the photo. Archaeologists today wear funny hats, walking boots and woolly jumpers; in most of these pictures Keiller is in suit and tie and golf shoes. He was fabulously rich, the heir to a marmalade fortune, a playboy who loved fast cars and the ski slopes. A good-looking man, too: wide, sexy mouth, oddly haunted eyes.

No wonder Frannie – if it was Frannie – looked awkward in front

of the camera. As well as being hardly out of school – fifteen? Sixteen?
– she wasn't from anything like the same background or class. How
did she manage to talk her way into a job on the excavation? I try to
remember what else I've gleaned about Keiller since I've been in
Avebury. He was an egalitarian employer, and at least one of his wives
worked alongside him as a professional archaeologist. Until he divorced
her, that is, and moved on to the next Mrs K.

I stare at the photo. No, it can't be Frannie. She'd have said
something.

But . . . the letter hidden in her armchair. **Anyone with eyes in
their head at the Manor knew what was going on.**

I pick up one of the box files, and set to work.

As well as Keiller's letters, the boxes also contain, in no particular order,
correspondence from other archaeologists, friends, tradesmen and the
occasional nutter. Keiller seems to have replied to everyone, even
the weirdos. Did Frannie really type some of these letters? And what else
might she have done for the Great Man? Wear a mask and cast a pentangle,
like something in sixties Technicolor starring Christopher Lee?

The room is darker. Outside, the sun has disappeared behind heavy
cloud. Almost two hours have passed. I stand up to stretch, wondering
if I can be bothered to go downstairs to the staff kitchen to warm up.
There are several large cardboard boxes in a stack by the door, waiting
to be transferred to the main storeroom. I kneel down to lift the lid
of one, catching a glimpse of about a billion polythene bags containing
tiny fragments of yellowish-white honeycomb, then scramble guiltily
to my feet as footsteps rap on the stairs.

Michael.

'I came to see how you were getting on.' There's a hint of reproach
in his voice. 'That's animal bone from Windmill Hill, by the way.'

'Sorry. I . . . was curious.'

'Thought for a moment you were after our skeletons too. Had
another missive this morning from those bloody Druids. Want a coffee?
Kettle's already on.'

I follow him downstairs. '*Are* there skeletons in the cardboard boxes?'

'Lord, no. Not human, anyway. We only keep Charlie in this building, in his glass case, and I'm sure the Druids aren't fussed by the dog and the goat on display. All the rest are in secure storage.' He puts his head round the door into the gallery where one of the volunteers is manning the till. 'Chris? Fancy a cuppa? Don't know anyone who'd do a couple of months part-time as assistant warden, do you?'

'Why won't you take me on?' I ask, as Michael returns to the kitchen and sets out a line of mugs.

'India, you are a splendid woman of many talents but you don't have the right qualifications. I don't mind letting you do the odd day, but I'd prefer someone with a grasp of landscape archaeology.' He dispenses instant coffee into the mugs with unnerving precision. Every spoonful probably has the exact same number of granules. 'Besides, I understand you're now archaeological consultant to a film crew.'

This is news to me. I'd been half expecting to hear nothing more from Overview TV. And, oh, shit, if Michael knows—

'Don't look so worried.' Michael clamps the lid onto the coffee jar and swings round to face me, but I can't look him in the eye. 'Daniel Porteus called me this morning and asked me to tell you he'd be in touch. He wants you to go to London for some meeting next week. And, no, I didn't tell them your main function for the National Trust was making cappuccinos. Indeed, I told them on the phone not ten minutes ago that you were labouring in the archive.'

'Thanks.' With some difficulty, I meet his eyes, and discover only amusement.

'We've all at some point embellished our CVs. By the way, I *like* your idea of putting up another stone. Don't look smug, though, you aren't the first to have it – nobody's yet succeeded in persuading a broadcaster to part with enough money to do it. Anyway, how are you getting on with the letters?'

'Slowly.' I cast around for milk. 'I can't help reading them. Hey, you know this woman who says my grandmother used to work at the Manor?'

'Said,' says Michael. 'She died in December. She was something like ninety, mind.'

Damn. 'Anyone else left who was around then?'

'That's what the TV people wanted to know. Gave them all the names I had, but everyone I could think of was at last night's meeting. Most of them were tots in the thirties. It's a pity your gran is so confused because, by my reckoning, she's the last surviving person who worked at the Manor then.'

At home, Frannie is ensconced in her favourite armchair, watching *Flog It!*.

'Why do you find it so fascinating?' I've asked her this more than once.

'All this stuff,' she says. 'People's treasures. Never think it was worth so much, would you? I live in hope, Indy. One day there'll be something come up and I'll think, Ooh, blow me down and bugger, I got one of those.'

On the television, someone's holding up a truly hideous pottery figurine, turning it this way and that so the camera takes in every porcelain dimple and simper.

'You know these television people want to make a film about Alexander Keiller? I've spent the whole morning in the archive sorting out his letters. Michael at the National Trust says you used to be one of AK's secretaries.'

Frannie rearranges her features to look more than ever like she should be serving drinks on a budget airline, face utterly bland and unreadable. Strikes me you can hide a lot of dirt in wrinkles. 'How's he reckon he knows that?'

'Somebody else who used to work at the Manor.'

'That'd be the interfering old bitch below stairs. Dead now.'

Well, knock me down with the duty-free trolley. 'So you did? Work for the Great Man as a secretary?'

'Before the war I did, yes.'

'You never told me. What was he like?'

'You never asked. 'Sides, told you, I prefer not to 'member those times. Bad for everyone.' She heaves herself out of the armchair. 'Thing about diggin' up the past, like Mr Keiller did, don't really know what you'm turning over with your spade, do you?'

'Where are you going? Your programme's not finished.'

'Call of nature.' She shuffles out of the room. 'You wait till you're my age. Getting old's no fun. No fun at all.'

I should wait till tonight, after she's gone to bed, but I can't. As the loo door closes, I'm across the room, hand diving down the side of her armchair.

My fingers come up empty. The letter has gone.

CHAPTER 10

1938

There's a man on *Flog It!* with a lovely Victorian cow-creamer. Black Jackfield lustre glaze, he says, little gilt flowers painted on its hide. It has a lid on the top, where you fill it, and the tail curls into a handle so you can lift her up by the arse end and pour the cream out of her mouth. Mr Keiller had one just like it. No, I'm wrong. Our mam had one just like it, and Mr Keiller wanted to buy it off her, but she wouldn't sell. Said it had belonged to her mother. I wonder what became of it. We never used it. It sat on the Welsh dresser with the Royal Albert.

Mr Keiller collected them. They had a whole room to themselves at the Manor. He had six hundred and sixty-six. Can't remember why I know how many. I surely to goodness didn't count the blasted things while I was dusting them. He was particular about who was allowed to touch them, wouldn't let the housemaid do it, said she had fumbly fingers and he preferred me, even though I was secretarial. I washed them once, with him stood over me while I did it. Made me uncomfortable. I told him to get out a tea-towel and dry them himself, if he didn't trust me, and that made him laugh.

Six hundred and sixty-six. The number of the Beast. Did he always keep just six hundred and sixty-six, and have to sell one every time he bought one? No wonder some in the village said he was the devil incarnate.

My mam used to say I had the devil in me. She didn't know the half of it.

My feet were dragging when I crossed the road after getting off the bus. I was about done in.

Mam was in the kitchen. The wireless was on, but you could hardly hear it because the Frigidaire was making a terrible racket, somewhere between a wheeze and a beehive-sized hum. It couldn't cope with the heat when Mam was baking.

'Any luck?' she said, without looking up from rolling pastry.

'No. They all said I was too young.'

I wanted a secretarial job. I couldn't go on working with Mam and Dad in the guesthouse. Not that it was going to be a guesthouse much longer. Heap of rubble was next on the agenda. Mr Keiller was our landlord, and Mr Keiller wanted us out, so he could knock the place down and put up more of his old stones.

Wouldn't have happened if it hadn't been for the day he came to call to try to persuade Mam to part with her cow-creamer that he'd heard about from one of his friends who'd stayed with us. Mam said ever so polite she wouldn't sell, but she was happy to show it to him. She took him into the front parlour where it stood on the dresser, and Mr Keiller spotted the big stone that made the lintel over our fireplace.

'Sarsen, Mrs Robinson,' he said. 'Mind if I take a closer look?'

Well, he's the landlord, she couldn't very well say no. Next thing, he's out of the door saying he'll be back in a tick. Came back trailed by the dark-haired young archaeologist with the pointed nose and prominent teeth, the one I'd watched surveying the stones, and introduced him as Mr Stuart Piggott. Close up, I didn't like the look of him. He had sly eyes, which peered into our inglenook and up our chimney while Mr K looked on approvingly. Then they put their heads together and eventually declared that the house was built around one of the stones used to be in the circle, broke up into bits.

'Well, isn't that nice?' said our mam, uneasily.

Mr Keiller looks at her like she's some insignificant species of small brown bird, interesting maybe to some but not to him; he's a man for hawks. 'I'd like to get a closer look at it,' he says. Standing in our parlour, he was even more handsome than he'd seemed that night in the Manor garden. 'See those grooves on your lintel? It looks like it may have been a *polissoir*.' Powerful clever, too, knowing all them foreign words.

'A polly-what?' says Dad, who's come in from the garden where he's been digging up a load of taters for the guests' dinners.

'A polishing stone. Where Neolithic people smoothed stone axes. There are several up on the Downs.' Mostly he sounded like any posh toff, but occasionally his voice took on a soft Scottish lilt; the *r*s sounding more like *w*s, but not in a pansyish way. 'They were probably considered sacred.'

But he's lost our dad. He has a polite, bemused look on his face, muddy boots dangling from his hand.

'Don't see how you'll get a closer look without climbing the chimney like Santa Claus,' said Mam, trying for a laugh. 'And getting your lovely suit all sooty.'

Mr Keiller was looking thoughtful. 'How much did you say you wanted for that cow-creamer, Mrs Robinson?'

'Not for sale, Mr Keiller.'

A week after, we had our notice.

Mr K was generous, though. He said if we could be out by the autumn, he'd give Mam and Dad the money for the first year's lease on their new place. Dad thought that was a good deal. Mam said she didn't see why they should be bought. Dad said they didn't have much choice, really, so better take what they could, and we didn't have hardly any bookings past August anyway. So they cancelled what there was, and found a tobacconist's shop in Devizes. Dad said he'd be glad to see the back of guesthouse-keeping, and Mam said she was sick to death of changing sheets for Mr Keiller's snooty friends who were no better than they ought to be, and some of them a lot worse.

That left me. There was a second bedroom in the flat over the tobacconist's. Bedroom? Boxroom, more like. It was where the old tobacconist stored surplus stock, and it stank – be like sleeping rolled up in a cigar box. You didn't need three to run a tiny shop like that. I had to find a job. Seemed an opportunity, at first. But now it looked like I was aiming too high.

'Never mind,' said Mam. 'Something'll come up. You're a clever girl, Frances. I was ever so proud when you came top in bookkeeping last year in school. Somebody'll appreciate your talents.'

The Frigidaire gave a cough and fell silent.

'See?' said Mam. 'It thinks you're something.'

'No,' I said. 'It says I'm useless. Too bloomin' young, like they all keep saying.'

Then Ambrose came on again playing 'Small Hotel' and Mam started to cry.

What came up was Mrs Sorel-Taylour, who was Mr Keiller's secretary.

Mind you, like the parson used to say, God helps them who helps themselves. I'd heard they was short-handed at the Manor, with the digging season to plan for and a museum being built in the stable block. I made sure I bumped into her in the high street, by accident as it'd seem, when I went for bread from the baker's – oh, what a coincidence – at the exact time I reckoned she'd be on her way down the churchyard path to fetch some of Jack's lardy cakes to go with Mr Keiller's morning coffee. The sky was pale blue over the church tower, and a cloud of early midges danced over the drying puddles as I came up to her by the lich-gate, with the loaves under my arm.

'Mornin', Mrs Sorel-Taylour.'

'Good morning, Frances. Shouldn't you be in school?'

'Left last year. Working for Mam and Dad, now, though I in't sure what I'll do when they move to Devizes.'

For a moment I didn't think my plan would work. She looked at me as if she had no notion what I was blathering on about. She was a short lady, but very straight in the back, who sang in the Choral Society and gave lectures all over the county on etiquette. Her cream silk blouse with its Peter Pan collar was done right up to the neck, a carnelian brooch hiding the top button. I was a bit scared of her.

Then cogs began to whirr.

'Rumour has it you're good with numbers,' she said, her large dark eyes fixed on mine.

'Did well in arithmetic in school,' I said. Won a prize, I did, and Mr Keiller presented it at speech day, which was how Mrs S-T remembered.

'And you have a neat hand?'

I looked at my fingers. The nail varnish I'd put on last night for seeing Davey was already chipped.

'I need someone who can write clearly,' she said. 'And shorthand would help.'

'I'm enrolled on a Pitman's course.'

'You type, of course.' I should have enrolled for that too, but there wasn't the time as I was still helping most evenings at the guesthouse. 'What speed?'

'A hundred and ten,' I lied. Her eyebrows shot up. Perhaps I'd overdone it. 'On a good day,' I added. She must have swallowed one of the midges, because she started to cough and turned away to find a hanky in her bag. 'Is there a job for me at the Manor?' I hardly dared hope.

'Mr Keiller is bringing his collection down from London,' she said. 'We need help with cataloguing and typing up his notes on the finds. And there are his letters. He dictates several each day.' She looked hard at me, not quite a glare but there was disapproval on her long, delicate oval face. 'You'll find typing easier with shorter nails. And hair off your face, please, not falling over your eyes. You could try Kirby-grips. Mr Keiller prefers his staff to have a modest appearance.'

What she really meant was that it was easier if Mr Keiller didn't notice his staff's appearance. I understood that when I told Davey I had the job. That gave him ants in his pants, all right.

'Why on earth d'you want to work at the Manor?'

'So I can stay in the village, not have to move away with Mam and

95

Dad and sleep in that smelly boxroom. I'll be able to see you more often.' He had a room over the stables. I'd never dared go up there yet, but I thought of evenings, cosying up with him, the cars gleaming in the dark beneath us, maybe one ticking quietly after Mr Keiller had given it a long run to London.

'Yes, but . . .' He lit a cigarette, cupping his hand round the match. Its flare showed his frown in the darkness. We were sat in the lee of one of the stones, on a rug Davey always brought with him for our courting. I hadn't yet done everything on that rug that he wanted me to do, but on a cold night we'd both found warm places for our hands.

'You do *want* to see more of me, don't you?' Perhaps he had his eye on someone else. By now Mam had met him, but she said he was one of those quiet 'uns, could never tell what he was really thinking. I thought I knew him, but maybe I didn't.

'It's not that,' said Davey. 'It's more . . . Well.' He looked down at the ground. 'I'm away a lot, driving Mr Keiller.'

'But when you're there . . .'

'No, Fran,' he said. 'At least . . . I never know when he'll want me to do some job. Day or night. You have to jump to it when he has one of his whims, and his temper . . .'

'I don't understand you,' I said. 'I thought you'd be happy to have your girl a bit closer. So what if he makes demands? It'll be all the easier to see me when we know each other's comings and goings. I'll be working late too sometimes, right across the yard from you . . .'

'You never seen a temper like it.' There was a desperate look in Davey's eye. 'Takes against people just like that. You don't want to work for him – he'll eat a little thing like you for breakfast. And they say he's got a roving eye.'

'I know how to deal with roving eyes,' I said, bolder than I felt. 'Get plenty of those at the guesthouse.'

'Do you now?' said Davey. He gave a sigh of defeat. 'How about roving hands? Any good at dealing with them?'

* * *

'Your young man,' said Mam. 'Can I just say this? Be careful, Frances.'

'Don't know what you mean.'

I'd brought Davey over for Sunday tea, and he'd arrived with his lavatory-brush hair oiled down and an eager smile on his face. Dad and he seemed to get on – there was a lot of man-to-man chat about horse-racing and cars. But Mam – I'd seen the way her eyes narrowed when she looked at him. I'd stopped telling her everything, and I knew that hurt her.

'I'd like to see you settled,' Mam said. She was looking out of the window at the line of hills beyond the stone circle. 'One of these days. But . . . Don't be a tease, Frances. Davey's a nice boy and he don't deserve it.'

'Don't know what you mean,' I said, mutinous.

'I mean he's gentle and kind. Like I used to think you were. But I don't know, seeing you together, strikes me to wonder which one wears the trousers, and I don't think it's him.'

'He was on his best behaviour for you,' I said, desperate not to seem mannish.

Mam's eyes softened. 'Maybe I don't understand girls today, then. But – oh, I don't know. Still waters, as they say. All the same, I worry he's too quiet for you. I worry that you'll set your sights on some-body more dashing.'

The minute it was out of her mouth, I knew she was right, but I wasn't going to give her the satisfaction of pouring my heart out. Davey wasn't girlish, but he had a soft side, and now we were seeing each other regular, he didn't seem as exciting as when I'd noticed him first on the back of a tall bay horse stepping delicate-hoofed up the high street, his bony knees and wrists controlling that gurt explosive mass of muscle and power. But I had him, and as Mam used to say, whenever we passed one of the sad spinsters in the village whose sweetheart had died in the Great War, a woman counts herself fortu-nate to find a decent man and keep him. Mam always said she'd been lucky with Dad, and there weren't anything exciting about him.

Fair to say, of course, that Mam didn't tell me everything, and don't

I wish she had. I reckon she already knew it wasn't right for her to be so tired at the end of every day. Blamed myself for not talking to her, once she was gone. But at that age you think everybody you know'll be around for ever.

Then again, sometimes it's right to keep your big gabby mouth buttoned, and if I had, the afternoon Davey took me to visit Mam in the hospital . . . But no use stirring over might-have-beens.

CHAPTER 11

Fran refuses point blank to discuss her time at the Manor. Doesn't stop me trying at regular intervals.

'My memory in't what it was.'

'You must remember something.'

She shakes her head stubbornly. 'Nothing worth the telling. Read the books. They'd have it right, mostly, I 'spec'.'

'What about the letters you typed?'

'Oh, Ind, you can't expect me to remember those boring old things. Thought they were all in the files, anyway, and you'd read 'em.'

'Some of them were burned, apparently.'

Something glitters in her eyes, but she shakes her head again and clatters her spoon into her bowl, signalling it's time to change the subject. 'Don't want any more of this porridge. Anyway, I was thinking in the night.'

'Always a dangerous thing.'

'Go on with you. Have me best ideas then. I thought, Why doesn't our Indy find a job on *Flog It*? They make it in Bristol. You'd be good on that. Such an interesting programme, one of me favourites.'

'Don't worry,' I tell her, scooping up the cereal bowls and dumping them in the sink. 'Might have a television job already. I'm off to London, remember, today.'

'By the way, Ind,' she says, casually, 'you in't seen them buggerin' lights lately, have you?'

Channel 4 is housed in a scary modern building on Horseferry Road. As we walk under the sheer concave glass sheet suspended above the doors, I keep thinking the whole lot will come crashing down and slice off my head like in *The Omen*. Even Daniel Porteus looks uncomfortable. He keeps running a hand through his white quiff, which is getting alarmingly spiky.

He's invited me to help explain my idea to the commissioning editor in London, because Ibby is apparently not good in meetings. 'Doesn't butter them up properly,' he told me on the train. 'If the commissioning editor suggests something stupid, she can't conceal her contempt. Tells them they're wrong.' As he said it, he shot me a doubtful glance. 'Your job is to sit there and look fresh-faced. Leave the talking to me. Unless somebody asks you to say something, in which case be brief. And enthusiastic. *Don't argue.*'

He marches up to the desk and tells them who we are. We sign in and are given name badges. Then we sit on low, curved armchairs in the atrium. Above, a high glassy space is diced by steel cables.

Daniel shifts awkwardly on his seat. 'They design these specially to make it impossible to get up gracefully,' he mutters. 'Puts you at a disadvantage from the start. Especially with dodgy knees.'

'I suppose you come here a lot?' I'm not sure how to make conversation with him.

'I'm not well in, if that's what you mean,' he says. 'The company's too small, and you need to be London-based to do serious business. Channel 4 commissioners are much happier conjuring ideas off the tablecloth at the Ivy with their mates. They give work to bright young things who remind them of themselves. Doesn't matter if *we* had the best concept in the world —' He breaks off at the sight of a tall, gangly bloke bouncing lithely over the floor as if he had springs in his heels, boing boing, coming our way at a terrific pace.

'Cameron!' says Daniel, struggling to his feet. A fork-lift truck would be useful at this moment. The red plastic seat farts as he finally manages to lever his bum up from it. 'Good to see you! Thanks for sparing the time!' I can hear the exclamation marks.

'Daniel!' Cameron is exclamation-marking back. He's wearing an oversized tweed jacket that suggests at first glance he bought it at

Oxfam, though at a second you're meant to recognize he paid a fortune for it brand new somewhere much classier. He claps the older man on the shoulder manfully, and kisses me – 'And lovely to see *you* again!' – like he knows me. Daniel sends me a fierce glance, warning me not to open my mouth and say we've never met before.

'Now – I would have bought you lunch in the canteen, but I'm supposed to be at the Ivy in half an hour.' Cameron makes it sound *such* a bore. 'Come up to the office. You have passes?' Even I find it hard to keep up as he leads the way at a gallop towards a glass barrier. A tarty brunette I recognize from the last series of *Big Brother* pushes between us as if she can't be bothered with these lumbering provincials, but fortunately Cameron waits, cooling his smoking heels and drumming the backs of his fingers against the security gate.

'You didn't see that Michael Wood thing the other night on BBC4?' puffs Daniel, as we hurtle through and head for the stairs.

'Meant to but we had people round,' says Cameron, to let us know what a sparkly social life he has. 'Recorded it, of course – in case I ever have time to watch. Got a pile of DVDs this high. Not enough hours in the day to see our stuff, let alone what the opposition's up to.'

'You should try and make time. Brilliant.' Surely a miscalculation, as now Daniel needs to justify why he liked it, although we're halfway through a punishing stairs workout at Cameron-pace. 'If the . . . rest of the series . . . is as . . . good . . . Did you see it, India?'

'No. We haven't—' Another warning look silences me. Presumably admitting you don't have digital telly casts you into outer darkness at Channel 4. But here we are at the top of the stairs and Cameron isn't listening anyway. He sweeps us through a huge open-plan office and into a glass-walled cubicle overlooking a leafy courtyard. Daniel and I sit with our knees by our ears on armchairs that are, if anything, lower than the ones in Reception while Cameron swivels to and fro in a high-backed leather chair.

'So,' he says. 'Archaeology, Daniel. What's hot?'

'Did you watch the DVD I sent you?'

'DVD? My assistant must have it.'

'Never mind. The point is, we've some original archive material, never been shown before. Keiller excavating Avebury.'

'Twenties?' Cameron is cool, giving nothing away.

'That's when Keiller first started work in the area, at Windmill Hill, you're right, but this film dates from 'thirty-eight, when he was reconstructing the stone circle. The film was shot by one of the villagers – only a couple of reels, but there might be more somewhere – and I want to use it as the basis of a programme about Keiller remodelling Avebury to fit his idea of how it looked in the Neolithic.'

'New Stone Age,' I chip in helpfully, because I can see Cameron is looking puzzled. 'Avebury's about five thousand years old.'

'Viewers aren't much interested in pre-history,' says Cameron, witheringly. 'We get better ratings on *Time Team* for digs that are post-Roman. More to see. Unless it's an execution site, of course. People like skeletons, preferably mutilated.'

I can hear the faint grinding of Daniel's teeth. 'Ah, but this is a story with a double layer,' he says. 'Not just Avebury five thousand years ago, but Alexander Keiller, playboy archaeologist, four times married, a string of mistresses, fast cars, pots of money, so obsessed by his vision of the past he moved half the village out of their homes and destroyed a community.' He's on a roll now. 'He entirely ignored what would be an archaeologist's approach today – the fact that monuments like these don't simply exist at a single point of time but represent continuity. That a village grew up in the henge, perhaps for defensive reasons, that people tried to bury the stones or destroy them, perhaps because they feared them . . . The story of Avebury doesn't stop with its abandonment in the Iron Age, or for that matter with Keiller. People are still using the monument as a sacred space today.'

'Pagans,' says Cameron. He chews a thumbnail and looks out of the window. 'We used to do a lot about pagans. Not sure . . . Though I did hear that one of the contestants in the next series of *BB* is going to be a practising Satanist.'

'There aren't Satanists at—' But Daniel kicks me.

102

'That isn't the best of it,' he says quickly. 'Cameron, I brought this to you before I approached the BBC because I think it's very much your thing, though I know they'd kill for it at White City. Keiller's vision was never completed. The Second World War got in the way, he ran out of money. The climax of our film is *our* reconstruction of his reconstruction. We excavate and re-erect one of the fallen megaliths Keiller didn't have time to raise.'

Cameron's gaze snaps back from the courtyard. 'Fuck me. Now *that*'s a good idea. Positively post-modern.'

I glare at Daniel.

'India's actually,' he admits. 'She works for the National Trust.'

'Access?'

'Sorted.'

'Presenter?'

'Narrated, not presented,' says Daniel.

'No way,' says Cameron. 'Needs a presenter. Someone authoritative but sexy.' He stares out of the window again in case he spots the right person swinging through the trees. 'There's this bloke who's done a brilliant job for us on a *Time Team*. Hasn't gone out yet, so you won't have seen him. Came in as a guest expert, but I'd like to try him on something solo. It's his field, too – he's strong on ancient religion and mystery cults. Name's Martin Ekwall. Big bloke, early forties, looks good on camera, though I'd like to get the beard off him.'

'That went all right,' I say, as we cross the concrete bridge back to Horseferry Road.

'Maybe.' Daniel Porteus doesn't look happy. 'He didn't even offer us a coffee.'

'Is that bad?'

'The breaking of bread signifies membership of the clan.'

'Oh.'

'But he did suggest a presenter. They only do that when they're interested. "Like to get the beard off him."' Mimicking Cameron viciously. 'Like to get the pants off him, more like.' He roots in his canvas briefcase. 'Look, here's a list of stuff I'd like you to find in the archive – stills, mostly, Keiller's own photographs of the excavations. I'm not going back to Bristol this afternoon – meetings lined up at the BBC, different project, though it won't do any harm to mention this one and put the willies up Channel 4. They all know each other and gossip like mad. I'd buy you lunch at the Ivy just to show that wanker I can afford it, but we'd never get a table. You don't mind making your own way back?'

He hands me the list, and embraces me with a double air kiss. Behind him, a vast black 4×4 draws up beneath the *Omen*-style portico. Out steps Steve's father, the ITN foreign correspondent, wearing dark glasses.

Wyrd.

He stares straight at me, over Daniel's shoulder, taking off the glasses, as if he recognizes me. He has Steve's eyes. Then his gaze slides over me, and he turns away into the building, like I'm nothing after all.

As I run up the escalator to the concourse under the sooty vault of Paddington, after detouring via Oxford Street to dispel paranoia by buying myself new jeans, I'm sure I'll miss the train. If I don't make this one, I'll be waiting hours because my cheap ticket isn't valid in peak period.

Platform four. Three minutes. Can do it if I run . . .

The doors are slamming but I hop into one of the first-class coaches and wheeze my way down the train. The standard-class carriage beyond the buffet and the one after that are packed, but further down the train, passengers thin out and, joy of joys, there's a table with only one person at it, head down and absorbed in a pile of printouts. I wriggle out of my coat, plonk it and my bags on the aisle seat, shuffle across towards the window and—

Something cold and liquid explodes in my chest. It can't be.

My buttocks, hovering an inch above the seat, squeeze instinctively to lift me out of it and, if possible, off the train before it leaves.

He looks up. Fuck. It is. *Fuck.*

He looks, if anything, more shocked than I feel.

'Sorry,' I say. 'I – I'll— Just realized. Wrong train. Need the later one.'

'Bollocks. We're moving. Sit down. How the hell are you?'

Grey eyes, the North Sea. Too late. Drowned. Turned to stone. Lost.

And, dammit, Mr Cool, acting now like nothing happened, like we never shared a bed, let alone the experience of nearly dying in that helicopter. The train starts sliding out of the station. My bottom, with a will of its own, slowly sinks onto the seat opposite him.

'Ed.'

The sun slants in through the train windows and sparks highlights in his dark brown hair. The cut's shorter, though somehow messier: he must have tried gelling it into spikes but instead it appears unbrushed, and his eyes seem muddy and tired – or could I really have forgotten what he looks like?

'You look . . . different,' he says.

'Do I?' Renowned for my sparkling wit and ready quips.

'More . . . substantial.'

'Fatter. Thanks.'

'No. Actually I'd say you're thinner. I meant, somehow tougher . . .'

'Great. Older.'

'More confident. Come on. Stop doing yourself down.'

'Then stop paying me such overwhelming compliments.'

He looks older, too, than I remember. He must be ten years my senior, at least, in his mid-thirties, maybe knocking forty. As for the attraction between us – well, it's a scent I dimly remember on the air, but now vanquished by a railway carriage reeking of microwaved baconburger and diesel fumes and frizzling brake linings as we slow for a signal on the track ahead. Or, at least, that's what I tell myself.

'You never returned my calls,' he says.

'I didn't think it would be a good idea.'

An awkward silence, as we both mull over why it wasn't a good idea.

Apart from my not wanting to be involved again with a married man, any real chance of a relationship went down with the helicopter.

'So what . . .' he starts, same moment as I say: 'Have you . . .'

'You first.'

'I was going to ask, what have you been doing?' he says. 'I mean – what have you been doing with your life?'

'I'm back in television again. With a Bristol-based independent. Been up for a meeting with Channel 4.'

'Great.' He actually looks impressed.

'You?'

'Oh, various stuff. The MA, mostly. Did I tell you I've been doing a part-time master's in landscape archaeology? On my way now to a job interview.'

'You're not working with Luke any more?'

'No.' He props his chin on his hand, looks out of the window. 'He . . . well, not to put too fine a point on it, he let me go. Company went bust anyway.'

Dangerous ground. 'I need a coffee,' I say. 'Can I fetch you one from the buffet?'

'No, let me get them.' He levers himself upright, feeling in his pockets for change. 'Bugger. Meant to stop at the cashpoint . . .'

'Here, I've a twenty needs changing.' As he takes it from me, our eyes meet.

'I kept calling you because I wanted to be sure you were OK . . .' he begins.

'I was fine. Well, maybe a bit wobbly to start with, but you know . . .'

'Yes. Me too.'

He lurches away down the carriage, long-legged in a pair of neat black trousers and a fine wool jacket that seems absurdly formal next to my memories of him in T-shirt and khaki combats, at the controls of the helicopter.

Interview clothes. He said he was going for a job interview. He's doing an MA in landscape archaeology.

No. Not that job. Please.

An impossible coincidence. Couldn't be.

Could it?

Wyrd. Never trust the bloody web of connectedness.

'Ed!'

Several other people in the carriage peer round their seats to see what's up. There must have been a note of panic in my voice.

He turns round and starts walking back.

'Where are you getting off the train?'

'Swindon.'

Where Heelis, the National Trust head office, is.

'But didn't you ask him?' says Corey. She's polishing the nozzles on the cappuccino machine again. Maybe it's one of those neuroses, like constantly washing your hands. 'Your roots need retinting, by the way. I mean, it might not be the assistant-warden job. You said he's really a pilot, studying archaeology part-time.'

'Of course I didn't ask. I jumped off the train at Reading before he came back with the coffees. Sat in the buffet and waited two and a half hours until there was another I could catch with my cheap ticket. Arrived home so late Frannie had already put herself to bed.'

Two customers walk in, a middle-aged husband and wife, shaking raindrops off their parkas. They start a muttered argument beside the homemade cakes. I slide into place behind the till, and Corey flips the top off the milk carton ready to spring into barrista action.

'So he doesn't know?'

'Know what?'

'That you're here.'

'Why would he? It was a one-night stand. We didn't exactly get around to exchanging life histories.'

'Apart from him letting slip he was married.'

Out of the corner of my eye I watch the male customer stomping off to inspect the sandwiches and organic crisps. I haven't been entirely straight with Corey. As far as she's concerned, Ed is someone I had a fling with in London. No one in Avebury, apart from John, knows I was caught up in the helicopter crash.

What made me act so brazenly last summer? The short answer is too much drink. Steve and I were down from London, overnighting at a pub near the airfield so we didn't have to wake too early. Very definitely separate rooms, though Steve would have liked it otherwise. Luke and Ed were already waiting in the bar when we arrived, Luke knocking it back like there was no tomorrow, Ed switching to Diet Coke after a couple of beers. Maybe I started flirting because I was nervous Steve might make a move on me. He'd been through most of the women under thirty at the TV company, and I was determined not to join their ranks.

'Anyway,' says Corey, 'if he's a flyboy, plenty of other places he could be applying for a job. Half a dozen small airfields round here on the lookout for drop-zone pilots or instructors.'

When I first saw Ed, I thought him good-looking in a neglected way: messy dark hair, a lived-in face, dangerously unshaven, deep lines scored either side of his mouth. He had on a crumpled linen shirt with the sleeves rolled up, and a leather coat was slung over the back of his chair. He wasn't looking at me when we first came in. He was talking to the girl behind the bar. She was one of those snap-me-in-two blondes, like Corey, half my size with hair so straight she must have ironed it and a chenille jumper the colour of butter, beneath which her tits bubbled up in two perfect little spheres. I loathed her on sight.

'How *did* you find out he was married?' asks Corey. The woman in the parka is wielding the cake tongs with an unnecessary amount of clatter as she lifts scones onto a plate.

'Post-coital confession.' My fingers hover over the till buttons, as the customer moves on to the lemon drizzle cake. '"I should have told you earlier": that sort of stuff. Marriage on rocks. Wife, she no understand me. Well, he didn't actually say that last bit, but it was sort of hanging in the air, in the hope I'd fall for the oldest line in the book. They live in some bloody palatial farmhouse in Oxfordshire, no land as such but two socking great barns with it, ripe for conversion. My heart bleeds.'

'Hot chocolate, please,' says the woman in the parka, arriving in front of us with a carbohydrate-laden tray. 'Ray?'

'Do they do filter coffee?'

'No, but we do an Americano, which is virtually the same. I should've told him at the time that if he was married he could forget it,' I tell Corey, as she spoons hot-chocolate powder out of the tin. 'But . . . you know how it is. You're so anxious they shouldn't be spotted leaving your room that you don't get around to saying anything. I – well, I ignored all his phone calls and texts afterwards, except to tell him to go away.'

'I'm glad to say I *don't* know how it is. Not from personal experience, anyway.' Married to a Devizes policeman for two years, Corey is a devotee of women's magazines that discuss this kind of thing.

'Men are so full of shit,' I say confidently. 'Their problem is they can't tell the difference between sex and love.'

The woman at the counter snorts.

'Or would he prefer a latte?' I ask her.

'In my book, he's unfaithful even if he isn't sleeping with someone else.' Corey shoves the milk jug under the nozzle of the steamer. She has to raise her voice over the machine's whoosh. 'Which would you prefer – a husband shagging you and thinking of someone else, or shagging someone else and thinking of you?'

My creative studies BA had finished a few months and a lot of marks short of what I'd planned when my tutor's wife started asking herself the very same question. Not that marks had anything to do with it. I'd fallen hopelessly in love with the sod. The exams were a wipeout; I only scraped a pass on coursework. Never again.

The customer's eyebrows are jigging up and down in a demented dance. 'Do him an Americano, dear. He doesn't understand the difference.'

'The real question is,' says Corey, spooning froth into the hot-chocolate mug, 'how do you feel about him now, supposing he had a job here?'

'I told you. It's over. I knew that the moment I looked at him and realized I didn't fancy him any more. Can't tell you what a relief that was.'

This time both Corey and the woman snort.

During my lunch hour, I cross the cobbles to the museum. Chris, at the till, raises his eyebrows. I hand him a mug of hot chocolate: bribery. 'OK if I go upstairs?' I ask. 'More research for those telly people.'

'Does the curator know?'

'Checked with her this morning. She said to go ahead.'

He gives me the nod.

Upstairs, I pull on a pair of blue vinyl gloves to leaf through the photo albums. The first item on Daniel Porteus's list is Destruction of Village. Doesn't take me long to find the pictures at the start of the 1938 album: black-and-white stills of brawny workmen, braces and cloth caps, fragments of wall and thatch, homes that look as if someone dropped a bomb on them.

Grandfather or no, Keiller really was a bastard.

PART THREE

Equal Night

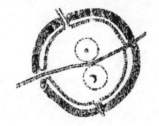

And that this place may thoroughly be thought
True Paradise, I have the serpent brought.

John Donne, *Twicknam Garden*

Let us be clear: there were no Druids at Avebury until the present day. Druids were a Celtic priesthood (and later a nineteenth-century re-invention) and Avebury fell into disuse long before the Celts arrived in Britain. Indeed, one of its most remarkable aspects is that no Iron Age artefacts at all have been found within the henge. Perhaps people steered clear of the circle at that point in time. So we can safely say that it is highly unlikely that Alban Eiler, the Celtic spring festival, was ever celebrated there during the Druids' heyday.

Having said that, most cultures celebrate a spring festival at or about the time of the vernal equinox. Certainly some Neolithic monuments – the passages in the tomb at Knowth, in Ireland, for example – seem to be aligned to sunset and sunrise at the equinox (literally, 'equal night'), on 20/21 March. There doesn't appear to be any such alignment at Avebury: but that is not to say categorically there was not one. Keiller never finished his reconstruction, and we have an incomplete picture of the other settings – the Cove, the inner circles and the stone row – that lay inside the main circle.

So when today's Druids meet to observe Alban Eiler, they could indeed be following a tradition observed through the ages at Avebury. The sun god meets the awakening spring goddess, Eostre – from whose name we derive both 'Easter' and 'oestrogen'. Sap rises, green things stir, the life force returns to the earth.

Dr Martin Ekwall,
A Turning Circle: The Ritual Year at Avebury,
Hackpen Press

CHAPTER 12

1938

You can't help who you fall for, can you?

To begin with I hardly saw Mr Keiller at the Manor. He was always somewhere else. Up and down to London, or off to Scotland. Most of the time we didn't know where he was.

'He'll be skiing,' said Cook, hopefully, if we hadn't seen him for three or four days. He'd been a champion when he was younger, and at one time trained the British ski-jump team. But, no, he'd turn up late that very evening, with guests, demanding supper at midnight.

Mrs Sorel-Taylour had introduced me, suitably Kirby-gripped, on my first day. 'This is Miss Robinson, who'll be helping with the cataloguing.'

He was in the Map Room, sitting on a high draughtsman's stool, looking at some photographs laid out under an Anglepoise lamp. Its light was the only splash of brightness. Everything in there was brown – velvet curtains, window seats, carpet. Even the walls were covered in brown leather.

He turned to inspect me, but I don't think he was much interested by what he saw, a fifteen-year-old girl in a cheap jacket-and-skirt costume, with finger-waved hair and a scrubbed country face. 'Do you write clearly?' You could hear the *w* in write.

'Very,' said Mrs Sorel-Taylour, before I could open my mouth. 'That's why I took the child on.' Did I imagine that tiny stress on 'the child'? 'She will, of course, be under my direct supervision.'

'Good,' he said. He was bored already, wanting to return to his pictures. The one on top was strange, but familiar too. It took a moment to work it out, then I saw it was a photograph of Avebury from the air. It had been taken late in the day because the shadows were long.

He must have been watching my face. 'You recognize it.' The soft upper-class *w* sound again, instead of the *r*.

'I can see our guesthouse. There.'

'Ah, that Robinson. I thought I'd seen you before.' I could smell the oil on his sandy brown hair, sweet and spicy. The parting, on the right, was straight as a metal rule, the hair slicked back from a high, smooth forehead. 'Do you know who you're descended from?'

'The monkeys, my mam says.'

He laughed. 'The biggest monkey round here in the eighteenth century was Tom Robinson. They called him Stonebreaker Robinson, because he destroyed so many of the stones from the circle – broke them up for building material and road surfacing. Did you know that?'

'No, sir.'

'It seems to me entirely appropriate that we should put a Robinson to labour setting right what he destroyed. You shall serve your time in the museum on his behalf.' He had a habit of dipping his chin and crinkling up his eyes when he smiled. 'Of course, you might not be descended from him, but we shall never know, shall we? So I shall always assume you are and, on high days and holidays, give you twenty strokes of the lash as additional penance.'

I looked helplessly at Mrs Sorel-Taylour. Her mouth was a tight red seam.

Mr Keiller turned back to his photograph but his eyes stayed crinkled and happy, a smile rippling round his mouth.

Big crates arrived from London, full of what Mam called 'stuff'. So many bits of broken pot and flakes of stone that Mr Keiller had dug up from Windmill Hill when he'd come there in the 1920s, or from Mr Peak-Garland's fields when he'd rebuilt the Avenue that leads up to the circle. Not to mention the bits and pieces they found from the circle itself in the last year, when they started putting back the stones. It was all *stuff* to me, too, to begin with, but after a bit what the archaeologists say starts to sink in, so you see how a sliver of flint has a serrated edge that some old fellow chipped there five thousand years ago, or the pattern of nibble marks on a piece of pot jabbed into the clay by an ever-so-patient woman with a tiny bird bone.

We didn't unpack it – that was a job for the men. All of them used to wear these dark green blazers, like a sports team, with a badge on the breast pocket that said MIAR: Morven Institute of Archaeological Research, after Mr Keiller's family home in Scotland. At first it made them hard to tell apart at a distance, but it didn't take long to sort out who was who. There was Mr Young, Mr Keiller's foreman, small-built, lean and leathery-skinned from the last season, who'd been promoted to supervise the museum. He wasn't posh like the others, and he had a proper Wiltshire accent, but he'd worked with Mr K for years, and Mr K always listened to his opinion. He was friendly but a bit shy around me, and Mrs Sorel-Taylour said he was awkward with women, never been married. But it was the two younger ones I saw most of: dark, heavy-browed, big-nosed Mr Piggott, who treated me like I wasn't there, most of the time, and Donald Cromley, the taller, good-looking fellow whose light brown hair used to flop over one eye because he didn't oil it back.

They would take out each piece from the crates and try to find it in the notes, which had always got lost or separated, then argue over what it was. Once or twice I half expected them to come to blows. Mr Piggott was the older of the two, and the more experienced, though sometimes he behaved like an overgrown schoolboy, but Mr Cromley was the clever young puppy snapping at his better's heels. Mrs Sorel-Taylour and I had to sit there writing everything down, and later type it all up. When she was satisfied I really did write neatly, she let me do the labels to go with the exhibits in the glass and mahogany cases.

We were in the museum one morning when Mr Cromley dipped his hand into the crate, and Mr Piggott started to giggle when he saw what he'd come up with. 'You know, Donald, the Americans have an expression,' he said, 'which we could adapt for this occasion. "Happy as a Don with two . . ."'

Mrs S-T shot them a disgusted glance. 'Gentlemen. Please remember there are ladies present.'

'She's a country girl,' said Mr Piggott. 'She knows what it is. Don't you, Miss Robinson?' The first time, I think, he'd ever addressed me by name.

Of course I knew. Didn't stop my cheeks being on fire, though. Mr Cromley placed the chalk doo-dah on the table where he had been laying out the finds. It was about four inches long, rough carved, with a bulging knobble at the end.

'Not amazingly impressive,' said Mr Piggott, with a scornful twist of his thick dark eyebrows.

'Ah, but I have four of them,' said Mr Cromley, delving into the crate, and the pair of them burst out laughing again.

'Where did they come from?' I asked, provoking more hoots and snuffles.

'These are from Windmill Hill,' said Mrs Sorel-Taylour. 'I'm sorry, Frances, you'll have to become used to this sort of thing.'

'Regeneration,' said Mr Cromley, recovering himself sudden-like. 'That's what ceremonies at Avebury would have been about, in all probability. They may have been left as offerings to the gods. Or the priest may have strapped on a chalk phallus for the ritual.'

'He never wore one of those!' I exclaimed. 'What would he have done with it?'

Mr Piggott went so brick-coloured I thought he'd explode with trying not to laugh. But Mr Cromley pushed back his hair and gave me a look that was almost respectful. 'That's actually a very good question.'

'But not one we should waste time answering this morning,' said Mrs Sorel-Taylour, briskly. 'It's nearly Miss Robinson's lunch break, and there are at least half a dozen finds in that crate you haven't begun to look at.'

At twelve thirty exactly Mrs Sorel-Taylour would send me off for lunch, and usually I'd wander across the cobbles to the barn in the hope of finding Davey polishing one of the cars. He wasn't often there.

He'd be on the road, maybe driving Mr Keiller to some dinner in Mayfair, or fetching more boxes of stuff from Charles Street where Mr K had his London house.

Today I wasn't sure if I was glad or not there was no sign of him. I kept thinking of the great big chalk thing Mr Keiller had been carrying the night Davey and I watched the ceremony in the garden. Whatever had he done with it when they disappeared between the box hedges?

I wanted to ask Mrs Sorel-Taylour what she'd seen. If she was there, it couldn't have been anything too dreadful, could it? Surely Mr Keiller wouldn't . . .

There was a step behind me on the cobbles. I whipped round to see Mr Cromley crossing the stable yard towards the Manor. He'd been there too that night, I remembered, the moonlight silvering his light brown hair. 'Mr Cromley!' I called.

He turned and came towards me. 'What can I do for you, Miss Robinson?'

He was delicate-looking, but strong too. I'd seen him lift them crates effortlessly from the floor.

'I was interested in what you were saying in there,' I said. 'But what I was wondering was . . . how you know what they did?'

His face lit up in a smile. 'Always pleased to enlighten the genuinely curious,' he said, eyes raking me like I was a seed patch. 'It's all conjecture, of course, but I've made a study of primitive magic, in various parts of the world.' I'd thought of him as cynical and knowing, but now he seemed surprisingly young and earnest. 'The urge for ritual is always close to the surface, even in modern life. There must be superstitions in the village connected to the stones.'

'Only superstition I know is not to go round them widdershins,' I said. 'My mam told me that. Always has to be sunwise.'

'Widdershins!' Mr Cromley was delighted. 'Must tell Alec. Widdershins is the direction he's chosen to take excavating the circle.'

'Well, my mam would say he was storing up trouble for himself.'

'Perhaps he is. In more ways than one.' He gave a rueful grin. 'Sorry about the ragging in there. Piggott and I don't entirely see eye to eye. For all his schoolboy bluster, he's a prude. Won't admit these places were about sex and death.'

'I think you're trying to shock me, Mr Cromley.'

'Merely making an academic case for ritual magic in the Neolithic.' He threw me a mischievous look, then glanced up at the church clock. 'I'm so sorry, but I'm expecting a telephone call in the Manor from my uncle. He's visiting friends in Wiltshire, and we're hoping to arrange dinner this week. Otherwise, I'd happily . . . initiate you in the mysteries. But there'll be other opportunities. Strikes me you're a lot brighter than you let on, Miss Robinson.' He raised an eyebrow like other men might raise a hat, and let himself into the Manor garden through the wrought-iron gate.

So I went back to the guesthouse and hung around the kitchen, pinching scraps for a sandwich, while Mam toiled over preparations for the evening meal, and ran in and out of the dining room with lunch for any guest who hadn't gone out for the day. She threw me an impatient glance and the tea-towel, and I ended up, as I often did, doing the washing-up. Then when I started shooting worried glances at the clock, she touched my hair and said, 'Go on, I can manage without you – you've more important things to do.' I can feel her fingers now, after all these years, smoothing my curls.

I ran across the road to the barns again, in the hope Davey was back and I'd sneak ten minutes with him before I had to return to Mrs Sorel-Taylour. But he was off to London again with Mr K, according to Philip the other driver, and staying overnight.

A few days later Mrs Sorel-Taylour and I were in the office upstairs, typing up notes Mr Piggott had dictated, when there was a terrible bang from outside. A couple of years later a noise like that would have sent us scurrying under the table, thinking German planes were bombing us, but this was still six months before Mr Chamberlain and his piece of paper and it hadn't sunk in, to me at least, that there was a war coming.

Mrs Sorel-Taylour rose straight-backed, flapping a hand to tell me I should stay sitting. She stalked over to the window – there was only one, in the end wall, with faded chintz curtains – but I dare say she couldn't see much, not being very tall.

There was another bang like the crack of doom.

'It in't the trees again?' I asked. Two years ago, they'd cut down the trees that grew over the banks and dynamited the stumps. A gurt piece of wood had gone clean through Mr Peak-Garland's cowshed roof, and Mr Keiller liked to tell the story of how Mr Piggott had been hit on the head by another lump. Pity it didn't bash some of his brains out, I thought. He had far too many of them, and knew it. I'd seen cartoons he'd drawn of people in the village and it seemed to me he always made us out to look fools.

'*Isn't*, Frances.' Mrs Sorel-Taylour was waging war on my Wiltshire ways. 'That wasn't explosives, it was a demolition ball. It'll be the black-smith's.'

'Can we go and look?'

She checked her watch. 'It's almost lunchtime. Make sure you're back a few minutes before half past one.'

I was down the steep narrow stairs and out across the cobbles before you could say Fran Robinson. I wanted to see this.

The blacksmith's wasn't the first building to go. Rawlins's garage, hard by the Adam and Eve stones, which Mr Keiller called the Cove, had already gone. Mr Rawlins didn't mind. Shabby wooden shack, yard full of old tyres and bits of cars, backed by a row of four cottages with leaky thatch. Rawlins needed space for his new petrol pumps, his second wife and all his kids, so he thought it a great deal when Mr Keiller offered him in exchange a piece of land outside the village on the Swindon road. Even lent him three hundred pounds to build a gurt new flat-roofed house that looked like an Egyptian picture palace. Our dad was impressed, but our mam used to wince every time she went past it. Mr and Mrs Tibbles from the cottages, Curly

119

and Mary King, and the old lady who always wore black, who also lived in the row, faded out of our lives. I thought they'd all gone to Marlborough, but I wasn't sure.

There was another bang as I came round the side of the church. It looked like there was a fog rolling down the village street, and the lich-gate was shrouded in yellow dust. A cheer went up, there was a creaking noise, then a crash.

By the time I was through the gate, there was no thatch left on the blacksmith's shop, except for one corner, and no front, and not much by way of side walls either. The straw clung to the last bit of chimney-stack like Mr Hitler's moustache. Half the village had gathered, far as I could tell, including all the lads who should've been in school, and the teachers with them too. There was a crane swinging a wrecking ball, and a group of our men, wearing dungarees and thick leather belts, were going to work with sledgehammers on what was left. The dust caught the back of your throat.

I was standing next to old Walter, who lived up Green Street. He shook his head. 'What a day. Never thought I'd live to see this.' His lip was trembling, and he wiped at the corner of his mouth with a wrinkled arthritic hand. 'Pigsties are coming down too before night-fall. An evil day. I'm going home while I still have one to go to.' He began shuffling up the street, blinking against the cruel dust. He'd served in Sudan under General Gordon, they said, and been wounded in the head, then come home and lived with his old mother until she died on the same day as the King two years ago. Suddenly he stopped and turned, taking in this time who I was. 'Why d'you work for that ol' devil? It'll be *your'n* next.'

Another great crash and the back wall of the blacksmith's came down. Now there was nothing left but a jagged amputation, a ghost of a house, rubble where people I knew had once lived and worked and had babies. And all the little boys in the village were cheering.

CHAPTER 13

He's waiting for me by the Land Rover, leaning against the open passenger door with one foot on the step. Jeans this time, black ones. A pair of aviator sunglasses. And those stupid cowboy boots he had on the night I met him.

'This wasn't my idea,' I say, before he can get a word in. 'Understand? This is the one and only time I'm ever going to mention what happened between us. I'd rather not be showing you round, but it seems nobody else has time to do it.'

He starts laughing. Bastard. Then he peers over the sunglasses and sees I'm serious.

'Sorry. Sorry, Indy.' He takes the glasses off, folds them, tucks them into his shirt pocket and strides round to the other side of the vehicle. 'Get in. By the way, I've the change from your twenty.'

'My what?'

'The twenty-pound note you gave me on the train. Remember? Before you did a runner at Reading.'

Ha, ha. I throw my rain jacket into the footwell, feeling stupid. But I had to say something to make the position clear.

'Why did you give the job to *him*?' I asked Michael, without thinking, when I heard last week. I'd strolled into his office hoping to persuade him to give me more work with the wardens, and it came as a shock to have my fears confirmed.

'D'you know him, then?' Michael straightened the photograph of his children, which I'd knocked off its precise axis on the desk.

I'd well and truly stitched myself up. 'I met him once. He struck me as a bit of a loudmouth.'

'Really? I wouldn't have said that.' Michael gave me a particularly beady stare, and I discovered I was kicking the leg of my chair like a petulant schoolgirl.

'And he's a helicopter pilot, not an archaeologist.'

'Which is an excellent skill to bring to the job. He's studying aerial survey, among other things, and it's about time we looked again at Avebury from the air, especially with these new Lidar techniques that can even penetrate woodland. You do realize this placement is part of his MA? We've an arrangement with the university.'

'Oh.'

'Works out perfectly to give us cover while Morag's away. He won't be here full time. There might still be a day here and there for you. But you'll be pretty busy, anyway, with those television people.'

Will I? Not a word from Daniel Porteus since I emailed him a list of the stills I'd found, and no dates fixed for filming.

'Tell you what,' Michael adds, with the gleeful expression of a man handing out sweeties. 'Why don't you do a day for us next Monday? You can show Ed round.'

'Hope the anti-freeze is topped up in this vehicle,' says Ed, as I climb into the Land Rover: his, not the National Trust's, and in only marginally better condition. 'Your expression could ice a small lake. Pardon me for asking, but what was so awful about what we did? You seemed to appreciate it at the time.'

'I wouldn't have, if I'd known you were married. You waited to break that snippet of news until afterwards.'

'Ah.' He clips on his seatbelt. 'Only . . . there didn't seem to be an appropriate moment to mention it.'

'You're doing it again.'

'Doing what?'

'Being flip about it.'

'I'm *never* flip about my marriage.' He starts the engine before I've closed the passenger door, and we're spraying gravel on the Manor driveway while I try to get the seatbelt fastened. It's become twisted somehow inside the reel, and I haven't managed to straighten it out when we come to a sudden halt.

I turn round to see him looking at me. 'What's the matter?'

'Which way? Left, right? You're supposed to be giving me the guided tour, remember?'

'Oh. Right.' Right takes us between the henge banks, past the massive diamond-shaped Swindon Stone, and into the circle. 'Follow the road round by the Red Lion, then we'll go down the Avenue to where the equipment's kept at West Kennet Farm. Graham asked us to pick up a chainsaw.'

He guns the engine and we move out between the Manor gates onto the main road. It's a sunny, blustery day, cloud shadows scudding over the high Downs, a bit chilly but what do you expect in March? At least it isn't raining. But those cowboy boots will take some punishment when we go up to the Long Barrow. There's a lake of mud at the bottom end of the track.

Anchors on again. Dead halt.

'What the fuck're *they* doing?'

'Oh, no. Druid procession.' I'm scanning the fluttering white robes in the hope of spotting a friendly face. 'I hope Michael knows . . . They'll be trying to Reclaim their Ancient Dead.'

'*What?*'

'Someone delivered a leaflet to the Trust. Part of the spring equinox celebrations – they're complaining about the skeletons in the museum. This'll be a protest march.'

Strung out across the road, at great personal peril given that it's the main route from Swindon, the Druids are doing a stately dance to the sound of a drum. They are led by a mountainous man with a grey beard and dreadlocks. Next to him, a fire-eater juggles blazing clubs, the flames deceptively transparent in the sunlight. Bringing up the rear, a man in a wheelchair is doing wheelies in time with the beat.

'This lot aren't from round here,' I say. 'The local Druids wouldn't let them interfere with the traffic. That's a blind corner – you can't see what's coming.' A screech of brakes behind underlines this. One massive supermarket lorry in a hurry could flatten us all. 'We ought to move them off the road.'

A car hoots angrily from the back of the queue. The grizzled Druid swings round and blows his horn in answer. His is bigger and louder.

'And sod you too,' says Ed, one hand on the steering-wheel, peering cautiously out of the Land Rover window, the new cowhand clasping the reins against the pommel of his saddle while he surveys the milling herd. 'Now I remember why I prefer flying.'

I open my door, ready to jump down.

'Hang on.' He turns off the engine. 'I think I should be gallant here. Allow me to exercise my natural authority.' He grins at me, unclips his seatbelt and hops onto the road.

The procession ignores us.

'Before I attempt to sort this lot out, do you know any of them?' he asks, as I join him. 'You sure there are no locals?'

'Might or might not help if the Avebury Arch-Druid was here because not all the Druid groups recognize his authority.' There are about twenty protesters, divided almost equally between men and women: several in white robes, and not a soul I've seen before. 'Sorry. You're on your own here, Ed.'

'What do you mean, I'm on my own? You'd better back me up.'

'Right behind you. But I thought I heard you volunteering to exercise your natural authority.'

'I'm not proud. This could be a two-person authority job.'

Judging by the rising chorus of hoots from the backed-up traffic, it won't take a Sainsbury's lorry to create bloodshed and mayhem if the Druids stay on the road much longer. Their dance is taking them slowly towards the crossroads in the centre of the village. They've almost reached the pub car park, the perfect opportunity to herd them out of danger, if only they'd pay attention. Ed could either jog ignominiously after them, or—

'EXCUSE ME!' He's gone for the more dramatic option, hands on hips to summon the necessary lung power. 'NATIONAL TRUST! WOULD YOU KINDLY GET OFF THE ROAD SO WE CAN DISCUSS THIS WITHOUT ANYONE GETTING RUN OVER?'

The only response is another contemptuous horn blast. The drum beats louder and faster, and there's a lot more energetic twirling of white robes. A she-Druid with a wraparound skirt seems to be deliberately flashing her knickers.

'Politeness doesn't always work,' I tell him. 'But don't be tempted—'

Too late.

At least he doesn't break into a run, which would be humiliating, but his long legs take him at remarkable speed through the twirling dancers and up to the grizzled Druid with the horn. Resisting the temptation to cover my eyes, I follow.

'. . . any *fucking* idea how fucking dangerous this is?' Ed is saying, as I catch up. 'This is the main road from Swindon, not a fucking pagan playground.'

'And who might you be?'

Oh dear. Mr Big has an American accent. I have a dim and hung-over memory of Ed telling me exactly what he thought of Americans with a mystical bent. The ones booked onto the helicopter had phoned his mobile painfully early to give him pre-takeoff grief about having to share their crop-circle flight with a film crew.

'Erm . . .' I have to intervene before injury is done. 'We're from the National Trust.'

'Yeah, I got that much.'

'Which means we have a duty of care to everyone who visits Avebury.' The novice warden is back in control of himself. 'For your own safety . . .'

'Safety? I don't take lectures on personal safety from thieves.'

'Thieves?' Ed is bewildered.

'We're here to represent the dignity of the ancestors.' The huge Druid has slung his horn over his shoulder, and planted himself as firmly as a sacred oak in the middle of the road. His eyebrows are a startling black, in contrast to his greying hair and beard. His full lips are plum red. 'How would *you* like it if, five thousand years from now, your earthly remains were dug up and put in an exhibition?'

'I'd quite like it, actually,' Ed begins, then catches my disapproving glare. He tries to look more serious. 'Of course, you've every right to express your views, but we'd prefer it if you didn't do it in the middle of the A4361. If you wouldn't mind stepping into the pub car park . . .'

Mr Big turns his back, and raises his arms to the sky, turning slowly sunwise. 'Spirits of the Circle, we invoke you.'

'What's he doing?' Ed asks, in a low voice.

'He's opening a circle to raise the elemental energies.'

'*Magic?* He's not trying to hex us, is he?'

'Don't worry, this is standard Druid stuff. But unless you want to clasp hands with a couple of men in frocks, it might be wise to retreat.' Ed takes a hasty step back.

'In the East, Air, who will lend power to our voices,' booms the grizzled Druid. *Pahhrrr*: the word flies out between the sensuous red lips like the fire-eater's flame. 'In the South, Fire – ' *fahhrr* ' – forge the purity of our hearts. In the West, Water, to wash clean our intentions . . .'

A snort from beside me. Mr Big wisely pretends he hasn't heard, but his arc brings him round to fahhrr the last salvo right in our faces.

'. . . and in the North, Earth . . .' *urrrth* '. . . whose solidity will confound our enemies.'

Druids don't go in for cursing, but this is about as close as they come to invoking a whopping great mound of mud to bury us and all our works. Spinning again, he rallies the troops, gripping the hands of the two pagans nearest him. 'Join hands, brothers and sisters, at this time of Alban Eiler, equal night, when dark and light are in balance.'

But hurrying down Green Street past the antiques shop, here's the cavalry. I never thought I'd be so glad to see a set of Avebury pagans.

John slips into the circle in front of me as the away team are about to clasp hands. Several others infiltrate from the opposite side: Beech

Tear and Wind Rose – no idea of their real names, but they live in a flat over a shop on Marlborough high street – and a woman in a fluffy scarf, who calls herself Moon Daughter. Half a dozen more are steaming along from the direction of the museum.

'Not joining us, Indy?' asks John, over his shoulder.

'I'm representing the forces of darkness today.'

'Don't joke. This is the heavy mob.'

'Where's the Arch-Druid when we need him?'

'Knee replacement.'

The grizzled American Druid is trying to look happy about how large his circle has grown. But he suspects something's afoot. He's right. Before he can carry on the ritual, John has seized the initiative. 'Welcome, brothers and sisters, to Avebury. Merry meet and merry part.'

'Merry meet,' says the American, uneasily.

'Will you join us in the Cove? We'll be opening a circle there, and in the absence of the Arch-Druid who usually leads our rituals, we'd be delighted if you'd preside.'

This is neatly done, and hard for Mr Big to refuse. All the same, he tries. He casts a helpless glance down the high street towards the barns and the Manor. According to John, the collective noun should be a dispute of Druids.

'Our plan was to hold a ceremony for the dead at the museum.'

'Perhaps you'd let us help you there, after you've celebrated Alban Eiler with us in the Cove?' The tiniest, most delicate stress on *after*.

The big Druid knows when he's outflanked. Besides, a strong contingent of local pagans will make his demo at the museum all the more impressive. Within seconds he's closed the circle and turned it into a long, hand-holding snake of pagans who file docilely off the road and through the gate. They reassemble themselves in three concentric circles in the lee of the massive Adam and Eve stones, a.k.a. the Cove.

'Bloody hell,' says Ed. 'That was impressive. Never seen Druids in action before.'

'They're not all Druids. Pagans follow lots of different paths. Two of those are Wiccans, Gardnerian, I think, and the one with the fluffy scarf is a Hedgewitch.'

Ed closes his eyes. 'I won't ask. Who's the bloke with the limp?'

'John Bolger. The pagans call him Wrongfoot because of his leg. Argie bullet in the Falklands – or possibly a police truncheon at the Battle of the Beanfield.' I decide not to reveal my connection with him. 'He's a shaman.'

'Sweat lodges and stuff? More American nonsense?'

'There's a Saxon tradition of shamanism too, you know.'

'No, I don't know. This is like being beamed onto another bloody planet.'

'Welcome to Avebury.'

'How come you know so much about this pagan bollocks?' asks Ed, as we chug away from the village, after warning Michael. The stones of the Avenue march alongside us in the field next to the road.

'I spent the first eight years of my life as a pagan.'

Anchors on again, right by the sarsen on the verge Frannie calls the Courting Stone.

'Just run that past me again. I thought for a moment I heard you say you were brought up as a pagan.'

'I was. My mother was a pagan. We lived in Bristol, but we'd hop in the van and head for Stonehenge or the Rollrights or wherever for the eight festivals. I'd never been into a church until I was eight, and the first time I went into one I was certain God was going to strike me down with a bolt of lightning.' A sudden memory of the coolness of St James's, on a hot summer's afternoon, my small fingers tracing the serpent carved on the font . . .

'*Eight* festivals?'

'Surely some of those people you flew over crop circles must have been pagans.'

'We didn't ask them to fill in a questionnaire – age, hair colour, religious persuasion.' He puts the Land Rover into gear again. 'You don't *believe* in it, do you?'

'I went to live with my grandmother after that, and she sent me to Sunday school. A few years of Anglicanism knocked anything remotely spiritual out of me.'

'Good.' He's looking at me warily, in case I suddenly whip a pentacle out of my pocket. 'Right. Better press on, then. Where to?'

I take a quick look at my watch. 'First, we should pick up the chainsaw from West Kennet, and then we'll drive back to see what's happening at the museum. Michael should have it all under control, but he might need back-up.'

Sacred geometry. Earth magic. It was so long ago when my mother explained it to me, and I've forgotten a lot, but some of it sticks. The Goddess's body, sculpted in the landscape; the Avenue a divine snake curving up the hillside. Sadly all utter bollocks, as Ed would say. Those theories were developed before archaeology revealed evidence of further ancient structures to confuse the pattern, including vast palisaded enclosures by the riverside at West Kennet, uncovered the same summer Margaret, John and I camped under the trees at Tolemac.

Ed touches my arm as I struggle with the padlock on the door of the barn where the wardens store equipment. 'Indy, can I say something without you biting my head off?'

'What?'

He rolls his eyes. 'That's exactly what I mean. You've been making me feel like an idiot all morning. This is my first day. You seem to be getting some twisted kind of pleasure out of seeing me flounder.'

I open my mouth, then snap it shut again.

'See?' says Ed. 'You were going to say something sarcastic *again*, weren't you?'

The key finally turns. I release the catch and swing back one side of the massive wooden doors.

'Look, you made your feelings utterly plain first thing,' says Ed. 'I take your point. That night . . . well. Sorry I didn't tell you sooner I had a wife. But chances are we'll keep running into each other while I'm doing this job for the National Trust. So *pax*?'

I kick a stone into place to prop the door open, then walk away from him into the barn. Stop. Close my eyes. Count to five. Turn round.

'Sorry,' I say. 'And . . . well, sorry.'

Light slants down through the gaps in the wooden walls, misty white spears stabbing the packed-earth floor. I'm trying to decide which chainsaw is the least heavy when Ed's voice startles me. 'What on earth is this?' He's at the far end of the barn, deep in shadow, examining an enormous mottled grey bulk propped against the wall. It's taller than a man, broader than an elephant's backside. Ed's goggling. 'Don't tell me they keep a spare stone for the circle, like a replacement light bulb . . .'

'Give it a push.'

He hardly touches it, but the megalith promptly falls over. I flip it with my foot and it wobbles like a giant lopsided rugby ball. After a shocked silence, Ed starts laughing. 'It's effing *polystyrene.*'

'It was a prop in a children's drama serial filmed here. The plot required the stones to move about. A tourist leaned against it, and nearly had a heart-attack when she knocked it down, but now it only comes out occasionally for staff Christmas parties.'

'It's so – lifelike. No, wrong word, stone isn't alive.'

'The pagans will tell you it is.'

'Your pagans are barking.' He gives it a kick and it rolls back against the barn wall. 'Hard to tell what's real and what's fake in this place. Indy—'

Somehow we've ended up standing very close in the darkened barn. I take a step back. 'What?'

'There's something else I'm sorry for. I *was* being a bit of a pillock this morning.'

'Well.' I can't think what to say.

'I'm finding this difficult too, you know.' Ed runs a hand through his spiky hair. 'Had no idea you were connected to this place. You told me about some television job on the train.'

'I may have bigged up my role, somewhat,' I say. 'Not even sure the programme's commissioned. It's about Avebury, when Keiller was digging here.'

'Keiller? One of my archaeological heroes.'

'You know about him?'

'Of course. Pioneer of aerial survey. Anyway, thought *I* was going into cardiac arrest when Michael mentioned your name. Didn't know whether you'd have told them about the crash. Then I'd have lost the job. Believe me, I need it.' He's watching me intently. 'Thanks for keeping quiet.'

'It's in my interests too, you know.' Suddenly my eyes are welling. 'I only want to forget that bloody day . . .' Damn, damn, damn. I shake his hand off my arm and walk out into the sunshine, blinking in the brightness.

A squelch behind tells me Ed has followed. It's a small comfort to think those cowboy boots are muddying up.

'One more thing to see here,' I say briskly, to prove I'm fine, really. 'Round the back of the barn we have the pagans' altar.'

No one has tidied its stone slabs for a while, and the wind has scattered withered flowers and grasses across the mud. Coloured ribbons and beads hang damply from the branches of the nearest tree.

Ed picks up a shell. 'So what's this about? Please don't tell me you facilitate them sacrificing the odd goat.'

'*Ed.* It's where volunteer pagans on litter duty put offerings that have been left in the stone circle – flowers, feathers, ribbons, pebbles, whatever. The Guardians didn't like the idea of throwing them away, so this altar gives them somewhere to bring them. Every month or so the Arch-Druid and the Wiccan high priest pop down and bless the offerings, before putting them on a sacred bonfire. And don't scoff. These people are serious in their beliefs. Talking of which . . .' I glance at my watch '. . . those Druids will have hit the museum by now. We should see what's happening.'

'Fine by me.' He starts back towards the farmyard where we left the Land Rover. There's a glutinous sucking sound. 'Oh, *fuck.*'

He's standing comically on one leg. Behind him an empty cowboy boot sits in a sea of mud.

'You idiot. That's the Goddess's revenge for disrespect.'

'Hey. Don't make me laugh. I'll fall over. Fetch my bloody boot, can't you?'

'Get it yourself.' But, of course, I pluck it out of the mud and carry it over to him. Somehow our fingers touch as he takes it from me.

Bloody Ed.

No sign of Druids on the main road or in the circle. The ceremony at the Cove must be over. We turn in through the gates and bounce down the gravelled drive towards the staff car park. White robes are fluttering outside the museum. One of the Druids is wielding a video camera, maybe hoping to sell footage to the local TV news. Ed gives me a sideways glance.

'Michael's there,' I say. 'It'll be under control.' Perhaps not the precise terminology when pagans are involved, chaos being an important magical principle.

As we're parking, someone blows a horn, and Michael disappears into the museum. The Druid with the camera is trying to film through the glass doors, though the sun's too bright and he'll only catch reflections.

John is leaning against the museum wall, chatting with a couple of white-robed women. When he sees us, he excuses himself and comes over.

'Any trouble?' I ask.

'It's all peaceful. Michael made it clear they couldn't have any skeletons, but he's allowed a few to go in and hold a ceremony of blessing over Charlie's bones. They're spinning it out as long as they can.'

The white bulk of the American, moving round inside the gallery, appears briefly through the glass of the museum door. 'What's he doing?'

'Bread and salt. Feeding the spirit.'

'Is that a good idea?'

John takes me seriously. 'It's safe if the American understands what he's doing. I wasn't too impressed with his technique at the Cove, though. Reckon he opened a vortex there and forgot to close it again. Magic's only as good as its practitioner.'

'Magic?' It comes out as a snort from Ed. John gives him a sharp look, taking in the tousled dark hair, the hint of got-up-so-late-I-failed-to-shave stubble, and the expensive Gore-Tex jacket.

'Sorry,' I say. 'John, this is Ed. New part-time warden, also, er, pilot.'

'Welcome to Avebury,' says John, who has worked out exactly who Ed is by now. Suspicion crackles between them. It's a shock to realize there are not so many years separating them: Ed in his mid- to late-thirties, John not yet forty-five. 'You from round here?'

'Not really,' says Ed. 'I'm borrowing a friend's place. At Yatesbury. Near the airfield. He gives me work sometimes, and it's quiet for studying.'

Only a mile or two away. My heart sinks.

'New helicopter pad opened up there, I heard?' John homes in for the kill. 'You a *family* man?'

Ed bends to free the cuff of his jeans, caught up on his cowboy boot. 'My situation's a bit complicated at the moment,' he says, to the cobbles.

The museum door opens and Mr Big and his white-robed cohorts sweep out. Michael is behind them, even more immaculate than usual in a tweed jacket with elbow patches and a striped tie. His brogues are blinding. He flaps a hand in a discreet shooing motion.

'Let's go.' I give Ed a shove, glad of an excuse to escape John. 'Coffee in the office.'

Wind Rose and Beech Tear are bringing up the rear of the procession.

'Indy! Merry meet!' Wind Rose gives me an enormous and faintly rancid hug. Beech Tear, who never washes on the principle that the body is cleansed by its own natural oils, embraces Ed with equal enthusiasm. He manages not to wince.

'Was that a man or a woman?' asks Ed. He reaches for the kettle, which is on the verge of boiling. 'Is there any real coffee?'

The kitchenette next to the wardens' office only stretches to a catering-size can of Nescafé. 'You'll have to bring your own,' says Graham, wandering in on stockinged feet. 'And if you're referring to Beech Tear, none of us are sure. First time I was hugged I was inclined to think female, because of the faint trace of patchouli, but most of the time the predominant whiff is elderly badger.'

'They're very good-hearted,' I say.

'But smelly,' insists Graham.

'So are you when you take your boots off.'

'Men's feet are meant to smell. It's part of our masculine allure.'

'I'll go for the hot chocolate,' says Ed, quickly, to avert bloodshed.

'Wouldn't recommend it. Been there nearly as long as the stones.' Graham frees a biscuit crumb from his blond beard and pops it into his mouth. 'Those custard creams were tasty. Excuse me, Indy, can I squeeze past? Good, there's another packet.' He tears the wrapping with his teeth and offers them round. 'No takers? You're seeing it all today, chum,' he says to Ed. 'I think the men in frocks have gone away satisfied. Still want their skeletons back, of course. They asked Michael to account for how many we've got, and weren't entirely happy he couldn't say exactly. I mean, how do you add the bloody things up? Thighbone here, jawbone there, sliver of scapula in the ditch. Prehistoric man did rather scatter human bone about. Get her to show you the storeroom – all the boxes of bits we don't put on display to Johnny Public.' He exits with a mug of builders'-strength tea and the packet of biscuits.

'He's very good with trees,' I say apologetically.

It seems to be my day for embarrassing encounters. Walking back to the Land Rover we see Frannie, who waves enthusiastically and totters along the cobbles towards us.

'Been to the post office. You heard these rumours it might close?' She eyes Ed keenly, as if she suspects him of being responsible. 'My granddaughter takes me shopping in the supermarket, but I tell her you have to support the local shop.'

So again I feel obliged to introduce him. She nods, not taking her eyes off his face. She looks tired today, her skin white and dry in the March sunlight.

Ed gives her a charming smile. 'Lovely to meet you, Mrs Robinson.'

As he climbs into the front seat, Frannie grabs my arm. 'He's not so bad,' she hisses, with a salacious and completely unjustified twinkle. 'Lovely green eyes. Reminds me of that doctor chappie on *Grey's Anatomy*.'

'Nothing like him. The eyes aren't green. And he's a *colleague*.' Ed has started the engine, so I squeeze Fran's hand and turn to climb into the passenger seat.

'Greeny-grey, then. Go on with you. I'd be after him meself if I was fifty years younger.'

'It was my fault,' Ed says suddenly, as we jolt down a rutted farm track, after a round trip involving Silbury, the Long Barrow, the Sanctuary, and finally the barrows along the Ridgeway, to check out Graham's theory that the beech trees on the Hedgehogs are dying because of climate change.

'What was your fault?'

'The helicopter crash, of course.' He doesn't look at me, keeps his eyes fixed on the track. 'At the time I thought a part had failed. Wrong. It was LTE – loss of tail rotor effectiveness. A problem with some choppers if you fly low and slow. Close to the ground, the main blades can create a vortex and there's not enough air for the tail rotor to work. The machine goes into a spin.' His hands tighten on the steering-wheel. 'It's in the training manuals – now. But it was my judgement call. I knew what Steve was asking was – well, on the edge. Shouldn't have let myself be persuaded. Showing off.' His eyes narrow as if they hurt.

'You are legal to fly, aren't you?' I ask. 'You haven't lost your licence?'

'Not *yet*. That could happen after the inquest. The Air Accident Investigation Board has to file its report first.' He chews a fingernail.

'Probably should find a solicitor, but I can't afford one. Flying's kind of gentlemanly. The decent thing is to ground oneself.'

'Which you haven't done.'

'I suppose I'm not a gentleman.'

He draws to a halt as we approach the end of the track, and I hop out to open the gate. The cowman is in the yard by the milking sheds; he waves as the Land Rover trundles through, and I clamber back in.

'This takes us back into Avebury now?' Ed asks, turning onto the metalled lane and changing gear with a grinding noise.

'Yep. Past Tolemac – the wood coming up on the left – and then into the henge.'

'Tollymack? That's a weird old Wiltshire name.' Ed slows as we draw level with the trees, peering through the windscreen into the thicket.

'Nothing weird, old or Wiltshire about it. Spell it backwards.'

His face screws up with effort. 'K . . .'

'C.'

'Oh, I see.' His mouth twists in a grin. 'Is this where the visiting pagans camp? I can smell woodsmoke.'

'Damn. Not *again*.' Graham has been complaining since Imbolc about what he describes as 'a couple of crusties' refusing to move on. 'They're not supposed to be there, let alone light fires.'

'Another chance to exercise my natural authority?'

'That would be the natural authority that worked so well this morning on the Druids?'

'Titter ye not.' He pulls the Land Rover onto the verge by the side of the wood. The sun has dropped behind clouds while we've been driving and the day has a sharp grey edge. Tolemac is gloomy and forbidding.

Ed jumps down. 'Can you manage to climb over the fence?'

'Of course I can.' Hanging onto the post for balance, I hook my foot onto the lower strand, and try for a contemptuous swing of the other leg over the barbed wire. There is a ripping sensation.

'Hold on, you're caught. Let me help you.' His hands run over the back of my thigh. 'There. All free now.'

He's let go and is jumping the fence easily, but I can still feel the imprint of his fingers. The tear in the back of my new jeans is wafting cool air onto my bum, a mixture of horribly embarrassing and bizarrely sexy. I glare at his back as he strides ahead under the trees towards a grey, ghostly shape. The smell of woodsmoke is strong.

'A bender,' he calls. 'Nobody home.'

It's made of thick transparent polythene sheeting, strung between tree branches. Stones hold down the edges to stop them flapping in the wind. Ed lifts one and ducks into the shelter.

'Hey, don't . . .' One of my earliest memories is Greenham, Frannie coming with Margaret and me to embrace the base. We camped, all three of us, in a bender like this, and then the bailiffs came and evicted us, chucking people's possessions into the back of a dumper truck. Watching Ed stroll confidently into someone's private space feels like a violation.

'A rucksack . . .' His voice is muffled behind the plastic. 'Cooking gear. Couple of books.' He lifts the sheet. 'Bit smelly in here. Come on in.'

I follow him inside, feeling it's an intrusion. The smell isn't that bad, damp earth with a sour undernote of wet dog. Now it's the outside world that's ghostly, grey and distorted through the thick polythene walls.

'We're not supposed to take this down, are we?' Ed asks.

'No. Looks like they'll be back.' A muddy black plastic groundsheet is spread underfoot, wrinkled and rucked, a couple of blankets in one corner, a sleeping-bag in the other, navy blue quilted nylon, greyish with age. 'The villagers would love it to be dismantled, but that's not the way to do it. You ask them politely to move on. Unless it's been abandoned.'

'None of this is exactly valuable. No self-respecting earthquake victim would be caught dead under one of these.' He prods the heap of blankets, meagre beige, so grubby and threadbare they do indeed look like Oxfam rejects, with the toe of his boot. A small rip in the sleeping-bag oozes filling. 'But the rucksack's a good one, brand new.'

Beneath its flap, the eyes of a small boy stare up at me from a creased photograph.

It's Keir.

No, of course it isn't. Keir's hair was fairer, almost white-blond. This lad has a mass of freckles but Keir's buttery skin tanned. For a moment, I was fooled by the smile, the chipped front tooth, like the one he broke coming off his skateboard going too fast round the corner into York Road when we lived in Bristol.

Fooled by Tolemac. The ghostly trees outside the bender suddenly seem dangerous. I drop the flap back on the rucksack. Ed has picked up the book that was lying on top of the blankets – a biography of Gurdjieff – and is leafing through.

'Leave it. Graham can come back tomorrow and tell them to clear off.' It feels like we're prying, and I want to be away before the owner comes back. 'Let's go.'

Ed tosses the book back but it misses the blankets, its pages flipping open on the dirty groundsheet. I pick it up, wiping a smear of mud off the cover. There's a name on the flyleaf, inked in rounded handwriting that's almost childish. **Bryn Kirkwood**. In charity shop pencil, '£1.99'. There was a Welsh lad at my school called Bryn. I thought it was such a pretty name, though everyone else called him Bryn the Bin because his dad worked for the council. I close the book carefully, not wanting to crease the pages, and lay it on the bedding.

Ed's waiting outside.

'We should track down the smoke before we go,' he says. 'I don't like people leaving unattended fires under trees.'

'Mr Backwoodsman, now?'

'I was a Boy Scout,' he says, with immense dignity.

'Until you got kicked out for cheating on your Pathfinder badge, I bet.'

'Actually, it was for smoking in the tent.'

Someone has built a ring of stones in a clearing a few yards behind the bender. There are turves banked over it, a thin stream of smoke escaping from the top. Ed kneels and peels one back. 'Whoever built this has been watching too many telly survival series.'

'Or he's genuinely ex-SAS.'

'Nah. Bender was too untidy.' Ed lets the turf drop back into place. 'Believe me, I've worked with some of the buggers. They're borderline obsessive-compulsive.'

'Come on, the fire's safe,' I say. 'Let's go.' The sun's dropped too low to penetrate the clearing and the trees are getting to me.

Ed straightens up, shooting me a suspicious glance. 'You're twitchy.'

'I need to be back.'

'You're behaving like the peasant in a Hammer vampire film. Any moment you're going to whip out the garlic and crucifix. The sun is setting, Ma-a-aster, it is not safe to be out of doors. Go on, roll your eyes, that's it. All you need is a baggy shirt and a big droopy moustache.'

That was why I slept with him. He made me laugh.

'We should tell Graham,' I say.

'So get out your phone and do it. No, silly me, you're a Transylvanian peasant. Long-distance communication by flaming arrow only.'

I explain about the mobile-phone black spot. He pulls out his handset, and looks at it, surprised. 'Bugger me, you're right. Hang on, two bars have just popped up – no, down to one now. What's that supposed to be about – mystic vibrations? Magnetic resonance from the stones? I'm sure your pagan pals have a theory.'

'Sorry to disappoint, but I think it's more to do with the ethics of erecting mobile-phone masts within a World Heritage site. You get a signal now and then, but it doesn't last long.'

'I was wondering why mine hadn't rung all day. Better check my voicemail while I can.'

And a sick, tired feeling washes over me. She'll have been calling him. Love you, darling. When are you coming home? The weekend? That's great. Missing you already.

I tug my cagoule down to hide the rip in my jeans and plod back through the trees to the Land Rover, leaving him in the clearing with the phone at his ear.

When I get home Frannie's in bed.

'You haven't had supper yet, have you?'

'Don't feel like any.' A ghost of a smile twitches her mouth. 'I liked your young man this morning.'

'Are you ill?'

'No. Tired.'

'It's only six o'clock.'

'Leave me, India. I had a bad night last night, and wore meself out walking to Big Avebury. Just need a bit of sleep and I'll be fine.' She rolls over and pulls the bedcovers up to her chin.

There's a frowsty, stale smell in here. The bedroom – dining room as was – is crammed with furniture. The drop-leaf dining-table is pushed against the wall, with a mirror hanging over it. As well as her bureau, there's a wardrobe, a chest of drawers by her bed, and an open-fronted cabinet with what she calls her 'knickknacks' – china figures I wouldn't give house room to, but she seems to think they're the last word in elegance, and a couple of really hideous pots I made for her at junior school. Everything seems to have accumulated a thick layer of dust since I was last in here, but Frannie insists she should be left to do her own cleaning.

I don't like this 'tired', though. She's been sleeping later and later in the mornings, and Frannie always used to be out of bed with the lark. Maybe she is ill.

'Let me take your temperature.'

'No.' Muffled, stubborn. All the same I open the top drawer of the bedside chest, where she keeps a variety of first-aid bits and pieces, to look for the thermometer.

My God. A nauseating smell pours out.

There's a half-eaten sandwich in there, green with mould. It might once have been ham. 'Frannie . . .'

'Aren't you gone yet?' she grunts.

'What's this?' My voice is sharper than I mean it to be.

'What's what?' She rolls over to look at me. 'Pooh, what's that stink?'

'There's a mouldy sandwich in your drawer. No wonder you're ill.'

'I'm not ill. And I didn't put it there.'

'For Chrissake, Frannie, who else?' I'm shouting now, I'm so angry. How dare she not look after herself? I'm always telling her to keep an eye on sell-by dates and chuck stuff out before it goes off – at her age food poisoning is *serious*, for God's sake . . .

'Oh, India, I don't know. Chuck it out and leave me to sleep.' Her eyes are watering, and now there's a horrible choking lump in my chest because I don't mean to shout at her, but I'm so frightened she'll go away and leave me.

'I'm sorry.' I reach out and stroke her hair. Her shiny eyes meet mine and there's fear in hers too. Then she smiles at me, as sunny as she ever was.

'My mam used to do that,' she says. 'You're a good girl, India.'

CHAPTER 14

1938

I was a good girl. Mam always used to say that. You sometimes have the devil in you, Frannie, but you're good-hearted.

I broke her heart, I know I did. She was in the hospital when I moved away from Avebury, later, and she knew why I was going.

There was only one conversation. 'I've eyes in my head, Frances,' she said. 'Don't think you can fool me, like you can your father. I won't tell him, though. It would kill him. I know I can trust you to do the right thing.'

It killed her instead. My lovely little mother, dancing with the tea-towel to Ambrose and Henry Hall. She waited and waited for me to do the right thing, and I didn't. I reckon *I* was what killed her.

The trees had gone and all our secret places was laid bare. It wasn't only the blacksmith's and the pigsties: no end of cottages came down, no end of people left the village. *Why d'you want to work for that ol' devil?* Walter had said, the day we watched the blacksmith's demolished. But there was plenty who would, a gang of maybe twenty local men already employed to start digging once the museum was finished, and others queuing behind for jobs, because Mr Keiller paid more than the farmers did, and sometimes he treated them better.

Mrs Sorel-Taylour had a cold, a real streamer. She was all pink round the eyes, and her voice was like a piece of cracked old pot. We were in the museum. Mr Keiller was in the back room talking to Mr Young about plans for the new season – I could see the brim of his Panama through the open doorway – and Mr Piggott and

Mr Cromley were on their knees unpacking another crate from Charles Street.

'Blow me down,' said Mr Piggott. 'Alec! I've found Felstead.'

Mr Keiller came through and knelt beside him. 'Well, I'm damned. I thought I asked them to save the skeletons till last.'

The crate seemed awful small for a whole skeleton. There was a screeching sound as Mr Cromley wrenched out the last nails, and began pulling out the protective straw. Mrs Sorel-Taylour sneezed.

Mr Keiller looked up. 'Mrs S-T! Would you kindly take your germs elsewhere. Any more explosions like that and Felstead will be dust.' I was trying for a glimpse of what was in the box, but Mr Piggott's big head was in the way.

'It's ody a head code,' said Mrs Sorel-Taylour, trying for dignity through sinuses brimming with snot.

'It sounds awfully bad,' said Mr Keiller. 'I'm serious. I'd rather you went home. I don't want to delay the start of the excavation if everybody goes down with it.'

'I really can't justify—'

'I can, and I will, Mrs Sorel-Taylour.' Suddenly he was really angry, shouting at her. It was terrifying how quick he'd gone from joking to blind rage. I shrank back against the table, and Mr Piggott began edging the box of finds out of the way. 'You work for me. At this moment, I would prefer you not to be working for me. Go home. You may come back when you're well again.'

'But . . .'

'On your feet, Mrs Sorel-Taylour. Pick up your pencil and your shorthand pad, and *walk*.'

Mrs Sorel-Taylour sniffed. Mr Keiller's jaw clenched. She walked, unhooking her coat from the peg by the door.

They ignored me.

'Bloody woman,' said Mr Keiller, as soon as she was gone. 'She knows my chest is delicate.'

'You have to look after yourself,' said Mr Piggott. 'God knows, Alec, you work hard enough for ten Sorel-Taylours, and you're irreplaceable.'

'Oh, hell,' said Mr Keiller. 'I needed her to type some letters. Cromley, be a good chap . . .' Mr Cromley jumped to his feet, delving in his jacket pocket and pulling out a small squarish package, wrapped in a brown envelope and bound with a rubber band. But Mr Keiller rocked back on his heels, shaking his head. 'No, dammit, don't go after her – she'd only spread her microbes over the Discavox.'

He would notice you if he needed you.

'Miss Robinson.' There was a wheedling note in his voice. 'How is your typing?'

'Excellent, sir,' I said, trying to answer like Mrs Sorel-Taylour would.

The package came whizzing through the air towards me. Luckily I caught it.

'Two blue carbons,' he said. 'Drop them with the fair copies into the Map Room for me to sign before you leave tonight. Now, Piggott, let's get this bloody dog out of its box.'

Canis familiaris felstedensis. I had to spell it out longhand among the Pitman's. Then cross it out again.

'Alec, you can't label it that,' said Mr Piggott. 'You got into trouble before.'

'Nothing wrong with naming the creature after a Derby winner. Looks like a greyhound, anyway.'

'Cross it out, Miss Robinson,' said Piggy Eyes. No sense of humour. Well, he did have one, but it was silly and cruel. 'It's called *canis familiaris palustris.*'

Whatever the blazes that meant.

I wanted to see the human skeletons that had been dug up at Windmill Hill ten years before, but those hadn't come down from London with the dog bones. There was supposed to be a child's skeleton, which they called Charlie, and a tiny baby.

'Yooman sacrifice,' said Mr Piggott, trying to mimic a village accent. 'Arr, Martha, 'tes awful strange what our great-grandmamas was up to.'

He and Mr Keiller were behaving like over-excited schoolboys, without Mrs Sorel-Taylour's presence to restrain them, and that display of temper might never have happened. I had the feeling they were both vying for my attention, Mr Keiller because he could never stop until he had caught you up in his web, Mr Piggott because whatever Mr Keiller did, he had to copy.

'Stop playing the fool, Stu Pig,' said Mr Keiller. 'Don't pay any attention, Miss Robinson. He knows perfectly well there is no evidence how those infants died. The puzzle is why their bones are complete when the rest of the human bone we found on Windmill Hill is fragmented. Still, we may find human remains to shed some light when we dig the henge.'

'You hope,' said Stu Pig. That was a good name for him, I thought. 'You hope, you hope, you hope.'

'Nothing so abstract as hope,' said Mr Keiller. 'I *plan*. Stop giggling. Young will disapprove. I've set him to draw a survey of where he thinks the buried stones could lie, and if the rain's cleared I could do with fresh air. Let's leave the delightful Miss Robinson to get on with my letters.'

Mr Cromley had been keeping quiet. When I got to my feet to fetch the dictation machine, I caught his eyes on me, cool, grey and thoughtful.

The dictation machine was an extraordinary fandangle that Mr Keiller had brought back from somewhere overseas, America, I suppose, or maybe Switzerland. It was his favourite toy, housed in a polished walnut box with a hinged lid. Mrs Sorel-Taylour had shown me how to work it. It was like magic. Mr Keiller recorded his voice on it, but instead of engraving it onto a phonograph, the machine used plastic tape. She told me you had to be careful not to hold it near a magnet or somehow it would all be gone.

By day it was kept in the Map Room, where he liked to work, but at night it was taken up to his dressing room so he could talk into it whenever the mood came over him to write a letter, which it often did. When he was full of enthusiasm he'd sometimes write to the same person several times in a day. He'd go on late into the night, his voice coming and going as he paced up and down the room, suddenly getting loud when he sat down and remembered to lean in to the recorder. It was a funny feeling being alone with him talking right in your ear, out of the machine.

I collected it from the Map Room and took it to our office above the stable block. The packet Mr Keiller had lobbed at me contained three of his little tapes. But which came first? One was marked '6 April, VGC'. The other two had question marks pencilled on their boxes, so I picked up the one that was dated. I had never used the machine before by myself, but I set everything up like Mrs Sorel-Taylour had shown me, and sat back with my shorthand pad at the ready. Mrs Sorel-Taylour was so fast at typing she could almost keep up with the machine, but she said I shouldn't try that because I'd make too many mistakes that way and Mr Keiller liked a nice clean copy without words xxxed out or smudges left by the correcting rubber.

I turned the knob to start and, with a clunk, the machine let out Mr Keiller's voice, hissy and a bit slurred, so I could tell this had been dictated late last night with a brandy in his hand.

'My dear Childe,' the machine said to me. 'So glad you rejected cannibalism . . .'

You got used to this kind of stuff. He was writing to one of his professor friends about some excavation up in the Orkneys. More old bones, more bits of pot. 'If you find yourself in this part of the world in the early summer, perhaps you would care to join us for the grand opening of our museum . . .' The smooth voice with its soft *r*s, hissing out of the machine like steam, made me sleepy. My shorthand looked like something that had been dug out of the ground too. 'Yours, Alec.'

Another letter began. Made me smile because it was to Mr Piggott's mother. She was always worrying about her precious Stuart – a gurt grown man, mind, and about to get married, though for the life of me I couldn't understand what kind of woman would want him – and it was a joke between me and Mrs Sorel-Taylour that poor old Mr K had to keep writing back to reassure her Mr Piggott was well

and happy and his fingers not being worked to the bone. 'This work
– I always prefer not to call it *my* work proprietorially – is a perfect
religion to me . . .'

That was him all over: our high priest, inspiring us to do The Work.
If Mr Piggott laboured all hours, it was because Mr K had bewitched
him, like the rest of us. Reckon I wasn't the only one half in love.

There was a clunk. Time to change the tape; they didn't last long.
Which came next? Judging by the question marks, Mr Keiller didn't
know either, though it wasn't like him to be muddled. He was usually
so exact.

I eeny-meeny-miny-mo'd. But this one couldn't be to Mrs Piggott.

'. . . a turmoil of apprehension. I have, at different times of my life,
made studies, more or less cursory and sometimes merely superficial,
of various branches of the erotic impulse—' I stopped the machine.
My face was hot, and I was glad I was alone in the office. What would
Mrs Sorel-Taylour have said? This had to be the wrong tape. I turned
over the box. There was a date, after all, in small neat letters, half
erased: '9 Oct'. Mr Cromley had picked up an old recording by mistake,
maybe one that Mr Keiller had meant to wipe and use again. I couldn't
imagine Mrs S-T typing a letter like this, but she must have.

What did he mean, studies of the erotic impulse? I remembered
ideas Davey sometimes whispered to me. I thought of that thing made
of chalk, and the giggling ladies, as they followed Mr Keiller into the
hidden part of the garden.

My fumbly fingers kept making mistakes so it was seven o'clock before
I'd typed clean enough versions of the letters, with the blue copies he
asked for. It was pitch black outside.

I shut off the lights in the museum. No need to lock the door:
who'd want all them bits of broken old pot? It was dark over the
cobbles, but soon as I came round the end of the stable block, light
spilled out of the Manor House windows onto the lawns.

I went up the path, and knocked.

The butler, Mr Waters, was too grand to answer the side door, so when it swung open there was the housemaid behind it. She came from over Bassett way, and was always snappy with me, for I was clerical, a career girl, and she was a domestic. 'The master's upstairs, dressing for dinner,' she said.

'I'll leave everything in the Map Room, then.' I'd brought the dictation machine over, and it was heavy. She stood back reluctantly.

As I was lugging it through the long, dark passageway, with its old maps and engravings on the wall, I heard heels on polished wood. Mr Keiller came off the bottom of the stairs and round the corner and nearly collided with me. He was in a beautiful black suit and I thought again of film stars. He was maybe a bit old to be in the pictures but he had a lovely strong jaw and if he smiled his eyes crinkled like Errol Flynn's. The fact he was so tall always made me feel a shy little thing. I could feel myself blushing.

'Miss Robinson! What are you doing cowering in the passage?'

'I'm sorry, sir.' I could hardly bring the words out because all I could think was what he'd said in that letter. '. . . various branches of the erotic impulse . . .' I imagined long lean ladies, draped in cream silk, lying back while Mr Keiller stroked their rounded breasts and soft ivory skin for his studies, turning away now and then to say a few words into his dictation machine.

'Oh, the letters.' He'd seen the machine under my arm. 'Come into the Library and I'll sign them.' He held open the door for me, and I had to pass under his arm, smelling the warm scent of expensive soap that came off him. Underneath was something darker, more bullish. It was nothing like the smell of Davey when we were snuggling with our backs to the stone and our fingers lacing like cat's cradle while I tried to keep his hands somewhere this side of decency.

I stood while he leaned against the table and read the letters through before dashing off his signature on each. There was one to some old colonel that had written complaining because Mr Keiller wouldn't let him bring a group to see the dig when it started.

'Claimed I was placing him and his ghastly friends on a level with a cheerio coach party of trippers from the Black Country,' said

Mr K. 'Which is exactly why I don't want his type here. Frankly, I'd much rather have the trippers. Can't stand snobbery.'

The shelves in the room were arranged to make six big bays, and held more books than I'd ever seen in one place, more than there were in the Boots Lending Library in Devizes. There were some by Charles Dickens and Rudyard Kipling, but most were dusty old things you'd never want to read. One title leaped out on the nearest shelf – *The Sexual Life of Savages* – and I dropped my eyes quickly, feeling myself beginning to redden again.

Mr Keiller put the top back on his fountain pen. I'd the feeling he was laughing at me. 'Interested in books, are you, Miss Robinson?'

'I'm a member of the lending library.'

'There are some here that should never be lent. Look at this one: seventeenth century. Belonged to the Bishop of Aush.' He pulled a fat leatherbound book off the shelf. It didn't look really old. I said so.

'Because I've had it rebound, you ninny. It's a classic of witchcraft.' He pretended to cuff me with the book; his hand skimmed my hair. '*L'Inconstance de Demons*. The faithlessness of demons.' He sighed, and handed me the letters. 'Now there's a lesson for us all. Don't sell your soul – or, at least, don't sell it cheap. Right you are, Miss Robinson. Pop them in the envelopes and deliver them to the post, if you would, on your way to see your young man.'

I felt myself go hot all over again. How could he know about me and Davey? And I'd been thinking of *that*, what we did by the stones, childish fumblings, comparing it to Mr Keiller and his studies, the dark secret things he did with ladies like Miss Chapman and, if gossip was to be believed, plenty of others, although he and Miss Chapman were supposed to be getting married.

'I see I've hit bullseye,' he said. 'So pretty Miss Robinson *is* courting. We shall have to start calling you *Heart*breaker Robinson from now on.'

I was too young for him, I knew, but did he really find me pretty? The air outside the Manor seemed warmer than it had been, positively spring-like. Reckon I wasn't the only one thinking that way, because when I came round the side of the barns, where the stones Mr Keiller had raised the year before loomed over the ditch, there was a soft giggle and a flash of white in the dark.

They were the other side of the big stone nearest the gate. Would have been hard to see them in the dark, as I went past, but for the petticoat and the glimpse of pale leg, hooked around his waist. I recognized the voices, though, hers high and excited, his low and controlled.

'Give I your coat to lean back on,' she said: it was the housemaid who'd let me into the Manor. 'This stone's powerful rough.'

'You like it powerful rough, do you?' said Mr Cromley's voice.

Mam was cross with me that evening. 'You're late back, Frances. Where've you been?'

She could always see into the belly of my thoughts. It made me sharp back. 'At the Manor, of course. Where else would I be?'

'Only asking. I made your supper . . .'

'Well, you won't be having to do that soon enough. When I've my own place, it'll be a relief not to have to answer all these questions.'

Mam's eyes widened and went shiny under the kitchen light. She turned her back to me and started stirring something on the stove. I didn't care. It was my life.

Spring was coming. The museum was almost ready. I'd thought of it as a job that would go on for ever, but now I could see I'd be let go after it opened. For all my bold talk of finding my own rooms, it looked like I'd be off to the cigar box in Devizes with Mam and Dad, come September. The thought of leaving the Manor was almost unbearable, for reasons I didn't want to put into words. But I found myself looking up, every time the museum door opened, to see who it was. When Mr Keiller's tall shadow fell across us, I'd feel the warmth in my face, and an extraordinary, unreasonable happiness.

Mrs Sorel-Taylour was running out of work to give me. The flow of crates from London had dried up completely. The last one, with the skeleton of Charlie, the child they found at Windmill Hill, had been unpacked last week. Or Charlotte, said Mr Keiller. Could as well be a girl. There was something funny about the head: a clever doctor who was down from London had been brought over to the stable block to take a look, and he said the skull was distorted, too big for the body; some disease had swelled the brain and pushed the bones out of shape. The skeleton had been laid out careful, in a glass case sunk into the floor, a strange last resting place for a little boy thousands of years old. Every time I went into the museum I took a look, poor little mite. I didn't want to believe he might've been killed deliberate, like Mr Piggott suggested. *Yooman sacrifice*: I hated the way he'd laughed, showing his large, prominent teeth. Instead I pictured Charlie's mother laying him to sleep in the ditch as the sun sank over Cherhill and Yatesbury, stroking his clumsy misshapen head. 'My special boy,' she said, her eyes wet and shining. 'You sleep quiet.' They said he'd been laid to face the sunrise.

It made me think different about Windmill Hill. I'd always liked sitting on the old barrow mounds, wind rippling the grasses and the wild flowers. But now I went up there and thought about Charlie. I could see him in my mind's eye, running through the tall grass, chasing butterflies. He was as real as real to me. This morning, we'd finished the last of the labels. Mrs S-T had to go to the dentist in Swindon and she told me I could take longer for lunch, only be sure to be back by three thirty when she'd show me how to type up the excavation notes Mr Young had found from last season's digging. I'd walked to Windmill Hill to enjoy the sunshine. Could've gone to look for Davey to see if he was free to come with me, but to be truthful I was no longer so keen on Davey's poky fingers. It was someone else's hands I'd have liked roaming, strong, manicured hands. I wondered what it would be like to be Miss Chapman, and have Mr Keiller come to my room late at night.

I lay back on the barrow top, and let the wind play with my skirt and tease my goose-pimply legs. Charlie was playing in the sunshine somewhere below. I could feel the vibrations of his running feet.

I sat up. I *could* feel vibrations.

The wind had blown the sound of the engine away from me. There were two of them riding the motorbike, bouncing at speed over the tussocks of grass. Davey was in front, controlling the bike, his hair blowing half over his eyes, and Mr K, wearing a leather helmet and goggles, was behind him. His arms were round Davey's waist, and as I watched he bent his head as if he would bury his face in Davey's hair. Neither of them had noticed me: they were travelling away from me across the top of the hill towards the stand of trees that tumbled down the northern slope.

I stood up to wave – then sat down again. Even if Mr Keiller had turned his beautiful head at that moment, I wasn't sure I wanted them to see me. The shifting wind tossed the growl of the bike back to me as Davey revved it towards the brow of the hill, like he was gearing it to jump into space and float through the air. Then they were gone. The sound cut out among the trees, and a cloud flicked its tail over the face of the sun so my arms went goose-pimply too.

CHAPTER 15

It's a fact of life that television people delay and delay and then want everything done right now, no matter whether their schedule matches anyone else's. The week after Ed's arrival, Ibby from Overview calls to tell me Daniel Porteus is coming to Avebury, presenter in tow, to talk to the National Trust. He's expecting me to be there, as Ibby herself will be otherwise occupied.

Corey is less than enthusiastic about rearranging my shifts. As I pant into the café, she gives me a glare from behind the counter and jerks her head in the direction of the tables. Daniel Porteus and another man, his back to me, are at the far end. A fluffy mic on a boom pole is propped against the wall. Seeing me, Daniel stands up. 'India, good of you to join us.' Said with a touch of sarcasm: I'm late. We exchange the obligatory double-barrelled media air kiss. 'This is Martin Ekwall . . .'

The other fellow stands too. He's a bear of a man, in beige chinos and a bright red sweater, holding out a furry paw, a smile splitting his thick but well-barbered beard. Even the backs of his fingers are hairy. 'Glad to meet you. Daniel says you're good with a camera.'

'Well, um . . .'

Daniel takes this for modesty. 'You don't mind shooting a few pieces to camera with Martin, while the sun's out? May never use them, but it gives him practice.'

Beyond the window is a lovely day, chilly for April, but under puffs of cloud in a blue sky the lime leaves are unfurling, juiciest green. Martin is a palish shade of green to match, and rooting in a leather satchel slung over the back of his chair.

'Standing, sitting or walking?' I ask.

'All three,' says Daniel. '*Can* you walk and talk, Martin?'

'About a minute, like you told me?' says Martin, his head buried in his bag. 'Sorry, need the loo . . .' He bolts.

'Want a coffee, India?' Daniel waves in a lordly fashion to Corey, who looks thunderstruck since the café is self-service. 'I'll take a flapjack.'

I pull up a chair, and he starts to examine the photocopies of archive stills I've brought him. Corey bangs the cup down on the table so coffee slops into the saucer. Martin emerges from the Gents, looking more confident.

'So what's the plan?'

'I've a ten-thirty meeting to talk the National Trust into letting us dig up a stone.' Daniel has to negotiate many strata of bureaucratic approval before so much as a skewer can penetrate the sacred soil. 'You two start filming.'

'Fine,' says Martin. He looks relaxed, but under the table he's picking at the skin round his thumb. There's a smear of blood on his chinos.

'Shall we go, then?' Daniel wraps the uneaten half of his flapjack in a napkin, then puts it into his pocket. He ducks under the table and emerges with a padded camera bag. 'You have used a mini-DVC before, India?'

My hands tense. It'll be the first time I've touched a camera since . . .

But of course I can do it.

I thought I'd feel more, but it's just grey plastic and cables, inert, innocuous, not an instrument of mass destruction. Maybe it helps that it's so small, nothing like the heavier on-the-shoulder camera I used in the helicopter. I hold it up to my eye, half expecting to see through the viewfinder a flash of Steve's head, welling crimson, but the frame is filled only with Martin's hairy, worried face.

'Fine,' I say. 'Know it like the back of my head. You ready, Martin?'

I'll take that croak as a yes.

As we leave the café, he hangs back and grabs my arm. 'Be gentle with me, India.'

'You have done telly before?'

'Yes, but only as the chap being interviewed. Now I'm supposed to be front man, every sensible word has flown out of my head.'

I'm scanning the camera furiously, running my fingers over the casing. 'Tell you a secret. I can't remember where the eject button is so I can load the tape.'

'Well, don't ask me. I'm useless with technology.'

Somehow between us we set up in the henge with the camera loaded and Martin semi-coherent, and Daniel hasn't noticed what a pair of idiots he has in his employ. Martin strikes a manly pose, staring into the far distance, while I position the camera.

'Take off your jumper.'

'You forward young thing.'

'It casts too much colour up onto your face. You'll look like a tomato. Can you hold this piece of paper?'

'What's written on it? "Beware, lunatic talking"?'

'It's for the white balance. Don't ask me to explain.' Daniel is wandering between the tall stones of the Cove. 'Does Mr Porteus make you as nervous as he does me?'

'Too right,' says Martin, fervently, throwing his sweater to land untidily next to his leather satchel by the tripod. 'Am I white enough?'

'Lily-like. Now, in your own time, speak.'

'Hang on – what am I supposed to do with the rest of me? Where do I put my hands? No, don't answer that.'

'Lean on the stone, looking casual . . . Oh, shit.'

A green Land Rover has pulled up on the verge by the gate. A pair of muddy cowboy boots descends from the driver's door: Ed, wearing aviator shades. Michael, togged up for telly in a Barbour so pristine the wax gleams, is walking round from the other side.

'What's up?' asks Martin, uneasily. 'Haven't got coffee froth in my beard, have I?'

'Nothing. I thought they'd be meeting in the office.' Another car parks behind the Land Rover, disgorging the National Trust's film liaison officer, in green wellies, and the curator, in pink ones and a long flouncy skirt. 'Carry on. We're rolling . . . and speed.'

'What?'

'Sorry. Something camerapersons always say. It means ready, steady, go.'

Not everyone's face works on camera, but Martin's does, even with the beard. He's a boyish mixture of earnest and enthusiastic, eyes warm and twinkly, and although the sun shows up the creases at their corners, he's fit and muscled for a middle-aged bloke. Ed's wiry, but nowhere near as buff.

'Oh, Lord, I see what you mean,' says Martin, coming over to watch a playback on the camera's LCD screen. 'I do need to smile more on a closeup.'

'Relax and enjoy it.'

'Easy enough for you to say. You try.'

'Fortunately no one is ever going to ask me to step round the camera to the other side,' I say. 'There's too much of me to be a presenter.'

'Bollocks, India. Most men prefer a girl with some meat on her bones. You're tall enough to carry it. You'd look great.'

Does he mean *he* prefers . . .? We're standing close. The smell of him is warm, spicy, male.

'One more?' he says.

I readjust the tripod and bend to the eyepiece, while Martin faces the camera. 'That's good . . . No, hang on a mo.'

Behind him, Ed has reappeared, strolling across the grass towards us.

'Before we carry on,' I say, straightening up, 'something else I want to show you. Watch the last take again in the viewfinder.' When he's beside me, leaning in to the camera, I lean in too, intimate. 'There – see that thing you do with your hand? It's a bit flouncy. Fine to use your hands, but you don't want to look too gay when you do it.'

'India,' says Martin, his breath tickling my ear, 'you do realize, don't you?'

'Realize?'

'I *am* gay.'

Shit. Cold, hot, entire body thermostat throws a breakdown. 'Oh. Sorry. I didn't mean . . .'

'It's fine, blossom. I don't make a thing of it, no need to shout it from the rooftops. I just don't want you getting the wrong idea, given that we'll be working together.'

'Right.' Whatever I say is only going to land me deeper in trouble. I stare fixedly at the LCD screen, my face on fire. 'I hope you didn't think . . .'

'Er, hi, India. How's it going?'

'Oh, hi, Ed.' At least my blush makes it look like something's going on between us. 'Martin's a natural.'

'Really?'

My eyes meet his – and find no hint of jealousy, damn it. Either he knows instinctively that Martin presents no threat, or he simply wouldn't care if we flung our clothes off and got down to it right now on the Bonking Stone.

Over lunch in the Red Lion, Martin flirts outrageously with the curator – is there a woman he doesn't count as a friend within two minutes of meeting her? The National Trust haven't yet committed themselves to a dig, but it looks hopeful: Channel 4 have come up with the money, Martin has promised students and expertise, and Ibby arrives tomorrow with a full crew. Filming will take place over the next few months depending on weather and Martin's academic commitments. Daniel, roughing out a schedule on the back of his paper napkin, leans across the table to interrupt. 'How are you fixed towards the end of June?'

'That's Solstice,' I say. 'You don't want to film then. The place is heaving.'

'Great!' says Daniel. 'Remember what Cameron said? Channel 4 want pagans. Know anything about modern pagans, Martin?'

'Not much.' Martin looks less than enthusiastic. 'My speciality's the ancient sort.'

'Well, now's your chance to learn. India, can you find out when the next stone-huggers' shindig takes place?'

'There's a Wiccan full-moon ritual, just before Easter, all comers welcome,' I tell Martin, after a conversation with John on the pub's pay phone. We're watching the stream of cars for an opportunity to cross the main road.

'That didn't take long.'

'I have a friend who's pagan.' I give a thumbs-up to Daniel, waiting for us among the stones on the other side. 'Well, more than a friend. My spirit-father.'

'Your *what*?'

'Equivalent of godfather. My mother held a naming ceremony for me at Stanton Drew stone circle when I was small. But, hey, you don't want to hear my family history.'

'Of course I do,' says Martin, with a brave grin. 'I'm a vicar's son. Trained to listen sympathetically from birth. Your mum was pagan?'

'My grandmother says it was a rebellion. Meg married too young, then walked out on her husband and met up with a guy who took her to Stonehenge for the free festival one Solstice. She went back again and again – well, until 1989.'

'Because the police set up an exclusion zone that year,' says Martin. 'Don't look so surprised, blossom – I was studying for my PhD and my supervisor was digging the outlying barrows. So I remember the good old Second Summer of Love – been there, done that, got the smiley-face T-shirt.'

A gap appears in the traffic, and we scuttle across the road, the camera bag bouncing against my leg. While Martin was excavating at Stonehenge, my mother and I were in Avebury.

Margaret laying out the crystals, offering me the shiny black lump of onyx, the stone for secrets. Me opening my mouth, and the memories of a June afternoon in Tolemac pouring out in a thin grey jet of mist, a helicopter glimpsed through the trees, a column of filthy black smoke pouring into the sky, soaked up by the dark crystal.

Her voice whispers in my head. *Time wounds all heels, but you don't have to go on limping for ever, do you?*

Martin has been saying something I didn't catch. 'Pardon?'

'I said, free festivals weren't my scene, but I once saw Angelfeather play Glastonbury.'

'You saw my mother then. She danced with them. The bloke who took her to Stonehenge was Mick Feather.'

'Mick *Feather*?' Martin's goggle-eyed. 'Your mother was friendly with Mick Feather? Mick Feather, as in "Calling in the Mothership"?'

'Yep, that Mick Feather.' One hit only, and that about aliens landing at Stonehenge.

'Bloody hell,' says Martin. 'You have touched glory, young India.'

Mick Feather, skin grimy-tinged as a coalman's no matter how thoroughly he washed, Keir's father. Laughing Mick. 'He wasn't that famous,' I say. 'And it was a crap song.'

'Iconic,' sighs Martin. 'Whatever happened to him?'

And a shudder runs down my spine.

'No idea,' I say, crouching on the damp grass to open the camera bag.

Daniel has definite ideas about what has to be said in this piece to camera. 'Tie it to 1938,' he says. 'Same year as the cine footage.'

'How about saying something about the Barber Surgeon?' Martin points across the circle to a huge lozenge of a stone. 'He was discovered that summer, over there. You don't look keen, India. What's wrong?'

'Nothing,' I say, prickles of electricity running up and down my skin. The Barber Surgeon stone has always been among the stuff of my nightmares.

'Well, hurry up,' says Daniel, over his shoulder. 'Rain's coming on.'

The clouds are threatening as Martin and I pick up the camera equipment to follow.

'Was 1938 really the year they found him?' I ask. 'Because my grandmother was working for Keiller then.'

Martin almost drops the tripod. 'Your grandmother worked for Keiller? Is there no end to your surprises? Are we interviewing her?'

'She refused.' The first raindrops are already pattering on the back of my coat. 'But I'm working on it.'

'Were you there?' I ask Frannie, at home in Trusloe. Filming had to be suspended after an unsatisfactory twenty minutes' dodging raindrops, Martin's beard getting damper and stragglier with every take. 'Did you actually see them dig up the Barber Surgeon?'

Her eyes are fixed on the TV screen.

'Oh, yes,' she says. 'I drew him, didn' I? Mr Keiller took his photograph, but my job was to draw a picture of him under the stone.'

CHAPTER 16

1938

That year the plan was to put back up the stones in the south-western quarter of the circle. There was only two or three showing above ground, but Mr Keiller seemed to think he could find the others that were buried, and even know where the ones had been that was gone for ever. He was like an old wizard: could tell you what had vanished simply by digging in the ground and looking at the soil. Those that had been broken up by old Stonebreaker in the seventeen-somethings, Mr Keiller would mark where they'd stood with a concrete pillar.

The workmen had already cleared the rubbish out of the ditch and dug right down to the chalk, flaying the banks of their green skin. A caravan had been trundled onto the field for a site office. I still had no permanent job, and was reduced to skivvy work all over again, sometimes, dusting Mr Keiller's collections. He used to watch me, to make sure I didn't break anything, his eyes narrowed and his lovely strong mouth a bit open, so you could hear his smoker's breathing sucking at the air.

Heartbreaker, he'd say, *you have a delicate touch.* I'd run the duster so lightly over the backs of them creamers you could almost see the cows shudder with delight.

Mrs Sorel-Taylour was hanging up her coat when I trailed back into the museum one afternoon after another lunchtime stroll to Windmill Hill. I'd taken my sketchbook: the barrows were a mass of spring flowers. She gave me one of her sterner looks. 'You're freckled, Frances. Didn't you think to wear a hat?'

'Didn't know the sun would be so warm.' While she went into the back office to look for Mr Young, I put my sketchbook down on the mahogany case nearest the door, and peered into the glass top to check my reflection.

The door behind me opened, and Mr Keiller walked in. 'Miss Robinson! We keep colliding, don't we?'

I straightened up and backed away. 'I'm so sorry, Mr Keiller.'

'Don't be. You've gone quite pink. Is it the sun or that beau of yours?' He picked up my sketchbook. 'Whose are these? Yours? Heartbreaker, you've been hiding proverbial lights under bushels. They're rather good.'

Hearing his voice, Mrs Sorel-Taylour and Mr Young came out of the back office, Mr Cromley trailing after. Mr Keiller held up a picture of a clover head I'd sketched. 'Look, Mrs. S-T. Did you have any idea your *protégée* was so talented?'

'He's summat,' said Mr Young. He was more used to me now, and always kind, maybe because he understood how it felt to be not so posh as the rest of them. He'd been Mr Keiller's foreman for years on the digs. 'Where did you learn to draw so well? That's almost as good as Miss Chapman could do.'

'Don't let her hear you say so,' said Mr Keiller, flicking back through the pages of my sketchbook. 'In all fairness, though, you're right. The portraits are awfully smart. Look at this one: it's the Brushwood Boy. You've really caught a likeness, Heartbreaker. May I have it?'

It was a sketch of Davey. I'd never heard him called the Brushwood Boy; maybe the name came from his mop of wiry hair. Mr Keiller didn't wait for my nervous nod, and tore the portrait out. He placed it carefully between the pages of his own notebook, and something about the way he did it made me uneasy. Why would he want to keep a picture of Davey? I remembered the two of them on that motorbike, disappearing over the brow of the hill and into the trees.

'Tell you what,' he said, his eyes crinkling in a smile. 'How would you like to help us out on the excavations? What d'you think, Young? Reckon we've got room for another artist on the team?'

I couldn't help it, I was grinning like a mad sheep. Out of the corner of my eye I could see Mr Cromley watching me again. He made me uncomfortable too. I never knew how to read his expression.

Mr Keiller had given the village some land for their cricket pitch, outside the circle on the other side of the bank. Evenings, he goes to watch the game. He stands under the limp leaves of the chestnut trees with their white candles poking through the green, watching the men practise. They've been home to wash the dirt of the digging off, and put on clean white shirts and trousers, dazzling against the grass. One or two wear grey flannel bags, and the bowler, a brawny farmhand, is in a navy blue singlet, sweat glistening on his hairy shoulders.

Mr K watched the men, but I was watching him. I'd never seen a tiger except in pictures, but I thought that was what he reminded me of, fierce and sometimes angry and always dangerous.

'Why does he call you the Brushwood Boy?' I asked Davey, beside me, waiting his turn to bat. He was all in white.

He shrugged. He'd been trying to catch hold of my hand, but I shoved it firmly in my cardigan pocket. 'Dunno,' he said. 'One of his funny ways. Come with me to the dance at the Red Lion?'

'No,' I said. 'We – there's guests arriving that night, promised I'd help Mam.'

'Suit yourself,' he said sulkily, his golden-green eyes like bruises.

A woman was making her way down the path. She was in trousers, something you didn't often see women wear then. She was tall and they suited her figure; they'd have concertina'd round my ankles like a comic turn. As she came closer, I recognized her.

'Miss Chapman's all dressed up,' said Davey. I'd seen her often enough at the Manor, but never to speak to, not that she'd have noticed someone like me. Her usual outfit wasn't so smart: skirt and clumpy shoes, with paint under her fingernails. She was a major-general's daughter, people said, who'd studied art in Paris.

'Alec,' she called. Mr Keiller took his eyes off the men at practice, and smiled. It lit up his serious face. At the same time, he saw Davey and me.

'Doris,' he said. 'Someone here you should meet. Heartbreaker!'

I trotted over, little lamb that I was.

'This is Miss Robinson,' he said to her. 'You remember, I showed you her sketches.'

Close up, she was languidly pretty. She had a haughty nose, and wide, knowing eyes, with long lashes and lids that drooped seductively. Those eyes slid over my face. 'Yes,' she said. 'I remember. Not a trained hand, but she has an eye. You should keep practising, my dear.'

'I do,' I said. 'Especially now Mr Keiller's asked me to help with the drawing at the dig.'

Her mouth froze. 'You didn't tell me you'd offered her a job, Alec.'

'You couldn't have been listening. I said to you we need another artist because you're not here all the time.'

'And Piggott, I suppose, can't be everywhere at once.' She said it with a little laugh, making like she was following his thinking, how sensible he was, but she was grinding the words out between her teeth. 'Pity Donald isn't any good with a pencil.'

'Donald has other talents. And Stuart may not be here the whole season, if he marries Peggy in the autumn.' Mr Keiller was losing interest in the conversation: his eyes kept slipping back to the men on the cricket pitch. 'So give Miss Robinson what assistance you can, won't you?'

There was factions at the Manor, I'd come to understand that already. Best to know who was in with who. I wasn't sure I was as good at drawing as Mr Keiller believed, and I thought I'd better improve, quick, on my own, because I could tell Miss Chapman wasn't going to be any help to me. So I'd gone to the museum to practise. Mr K was in London again, and Davey with him.

I'd brought a chair out of the back room, and perched on it to draw Charlie in his glass case. His skull, distorted and almost as big as an adult's in spite of his tiny child bones, fascinated me. Miss Chapman's speciality was facial reconstructions: she imagined what the dead had been in life, and painted them. I'd heard her tell visitors that the shape of the skull determined the shape of the fleshed face. What had Charlie looked like? I wanted to give him the soft gaze of a baby deer, but that swollen head brought to mind instead Charles Laughton's froggy face and bulging eyes. That sent me off on another train of thought altogether: I'd seen *Vessel of Wrath* at the Palace cinema in Devizes with Davey, and somehow Laughton's slack, drunk mouth in that film had become associated with Davey's attempts to give me a kiss in the darkness.

Mam had been right. I was outgrowing Davey. It had all started to go wrong that day I'd seen him and Mr Keiller on the motorbike. He was a good-looking lad, but that was the problem: he seemed only a boy, compared to the others at the Manor. He kissed in a soft wet way that could sometimes make me queasy. In the cinema foyer there'd been a poster advertising *Mutiny on the Bounty*: Charles Laughton's full-lipped face next to Clark Gable. No prizes for who *he* reminded me of. Davey was devoted to me, but there in't anything about devotion makes the heart beat faster.

The overhead light reflected off the top of the glass case, making it hard to see Charlie clearly. I stood up to turn it off and found myself inches away from a shirtfront.

'Mr Cromley! Didn't know you'd come in!' Didn't even have to lift my eyes to his face because, up close, Mr Cromley had a smell all of his own, a pleasant, tangy, floral scent different from Mr Keiller's spicy hair oil, and Stu Pig's cabbagy old-socks stink. 'Was you – were you watching me?' Trying to mind my grammar like Mrs Sorel-Taylour told me.

'I hope you don't mind, Miss Robinson.' Ever so respectful, unlike Mr K and Stu Pig, who'd taken to calling me Heartbreaker most of the time. Polite, but I still had a funny feeling he was laughing at me. 'Alec's right. You might not be trained, but your pencil captures the soul of what you draw.'

'Have you been watching long?'

'Only a minute or two.'

But I'd a feeling it'd been much longer. And my pencil had been idle, with me musing about Davey. Mr Cromley's special gift seemed to be to catch me at those moments when my thoughts ran naked across my face. No comfort that my back had been to him – every last little frown and pout would've been reflected in Charlie's glass coffin.

He picked up my sketchbook. 'See? You've drawn a small boy, probably disabled, possibly hydrocephalic. If that's not capturing a soul, I don't know what is. Charlie's tribe would have been terrified of your power.'

'Oh.' Didn't know what to say to any of that. Didn't seem to me I'd ever been thought of as powerful by anyone before.

'Though that's not actually Charlie's own skull,' he said. 'It's a copy, a plaster cast. Alec keeps the original in his dressing room.'

'What for?' I asked, shocked.

'No idea. Maybe he drinks out of it, as sorcerers do.' He tossed the sketchbook back onto the seat of my chair. 'Do you know what aboriginal people believe about souls? That they can literally be caught. In the Pacific islands, sorcerers set snares for them, with netting sized to suit the different measures of soul. Big fat loops for big fat souls, tiny loops for thin ones. What's your soul like, Miss Robinson?'

'A strong soul,' I said, surprising myself with my daring. 'One that would rip through the net to be free.'

He shook his head. 'Impossible to escape. There are knives and sharp hooks in the traps, which tear and rend the poor soul. The more it struggles, the more likely it is to die. In Hawaii, the sorcerers shut the soul in a calabash, then give it to someone to eat.'

'That's horrible,' I said.

'I've seen a soul eaten,' he said. Such long eyelashes, for a man, sweeping downwards. 'They say it's very tasty, a bit like an oyster.'

I laughed uneasily. 'I wouldn't know what an oyster tastes like.'

'Salty and slippery.' His pale grey eyes were deep traps, sucking me in. 'Alec's a man for oysters.'

We were very close to each other. All through the conversation, he hadn't stepped back, and nor had I. There were tiny beads of moisture above his light brown moustache, and the pupils seemed huge in his clear grey eyes. In a moment—

But I turned away and picked up my sketchbook. 'I was finished,' I said.

'No, you aren't. I'm sorry. I startled you.'

'I was going to turn the top light out,' I admitted.

'Is that wise?' He laughed. 'People will talk.' He caught sight of my expression. 'Oh, Miss Robinson, I know I'm safe with you. After all, I'm not Mr Keiller, am I?'

'What do you mean?' I was suddenly hot and panicky.

'Don't worry, your secret is safe.' He tapped the side of his narrow, aristocratic nose. 'Mum's the word. I won't tell the Brushwood Boy.' In one quick movement he pulled the Kirby-grip out of my hair so my fringe fell across my forehead. 'Poor old Alec. He's no idea what he's missing.' Then he was gone.

I sat down on my chair by the glass case, plonk. I didn't understand what had just happened. Charlie's sightless eyes bored into mine, like Mr Cromley's had. I felt a lot safer with Charlie, even if he did look like Charles Laughton.

The dig had begun. First, all manner of stuff came out of the ground: broken crocks, coins so worn you couldn't read the dates, a whole brown glazed beer mug Mr Piggott said was two hundred year old, even a marmalade jar, Keiller's, of course, and that gave us all a laugh. He and Mr Cromley went about pushing pegs into the ground, probing for hidden sarsens, then marked where they found them on pages of squared paper in what they called the Plotting Book. When the buried stones were uncovered, lying in their shallow graves, they looked like the pits in a fruit.

'Question is, why?' The usual warmth flooded me when I heard Mr Keiller's voice. 'If eighteenth-century entrepreneurs like Robinson, Fowler and Green are profiting by breaking up stones for building material, why were these buried?'

I looked up from my sketchbook to see if he was talking to me, but no: he had his acolytes tagging along. 'Don, what's your theory?'

The field was humming with activity. One gang of men was returfing the bank. Another group was digging down to uncover a new stone further along. In front of us, the workmen had a big stone already bared and trussed up in ropes and pulleys, and Mr Keiller and his young men had arrived in time to watch them struggle to lever it upright.

Mr Cromley had affected a pipe, a useful prop for a young man who wanted to be taken serious like. He took a long draw on it, exhaled slowly, and said, 'Concealing the stones is about power, of course. They're buried to break the geometry of the circle, and to destroy their mystic hold over the community – to wither the stone's souls, if you like. The priest takes their power instead.'

'Stones with souls?' scoffed Mr Piggott. 'Sorcerer-priests? I don't subscribe to Don's *Golden Bough* fixation. That sort of thinking is twenty years out of date. The motive's economic, not spiritual. Eighteenth-century farmers are behind the burials, freeing up more land for cultivation. Some they bury, some they break, depending on the market's demand for stone.'

Didn't dare join in the conversation, but I was with Mr Cromley. Anyone who'd lived among them stones knew they had souls, all right. That big bugger they were about to lift: he'd been sleeping, but you could see he was coming awake. People like Mr Piggott would think they were clever to fetter the stones, but the stones were stronger, and they had time on their side. That old stone could shrug off all them ropes and pulleys, if he felt like it.

Mr Young was supervising, puffing at a pipe too – it looked much more natural in his mouth. 'Bring him up slowly,' he called, waving his arm like a man directing traffic. His bandy little legs had begun to turn a deep golden brown below the turn-ups of his shorts. 'Slowly, Reg! No bloomin' rush about it. Ready with the timbers?' The stone began to rise out of its bed like Lazarus. 'That's it! Now get that prop under there – Arthur, mind yourself, you don't want to be under this old chap if one of those hawsers snaps – quickly now! OK, George, take the strain – and pull . . .' Gradually the stone started to heave itself upright. Mr Keiller put his camera to his eye and began prowling round, looking for a good snapshot.

There was a shout from further down the field where the men were digging for another stone. 'Mr Keiller! Come over here. You'd better see this.'

People called back and forth all the time while the digging was going on, but there was something in this shout that made everybody stop. Mr Keiller lowered the camera. Young took his pipe out of his mouth. Mr Cromley and Mr Piggott broke into a run, and Mr K wasn't far after them. I felt a shiver go down my spine. The pencil fell out of my fingers, and the sketchbook slid off my knee.

'Well, I'll be blowed!' said Mr Cromley, as they reached the diggers.

'Bugger me!' came Mr Piggott's voice.

Mr Keiller stood stock still with his hands on his hips, at the edge of the excavation pit, slowly shaking his head as if he couldn't believe what he was seeing.

Hampered by my skirt, I arrived a few seconds later.

A grinning mouth full of teeth, a bony eyeless socket staring up at us from under the stone.

CHAPTER 17

'The Barber Surgeon,' says Martin, authoritatively, staring into the lens of the camera, 'was a shock to everybody.'

Nobody pays the slightest bit of attention. The crew are too busy setting up, and early on a sharp April morning, there are no tourists about. The camera stands unattended, while the intense young cameraman from the film show at the Red Lion wanders round the field, looking for good angles. The soundman, wearing headphones, has propped the woolly boom microphone on its long pole against a stone, and is sitting with his back to it, playing some shoot-'em-up game on his mobile phone, his thumbs a blur. Ibby is with Michael, leaning on the bonnet of the crew's Range Rover, deep in conversation over a map.

'His skeleton was discovered buried with this massive stone,' Martin continues, gesturing into empty air behind him, the camera being nowhere near the Barber Surgeon's stone. 'Crushed or suffocated, his leg trapped beneath it, his pelvis cracked, his neck broken, the tools of his trade, his scissors, spilling from his pocket—' He sees me and breaks off. 'Blossom! I rewrote the whole piece last night. Better, don't you think? What did your grandmother have to say?'

'Not much. Except that she drew his picture, under the stone.'

'Not much! That's remarkable. Where is it?'

'She was vague. Said Keiller took it.'

'Well, it can't be in the archive, or it would have been published.' Martin takes my arm and steers me across the grass towards the Range Rover parked on the high street. 'You only ever see the photographs Keiller took – there's a splendid one of Piggott holding the skull, pretending to be Hamlet – alas, poor Barber Surgeon . . .' He bows me through the gate with a flourish.

'. . . the ground's too wet,' Michael is saying as we close on the Range Rover. 'We'd achieve better results later in the summer when there are clear parch marks.'

'I need aerials sooner than that,' says Ibby, her tone firm and confident. Like the first time I saw her, she's wearing red – a long-sleeved T-shirt, this time, under a khaki waistcoat with lots of bulging pockets, a walking store-cupboard for batteries, videotapes and fold-up headphones. Sunglasses nestle in her short dark curls, and reading specs dangle on a chain round her neck. 'Shit, Harry doesn't look happy.'

The cameraman, on the other side of the field, is giving the sky over Cherhill a worried once-over. Trails of high cirrus are forming against the blue. There's something flat and unappealing about the light.

'We need to crack on with the PTC,' says Ibby. 'Michael, if it pours, can we film in the museum?'

'Shouldn't be a problem.' Michael checks his watch. 'Sorry I can't hang around – meetings.'

Ibby folds her map and puts it into another of her bottomless pockets. 'And rostrum the Keiller stills?' she calls, to Michael's retreating back.

'She speaks an entire new language,' whispers Martin, in my ear. 'I'm terrified of her already.'

'I heard that,' says Ibby. 'Good. It might persuade you to do what I tell you. Now get your arse over there and put your mind to this piece to camera. India, the mini-DVC's on the back seat. Can you film at the same time as Harry from the other side?'

'Oh, God, it's going to be modern,' says Martin. 'Funny angles and jump cuts.'

'It's for Channel 4, Martin,' says Ibby. 'They like to push the boundaries of technique. And for a man who claims not to know the language, you seem remarkably versant already with the basic grammar.' One side of her mouth goes up in a kind of smile. 'Arse. Gear. Joined by the preposition "in". Harry! Can you come and set up?'

The cameraman folds the tripod, picks up the camera and mean-
ders towards us, the soundman trotting at his heels like an eager puppy,
attached by a lead to the camera. I sneak a glance at Ibby's clipboard
on the bonnet of the Range Rover. The top sheet is a mind-bogglingly
organized list of shots.

'I'm not used to this,' I say, reaching inside for the smaller camera.
'Never worked on a production with budget for a full crew.'

Ibby gives me a withering look, opening the tailgate and loading
big flat camera batteries into her pockets. 'I do things professionally.
But that doesn't mean wasting money.'

She *is* scary. I unpack the camera in a hurry.

'Where do you want him?' asks Harry.

'That diamond-shaped stone. Two sizes, please, wide and MCU.'

Martin raises anguished eyebrows.

'Medium closeup!' yells Ibby. 'But I haven't the time to nursemaid
you. From now on, it's never apologize, never explain.'

Harry wanders around, stopping now and then, bending his knees
to dip and squint, framing possible shots. So far he's not smiled once.
Ibby's eyes follow him hungrily. He's probably only a couple of years
older than me, which makes him at least ten years her junior, but that
doesn't seem to bother her.

We're onto the fourth or fifth take before Martin overcomes his
nerves and hits a rhythm. '. . . The stone weighs approximately thirteen
tons. Hard to know what happened, but the likeliest explanation . . .'

'Cut.' The soundman pulls off his headphones. 'Aircraft.'

'You sure? I can't hear anything,' says Harry.

'Long way off, but could be coming in this direction.'

'Shit. That was going really well.' Ibby straightens up from the
portable monitor on the grass. 'You're starting to look like you're
enjoying yourself, Martin.'

'Actually, I *am*.'

In the distance there's the high mosquito whine of a microlight.
'Just what we need,' says Ibby. Her voice sounds relaxed, but she's
massaging the back of her neck as she glances at her watch. 'I hate

the little bastards. They should issue an anti-aircraft gun as standard filming kit.'

'We're going to lose the sun if he doesn't get a move on,' says Harry.

'Engine note's changing,' says the soundman, clamping one head-phone to his ear. 'He's heading away.'

'OK, ready to go again when Keith gives us the all-clear,' says Ibby to Martin.

'Hold on,' says Keith the soundman. 'There's a chopper as well.'

My stomach tenses. The helicopter is a long, black-bodied machine flying high and fast.

'You seen that footage on YouTube, Harry?' asks Keith. 'Round here it happened, wasn't it?'

'Bloody terrifying,' says Harry. 'Is it still there?'

'What footage?' asks Ibby, but my gut has already turned to ice.

'Helicopter crashed while it was being used for aerial filming.' Harry applies his eye to the viewfinder again. 'Cameraman let go of the camera, and it bashed the director's brains out – tape still running. Someone posted it on YouTube last week. Bound to make 'em take it off once the family finds out. You don't see much, but it starts with a clear shot of the bloke's face as the helicopter goes into a spin, and the sick bit is knowing the poor bastard dies.'

'Cameraman's revenge,' says the soundman. 'Now you know, Ib, what happens to directors who demand too much.' He draws a finger across his throat and guffaws.

My hands are shaking as I dial Ed's mobile number in the ladies' loo at the Red Lion. Somehow I managed to hold it together through the morning's filming until we broke for lunch. My head's pounding and I'm too nauseous to eat.

Nothing happens. I look down at the mobile screen, already knowing what I'll see.

No bloody signal.

*　　*　　*

'You all right, blossom?' asks Martin, at the picnic table outside the pub, veggie burger in one hand. 'You're a bit pale.'

'A bug.'

I sit down, my knees wobbly. Why did this have to happen when I thought I was over it? I didn't know the camera had gone on recording. Who put the video on YouTube? What does it show? Not much more than a blur, the camera jerking and tumbling, a final glimpse of Steve's lolling head, a red flower on a broken stalk? Please God, don't let it be in focus . . .

'Have a chip,' says Martin.

'Really, I don't want anything.'

'What's the plan for this afternoon, Ib?' Harry returns from the bar with a tray of drinks. 'Shoot the shit out of the stone circle?'

'Martin, I'd like an introductory piece from you,' says Ibby. 'What was Avebury for? Feasting? Healing? Giant astronomical computer?'

'Forget all that seventies bollocks,' says Martin. 'It's the place of the dead.'

'How d'you reckon that?' asks Harry.

'It's a stone monument. The theory goes, wood for the living, stone for the dead.'

I didn't go to Steve's funeral. His parents had him cremated at Golders Green, then scattered his ashes in a park near Elstree. Essence of Steve floating on the breeze, drifting across the garden of the *Big Brother* house. I check my phone again for a signal, and imagine his open, dead eyes staring back at me from the screen. Haunting me, like Frannie's buggerin' lights. Like the ghosts that whisper to me from the trees at Tolemac.

'Ten minutes,' says Ibby. 'Then we need to make a move.'

'Slavedriver,' says Martin, sounding completely happy about it.

As soon as we leave the pub the rain starts, sheets of it, sending us scurrying for the shelter of the museum.

Martin and I, trying not to get in the way, stand next to Charlie's glass coffin while Harry sets up to film the Barber Surgeon's scissors.

'What you said about Avebury being a place of the dead?' I ask, sidestepping as Keith the soundman comes past with a couple of lighting stands. 'Literally? Are there burials?'

'Well, there's the odd thing,' says Martin. 'The burials seem to be almost entirely outside the henge – like Charlie here, on Windmill Hill.'

As if on cue, the whole room is washed in a harsh glare as Harry switches on one of the lamps, shining through the side of the glass and illuminating the child's skeleton in its foetal crouch.

'But inside—' Martin stops suddenly, narrows his eyes, whips out his glasses and peers at the skull. A trick of the light makes it a different colour from the rest of the bones, emphasizing its grotesque distortion. He frowns, then shakes his head. 'Sorry, petal, thought for a moment – never mind. Thing is, *inside* the henge there seem to be hardly any burials, apart from the odd jawbone. The only complete prehistoric skeleton found was at the bottom of the ditch, near the southern entrance. The diggers almost missed her in the mud – one of them actually stood on the skull, unfortunately. This was years before Keiller and his more thorough excavation techniques. It was a woman, lying on her side, surrounded by a ring of small sarsens.'

'Meaning what?'

'Who knows? A ritualized burial right by the entrance suggests a deliberate killing. Maybe the stones round her are a miniature Avebury, confining her spirit, so her ghost focuses the magic of the place.'

'Wow.' Easy to forget, seeing visitors in floral wellies patting the stones in sunlight, that Avebury could have so dark a past. 'So when Keiller's team finds the Barber Surgeon *under* a stone . . .'

'Exactly,' says Martin. 'They get the wrong end of the stick altogether, at first.'

CHAPTER 18

1938

'I told you,' said Mr Cromley. 'Sacrifice. The killing of the priest-king. Blood feeds the corn.'

'Tosh,' said Mr Piggott.

'Peace, children,' said Mr Keiller. The three of them stood on the lip of the pit, staring at the skeleton under the massive stone.

'Well, what else could it be, Alec? Frazer cites examples from every culture. The Marimo Indians, for example, always slaughtered a short fat man: sympathetic magic, to represent the desired shape of the young ears of ripening corn.'

Stu Pig snorted with laughter.

Mr Keiller took Mr Cromley more serious, though. 'We must allow the possibility, Piggott – though I have to agree with you that Don's a touch too keen to smell magic in the air. We need to lift this chap out.' He looked away and closed his eyes, as he did when he was thinking hard. 'Our first skeleton from the circle. Something for you to sketch, Heartbreaker, and don't linger over it. We should parcel this chap off *toute suite* to find out how he died and, if possible, when. Don't want the padre finding out, in case he tries to commandeer the bones for immediate Christian burial.'

Terrible disappointment. They brought him out, bone by bone, and with him came a bodkin and a pair of scissors and three silver coins, dating to thirteen-something. So he wasn't near as ancient as Mr Keiller hoped.

'A tailor, maybe. Or a travelling barber surgeon. Yes, I like that explanation better. Cuts hair, pulls teeth, sets bones.' Mr Keiller tapped the rough sketch I had done. 'This is good, by the way, Heartbreaker. Can you work it up into something that shows us what might have happened? Passing one day, sees the villagers toppling a stone, lends a hand and gets in the way as it comes down. Dead as a doornail, they can't pull him out – his foot is trapped underneath. So they bury him with the megalith.'

Mr Cromley raised one elegant eyebrow. 'How do you know it was an accident?' We were watching Mr Young treat the bones with a solution of acetone and cellulose. It came out of the glass jar thick like honey, the sharp smell making our eyes water. When the preservative had dried, the skeleton was to be sent to the Royal College of Surgeons.

'Don,' said Mr Piggott, witheringly, 'leave off, will you? Not everything in the world has to be sinister.'

'*So* much more fun if it is, though,' said Mr Cromley.

Davey had taken to hanging around the dig when he'd nothing else to do. If I saw him in time I found myself an errand, anything to look busy. Sometimes I couldn't avoid him. Mr Darling's stables at Beckhampton had trained the Derby winner, Bois Roussel, and Davey, like half the village, had put a couple of bob on him.

'Come on, Fran, we got to celebrate. Slap-up tea at McIlroy's in Swindon? Pictures? *Too Hot to Handle* is showing – we'd be in time for the bus . . .'

'Not tonight.'

'You told me you like Clark Gable.' Wide, hopeful eyes. He was so sure I'd say yes.

Mr Keiller appeared from behind the newly erected Barber Surgeon's stone, deep in conversation with Mr Cromley. Mr K was wearing his blazer, MIAR embroidered on the pocket. Handsomer than Clark Gable. If I went blonde like Carole Lombard, would he want me? He saw Davey and me, and smiled. Something went cold and uneasy in me. Which one of us was he smiling at?

'In't every day a man has money burning a hole . . .'

'I told you, not tonight.' It came out sharp.

Davey tried to be light about it. 'Later in the week?'

'I'm not interested, right? Too busy here.'

The hope died in his eyes, and his jaw tightened with the effort of hiding he was hurt. I felt bad, but sometimes his smooth skin looked so girlish I wanted to make him cry.

Mr Cromley caught my eye, and winked.

When I wasn't at the site I now had a desk in the Map Room to work up my sketches of the dig. All that brown made it a dull place to me, everything laid out neat and tidy and just so. If someone moved anything, Mr Keiller'd come and rant at Mrs Sorel-Taylour. She'd do her best to soothe him, but he'd sometimes sulk for days.

I drew the stones one by one as they were stripped bare, shading the sides of the pits with neat cross-hatching, making sure everything was to scale according to the measurements Mr Piggott and Mr Cromley supplied. The leather brownness of the room was oppressive. Sitting at the tall stools in there, bent over my drawings, sometimes I caught myself looking down to check there was a skirt on my legs, afraid the place would have redressed me in a brown woollen suit too, like a man.

The consolation was Mr K. He was often in the Map Room. He worked there himself, hunched over big charts with his set-squares and rulers, his big hands tracing delicate lines with a fine-nibbed pen.

'I learned my draughtsmanship in an engineering factory, Heartbreaker,' he'd say. 'No room for inexactitude in car design or archaeology.' I became used to him standing behind me, watching me as my hands moved nervously over the paper. Sometimes he'd lean over to correct a detail of my drawing, and the spicy smell of his hair oil would lift me like incense. Or he'd explode on the room, filling it with colour.

'Miss Robinson! Haven't you finished that drawing of the Barber Surgeon yet? Never mind, too fine a day to hang about indoors. Come for a jaunt.'

Mr Keiller believed in jaunts. If he had to give a lecture, he preferred not to go alone; it was an excuse for a trip with a whole party of pals. They'd stay in some posh hotel, seeing the sights, maybe traipsing out in the evening after cocktails to a boxing match. Or he'd chivvy Mr Piggott and Mr Cromley and anyone else he favoured that week into a convoy of cars to visit a cathedral or castle, or some other archaeologist's site. I'd never been invited, though sometimes Mrs Sorel-Taylour would go with them because she was friendly with Miss Chapman.

So when he come bursting into the room announcing a jaunt that sunny morning, I could feel myself puffing up with excitement.

'Bring the drawing with you. We can look at it over lunch,' said Mr K. 'The Kegresse is outside.'

Oh. My spirits was sinking already. Couldn't go far in the Kegresse, which was a funny old car Mr K used to trundle about the fields. He'd bought it years ago for the snow in Scotland; instead of proper wheels at the back, it had a caterpillar track like a tank, so it'd go anywhere. Mr K loved it, called it the Caterpillar, and claimed he'd even taken it up a mountain for a shooting party.

'We'll have a picnic at the Long Barrow,' he went on. 'You look like you need fresh air – far too pale and peaky. The course of true love not running smooth, eh, Heartbreaker?'

I coloured up then, like I always did, and that would usually make him torment me more. But today he was in too much of a rush. All he said was 'Be outside in ten minutes,' then disappeared into the main part of the house, calling for Waters the butler to bring the hamper out.

There was room for four in the Caterpillar, two in the front and two in the back. By the time I left the Manor, the drawing of the Barber Surgeon tucked safely inside my handbag, the car was parked in the stableyard on the cobbles, its engine already running. Mr Keiller hadn't arrived yet, but Mr Piggott had settled himself in the back seat, and Mr Cromley was leaning against the museum wall, smoking a cigarette. When he saw me coming down the path between the lavender beds he threw it down. 'Miss Robinson! How delightful.'

The sulky housemaid from Beckhampton was strapping a hamper onto the side of the car. She gave me a look like she hoped I'd burst into flames on the spot, and I give her a haughty look right back that said she had no right to be smart with me. I was *one of the party* today, off on a picnic with Mr Keiller, and with the man she'd dropped her knickers for – that hadn't done her much good, had it? Mr Cromley was acting like she wasn't there, holding open the door of the Kegresse for me so I could sit up front.

Mr Keiller came down the path at a lick. 'Donald! Did you bring the rugs?'

'Strapped on the back.'

My foot was on the running board, and I was ready to swing myself into the front seat. Then I saw who sauntered behind Mr Keiller, wearing her lovely tailored trousers, as doe-eyed as Bette Davis.

Miss Chapman was coming with us.

Bright red, I stepped down. Mr Piggott leaned over and opened the rear door for me, looking his usual crosspatch self. Mr Cromley climbed in after me; the warmth of his leg pressed against mine. I shuffled further along the seat towards Mr Piggott, who squeezed himself against the far door like he didn't want to be touched. Wasn't no good doing that, because we all had to squash up together. Miss Chapman slid into the front seat, the loose material of her trousers draping her long legs. She nodded to the men – 'Hello, Stuart, morning, Donald,' – and ignored me. Mr Keiller jumped in the other side, put the car into gear, and as the caterpillar tracks ground over the cobbles he took one hand off the wheel and laid his arm along the back of the seat behind her, his fingers loosely touching her shoulder.

I killed a hundred times, as we bounced down the fields alongside the stones of the Avenue, suffocating the stupid fantasies I'd made up in the ten minutes between Mr Keiller inviting me to go with them and Miss Chapman following him down the path, and I died myself with every one of those little murders. The pressure of Mr Cromley's knee against mine was a strange comfort. Seemed to me he understood.

We parked up in the lee of the Long Barrow, out of the wind. There had been showers that morning, and the grass still sparkled with raindrops. Mr Piggott went walking round the barrow, counting to himself as he paced its length. Mr Keiller spread out the rug. Miss Chapman unloaded the contents of the picnic basket, a smug little smile on her face all the time because she was his consort, his Wallis Simpson. She'd even done her hair the same, though I didn't reckon the Marmalade King would abdicate for love of a woman, the way King Edward had, two summers ago. I'd thought it was romantic, but Mam said Mrs Simpson must have bewitched the poor man.

Mr Cromley was standing next to me. He took his silver cigarette case out of his pocket and offered me one.

'Heartbreaker,' called Mr Keiller. 'Come and lay out the cutlery, will you?'

We sat on the tartan rugs to eat our lunch, cold chicken and late Scottish asparagus that Mr Keiller had had sent down from his estate at Morven, with a buttery mayonnaise, but it was all salt to me, near inedible. There was chilled white wine, too, with a soft smoky taste, and I drank a glass or two of that, until it smudged the sharp edges of my hurt like a wet finger on a line of pencil.

Afterwards there was a Thermos of hot, bitter coffee. Mr Piggott took his cup away with him, wandering round the other end of the mound to look at the massive stones blocking the entrance. The barrow was all stopped up with earth, always had been, and I wondered what he found so fascinating about it.

I had forgotten my drawing, but Mr Keiller hadn't. When I opened the clasp of my handbag to look for a handkerchief, he spotted my sketchbook. 'Let's see it, then,' he said. 'Doris, Miss Robinson has been working up her picture of the Barber Surgeon. I asked her to visualize what he might have looked like.'

Miss Chapman's face froze. I was usurping her skill, laying flesh over bone.

'No,' I said quickly. 'It's not finished. I'm not at all happy with it.'

'Not how it looked to me this morning,' he said. 'You seemed pretty pleased with yourself, told me it was almost done. No need to be modest—' and he lunged to snatch the sketchbook.

I grabbed the bag closed against my chest.

'Donald,' said Mr Keiller, 'pin Miss Robinson's arms to her sides, will you?' He had a wicked smile on his face. Miss Chapman's lips were so tight I thought they'd bleed.

'Happily,' said Mr Cromley, and I felt his long slender fingers on my arms, digging in hard, pulling me off balance, though I still held onto the bag. I wriggled against him as Mr Keiller came forward on hands and knees across the rug, a stalking tiger. As he seized the bag, his fingers slid under it and against my breast. His eyes met mine.

'Alec,' said Miss Chapman, from the other rug, 'for God's sake, leave the child alone.'

'Oh, I don't think she's a child,' said Mr Keiller. 'She's a very determined young woman.' He took a firmer grip of the bag, his knuckles rubbing against my nipple, hard as a little cherry pip through the thin material of my blouse. 'She doesn't want to let her employer have what is rightfully his.' His eyes were on fire, burning into me. 'I might have to chastise her.'

I tightened my grasp on the bag. Mr Cromley's breath was hot on my ear.

'I think you should let go, Miss Robinson,' he said, 'or neither of us shall be answerable for the consequences. Shall we, Alec?'

'Hold her firmly,' said Mr Keiller, teeth parted, a glimpse of his tongue running against their edge, back and forth, like it always did when he was absorbed in something. 'Very firmly. I'm going to have to . . .' He moved his hand again, sending an electric thrill through me, and I could tell it was deliberate – he knew all right what it was doing to me.

'I'm going to have to slowly . . . very slowly . . . prise her fingers away, one by one . . .' He winked at me. 'Maybe with my *teeth*.'

'No,' I said, giggling now, as Mr Cromley hauled me backwards until I was almost lying flat on my back on the ground. Mr Keiller straddled my legs, looming over me, blocking out the sun. The material of his trousers was stretched tight over his thighs, his crotch in shadow. 'You wouldn't dare. I can bite too . . .'

'Oh, wouldn't I just?' His strong fingers were lacing with mine, pulling them away from my bag. 'You'd be surprised what I'd dare do, Miss Robinson . . .'

'Alec!' Miss Chapman's voice was ice splitting. 'I said *let the girl alone*.'

Mr Keiller wrested the bag from me and rocked back on his heels, breathing hard. 'Success, Doris,' he said. 'The sketchbook is mine.' Never taking his eyes from my face, he pulled it out of the bag with a flourish, and shook it so the drawing fell onto the tartan rug.

It was good: the best I'd yet done. I'd drawn the Barber Surgeon still alive under the massive stone, his leg pinned, pain streaked into the deep creases either side of his mouth, his eyes pleading through the long, straggly hair that fell across his face. He was stretching out one hand, and you'd almost swear that if you'd reached out to him, his fingers would have come up from the paper and seized yours.

Fingers tipped with paint-rimmed, bitten nails snatched up the drawing and crumpled it. Miss Chapman, standing over us, was white with anger. 'How dare you?' she hissed. 'How dare you flaunt her in front of me?' She gripped the balled picture with both hands and pulled, digging her fingers in so the paper tore, and my heart tore with it.

'Doris,' said Mr Keiller, in a surprisingly quiet, dangerous voice, 'you are a first-class fucking bitch. Get out of here.'

'I'm going,' she said, throwing the destroyed drawing onto the wet grass. 'For Christ's sake, Alec. She's young enough to be your daughter. Who do you think you are? The lord of the Manor, exercising his seigneurial rights? You and your bloody pimp there – do the pair of you both fuck her together?'

Mr Piggott appeared round the corner of the barrow. 'Are we going home now?' he said, in a surprised tone.

'Stuart,' said Miss Chapman, 'would you mind driving me back?'

Mr Piggott looked uncertainly at Mr Keiller. 'Alec?'

'I'll drive her back.' He stood up, frighteningly tall, face like thunder. 'Doris, get in the Caterpillar. I'm not going to ask you to apologize to Miss Robinson immediately, while you're still overwrought, but you will. She has nothing to do with this, and I certainly have not fucked her, as you so charmingly put it. Stuart, you and Donald look after the girl. She doesn't need to come back into the office this afternoon, and I'd be grateful if you'd see her home. I'm sorry for the language, Miss Robinson.'

He climbed in and slammed the driver's door shut. Miss Chapman's face was white and terrified. The three of us watched the Kegresse bump away down the slope. Why couldn't he have let Stu Pig go with her?

'What was all that about?' asked Mr Piggott. 'Why is Miss Robinson crying?'

'Stu, why don't you carry on measuring your bloody barrow?' said Mr Cromley. 'I'll see Miss Robinson safely home.'

'I'm not crying,' I said, setting my jaw tight so my mouth wouldn't tremble and more tears spill out of my brimming eyes, 'and I don't need either of you to see me home. I'd rather be on my own, if you don't mind.' I stood up; my legs were shaking. Beside the path, where Miss Chapman had flung it, lay the crumpled drawing. I bent to pick it up, then changed my mind and left it on the grass, all shredded and smeared. Don't know what happened to it. I suppose Mr Piggott and Mr Cromley threw it away when they cleared up the rugs and the plates from the picnic.

CHAPTER 19

Driving through intermittent, hammering showers, I keep wondering what happened to Frannie's picture of the Barber Surgeon. It came as a surprise that she was considered a good enough draughtswoman to work as an artist for Keiller. She used to sketch clever little doodles for me when I was a child, but I haven't seen her draw for years, her fingers now too arthritic to hold a pencil comfortably. The rosewood watercolour box in the drawer where I found Davey's photo looked as if it had been retired half a century ago.

Unable to find Ed to tell him about the YouTube footage – it's his day off, the office said – my only option is to track him down in Yatesbury. He probably goes home to his wife in Oxfordshire at weekends, but I guess he spends time off midweek studying in his friend's place, wherever that may be. All I know is that it's somewhere 'near the airfield'. I bypass the main part of the village, and the church where Davey Fergusson is buried, and drive along the airfield's perimeter road, past the microlight centre, looking for clues.

Little is left to show that this was once a bustling RAF training base, apart from a few skeletal hangars that might be contemporary with its heyday between the wars, when Guy Gibson of the Dambusters learned to fly there. The far end of the field has a sad, neglected feel, the perimeter road not so much a lane as a collection of loosely assembled potholes. Midges dance over the puddles. Wincing at the likely effect on what's left of the Peugeot's shock absorbers, I bump slowly down the track towards a pair of mock-Tudor semis, faced in grubby white plaster cladding. A man comes round the side of one of the houses, a shotgun crooked over his arm, a Jack Russell at his heels. The dog starts barking as soon as it sees the car.

'Sorry.' I wind down the window, trying not to feel intimidated by the gun. 'I'm looking for Ed Raleigh.'

The man jerks his head towards a clump of beeches. 'Down there. Shut up, Bingo.' He starts up the road in the opposite direction, but the dog stands his ground, waiting to see me off his territory. As I put the car into gear, the man calls over his shoulder, 'I'd walk if I were you. The potholes get worse.' He whistles to the dog. It bares its teeth at me in a soundless snarl, then trots after him.

The beeches are about five minutes' walk away, at the lane end. On the opposite side of the road a cluster of hangars stands behind a rusting chain-link fence with a notice hung on it: *Yatesbury Helicopters. Private Charter, Pilot Training. Positively NO admittance to unauthorized visitors. Premises patrolled 24 hours.* The last sentence is printed under a picture of a ferocious Alsatian. But the gate is sagging open, and Ed's Land Rover is parked on the cracked concrete forecourt between the buildings. He can't be living here, can he?

There's no sign of anyone, and all the doors are padlocked. I call Ed's name. No one comes. Somewhere in the distance music is playing. It sounds like Radiohead.

I walk behind the hangars, and find myself looking out across an apron of concrete and a flat, empty field. Wrong direction: the music has disappeared. Going back round the other side, it's audible again: definitely Radiohead. Someone's turned it up. Now I see what I missed before – outside the fence, under the trees on the far side of the road.

Close up, the caravan is distinctly seedy, even by the generous standards of a childhood spent moving from festival to festival in a convoy of travellers' vans. It was probably once a smart two-tone cream and brown tourer, but a layer of algae and grime has painted it a dull greenish-grey all over, like camouflage. There are no wheels: it's propped on bricks. It seems to have suffered a road accident, its skin buckled and creased at one corner like crumpled paper. At the grubby window, curtains printed with Thomas the Tank Engine are drawn closed. 'Creep' thunders through the thin walls.

I bang on the door. 'You there, Ed?'

No answer. I hammer on the door again. Eventually it opens. Ed stands there, swaying, blinking, bemused, stubble darker than ever.

'You look awful,' I tell him, as 'Creep' finishes.

'How did you know where to find me?'

'Mystic pagan powers. Aren't you going to invite me in?'

He steps back, stumbling a little, catches the side of the door and rights himself. On the stereo, the Smiths strike up 'How Soon Is Now?'.

'Boy, we *are* feeling cheery this evening.' I mount the steps into the caravan, catching a whiff of stale beer, damp carpets and a thick, chemical odour. 'Are you drunk?'

'Wish I was.' Ed runs a hand through tousled hair. 'Only just out of bed. I've the mother of all hangovers.' He disconnects the iPod from its docking station. '"Heaven Knows I'm Miserable Now", etc.'

'What the hell did you drink last night?'

'Don't ask.'

No need. The evidence is piled in the tiny sink: a sandcastle heap of lager cans. Sticking out of the top, like a flagpole, is a vodka bottle. At one end of the van there is a rumpled double bed, at the other a narrow fold-down table between two bench seats.

'Is that Pot Noodle on the table?'

He has the grace to look ashamed. 'Didn't actually eat it. I only thought about it, like you do when you're drinking.'

'Christ, Ed, you must have put away enough to knock you out for a week.'

'Take your pick of my excuses.' He gestures towards the table, and a scatter of letters and torn envelopes next to the Pot Noodle. The top sheet of paper has a Barclays Bank logo. 'On second thoughts, don't look. I'd prefer you not to know the extent to which my life is falling apart. Sorry, it's a pit in here. I probably stink, too. Let me get showered.'

'I'm not staying long.'

'Can hardly blame you.' He wrinkles his nose. 'No, even I can smell me, so unless you want one of us to stand outside and conduct this conversation at a safe distance through the open door, I'm going to have to insist you give me two minutes in the shower. Don't panic, it's perfectly private – you won't have to see bits of me you'd rather forget.'

Can't help a smile. 'Really, Ed, no need . . .' But he's already pulling closed the sliding door that shuts off the bedroom end. I immediately start thinking about all the bits of him that I actually wouldn't mind seeing again: what he looks like pulling his T-shirt over his head . . .

No. To distract myself, I concentrate on the utter squalor around me.

The caravan would smell sweeter if the lager mountain in the sink was levelled. There's a Waitrose carrier bag on the floor so I scoop into it as many empty cans as will fit, and drop it into the overflowing dustbin outside the door. From the other end, creaks and the sound of trickling water announce that Ed's ablutions are under way. I don't mean to pry into the pile of papers on the table, really, but I can't help noticing—

Oh, my sweet Jesus. *How* much?

. . . would point out that you also already have an unsecured loan for seventy thousand pounds, the repayments on which are in default, and therefore on this occasion we are unable to advance any further monies . . .

Seventy thousand pounds? No wonder the poor bastard's in a caravan. And it's not the only letter with a bank logo.

'Don't rub my nose in the shit I'm in, will you?'

I spin round, guilty. 'Sorry, I—'

'Kinda leaps out at you, doesn't it? It's been leaping out and twisting my balls for the last three months.' Ed towels his hair, in damp black ringlets from the shower, releasing the clean scent of coal-tar soap. His shirt's hanging open, revealing low-slung jeans, a flat stomach, a sparse fuzz of dark chest hair. Another cloudburst starts to hammer on the caravan roof.

'How –'

' – did I get into this mess? Nothing too dreadful, honest, guv, no gambling habit, no cocaine addiction, no drink problem, despite the evidence to the contrary in the dustbin. Costs roughly fifty thou to train as a helicopter pilot, more if you get a commercial licence for fixed wing as well, as I did. The idea is to pay off the loan with the fabulous wages we earn from our difficult and dangerous trade, and eventually take out another to buy our own chopper. Reality is that most of us lurch from financial crisis to financial crisis, and in my case to ultimate disaster.'

'So the crash was the last straw?'

'Give the lady a coconut. I was keeping up repayments until Luke sacked – sorry, let me go, as he so politely put it. The euphemisms people use. Lost the Bell, couldn't afford to have it repaired, insurance people wouldn't pay out until after the accident report, etc., etc. Only way I'm earning anything is because the guy who runs the show here took pity. Not that's he's doing so well himself at the moment.'

'You're an instructor? Teaching people to fly helicopters?'

It sounds more like a spit than a laugh. 'Oh, I could. I'm qualified. But he thinks it's better I don't for the moment. I'm the fucking night security guard.'

Light dawns. 'I saw the notice on the fence. Where's the dog?'

'It's the Jack Russell at the cottages along the road.'

Can't help it, I burst out laughing. 'Oh, I'm sorry, Ed, it's just—'

'I know, I know. It *is* bloody funny, when you think about it. I'm being paid for doing nothing – there's never been a security guard here before, not much need. I suppose somebody might come along and steal a chopper, but good luck to them – they'd have to know how to fly it, and there's an alarm system in the hangar that'd wake the bloody dead, let alone old Alan at the cottages. He's up half the night anyway, killing small inoffensive creatures.'

'I met him.'

'Yeah, well. Man of few words, but generally to the point.'

'Don't you fly at all?'

'Occasionally. My boss had great plans to run an executive air-taxi operation, as well as the flying lessons, but he hasn't really pulled it together. There are a few charters flying rich gamblers to and from race meetings, and a couple of dodgy businessmen and the odd pop group have used his services, but there's hardly enough work for him, let alone me. If it's a weekend or a night-flight and he can't be bothered, then it's mine.'

A silence falls. The rain has stopped as suddenly as it started. Ed puts down the damp towel – on top of the letters, to block my prying eyes – and starts to button his shirt. In the corner, a fat droplet of water oozes through the metal roof-seam.

'I hesitate to offer you a drink,' he says, 'but would a cuppa do?'

'Lovely.'

While he's putting on the kettle, I look round at Ed's private world. There isn't much of it, and what little there is is untidy. To sit down I have to shift a pile of box files onto the floor, next to a black bin-liner of washing – clean or dirty, impossible to tell. There are no books, no television, only the iPod and dock on a shelf, and a laptop computer, hiding under the papers. A half-open cupboard door reveals a tangle of boots and shoes.

But, of course, this isn't the whole of his private world. Somewhere else, there's a wife and a farmhouse. Although, if he's in debt, maybe the farm and barns have already been sold. Or repossessed. Perhaps his wife is in a council house on the outskirts of Slough.

He flashes a bruised grin over his shoulder. 'Sorry, have to rinse the mugs. There's only two. Helpful in that it simplifies washing-up, but makes entertaining challenging. What brought you here?'

It hits me in the gut like a fist. I'd completely forgotten. For a moment I can't find breath to speak.

Ed catches sight of my face. 'What's the matter?'

'Maybe you'd better break out the vodka again.' Then to my horror my eyes start to fill with tears. 'Bloody vultures. Voyeurs. Sick. Don't know how they got hold of—'

'This about YouTube by any chance?'

'You *know*?' Surprise stops the emotional leakage.

'It's been there a fortnight. Or, rather, it was. The Air Accident people managed to have it taken off earlier this week. I had about eight emails, sending me the link, from so-called friends.'

'And you didn't bother to tell me?'

'It would have upset you. Don't give me that look – it's on your face that it upsets you. Only a matter of time before someone had it removed, if not the AAIB, then the family – though I bloody well hope *they* never heard about it. It was the last couple of minutes, mostly the crash itself, not what led up to it.'

'You *saw* it?'

Ed looks uncomfortable.

'You did, didn't you?'

He sighs. 'Yes, I watched it. Once, if that makes it any better.' He picks up a tea-towel from the floor, wipes the mugs and drops a teabag into each, his back to me. 'Shouldn't ask this, but . . .'

'Oh, my God,' I say. 'You want to know what I'm going to say at the inquest, don't you? What I told the police?'

'*No,*' he says. 'Well, yes. It would be helpful.' He swings round to face me. 'More to the point . . . Any chance you could get me a copy of the rest of the video?'

No way. I feel sick at the thought of it.

'Jesus, Ed, even if I could . . . What the hell would you do with it?'

His fingers are worrying at a piece of loose skin by his thumbnail, reminding me of Martin on the first day of filming. 'I thought I explained the shit I'm in. No money, no lawyer. If I lose my licence, I'm bankrupt for sure. Do *you* remember the exact conversation immediately before that last run across the crop circle? I sure as hell don't, not word for word, but if it's on the tape, the Air Accident Investigators will know precisely what Steve and I said to each other. I have to know what they know: it's the only way I can plan my defence.'

'You said OK. I remember that, I think – you said OK, like it was . . . a challenge.'

'Is that all? Didn't I say – that's not a good idea? It's dangerous? Nothing like that?'

'I don't know. You might have done. I don't remember. But the conversation wouldn't be on the tape anyway. We were planning to dub music and commentary over the pictures so we didn't bother to take a feed from the headsets.'

Ed closes his eyes in relief. 'I thought . . . There were screams on the YouTube piece.'

'But muffled, right? The camera's inbuilt microphone might've picked up the odd sound at high volume, but any normal chat would have been drowned on the recording by wind and engine noise.'

The kettle starts to whistle. Ed crouches to open the tiny fridge for milk. He says something I can't hear.

'What was that?'

'I said, would you be prepared to back me up at the inquest if I told the coroner I warned Steve about the danger but he insisted? I know it's a lot to ask . . .'

My heart stutters. 'I can't do that. I told you, I don't remember who said what.'

'It wouldn't exonerate me but it might make a difference.'

'You're asking me to lie for you.'

'It's not a lie. It's what I'm sure happened.'

The kettle's still shrieking. I reach over and turn off the gas. 'Don't bother with tea on my account,' I say. 'I have to go. You're right. It *is* a lot to ask. Too much.'

He stands up and, for a second, I think he'll block my way, but instead he flattens himself against the kitchenette so we don't have to touch. There's sadness in his eyes, but they crinkle up with his usual lop-sided smile. 'Sorry,' he says. 'Friends, Indy?'

'I'll have to think about it.'

As I walk down the road towards the car, the Smiths blast out again from the caravan, singing about being human and needing to be loved.

CHAPTER 20

1938

I was so upset that I couldn't summon enthusiasm for church that Sunday. Hard to kneel in front of God, remembering the thoughts in my mind when Mr Keiller tried to wrestle my handbag from me. Whenever I closed my eyes, I saw his handsome face leaning over me, felt his hand slide across my bosom, accidental like.

Mam and I usually went to St James's, where the serpent writhed round the old font and the saint trod on its wicked head. Dad never went; said he'd seen all he wanted of God in the trenches. Nor did Mr Keiller. Sometimes, like this week, we were too busy with guests expecting roast Sunday luncheon. Then I'd go to evensong instead, on my own if Mam was too tired. Sunday supper was always serve-yourself, a cold collation, sandwiches made from the left-over roast, and salad and cheese and pickles, and once we'd laid it out Dad looked after everything while I went to church and Mam put her feet up.

'I'll be glad when we've done with the guesthouse,' she'd taken to saying. 'It's a chore and no mistake, these days.'

Tonight the evening was too lovely to sit in the dark nave of St James's, I told myself, knowing it was only an excuse to have an hour to myself, thinking about Mr Keiller and imagining his fingers doing much more than brush accidental against my chest. So I went walking, the laburnum flowers in yellow drifts and the air smelling of fresh-mown grass. Over the footbridge, the Winterbourne shrunken to a reedy trickle, the ground was already pegged out at Trusloe for the foundations of the new houses. Lawrence of Arabia's brother had put up some of the money. Strange to think these empty fields would one day hold a village.

I'd reached the far side of Longstones field – two big old sarsens down there, facing each other like wary boxers – when I heard bells floating across the air. Not St James's: these were from the next village on, Yatesbury. My conscience tugged me. It was a fair step, but a pretty church. I'd be too late for the start of the service but I could slip into a pew at the back.

It was further than I'd thought. As I walked up the path between the yews, limping a little on blistered feet, the sun was dipping below the treetops. The wooden door was ajar, and I could hear the deep voice of the vicar intoning the words of the Collect: *Lighten our darkness, we beseech thee, O Lord, and by thy great mercy defend us from all perils and dangers of this night.*

Leaning on a box tomb with his back to me, Mr Cromley was smoking a cigarette; I knew him by the slope of his shoulders in the dark green Morven blazer. I hesitated, but he must have heard my step on the gravel. To my dismay, he turned, dropping the glowing cigarette end onto the ground.

'Miss Robinson! Beautiful evening.' He had a winning smile, and I reminded myself it wasn't his fault, what had happened at the picnic.

'Didn't have you down as a churchgoer, Mr Cromley.'

'I don't go into the service. I prefer to shrive my soul out here in the churchyard.'

'You have a soul, then?'

'You're very cruel all of a sudden. And you've been avoiding me, Heartbreaker. You've missed most of the service, so come and sit down on –' he looked at the slab between us '– William Cullis and his fine family and watch the sun go down with me. We can discuss the state of our souls.'

It was the first time he had called me Heartbreaker. The organist was hammering away at the closing hymn, 'And Now the Wants Are Told'. I felt a snake twist in my belly, and I held his gaze, without saying anything, though the sun was against me and I couldn't make out the expression in his eyes. I remembered the feel of his hands on my shoulders, pulling me down onto the grass while Mr Keiller knelt over me.

'I have to be back before long,' I said. But all the same I sat next to him on the flat surface of the box tomb. Birds sang all around, threatening and warning each other: *don't* let me catch you at *that*, *don't* let me catch you at *that*.

Between us and the sun was a row of white headstones.

'You know who they are, don't you?' said Mr Cromley. 'I come here to pay my respects, because who else will, apart from their families?' He pointed at a stone carved with a pair of wings in a laurel wreath. '*Per ardua ad astra*. The hard way to the stars.'

'Royal Air Force?' I asked.

'Royal Flying Corps, when they joined up. These are men – boys, probably – who were learning to fly here in the Great War. Died before they made it to the front line. Some might've come down in that field beyond the fence.'

I jumped down to look. He was right, boys, most of them: you could see from the dates. Some headstones carried a message from their mams and dads. A pressure came in my chest, and my eyes prickled. 'They never got to fight?' I asked, climbing back onto the box tomb next to him.

He nodded. 'I can see them, can't you, carrying their kitbags into the barracks, with such hopes of glory? Maybe they'd weighed up their chances in a dogfight against a German ace. But a mistake on a training circuit? Nobody imagines he'll go that way.' He shook his head. 'Poor sods. I find it inexpressibly sad.'

O wondrous peace, sang the congregation in the church, in thought to dwell on excellence divine; to know that nought in man can tell how fair Thy beauties shine.

'Will there be another war?' I asked him.

He blew air down his nose like an impatient horse. 'Of course there'll be another war. The Jewish financiers who run this country will see to that, whatever the old appeaser Chamberlain hopes. And another row of headstones. Another bad joke on the part of God. More brave souls, who hoped for glory and never touched it.'

'You have souls on the brain,' I told him.

He glared at me. 'Maybe because it could be my soul hovering over a chunk of white marble. Everything will change, you know.' Then he sighed. 'I forget you're so young, Heartbreaker. How fair *thy* beauties shine. Smoke?'

I shook my head. He selected a cigarette from a silver case and slipped it between his lips; he'd given up that silly pipe. There was the creak of the church door behind us, footsteps in the porch. The service had ended. As Mr Cromley took out matches and lit up, we could hear the congregation crunching down the gravel path, chattering away to each other. Goodness knows what they thought of us, silhouetted against the sinking sun like a courting couple.

'I blame the Communists,' I said, hoping to prove I knew something about politics. I'd heard Dad say that to Mam, listening to the news on the wireless.

Mr Cromley laughed. 'There you go again, Heartbreaker. No, Mr Hitler's the villain, and will have to be stopped somehow, or we'll all be speaking German in ten years' time.' He took a pull on his cigarette, then blew a perfect smoke ring into the still air. 'I don't like dancing to the tune of our Semitic brethren, but that's a far lesser evil than a mad housepainter in charge.'

A robin fluttered from a chestnut tree and perched on one of the white headstones. Mr Cromley twisted round to watch the last of the congregation pass through the lich-gate.

'I hate it,' he said. 'All this pious bleating, hoping to save their souls. It achieves nothing. My father was a churchgoer, but it didn't stop him being blown to bits the week the armistice was signed.'

'How old were you?' I asked.

'Six.' He sounded cold and dismissive, like I'd asked a stupid question. 'War's the great leveller, Heartbreaker. And maybe that's not a bad thing. D'you know, where I'm lodging in Trusloe Cottages, farm labourers can't afford the rents of the houses the council built for them? Things have to change, and perhaps war's the only way to do it.'

I didn't know what to say. Times was hard for a lot of families on the land, I knew that. But they always had been. How was a war going to sort that out? But Mr Cromley was looking at me intense, like. 'Haven't seen you since the picnic,' he said. 'Alec is right, she is a first-class bitch.'

'He's going to marry her, isn't he?' I said.

' 'Fraid so.' He tapped me lightly on the chin. 'Thing is, Heartbreaker, you're younger and prettier, but her father's a major-general. Your father keeps a guesthouse, and soon he won't have even that questionable status. I hear he'll be a tobacconist.' Mr Cromley said it like you'd say 'toilet attendant'.

Tears pricked behind my eyes. Dad, in his cheap off-the-peg suit, Mam ironing the hand-stitched table mats. All they'd worked for, the guesthouse with its clean sheets and towels changed every day, meant nothing. Clean sheets could never take me where I wanted to be. I swung my legs up onto the tomb, and wrapped my arms round my knees, looking away towards the dipping sun at the end of the grave-yard, willing the tears back where they came from. The row of white headstones confronted me like a row of sinister, even teeth.

'You really have fallen for him, haven't you?' Mr Cromley sounded amazed. 'You poor little thing.'

Best not to say anything. I wasn't so green I didn't see Mr Cromley as a dangerous fellow to confide in.

'How old are you, Heartbreaker?'

'Sixteen,' I lied.

'A mature woman in the Neolithic. You'd probably have at least a couple of babies by now. In fact, you could be considered middle-aged, given that life expectancy wasn't much over thirty.' He threw away his cigarette. 'Are you still a virgin at sweet sixteen?'

I went hot. 'No gentleman would ask that.'

He reached out a hand and lifted my skirt back from my knee. I went completely still. The evening breeze played over the bare skin above my stocking top.

'Do you know how I made Alec's acquaintance, Miss Robinson?' Every time he repeated my name it was like an incantation. 'We were both members of – how shall I put it? A small group of gentlemen with certain interests in common. My uncle recommended me. We would meet for drinks at someone's club, then repair to a flat in South London where a young woman would assist us in our experiments in ritual. And I'm not talking about what goes on in there . . .' He nodded towards the church. 'Religion's a crutch. I'm talking about a *tool*. There are ways of harnessing the cosmos to help someone determined. What you will shall be.' His finger began stroking my thigh, circling above the top of my stocking. 'We'd take turns, Miss Robinson. One after another with the same woman. Do you know what I'm talking about?'

'Enough to know I don't want to hear it.' But my breathing gave me away. I was remembering what had happened at the picnic, Mr Cromley holding my arms, Mr Keiller towering over me . . . The two of them becoming confused in my mind, changing places, turning in mazy circles like Mr Cromley's insistent finger.

'Alec is a highly sexualized man. He's curious, likes to try different experiences. Sometimes our experiments would be about withholding.' The finger abruptly stops stroking. 'Withholding can create very powerful magic. And sometimes –' the finger lightly brushes my skin again, this time on the inner thigh '— sometimes it would be about giving.'

Our breath hung in the air between us, his finger a light pressure on my leg. My skin ached. I wanted that finger to move again, but it didn't.

'Are you a giving person, Miss Robinson?'

'I don't think you should be talking like this.'

'I could make a gift of you to Alec. Or vice versa.'

I lifted his hand off my thigh, swung my legs off the tomb and jumped to the ground, dusting fragments of stone off the back of my skirt. 'I'm not a parcel, Mr Cromley.'

I didn't turn round as I stalked away into the glimmering evening, but I knew he was watching me all the way down the yew-shaded path.

CHAPTER 21

'Not Druids,' says Martin, as we approach the Red Lion. 'Please tell me there won't be Druids.'

A lively wind shoos the clouds across the night sky. Wiccans celebrate rituals according to the moon, and tonight is the first full moon after the vernal equinox – which also makes it Easter on Friday. The campsite behind the car park has already sprouted a few tents: pagans of various persuasions who've started their bank-holiday break early.

'Of course there will be Druids. Also witches, goddess worshippers and—'

'Enough. My father will be rotating in consecrated ground. I told you he was a vicar, didn't I? Broad-minded, ecumenical, but nevertheless drew the line at sacrificing goats.'

What is this masculine obsession with goats? 'There will be no goats,' I say firmly. 'Not so much as a gerbil.'

But Martin is clambering onto an archaeological hobby-horse. 'The point is there never were Druids at Avebury. Druids came several thousand years later, and hung around sacred groves, not stone circles. And, frankly, what we know of Druids today is all nineteenth-century construct – started by a load of rich, middle-aged Victorian men with nothing better to do than dress up in white sheets and silly hats and hold secret rituals.'

'Don't let our Druids hear you talking like that. They take it very seriously.'

'Is your chum the shaman going to be there?'

'Not tonight. He's taken a party of men to camp in the Savernake Forest on a discover-your-inner-wild-man weekend.'

'Wish I'd known. Sounds right up my street.'

The cottages look cosy, glowing curtains drawn against the night, chimneys emitting thin streams of smoke that the wind tosses into the ragged clouds. Sensible villagers, warm villagers, unbothered by the full moon, hunkered around their fires watching the *Ten o'Clock News* and the late film. On the corner of the main road, the pub is a blaze of light. The pagans generally gather at the tables outside, but we're early.

'Inside for a drink to warm us up?' suggests Martin, as we cross the road. 'Or, put it another way, I am not freezing my bollocks off on a bench waiting for Druids. I've more time for Wiccans, mind. Another completely made-up faith, invented mid-twentieth century, but there's something about a Wiccan that appeals to my lapsed Anglicanism. Did you know there are actually Christian Wiccans too?'

He gives me a naughty sideways grin as we go inside.

Martin's all right, really. Now I know him better, I can't imagine why I fancied him, except that something can happen between the filmer and the filmed. They spend so long staring into each other's eyes through either end of a camera.

'Have you got a boyfriend?' I ask, as he sets two whiskies on the table. 'If that question isn't off-limits.'

'It is, actually.' Martin's voice is unexpectedly sharp.

'Sorry, I didn't mean . . .'

'No, no.' He sits down heavily. 'I should be saying sorry. It's a sore point at the moment. Tell me about the men in your life instead. I couldn't help noticing there seemed to be something between you and that bloke from the National Trust.'

'What, *Michael*?' My best Outraged-of-Avebury. 'I like older men, but he's old enough to . . .'

'Don't come the innocent with me, flower. You're far too young to pull it off.' Martin raises his whisky glass. 'Here's to bad boys who break our hearts. No, I mean the other one. The Midnight Cowboy. Mr Stroke My Stubble in his fancy boots. My, don't you blush easily?'

'Oh, him. Well, there is a history. Past tense.'

'Sorry, now I'm being appallingly nosy. You don't have to tell me anything.'

'No.' The level in my whisky glass is sinking unnervingly fast. 'Well, yes. Thing is, he's married. Works here, goes home every weekend. Anyway, it was a one-off mistake. I'm not stupid enough to think he's going to leave her.'

'Oh, petal, they never do. Believe me, been there, done that. You're better off without him. Good God, was that a pair of antlers going past the window?'

'It'll be Trevor.'

Outside, pagans have started to assemble: some thin girls in jeans sharing a spliff with an even skinnier bloke with dreads; three or four middle-aged Druid couples in white robes; a group of wary-eyed young men kitted up in heavy fleece jackets against the biting wind. There are about twenty in all. A few I've met through John: Beech Tear and Wind Rose, always stalwarts on such occasions, Moon Daughter, again, sitting by herself, and a rather scary woman who lives at the other end of Trusloe, with long white hair and piercing blue eyes.

As this is a Wiccan occasion, Trevor, a former estate agent and now a full-time practitioner of Gardnerian witchcraft, is presiding.

'I was expecting something . . . well, a bit more sinister,' murmurs Martin. 'He looks like Eric Morecambe. Jolly with glasses.'

'Eric Morecambe was before my time, but I don't imagine he had waist-length hair.'

'And the – er – reindeer on the top of his staff. I'm sure it started life as a Christmas-tree ornament.'

'Pagans believe in recycling. Live lightly on the earth is one of the Wiccan tenets.'

The outfit changes with the season, but tonight Trevor's resplendent in furry moon boots, velveteen dressing-gown, and a Bob-the-Builder hat, sprayed silver, to which he has Superglued a pair of antlers, thus representing the Horned God. His consort, Michelle, who shares his Georgian house in Marlborough, is either Diana or Hecate: John did explain Wicca to me once but I wasn't paying attention. She's in a full-length dark blue cloak, with the hood thrown back, her bobbed hair dressed with a diaphanous blue scarf sewn with silver stars and moons. Rumour has it she's someone important in marketing at Asda's head office.

Trevor raps his staff on the ground. 'Think we ought to get going in a minute or two, people. Drink up and, if you wouldn't mind, save the bar staff a job on a cold night, take your glasses back into the pub.' He turns to Martin and me. 'Haven't seen you two before, have I? Merry meet. Oh, sorry, it's India, isn't it? You look different somehow.'

'I was blonde last time.' I introduce Martin. Trevor's delighted: he's addicted to *Time Team*. Scratch a pagan and you find an amateur archaeologist – and sometimes vice versa. I wander off and leave Trevor explaining why, in his opinion, dowsing can be as reliable as geophysics in revealing archaeology under the soil. Martin has a polite but strained expression on his face. Lady pagans are popping into the pub for a last pee, while the gentlemen head into the darkness to water Mother Earth; coats are being buttoned against the chill, hats pulled down over ears, bottles of mead, the midnight tipple of choice for your average Wiccan, already stashed in backpacks.

I sit down on one of the benches, remembering drums at dawn, the eastern sky flushing gold, Margaret dancing, a land of lost content. Until I turned eight, this was a way of life. Now all I feel is cold and bored and faintly resentful. If I were a pagan still, I'd be a Hedgewitch, like Moon Daughter: do-it-yourself rituals alone under a starry sky.

The moon pops out like a white traffic light, and Trevor leads his ragged troop across the main road and through the gate onto the grass. Someone flashes a torch; someone else stumbles with a muffled *shit*. I stir reluctantly from the bench and attach myself to the end of the procession. Moon Daughter holds open the gate to the stones, with a shy smile. Moonlight pouring down over the circle reveals Trevor and Martin a long way ahead, already passing through the massive entrance stones, deep in conversation. Trevor breaks off to pat the Devil's Chair as if he's reassuring an old friend – *all for the best in the best of all possible worlds* – then he and Martin are hidden in the shadow of the beeches. A ewe calls to its lamb, the gate clicks again, the moon flicks behind a cloud and disappears.

And the skin over my shoulder blades is prickling because, although I was the last to leave the pub, there is someone behind me.

Steve.

Don't be silly. I know it isn't Steve. Steve is dead and the dead don't come back – at least, not to people like me. I turn my head, catching no more than a glimpse of someone disappearing between the stones of the inner circle. The breeze rattles the beech branches. High overhead, winking lights and the distant rumble of a plane returning to Lyneham.

Suddenly Moon Daughter, too, seems a long way ahead in the darkness, an indistinct shape passing the Devil's Chair.

That *is* Moon Daughter, isn't it?

The far-off note of the plane's engine changes as I run to catch her up. The winking lights are losing height, wheeling, dropping steeply downwards, coming closer. And then the throbbing starts, a great white beam stabs down out of the sky, my heartbeat ratchets up, I can hardly catch my breath—

Not a plane at all. A helicopter.

There it is, over Waden Hill, racing towards me, following the path of the stones in the Avenue, its white searchlight fingering the contours of the muddy fields. I shrink back against the Devil's Chair, convinced against all sense it's hunting for me. But then comes the roar of a car engine, screaming into a gear change as it shoots round the bend. Headlights blaze across the grass as it takes the road through the circle. The helicopter sweeps overhead, trying to pin the car with its searchlight. For a moment it catches it, a silvery hatchback with four baseball-capped heads silhouetted inside, and then the car skids across the curve by the Red Lion, narrowly missing the car-park wall, and disappears in the direction of Swindon, the helicopter in pursuit.

'Bloody pigs,' says Moon Daughter, child of the rebellious sixties, waiting for me and holding the gate by the bank open. 'Hope they get away.'

Fifteen seconds earlier, if she hadn't waited for me, she'd have been crossing the road as the silver car raced round the corner.

If there was anyone behind me, they've gone. I let the gate shut, *click*, and follow Moon Daughter in the wake of Trevor's ritual procession, sunwise, round the perimeter of Avebury.

It's an involved route: past the social centre, through the visitors' car park, along the side of the village cricket pitch, across the high street, then through the tall wrought-iron gates onto the Manor driveway. Eventually we end up at the main road again, at the northern entrance to the circle. Trevor recommends the agile enter by crawling under the side of the Swindon Stone. The megalith is diamond-shaped, and one corner juts to meet the fence, leaving a gap just big enough for—

Martin emerges with mud on his knees and elbows, and a happy grin.

'I wouldn't have thought you'd squeeze through that,' I tell him.

'I'm a caver. You learn Houdini wriggles for tight spots. Your turn, I think. Go back and come through the proper way.'

'Not on your nelly.' I'm not risking another pair of jeans.

Trevor leads us to the Adam and Eve stones, all that remains of the three-sided Cove at the heart of the northern inner circle. He stretches out his arms, beaming. Obediently we form a circle, my left hand clasping Martin's hairy paw, my right in the clammy grip of one of the stick-thin girls, who's giggling a lot.

'Merry meet!' Trevor casts an approving eye round his enlarged coven. 'No, hang on a minute – first full moon since the equinox, we should balance the circle. Can we rearrange ourselves so we go boy, girl, boy, girl?' There's some shuffling and I end up with a white-robed, spike-haired Druid on my right.

'Merry meet!' calls Trevor again.

'Merry meet,' we all chorus obediently. Two deep voices are coming from behind us: tallish lads wearing sheepskin caps with earflaps, standing self-consciously apart. Martin raises his eyebrows enquiringly.

'Northern tradition,' I whisper. 'Odin, Valhalla, all that manly stuff. Big in Yorkshire. They think it's cissy to hold hands in a circle.'

Trevor invokes the elemental spirits: East, South, West and North; Air, Fire, Water and Earth. He does it in a quiet, thoughtful way that I much prefer to the American Druid's bluster on the day of the museum protest. With each invocation we drop hands and spin to face in the correct direction. At the end Trevor's partner, Michelle, lights a lantern and sets it in the middle before stepping back and joining hands to complete the circle.

'We've got some good energies going already tonight,' says Trevor. 'Everybody step back one pace. No, keep holding hands – feel the pull on your arms. It's all about balance. Dark and light in equilibrium . . .'

Across the circle, clear eyes in the lamplight meet mine. The corkscrew curls under the woolly hat seem familiar but I can't remember why.

'Stirring the energy . . .' Trevor starts to move the circle, sunwise. The man opposite keeps his eyes fixed on me as the circle moves faster and faster. 'Opening the vortex,' calls Michelle, her scarf slipping, hair flying round her face. 'Let's hold it within ourselves . . .' I have no idea what we're supposed to be doing, but the motion is dizzying and exhilarating. The moon comes out again, the clouds have silver rims, stars wink between the branches of the trees, and I can hear a soft panting growing louder in my ears, like the breathing of the whole universe . . . The Druid next to me stumbles on the uneven ground, jerking my arm, and the movement somehow communicates itself round the circle to Trevor. He starts to slow, brings the circle to a halt, then drops his arms.

'Brilliant,' says the spike-haired Druid, squeezing my hand in a bone-crunch grip. 'Utterly brilliant. Trev, I've some mead in my backpack, shall I pass it round?'

'Have ours instead. Made from our own honey.' Michelle flourishes the bottle, Trevor produces a cup from his furry satchel, pours the mead into it, holds it up to the moon, then both he and Michelle take turns in stirring it, he with a black-handled knife, she with a white. The cup goes from hand to hand round the circle, while one of the stoned girls reads a poem. The Druid produces his bottle anyway, and that, too, is passed round. The mead scalds my gullet like sugary heartburn. I offer the bottle to Martin, who hesitates, then wipes its neck surreptitiously on his sleeve before drinking.

'All we need now is some drumming,' says the keen Druid next to me. 'I brought my bongos.'

Trevor nips the idea firmly in the bud. 'Bit late at night for drumming. Sorry.'

'Aw, we always have drumming. Wouldn't be the same without drums.'

'We get complaints, George. Some of us live round here. You can drum at the campsite if you want to – that's far enough away from the village.'

'Always have drums,' repeats George the Druid, in a sulky mutter.

'Is that it?' whispers Martin, in my other ear. 'Bloody hope it is, before I have to freeze my bollocks off listening to another poem.'

Michelle has hooded the lantern. Trevor begins his closing incantation, sending the elemental spirits back to the four quarters. The circle breaks up and with shouts of *merry part!* echoing in our ears, we stumble across the uneven ground towards the gate in the lane and make our way back to the cottage where Martin is staying, a National Trust property that was once home to an eminent academic in her declining years, now used to house visiting archaeologists.

'Well, that was an experience.'

'Did you enjoy it?' I ask.

'I could have done without the hug-a-hippie bit at the end.'

'You wouldn't have said that if it had been those lads from the northern tradition.'

'Or that pretty boy across the circle, who was giving you the eye.'

'Did you think so? Not really my type,' I say regretfully. 'Tediously predictable, looking for a dad and all that, but I usually go for older men. Preferably bastards.'

'Oh, I don't think the Midnight Cowboy's entirely a bastard,' says Martin, as we walk up the path. He stops under the porch light, fumbling for the key. 'Can I tempt you in for a farewell jar? I'm away early tomorrow.'

'Don't want my gran worrying.'

'Won't she be asleep?'

'Oh, all right, then.'

The cottage is essentially one up, one down, with kitchen and utility room tacked on like an afterthought. Martin tickles the fire in the living room, while I uncork the bottle of red wine on the table. There is a small sofa, but Martin sprawls on the floor.

'So how did you wind up with these TV people, petal?' he asks. 'They're exploiting you ruthlessly, you know.'

'It's the way television works now.' I swirl my glass to make a whirlpool in the wine. Another vortex: one I can control. 'You have to prove your worth before they give you a job. And I couldn't take on a contract in Bristol or London for the moment. I'm starting to think Frannie's too old to be living alone, but an old people's home would kill her.'

Martin says nothing, looking at me steadily. It's the first time I've articulated my dilemma, and I'm grateful he doesn't offer advice.

'Anyway,' I continue, 'there is this – other reason. Bit of an obsession of mine. My grandfather.'

'You know, you sound like you're half in love with Keiller yourself.' Martin has a dubious expression on his face, after hearing me out. 'He could've had a fling with your grandmother, I suppose, he was free with his favours. Four wives, numerous mistresses, and I've always suspected he might've swung both ways as well. But you do realize there are no known Keiller offspring, legit or otherwise? Either he really didn't like kids or he was firing blanks.'

It doesn't sound promising.

'And that anonymous letter doesn't really say much, does it? Any idea who sent it?'

'There was this woman who was a housemaid at the Manor, died not long ago. I don't know anything about her, but Frannie practically snarled the only time she mentioned her.'

'Dead end, then.' Martin sounds disappointed: another lost interviewee. 'But the line that implies devil worship at the Manor – Keiller *was* interested in witchcraft, and there's an account of at least one bizarre ceremony in the garden, though I doubt he was taking it seriously.' He leans over to pour more wine into my glass. 'Ritual magic was one of the growth spiritual industries of the twenties and thirties. James Frazer's *Golden Bough* had raised interest in anthropology and magic. There was an idea that Eastern mysticism held the key to knowledge Westerners had lost, and the Ordo Templi Orientalis were invoking Isis and Ishtar and God knows what else in London and Paris. Aleister Crowley – and don't give me any of that pagan tosh about how he had an unfairly poor press, he was a deliberately bad lad into cocaine and shagging anything on legs, and he *loved* being called the Great Beast – was supposedly the most accomplished ritual magician of his time. If you ask me, it owed a lot to hypnotism, and Tantric sex technique. But these people genuinely thought they were onto something, tapping into the hidden forces of the universe. Crowley supposedly managed to summon the goat god Pan, but the experience nearly destroyed him. Mind you, we only have Denis Wheatley's word for it, and you should never trust a novelist, especially one who admired Mussolini and wrote spicy thrillers with titles like *The Devil Rides Out*.'

'Was Christopher Lee in that one?'

'Probably. All sounds deeply iffy now, but some of Crowley's beliefs, like the power of will, are the ancestors of modern fads like cosmic ordering.'

'You're saying it was exactly the kind of fashionable hobby Keiller would have thrown himself into?'

Martin lifts up his glass to admire the colour of the wine. 'Well, yes and no. In some ways they had a lot in common – neither had to work for a living, both were borderline psychopaths who flew into a tantrum if crossed, and blew an inherited fortune on their obsessions. Keiller was certainly interested in magic, from an academic point of view. But he was too much a rationalist to be the Beast of Avebury. Though, mind you –' he puts down the glass, and levers himself to his feet to peer out of the small back window onto the stone circle '— I'm not a superstitious bloke, but in a long career of digging up ancient places, this is one of the strangest. It's something to do with people living inside the henge. Not many stone circles where you can do that, are there? You could take a tent and doss down temporarily inside the Rollrights or Stanton Drew – but there isn't a village built inside either. Nobody ran a high street through the middle of Stonehenge. People have been going to bed every night inside this circle for a couple of thousand years – leaving layer upon layer of history and belief all over the site.'

He blows out the candle on the window ledge, draws the curtain to shut out the darkness, then throws another log on the fire. 'It's not just ghosts of Neolithic farmers, doing whatever they did. It's generation after generation, reshaping their beliefs on these stones, but probably coming up with remarkably similar stuff. Fertility and death. The endless round.' A rueful smile twists his mouth. 'Sorry, petal, ignore me – it's the vicar's son lecturing again, I'm afraid, after several glasses too many. Blame the mead.'

'So what kind of rituals did they go in for when it was first built?' I ask, reaching for my coat. 'Sacred mysteries, I suppose. A socking great bank and ditch, to keep the uninitiated out.'

'There's another way of looking at it,' says Martin. 'Maybe the bank and ditch were supposed to keep something *in*.'

CHAPTER 22

1938

Miss Chapman never did apologize. She avoided me from then on, whenever she came to see the excavation work, stalking around with her arm through Mr Keiller's and her nose in the air. Mr Cromley was keeping his distance too. That irked me. I needed him to explain what all that weird talk in the graveyard had been about.

They'd found a barrowload of broken bits of stone under one of the cottages they'd taken down, which Mr Young was putting together like a jigsaw puzzle by the gate onto the high street. Mr Cromley was helping him. How did they know which bit went where? Peculiar old thing it looked, too, when it was finished, stuck together with metal rods and seams of cement. It was time to pack up for the day, but Mr Keiller was back from a trip to London, doing the rounds to see what had been going on in his absence, and nobody dared stop work while he was on site. Mr Cromley and Mr Young were still hard at it, and I was trying to finish a drawing of a newly discovered stone hole, further along the circle. I'd lost confidence, and it wouldn't come right, especially with Mr K breathing down my neck.

'You know, young Donald's going to be a brilliant archaeologist, eventually,' said Mr Keiller. 'He has a questioning mind, and he doesn't give up.' Mr Cromley was holding up a piece of stone, turning it this way and that, running his long fingers over the broken edges. 'He'll puzzle away till he finds an answer. Loses me, though, when he starts on about theoretical physics and all the other gen he picked up at Cambridge. Too clever for his own good sometimes.'

'He doesn't seem a happy person,' I said.

'No,' said Mr Keiller. 'Well, losing his father so young – he and his mother having to rely on that uncle of his . . .'

'He said something about his uncle.' I remembered what Mr Cromley had told me, about the men and their club. I didn't believe it for a minute – nobody would do that, would they? Not Mr Keiller, surely.

I have made studies of various branches of the erotic impulse . . .

Mr Keiller stopped smiling. 'Yes, his uncle's a strange chap. Has a high-powered post with the Air Ministry, but he's also said to be one of the foremost ritual magicians in London.' He laughed at my disbelieving expression. 'Well, maybe civil-service politics and the occult aren't such strange bedfellows after all. Can't say I took to him on either of the occasions I met him. Donald won't hear a word said against him, of course. Hero-worships the man.'

Miss Chapman had come through the gate, and stopped to talk to Mr Cromley. My jaw tightened with jealousy. Seemed to me she wasn't happy unless she had everyone dancing attendance. Her smile was lazy, confident.

'Excuse me, Miss Robinson,' said Mr Keiller. 'Doris has probably come to remind me we have dinner guests tonight.' He started across the grass towards her, then checked himself and turned back, his hand delving in his blazer pocket.

'Almost forgot. I picked up something for you in London, at Mowbray's.' He pulled out a square, flattish rosewood box. 'Go on, open it.'

Stamped on the inside were the magic words 'Winsor & Newton'. It held a tray of coloured pans and a ceramic palette, even a tiny dish to hold the water. A slip of paper fluttered to the ground; I picked it up. The names of the paints on it were like an incantation: cerulean blue, cadmium yellow, alizarin crimson, burnt sienna, raw umber, Payne's grey.

'It's a field set,' said Mr Keiller, looking pleased as punch at my delight. 'All the basics, so you can paint wherever you please. Open the drawer – there's a sable brush in there and a sponge, and space for your pencils. I've had your name put on the lid, too.' There was a small brass square set into the rosewood, *Frances Robinson* engraved in sloping script. The watercolour set was far more expensive than anything I could have afforded. I couldn't speak, my eyes filling with tears. I had never seen anything so beautiful.

'There,' said Mr Keiller. 'And now I really have to answer Doris's call.'

'Thank you,' I croaked after him.

Mr Cromley had put down his jigsaw piece of stone and was staring. Miss Chapman leaned towards Mr Keiller as he came up to them, and whispered something in his ear. He looked back towards me, and waved.

'Would you mind awfully, Heartbreaker? Doris thinks she left her sketchbook at the bottom of the Avenue. Could you fetch it? Leave it at the side door. One of the housemaids'll take it if we're dressing.'

The sketchbook was there, by the very last stone in Mr Peak-Garland's field, and so was a case with a broken pencil in it, a banana skin, a glass with her lipstick on the rim, and a dirty handkerchief. Abandoned, for someone else to pick up, a menial like me. I threw the banana skin and the handkerchief into the hedge, picked up the glass and the drawing things, and set off back uphill.

Mr Cromley was waiting for me, about halfway up the Avenue, leaning against one of the tall stones that Mr Keiller had put back up when he began work at Avebury. The light was fading over Waden Hill in the west. A wind shivered the grasses.

He didn't say anything, for once, only linked his arm in mine. We walked up the slope together. There's a trick of the land, where Mr Peak-Garland's field levels out: the Avenue twists, and the henge comes into view all of a sudden. It never fails to take me with a shock, and I always draw breath, like I've never seen it before, though I've come up that slope a thousand and one times. Mr Cromley's arm tightened and drew me against him.

'Magic,' he said. 'The circle builders wanted to hide it until the very last moment.' Over a dip in the bank we could see the new stones

Mr Keiller had put up that summer, and beyond them the backs of the cottages and the church tower poking through the trees. 'But look how the terrain rises again, concealing what takes place in the inner circles. You think you've arrived, but there's still a way before you're admitted to the sanctum.' His breath was warm on the side of my face. We crossed the road and came into the circle.

As we passed between the two big entrance stones, I dropped Miss Chapman's sketchbook and bent to pick it up. Mr Cromley's hand touched my back and his fingers danced along my spine. 'I'll take those to the Manor for you,' he said. 'I might owe you an apology. For some . . . rather wild things I said last time we talked.'

'No apology necessary.'

'Shall we stroll through the stones?' His grey eyes took the clothes off me, and I didn't care one bit.

There was a three-quarter moon rising already like a screaming face. We skirted the backs of the cottages, in the wild part of the circle the dig hadn't yet reached. Only a few tall stones still stood there, as they had for five thousand years. It was the heart of the circle, Mr Keiller had said, where a tall obelisk had towered above everything else. A yellow lamp shone in Mam's kitchen window; I could see her moving between refrigerator and table, setting out plates for the guests, lifting lace doilies to unveil the supper dishes. Mr Cromley's hand was fire on my arm. A flock of sheep glimmered in the last of the light. Bats skimmed over us on their way to the ditches.

'Your uncle,' I said. 'Is he really a magician?'

'Oh, yes,' said Mr Cromley. 'He's taught me a lot about understanding the laws of the universe. We work with energy, like a physicist. Some people would call those powers gods or demons, but I prefer to think of them as . . . natural forces. If you understand them, you can manipulate them, and bend the cosmos. What you will shall be.'

A shiver ran through me. He made it sound so logical, like anybody might do it.

'Have you heard of the Ordo Templi Orientalis?' he went on. 'Never mind. There've been some remarkable experiments . . . the results not so far removed from what physicists themselves have begun to consider. At Magdalen College in 1933, I met a remarkable man, Erwin Schrödinger, with an interest in Vedanta, a Hindu philosophy. He didn't last long there. The university couldn't swallow him living with two women at once. His theories, though – extraordinary. He believes scientists influence the results of their experiments simply by acting as observers. What you will shall be.'

'Show me,' I said. 'I won't believe it else.'

'Are you sure you want me to?' His cool grey eyes looked into mine to dig out the truth.

'Yes.' My arms were rippling with goose-bumps and there was electricity at the root of every hair on my head.

He led me through the field behind the cottages, to the edge of the circle, where a single stone lay fallen among the bushes under the shade of deep-skirted trees. It was full dark under there, and the screaming moon peeked at us through the branches.

'Lie on the stone.' Mr Cromley took off his green Morven Institute blazer, and spread it carefully across the sarsen. I climbed onto the stone, afraid to make myself so vulnerable, so instead of lying I sat with my knees drawn up again, like I had on the tomb in Yatesbury churchyard. Mr Cromley sat cross-legged opposite me at the lower end of the fallen stone. His white shirt glowed faintly in the darkness. 'You thirsty, Heartbreaker?' He pulled a hip flask out of his back pocket and unscrewed the top. 'Only a mouthful, it'll warm you up.'

He leaned towards me, and I saw the light of the moon reflected in his eyes. I took a deep swallow, for courage, anticipating the fire of whisky or brandy to run down my gullet, but whatever Mr Cromley kept in his flask was sweet and cold, a sword of ice through my warm core. It matched the white moon in his eyes. I took off my cardigan and folded it for a pillow, feeling in its pocket the comforting shape of the rosewood watercolour set. The thought of who had given it to me made me warm. I lay back, feeling unexpectedly dreamy under the rustling trees.

Mr Cromley had slipped off the stone without me noticing.

'What are you doing?' I asked. His movements seemed slowed. He

214

was circling the stone, sprinkling droplets from the flask at each quarter rotation, saying something so quiet I couldn't catch it, a rhythmic kind of mutter that was like soft fingernails scratching gently inside my head.

'I've opened a circle,' he said, coming back to sit on the stone by my feet, and leaning over me, 'and called elemental energies into it. Air, Fire, Water, Earth. Can you feel them? Wind, heat, tides and gravity.' Seemed to me I felt a breeze rippling the leaves and running over my skin, a warmth spreading through my body again, the flow of my blood, the weight of my body holding me down on the stone.

'This is not a trick,' he said again. 'This is how it feels to enter the vortex, at its shallowest rim. I love this time for working magic: neither full day nor dark night. We're between worlds, Heartbreaker.' His fingers moved over my face. 'Can you feel it? It's like dipping your toes into the edge of the sea, letting the shallowest of waves break over them, feeling the suck of the water as it recedes again, while your feet sink into wet, sliding sand . . .'

His voice was like slow, soft piano music, the fingers of one hand stroking my cheeks and lips, the other cradling the back of my head and kneading the bones of my skull. He was leaning right over me now, and I couldn't see the moon in his eyes any longer, but I could feel his lips brushing gently over my skin, the lightest of pressures. He let his torso sink against mine, hardly touching me, his body almost no heavier than his breath on me. All my nerves were alive, my skin trying to reach up to mould itself to his through our clothes. I opened my eyes – when had I shut them? – and saw his were closed above me, the eyelids fluttering, his mouth slightly open, his face concentrated and ecstatic, like pictures of saints when they go to their martyrdom.

'Sssh,' he whispered. 'I know what you're thinking, now, Heartbreaker, when we breathe together like this . . . You want this to go on for ever, and it will, so long as we're in the vortex, but I don't want to take you all the way in. It'd be too much for you yet.'

The chill of evening air slipped between us as he lifted himself off the stone. Drowsily I watched him moving round it, whispering again to the four quarters. I tipped my head back and looked upwards, with a deep sense of peace. The moon lifted itself above the branches. It was no longer screaming: now it smiled.

Mr Cromley came back and sat on the stone. 'How are you feeling?'

'Marvellous,' I said. 'What did you do to me?'

'Nothing,' he said. 'You did it all yourself. Remember, what you will shall be.'

He helped me sit upright. I'd expected to feel woozy, but I was amazingly clear-headed. I could've done anything. Miss Chapman? She thought she was something, but if she treated me like a slut again . . .

'Take it easy,' said Mr Cromley. 'You've only had a taster.'

'Did your uncle teach you that?'

'Yes, but it's only basic technique. If we went further . . .'

'Is this why you came to Avebury?'

He shook his head. 'An experienced ritualist can act anywhere. It gives me a thrill, that's all, to use the energies of once-sacred places: they can be very powerful. I'm sure there's something here, something the circle-builders left behind. Maybe something they were afraid to take with them. Next time . . .' But then he shook his head. 'Perhaps not. You're very young.'

'You told me that back then, I'd have been an old married woman by now.'

He laughed. 'What I meant was that next time we'd be going further in all sorts of ways. It's customary to . . . you know. Have sex. It feeds the energies in the circle.'

Silence hung between us. There was a pulse beating between my legs. I took his hand. 'Feel that.'

His fingers slid over the silky surface of my knickers. He leaned forward and whispered in my ear, 'Maybe I could persuade Alec to be there as well. He has a keen interest in ritual magic.'

Seemed to me the night was full of whispers as he moved down the length of the stone.

CHAPTER 23

Steve's eyes, deep black holes containing the immensity of all space, are haunting my sleep again. I mention it casually to John while he works on my feet.

'I keep telling you,' he says, 'belief's a powerful thing. Creates crop circles, starts wars.' He pulls on my toes, one by one, rotating them in their sockets. 'Way I see it, all of you in the helicopter that afternoon were in the space between worlds. One of you died in the vortex, the rest came out. Whether that's mysticism or psychology, I don't give a fuck. Nobody's unchanged after an experience like that.'

As I leave his cottage, he presses something into my hand. A purple crystal.

'What's this for?'

'Amethyst. Helps you sleep. Also very powerful protection, if you think you're under psychic attack.'

'Don't be daft. Who'd be attacking me?' I try for a light, sceptical laugh.

'You tell me.'

Utter, utter crap.

It comes as a shock to find a letter at home, forwarded from London. It's from Steve's father, accusing me of putting the crash footage on YouTube.

I storm down to Big Avebury to buy a stamp and post my reply, an indignant rebuttal pointing out that as I no longer work for Mannix TV I don't have access to their video. The post office is already shut for the day.

I sit on a bench in the churchyard to calm down. It's a balmy evening, warm for late April. A lawn mower buzzes from one of the gardens off the high street, and the scent of cut grass fills the air. A man on the opposite side of the road is trying to unload a slab of granite worktop from the back of a Range Rover, with the help of a woman in True Religion jeans moaning that it's too heavy, he'll have to wait until Joshua turns up from London at the weekend. The stereo is blasting Robert Miles's *Dreamland* across the street. I've never seen either of them before. Avebury is becoming a village of second-homers, with stainless-steel cooker hoods and fridges with water-coolers. I wonder if this couple has yet experienced an Avebury Solstice, and if it will chase them back to London in a hurry.

The letter to Steve's father is still in my hand. Perhaps I shouldn't send it or, at least, wait a day and write something more considered. Folding it and tucking it into my pocket, my fingers encounter a smooth, cool shape: John's piece of amethyst. It's a deep purple with layers of white streaks folded into it. Margaret used to tuck similar stones under our pillows in the van. Keir was fascinated by Mum's crystals and used to squat on the floor for hours, lining them up, rearranging them.

As usual, the thought of Keir makes the black crystal, the shiny lump of onyx in my head, twist for the light. Fathers and sons . . . By an enormous effort, I shove it back where it should stay, in the darkest corner, and reach for one of the brighter memory crystals instead, one that shows Keir and me racketing around the Downs that summer of 1989. We roamed all over by ourselves. In Bristol you had to tell Mum where and with whom and what time you'd be back, and mostly she said no anyway, so this was paradise.

'You can go anywhere you like,' she said, tidying away Keir's sleeping-bag. He'd left it in a heap on the floor of the van in Tolemac. 'But stay together. And watch out for the cars when you cross the road.' No problem – we were used to traffic. 'And don't go in the church,' she added, as an afterthought. 'That's a *bad* place for pagans.'

So that was one of the first places we went.

*   *   *

Going into the church was Keir's idea. *Dare you.*

I'm not afraid.

I'd never been into a church. It felt wrong. It was where the other people went, Christians. The ones who stole places like Avebury, stamped out the old religion. As we chased each other between the gravestones in the churchyard, I kept hearing Mum's voice in my head. Mind the traffic on the main road, mind your manners, and don't go in the church.

Why not?

Because they don't like pagans.

Frannie had wanted to take me to church once, when I was visiting her, but Mum had found out the night before and kicked up a terrible fuss. Put your grandmother on the phone *this minute.* I'd handed it over, shaking already. Mum'd screamed down the phone, so loud I'd heard all the words. How DARE you docternate her? Frannie had held the phone away from her ear, wincing. Afterwards she said, maybe when you're older, Indy. Or your mam'll call down forty terrible curses on my head.

Keir stepped out of the sunlight into the darkened porch. His hand was hovering near the heavy iron door handle.

I was afraid. You didn't know what kind of bad things might happen to you if you went in a church. You might get nailed to a cross.

Don't, I said. Keir turned his head and gave me a wicked smile from under his tousled fringe, bleached by the sun. Keeping his eyes fixed on me, he stretched out his hand and grasped the iron ring. Slowly he turned it. It made a rusty clunking noise. I could hardly breathe. Mick'll be furious with you, I said.

Keir stuck out his tongue, leaned his shoulder against the door to open it and slipped through the gap. I waited for the strangled scream that would surely come, but there was silence. I gave it a moment longer, then followed him in.

It was huge inside, much bigger than I'd expected, and not as dark, though there were rows of hard, forbidding pews. Sunlight filtered into the nave from a tall window, but the chancel was much darker, behind a fretted screen of age-polished wood. I nearly yelled when I looked above it: there was a huge metal cross on the wall, wrapped with barbed wire. That must be where they hung the pagans.

There was no sign of Keir, not even a puddle of melted flesh on the floor. They'd got him then.

'Yaaah!'

I almost wet myself with fright. A figure bobbed up like a jack-in-a-box from the rows of pews, waving its arms. 'Caughtcha!'

'Sssh. They'll *hear.*'

'There's no one. We're on our own.'

'That could be . . . as bad.' Christians, after all, were people. But Jesus – Jesus was a dead person who'd come back to life. What if Jesus was lurking in the shadows behind the wooden screen? I'd seen *Dawn of the Dead*. They ate you. I said as much to Keir.

'No, you got it the wrong way round. Christians ate Jesus.'

I hadn't realized they were cannibals. This was getting worse.

Keir pranced off along the pews, giggling. There was a big book, open on top of a high stand. 'Double dare me?' he called.

'To what?'

'Touch the book.'

'*No.*'

He was on tiptoe already, trying to reach up to it. Desperate to distract him from this almost certainly lethal experiment, I ran in the opposite direction.

'Hey, look at this,' I called.

I'd only meant to grab his attention with a cartwheel in the aisle, but then I saw it, this beautiful stone tub with a wooden lid, and carvings on the side. It stood in a shaft of sunlight under the tall window.

'I mean, *wow*. It must be really old.' I walked round it, tracing the patterns on it. The stone was wonderfully cool under my trailing fingers. 'There's a *snake.*'

I couldn't have said anything more likely to attract him. He forgot the book and belted after me, thinking I meant a real one.

'Oh.' Disappointment in his voice when he saw it was only a pockmarked stone carving.

'Yeah, but look. There's a bloke stabbing it with his spear.'

'Maybe it's a *dinosaur.*'

There was another rusty clunk, a rattle. Somebody was turning the handle of the big wooden door, the wrong way, trying to open it. Keir and I looked at each other. There was panic in his eyes. I'd have felt smug, if I hadn't been scared shitless too.

'Hide,' he hissed.

'Where?' The tub wasn't big enough to conceal even one of us, or I'd have lifted the lid. Keir was already darting through the wooden screen, and I followed him into the part of the church that was darker and spookier. I didn't understand why the seats here faced inwards, instead of forwards, though I supposed the table with a cross must be the altar.

The heavy church door swung slowly open. In came the curly-headed friend of Keir's father, one of the others camping in Tolemac. He'd been with us when John had made a crop circle, a couple of nights ago, right after Solstice. He had his back to us, looking at leaflets on the stand by the door, but at any minute he could turn and see us through the screen, two splashes of brightness in our yellow and red hippie kids' clothes. I looked for somewhere better to hide – under the altar cloth? – but it was too late.

'It's only Riz.' Keir was walking out into the middle of the church. 'Hi, Riz!'

A frown screwed up Riz's face, only for a second, to be replaced by a wide smile. 'Whatchoo doin' in here? You pair of monkeys, Meg'll give you what-for.'

'What are *you* doin' in here, then?' asked Keir. Hadn't given him credit for so much boldness: he never had a problem talking to me, but was usually shy with grown-ups.

'Sizin' up the opposition,' said Riz. He pulled open the top of his shirt, revealing a peace symbol on a chain. 'See, I'm protected. You two got summat like this? If you ain't, you better get out quick because the old man with the long white beard don't like pagan kids.'

'Nothing happened to us yet,' said Keir.

Riz looked at his watch. 'How long you bin in here?'

Keir looked uncertainly at me. 'How long, Ind?'

'Maybe ten minutes,' I said.

Riz shook his head slowly. 'You bin lucky. Good thing I found you. Reckon you got three, four more minutes at most before he sees you. It's like a searchlight, see – God's eye swings back an' forth, but there's a lot of churches for him to keep his eye on.'

'I don't think that's right,' I said. 'My gran told me God can see everything at once.'

Riz's dark button eyes narrowed. 'You doubtin' me, Ind? Because God and pagans is at war, see? You seen that big book up on the stand there? You go take a look in that. Genesis three, thirteen.'

'What's that?' I said.

'You're good at readin', intcha? Flip back near the beginning of the book.'

There was a step behind the reading stand. Riz made me drag it over and stand on it to reach the book. It had flimsy, fragile pages.

'Keep turnin' back to the beginning.' He was at my side, not much taller than me now I was on the step. 'There – read that bit. From where it says thirteen.'

'"And the Lord God said unto the woman, What is this that thou hast done? And the woman said, The serpent be – beg—"'

'Beguiled me,' said Riz. He seemed to know it by heart.

'"And I did eat."'

'Go on. What does it say next?'

'"And the Lord God said unto the serpent, Because thou hast done this, thou art cursed above all cattle, and above every beast of the field; upon thy belly shalt thou go, and dust shalt thou eat all the days of thy life . . ."'

'See?' said Riz. 'That's God cursing the serpent. And you know who the serpent is?' From the lectern, I could see the stone tub, with the serpents carved around its base. The man sticking his spear into one of them was hidden on the far side. 'That's us. The pagans.' He reached over my shoulder and tore the flimsy page right out of the book, flipping the pages back to hide what he'd done. 'Upon thy belly shalt thou go, Ind. I reckon you got about thirty seconds left to leg it out of here. Before you ain't got any legs left to leg it on.'

Keir had turned pale under his tan. He tugged my arm. We legged it and, in our hurry to put distance between ourselves and God, almost collided with the other man in the leather jacket who was coming into the porch.

He was a black man. And that was weird because although there were plenty of black people back home in Bristol, I hadn't seen a black man in Avebury all summer long.

The sound of the church door scraping on stone hauls me back to the present, shivering, because by now I ought to know that the brighter memories of that summer all turn dark in the end. An elderly woman comes out of the porch, carrying a bucket filled with dead flowers. She nods at me as she comes towards the bench. 'Lovely evening.' The nod turns to a smile, and she stops. 'India, isn't it? Frances's granddaughter?'

I vaguely recognize her from the film show in the Red Lion.

'You've been working with that TV crew, haven't you?' she says. 'Someone rang me the other day to persuade me to be interviewed. Said I'd think about it.'

'You should do it,' I say, moving up the bench to make room for her. 'I've been trying to talk Frannie into it.'

'Won't stop, I must take these to the compost heap and get on home.' Nevertheless, she puts down the bucket. 'Those kids running towards the camera in Percy Lawes's film? One of them was me. Your gran always seemed so grown-up to us – such a pretty girl, she was, quite the young lady, especially after she started at the Manor. And she had spirit, still does. Though it wore her down eventually, I reckon, working for that old devil.'

'Keiller? What did he do to her?'

'What I mean is, I shouldn't have liked it. He used to stand on a box among the stones, bellowing instructions through a megaphone. And in the end he did the same to her as he did to the whole village.' She picks up the bucket of dead flowers. 'Tore the heart out of it. I remember it ever so clearly, that September he had her parents' guest-house demolished, and we all stood and watched.'

CHAPTER 24

September 1938

I thought it would be in the Manor. Mr Cromley said that when Mr Keiller carried the chalk phallus out that night in February, the dinner guests made a circle, and they all kissed it before Mr K presented it to the statue of Pan. You could feel the energies swirling and crackling, he said, because the stone circle is like Mr Rawlins's big Crossley generator, making invisible power that spills over the henge banks through the whole village. But the ritual can't be there this time: the Manor's not private enough. If Davey and I could spy, who else might be watching?

So it's a house in Swindon, an anonymous terraced house in a row on the north side of the town. Respectable, characterless. Behind it is a park, with trees, which seems nice, only when I look closer it's not a park after all: it's a cemetery.

I let myself in with the key Mr Cromley gave me. A long, dark, spooky hallway that smells of furniture polish. Kitchen at the back, abandoned in the middle of a meal. There's a plate on the oilcloth with half a piece of buttered toast, an eggcup of white powder covered with a saucer, a cup in the sink. But maybe I wasn't supposed to go in here. Upstairs, Mr Cromley said. Front bedroom.

The curtains are already drawn across the bay windows, worn crimson damask. The satin eiderdown on the bed is a purply red that clashes. The carpet is dark blue with swirly gold leaves, not quite enough to cover the room so there's a border of stained dark brown floorboards round the edges. It's a large room for such a little house, hardly any furniture except a wardrobe with a mirrored door and an old-fashioned dark oak washstand in the corner, but still the bed seems to fill most of it. Someone's left a long white nightie on the pillow, freshly washed and ironed. I slip off my shoes and sit down on the end of the bed to wait.

The village turned out to watch the wrecking crew bring down Mam and Dad's guesthouse. The first people were already gathering on the road outside at half past seven when I came downstairs, and they looked surprised to see someone coming out of the empty house. Mam and Dad had moved out weeks ago, gone to Devizes with all their furniture and bits in a van, apart from what was thrown out for the rag-and-bone man. I'd found lodgings less than a mile down the road at Winterbourne Monkton, under the roof of a widowed lady who rattled around in a house she couldn't afford to keep up. I had my own gas ring and she let me have the back sitting room all to myself, so I never saw her unless it was on the way to the bathroom. She didn't seem to care about my comings and goings. The night before they was due to knock down the guesthouse, I'd gone home with a stub of candle and blankets and slept on the bare boards of my old room.

Mr Cromley had said it took time to arrange these things. He said it wouldn't be the same as the ritual on the stone under the trees. That was a makeshift demonstration of what the energies could do; this had to be more formal, like, more special. It should take place near the autumn equinox, when light and dark were in balance, between summer and winter, to help us slip between worlds.

He'd never taken me into the circle again, but sometimes he caught me in the corridor in the Manor, and would press me against the panelled wall and kiss me, slipping his hand under my skirt. It excited him all the more if there were people not far away. Once, we heard Mrs Sorel-Taylour's little feet clacking down the wooden staircase, and I tried to push him off but he kept sliding his fingers against me and only stepped away a moment before her shape blocked the light at the end of the passageway.

'Mr Cromley!' I said, a little breathless, the minute she'd gone. 'That was—'

'My lovers call me Donald,' he whispered in my ear. 'But you still can't bring yourself to do that, can you, Heartbreaker?' His fingers resumed their relentless circling. He never called me Frances or Fran, and he never finished what we were doing. That was for the equinox.

I'd had cold feet about it since September blew in and swept the stone circle with drifts of golden leaves. What was I letting myself in for? This wasn't black magic: Mr Cromley was clear on that. I wasn't putting my soul in danger, oh, no, there was a long tradition of Christian magicians, like John Dee, whose magic mirror Mr Keiller kept in his study. Occult didn't mean bad: it meant secret, hidden. Knowledge that had to be hidden from ordinary people because it was powerful and, in the wrong hands, dangerous. Like electricity, from Mr Rawlins's generator: it lit the house, but it could kill you too, if you pushed in a plug with wet hands.

Had to be done with proper ritual, he said. They would wear robes and masks. I was to be masked too, dressed in white. Masks were important, to make us not entirely ourselves: we would become vessels for the forces we were calling on. I was to be the Goddess made flesh, and I would draw down her power into me.

What you will shall be
Between worlds.

The front door rattled with the key in the lock, the hall light went on downstairs, and I jumped up and threw off my coat because I wasn't undressed yet like he'd told me.

'Hello. You there?' Mr Cromley's voice floated up the stairwell. I didn't answer. He muttered something, then I heard a foot on the stair.

'I'm here,' I called. 'Getting myself ready.'

'Good.' I could hear the relief in his voice. The floorboards creaked as I took off my coat and dress, my fingers fumbling with the buttons. I was in a panic. I wouldn't be ready, they'd come up and find me in my vest and knickers . . . But they could hear me moving around, and they wouldn't come straight up because they were getting ready too, in the front room downstairs.

Robes and masks. Masks make you free, Mr Cromley had said. You can do what you like wearing a mask. Mine was tucked under the white nightie. I'd imagined it would be a little black Burglar Bill mask, just covering the eyes, but it was a great sparkly thing with sequins and feathers, and it came down over my nose and cheeks, so there was only my mouth exposed. I'd put on red lipstick before catching the bus to Swindon, but it was all eaten off now. I looked for my bag that I'd kicked under the bed, but I heard their feet on the stairs.

There was only the two of them, like he'd said. They had hoods on their dark blue robes, and under them masks, like balaclavas made of leather, that covered the whole head. A smell came off them, a tannery smell overlaid with whisky fumes, a hot chemical stink of excitement. Eyes gleamed through the eyeholes, lips glistened in the wide oval cut in the masks for the mouth; they looked like blacked-up minstrels from an end-of-the-pier show. One was taller, one was younger; and anyway, I'd have known which Mr Cromley was because he spoke, he said the words, he told me what to do, and he was first.

The dagger, he'd told me, is called an athame, a ritual tool from earliest times. The dagger and the cup. You mix the fluids in the cup with the dagger. A little mead, a little blood and, afterwards, a little seed. We shall smear it on your forehead, Heartbreaker, and on your breasts, and call down the Goddess into you. In the space that hangs between worlds, you shall have infinite power. What you will shall be. Demand the universe gives you whatever you desire.

At the empty guesthouse I woke before the dawn, and washed my face in cold water from the jug I'd brought in from the pump the night before; the mains water had been turned off when Mam and Dad left. No power, either, and the range was long out, so I drank water from the jug for my breakfast and ate the bread and jam sandwiches, soggy now, I'd made at the widow's house. The early sun was coming through the kitchen window, making patterns on the dusty flagstones where Mam had danced. There'd been a frost in the night – no wonder I'd been cold under the thin blankets – and the stalks of the runner beans had turned black.

I took out my rosewood watercolour set that Mr Keiller had given me in the summer, filled the little tray with water, and began to paint what I could see. Beyond the fence at the back of the garden, the trees on the main road hid where the workmen was still busy with the digging. At the end of the field was a single stone, trussed and bound and propped with planks. A cement mixer and a wheelbarrow stood a few yards away, ready for making the concrete base so it'd never fall down again. Mr Keiller had said he'd carry on till November if need be, so he could say he'd finished the first half of the circle by the end of 1938.

We all understood why he was in a rush.

Mr Cromley's dagger was an old bronze thing. He'd stolen it from a museum in Oxford where he'd worked for a time. He had a pewter cup, and he mixed the stuff in it with the dagger. It wasn't like before, at the stone, when I could feel the control radiating from his hot skin, and the strange dreaminess carrying me along with all the weirdness. This time something was making him tense, like he was afraid of getting it wrong. He'd lit candles all round, fat white ones like they have in church. They dragged the double bed away from the wall, into the middle of the room. Then Mr Cromley opened a circle around it, like he had around the stone. North, East, South and West. Earth, Air, Fire, Water. The tall, older man stood watching, nodding, like he approved. He didn't say a thing.

I was scared, but I couldn't help myself laughing, because Mr Cromley was so solemn. In the cut-out eyeholes his eyes narrowed like he was cross with me for not taking it more serious. There was an insect, a big late-in-the-season blowfly, buzzing round and round the room, swooping at the candle flames and bumping into the windowpane.

They laid me back on the bed, and I went limp like Mr Cromley had told me to, while they lifted my arms above my head and tied a cord round my hands. He had explained what would happen weeks ago, but it had sounded special then. Now I could see myself in the cloudy mirror on the wardrobe door: I looked like a plucked chicken, shivering in the unheated bedroom, goose-bumps on my skinny arms and legs. Mr Cromley drew a pattern on my stomach, and on each breast, and on my face, with the dagger. His hand was shaking so much I was afraid it would slip and cut me. Then he stood up with a sigh of relief, unravelled the cord around his waist, and opened his arms wide, so that his robe fell open. The other man, silent still, lifted the robe off his shoulders, picked up the cord from the floor and, as Mr Cromley leaned over me, lashed his back with the knotted end.

It hurt like a dagger, and he couldn't seem to get it in properly, and then it was all gush and stickiness.

He collapsed onto me and I brought my bound arms down over his head in a clumsy embrace, because it seemed like the thing to do. His back was rigid under my fingers like a boy who's messed up.

The tall man was angry, I could tell. Donald had spoiled the ritual. He didn't say anything, but his eyes glinted through the eyeholes of the mask, and his mouth was set hard beneath it.

But the tall man was gentle with me. He smoothed my hair, and he let his finger trail over my dry lips.

'Spit,' he said, a whisper. The first time he'd spoken. 'Lick my finger.'

The wrecking ball was there by half past eight. I stood outside with the others, the wind nipping at me through my thin cardigan. Old Walter was letting himself out of his little cottage across the road. He shuffled through the wooden gate, and smiled a bleak smile when he saw me in the waiting crowd. He didn't stay to watch but shuffled down Green Street towards the crossroads.

This time the crowd was silent, not like when the blacksmith's place came down. There was dread in the air, a dull resentment, and a sense of awful expectancy, like they were waiting for an execution.

'Anything on the wireless this morning?' I asked the woman standing next to me, Mrs Paradise, the blacksmith's wife. She shook her head.

Yesterday Hitler's troops had rolled into the Sudetenland. The BBC had broadcast the sound of an air-raid siren, an awful howl that set your teeth on edge. We were expecting to be at war any day now, though Mr Keiller's view was that Hitler and Mr Chamberlain probably had a secret understanding, and would carve up the world between them. 'Let 'em have Russia,' he'd said, standing outside the caravan on the dig site, hands on his hips, as he often stood when he was making a pronouncement. 'That's what the Germans would really like to get their hands on, to give old Joe Stalin and his Communists their marching orders.' He spoke like he knew what was what. Mrs Neville Chamberlain had been to see the dig in August; maybe she'd let slip something over lunch.

Three men set ladders against the side of the guesthouse, and began to strip the lead off the roof. When they had finished, the wrecking ball was trundled into place.

I turned my face away, felt as much as heard the swish of air, the crumbling impact. Someone put an arm round me. When I looked up, there was my bedroom, a yawning cave with smashed floorboards and torn flowered wallpaper.

Couple of days after the guesthouse came down, Mr Chamberlain was on the radio and in the newspapers. Peace for our time, he says. Flapping a piece of paper like a magician producing a dove.

'You lied to me,' I said.

Mr Cromley, still in his leather mask, was coming out of the bathroom, a towel round his waist. The other man had already gone.

'Don't pretend,' I went on. 'Who was that? I know it wasn't Mr Keiller.'

Mr Cromley sighed. He reached up, unfastened the back of his mask and took it off. His hair was damp and flattened to his head.

'It was my uncle, of course. You're very lucky, Heartbreaker. Your virginity was taken by the best ritual magician in Europe.' There was bitterness in his voice because it should have been him.

'He smelled wrong for Mr Keiller,' I said. 'I'm not stupid.'

'No, of course you're not,' he said, his voice as cold as his uncle had felt, pushing into my warm core. 'A stupid girl is one who doesn't understand how fragile her grip is on what she holds dear. How easy it would be, for instance, to lose her job because of a careless mistake, a thoughtless word to the wrong person. How disappointed her parents would be in her. How shocked people in Avebury would be if they knew what she had allowed herself to do. *Begged* to do, as I recall.'

I was barely sixteen, and I believed him.

PART FOUR

Fire Festival

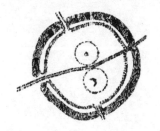

Beltane – May Eve, the night of 30 April – is a fire festival. It marks the point in the agricultural year when cattle were moved to new pasture to graze the spring grass. Bonfires were lit; young men and women jumped over them to prove their bravery, then paired off in the darkness.

Today May Day is associated with jolly folk customs: maypole dancing, morris men. We have a vague sense that all this phallic symbolism must be something to do with fertility, and indeed it is. The main concern of agricultural societies is always fertility.

Whether our forefathers (and mothers) actually carried out sexual rituals in stone circles like Avebury is a moot point. Every time an archaeologist discovers rock carvings that appear to show men copulating with women, or each other, or even, in one celebrated case, cattle, it is hailed as proof that sex was an integral part of prehistoric religious ritual. On the other hand it could also be prehistoric graffiti, of roughly the same significance as a spray-painted penis on a warehouse wall.

Dr Martin Ekwall,
A Turning Circle: The Ritual Year at Avebury,
Hackpen Press

CHAPTER 25

1939

May's a white month in Wiltshire. Stitchwort and three-cornered leek and wild garlic in the hedges, horse-chestnut candles bowing down the branches above. On the juicy green Downs, lambs looking like they've been laundered. None of it lasts.

May Eve 1939 was cold and stormy as a curse, though.

'The witches' Beltane, Miss Robinson.'

'I wouldn't know, Mr Keiller.'

'My dear girl, call yourself a countrywoman? Rural types are supposed to be in touch with the pagan calendar.'

'Not me. I go to church.'

We were in the library, rain lashing the diamond-paned windows. I was delivering another batch of typing, waiting by the table with his fountain pen for him to sign the letters. Mr Keiller was all restless energy, pacing round making plans and pulling out books from the shelves instead of getting down to his correspondence. He'd wanted to know where the maypole went, and did we still do the dancing? He come over all of a tizz when he discovered it used to be set up at the back of the Methodist chapel, right by the tall obelisk stone he reckoned marked the dead centre of the circle – or would have, if it hadn't been pulled down and broken up hundreds of years ago.

In the lamplight, his eyes were golden, on fire.

I held out the fountain pen. He took it, his fingers touching mine needlessly, lingering a moment. Last summer I'd have revelled, but now I flinched: when Mr Keiller touched me, my mind had lurched sickeningly to Mr Cromley. He hadn't been seen in Avebury since the end of last year, thank God.

Mr Keiller let go my hand. 'Poor little Heartbreaker. How are you going to manage now your Brushwood Boy is leaving?'

'Leaving? Who?' It didn't sink in immediate.

'Your young man.' Mr Keiller's face furrowed. 'Good Lord, I'm sorry. I assumed you knew Davey's enlisting with the RAF. He came to me for a reference last week.'

'I didn't know,' I said. 'But Davey and I . . .' I wasn't sure how to finish.

'Is that what this is all about? A lovers' tiff? I *am* sorry – I've made it worse, haven't I?' His rueful grin made my stomach muscles twist. I was glad it hadn't been him, in the house by the cemetery, but then again, part of me wished it had.

'No,' I said. 'No reason he should tell me. It's . . . been that way between us for a while.'

'Well, fair enough.' Mr Keiller was embarrassed. 'I thought . . . Davey's a handsome young fellow and he said to me a while back . . . but you are young for an understanding, I suppose.'

'There's going to be a war, Mr Keiller,' I said. 'Nobody's too young for anything.' He was looking at me, puzzled. I didn't know what I was trying to tell him either. Everything seemed so mixed up now: Davey going, the place I'd been born rubble. The Blackshirts had been marching for peace, or so they claimed, in London, someone had carved MOSLEY WILL WIN in the side of Silbury Hill, and it seemed to me there were no certainties left in the world. Not even love, whatever that was. People said Mr Keiller and Miss Chapman – I couldn't think of her as Mrs Keiller – were already arguing almost every night.

'Don't be too quick to grow up, Heartbreaker,' he said.

They'd married in the autumn, as soon as the dig was over. No fuss, no grand wedding. I'd always thought her a bit of a ragbag, preferring comfortable clothes to fashionable, but when she came back to Avebury after their November honeymoon in Paris, she was as smart as silk drawers, in a toque hat and fur coat. The gossip was that Mr

Keiller made her sign an agreement before they married to say she wouldn't use her allowance to buy furs and jewellery without his consent. I don't think he trusted wives, and we all understood that, in spite of her father being the major-general, the new Mrs K wasn't out of the very top drawer.

The smile was triumphant, when she arrived back at the Manor with varnish on her nails instead of paint under them. The eyes were scared.

'She's a clever woman, or he wouldn't have married her,' said Mr Cromley, half under his breath, standing behind me at the 1938 MIAR end-of-season party. 'But I reckon it's only just dawned on her what she's taking on. Wouldn't you say so, Piggott?'

He'd done it deliberate, come up behind me unexpected when the toasts were due, so it would look odd if I walked away. This was the first time I'd seen him for weeks, because he'd vanished from Avebury only days after the ritual in Swindon, well before the season was finished, and I'd prayed he wouldn't come back for the party. My skin crawled to have him so near.

We were supposed to be celebrating but no one seemed very cheerful. There was little huddles and whispers about how the marmalade money was finally running out.

'None of our concern what happens in that marriage,' said Mr Piggott, tartly. Mr Cromley's remark might have been designed to catch him on the raw, because Stu Pig'd recently married too, and he didn't look like my idea of a radiant husband. His wife Peggy was over the other side of the room, and there was an atmosphere between them. 'You planning on coming back for the dig next year?'

'Bet you ten bob there won't *be* a dig next year,' said Mr Cromley. 'Even if she doesn't bleed him dry. Word to the wise. Don't wait to be conscripted. Grab yourself a commission before the balloon goes up. That's what I'm doing.'

'Easy for those with an uncle in the Air Ministry.'

'Connections, Stu. That's what it's all about.'

Mr Cromley had behaved as if nothing had happened between us.

He seemed sure enough he'd frightened me into keeping quiet. And me? I'd never speak out – it'd kill Mam. The tobacconist's shop in Devizes was dragging her down. She was thinner. Her hair looked dry, like dead moss in a bird's nest. Her skin seemed papery, and she had a yellowy colour. No, I'd do anything to protect her from knowing what I'd done, but I never let myself cry over that day. They were scum, him and his uncle. Magic, my arse. It was a game to them. Pass the Parcel. Unwrap it. Take turns.

Davey was there at the party, face like misery. I felt sorry for him: he always gave his heart too easy. He idolized Mr Keiller, didn't think Miss Chapman was right for him at all. I thought I guessed how it had been: driving about together up and down to London, stood to reason they was close and Davey had opinions. But I'd never seen him so wretched. If he could have sunk into the wood panels of the wall, clasping his beer glass, he would have.

He and I weren't clever. We didn't have connections. I went over to him and laid a hand on his arm. He put his hand over it, slopping some of his beer on the polished oak floor.

'It's all over, Fran.' His golden eyes were swimming; he was very drunk, and I'd never seen him that way. 'You, me, and – Mr Keiller, he was special, deserves better than her. Didn't think I'd mind, but I do.'

'I know you do,' I said. There was plenty to mind, for both of us. We'd both had our souls caught and eaten, one way or another.

So, as the new season started, we were a depleted team – no Mr Piggott, no Mr Cromley – and the atmosphere on the dig was jittery. No one was sure when the fighting would start, but for all Mr Chamberlain's bits of paper, there wasn't a living soul optimistic enough to think we could avoid war now.

And Davey going, too. The day after my conversation in the Library with Mr Keiller, I found him in the barn, his legs sticking out under one of the cars.

'What's this I hear about you joining the air force?'

He trundled himself out and sat up, propping himself against the side of the car. Oil had dripped on his hair, making it look like wet corrugated iron. 'What's it to do with you?'

'Well, I hope it *isn't* anything to do with me. I don't want you flying off and getting killed on my behalf.'

'I won't be flying anywhere. I'm going in as ground crew. And, no, it's nothing to do with you. When I heard Mr Cromley had enlisted, I thought it was the right thing to do.'

'Oh, for God's sake.' I kicked the car tyre, inches away from his thick head. 'You don't mean to tell me you admire that . . . that . . .'

'He went in because there's a war coming. I call that brave.'

'He went in so he could grease his way into a cushy desk job, like his uncle.'

'He's a pilot, Fran. Nothing cushy about that. Stop kicking the Hispano's tyres. They cost a lot to replace. Anyway, we'll all be in sooner or later.'

'But what about the excavations? Mr Keiller needs you.'

'No, Mr Keiller doesn't need me, not any more. He says he's proud to spare me for the RAF. He has Philip to drive him if he dun't drive himself, and he won't be racing the cars this summer. Everything's different this year.'

It was. Mr Keiller's inconstant demons let him down, and stole away both his time and his money before he could finish. He dug up the stones of the inner circle on the south side of the village, many as he could find, and set them in concrete. But he didn't get round to finishing the rest of the great outer circle. Before summer was over, he'd joined up himself: part-time duty with the Special Constabulary. There was tanks chewing the grass along the Avenue, and the soldiers scratched their initials on the stones.

'Have you ever noticed, Miss Robinson, that the *Encyclopaedia Britannica* classifies intelligence into three separate types?' said Mr Keiller. 'Human, animal and military. In that order of preference, I think.'

On the first of September, the first evacuees arrived in the village, seventy girls and boys from the East End of London, along with their teachers. The blackout was already in force. In Devizes, Dad and Mam walked me to the bus stop, late at night, and it was so dark we went in a chain, holding hands.

A couple of days later, we was at war. Seeing as how everybody else was doing their bit, I thought it time to do mine too. I found a job in the almoner's office in the hospital at Swindon.

CHAPTER 26

Beltane approaches, and weekend pagans gather again. Ed's on camp-site patrol Friday night: as I leave the café, I see him in the distance, climbing into the National Trust Land Rover and gunning it down the gravel drive, aviator shades in place like a cop in a seventies movie. Asking me to lie about what I remember of the crash is unforgivable. I'm annoyed with myself for wanting to wave him down and jump in beside him.

Martin and the film crew appear briefly, shoot some fire-juggling in the circle on Saturday afternoon, then leave once dusk falls, Martin heading for Bath to spend the rest of the weekend with a friend of his, caving in the Mendips.

But by quarter to ten on Sunday it's raining heavily. Martin won't be potholing today.

'Better drive you down to church,' I tell Frannie, though I'm still in my pyjamas, an old towel wrapped round head. 'Give me twenty minutes to rinse the colour off and dry my hair.'

'That'd be smashing,' she says. Her voice is bright, but her eyes have loose brownish-purple pouches beneath, and her skin has a tired, yellowy tinge. The doctor can find nothing physically wrong, but has suggested a social worker should call to see her this week, and she's been worrying about that. 'You don't have to wait around, though – Carrie Harper'll give me a lift back. Her sister usually gets out the car for church.' She spoons down the last of her porridge. 'Must find me collection money.'

'I *will* wait around,' I call after her. 'I could put in some time at the museum . . .' Sorting out the Keiller archive for Michael has taken

241

much longer than expected, my days off from the café usually occupied with filming.

'Not your television thing again.' Frannie can't understand why the programme isn't finished yet. But Ibby is working on several other productions at the same time.

'Not exactly. You know, they'd still like to interview you.'

'I told you, *no*,' says Frannie. 'Don't like this digging over the past. Get a job on *Flog It!*, that's my advice. I'm sure they don't spend nearly so much time on that. Anyways, you take long as you want in your old archive. Carrie Harper'll offer me a roast lunch, if I know her.'

'*I* could cook a roast . . .'

'No need, Margaret.' Frannie's briskly in control, the raspberry hat jammed over her curls. Shame she has me confused again with my mother. 'Just because we live in the same house doesn't mean we have to be on top of each other. You do your thingy, I'll do mine.'

Having dropped Frannie at the lich-gate, I drive round to the staff car park. Graham's red Mazda is about to pull out. I draw up beside him and wind my window down.

'What are you doing here?'

'Trouble at the campsite in the wee small hours. Over-enthusiastic drumming. One of the locals rang and hauled me out of bed first thing this morning to read the riot act. Not that it'll make any difference. They wait till I'm gone, then start up again.' He sighs. 'Thank God I've an appointment with a chainsaw tomorrow. This wind'll bring down a hell of a lot of dead wood.'

He drives off. In the distance, the sound of drums pulses raggedly from the campsite, as I battle with gusts to open the car door before letting myself into the staff entrance of the building.

The museum is open, but there are hardly any visitors, and the volunteer manning the desk has his nose buried in the Sunday papers. Upstairs, the attic office is cold and gloomy, but this time there's a convector heater under the table and I plug it in before settling down with the last unsorted box of Keiller's correspondence.

I like offices when no one else is around. In London I often used to tube or bus it into Mannix TV at weekends. I could have finished the same tasks in the flat, on my laptop, but the Australians were always around. Six months on I can hardly remember their names.

I work my way through the letters, sorting them into piles by date. You can almost smell the late-night brandy on the blue copies, Keiller's personality pushing through the page. He's so obviously a charmer, used to getting his own way; also, less attractively, an obsessive and a hypochondriac. An extrovert, by all accounts, yet he'd grown up a lonely boy, both parents dead before he was eighteen, fascinated by witchcraft and the stone circles he found on his solitary walks on the Scottish moors. Loved flying, skiing, fast cars. Opiniated, a ruthless enemy waging war on slipshod archaeology, a tyrant with an explosive temper . . .

Somehow it's nearly one o'clock already. By now Frannie will be comfortably ensconced at the Harpers' with a glass of sweet sherry in her hand, admiring the Crown Derby dinner service and chattering through the open doorway to Carrie in the kitchen.

Or will she be sitting silently in the living room with that vacant, preoccupied glaze on her face?

Of course not. She's fine. She's become forgetful, but all old ladies are forgetful. She's still the same Fran she's always been . . .

Always? Fact is, Fran was nearly sixty when I was born. I've only ever known her as an elderly woman. And now the active, vigorous Fran who helped raise me is disappearing too, all her different personas fading: the walker who taught me the names of wild flowers, the china collector who used to raid Devizes junk shops, the Greenham granny who took the bolt-cutters from Margaret to snip the perimeter fence, and held my small hand when we embraced the base.

Under my fingers, thin blue paper rustles as I lay it on the appropriate pile. May 1939. Who were you then, Frannie, when you typed some of these? The person who had sent the anonymous letter knew.

anonymous with eyes in their head at the Manor knew what was going on the Devil was at work there

As I lift out the last set of blue sheets from the box file, one slides from the sheaf, and a name jumps out at me.

Davey Fergusson.

Thank God it's raining. When I dial Martin's mobile, he answers almost immediately. A background of music and chatter makes it difficult to hear what he's saying.

'We're in the pub, petal. Would've been mad to go underground today. Hang on . . .' The chatter peaks as he turns away from the phone. A male voice is asking him what he wants to eat. '. . . sauté, not fries. Sorry, India, I'm back with you.'

'Who was that?'

'Nobody for you to get excited about. My friend's boyfriend.'

'I thought you were staying with someone special this weekend?'

Martin sounds like his teeth are clenched. 'That fell through. He had cold feet.'

'Anyway, look, I found something in Keiller's letters,' I tell him. 'My grandfather's name. I mean, the name of the man Frannie says is my grandfather. But the context is . . . weird. Keiller's going on about someone he calls the Brushwood Boy, who might or might not be Davey Fergusson, and there's someone else mentioned whose name is Paul. It's kind of confusing, and not clear which of them he's talking about, but he says: *His eyes are lustrous* . . . lots of stuff about the effect on Keiller being electric and bursting into song with an ecstatic expression on his face.'

'Is this by any chance a letter to Piggott?' asks Martin.

'How did you know?'

'It's the way they wrote to each other – homoerotic public-schoolboy banter. Although I sometimes think there was more to it than that: they were genuinely trying to define the mysteries of love in an age that sent you to prison for touching another man's willy. Keiller had an engineering background, remember, so he wanted to understand the mechanics of attraction, be it male to female or male to male. Poke it, probe it, give it a test run, see if it fell to bits. Look, scan the letter, email it, and I'll take a closer look.'

'Do you understand this reference to the Brushwood Boy? Was it a song, or something, of the period?'

The sigh coming down the line almost blows my ear off. 'Don't suppose they teach Kipling any longer in schools?'

'I saw the film,' I say defensively. 'When I was about five.'

'I don't mean *Jungle Book*, idiot. Kipling also wrote a lot of short stories about manly young chaps keeping the Empire going. The Brushwood Boy is about a handsome fellow, frightfully good at cricket, et cetera, who resists the charms of all the ladies swooning over him. Instead he longs for an ideal woman whom he meets in his dreams, by a brushwood fire on a beach. Eventually he meets her for real. And she's been dreaming the exact same dream – he's her Brushwood Boy. Their souls have been meeting every night since they were children, and they know each other immediately.'

'I don't get it.'

'God, your generation have *no* bloody souls, do you? Yes, yes, it's hideously sentimentalized, but it's about falling in love.'

So now I'm more confused than ever. Instead of being dazzled by my grandmother, it's my grandfather Keiller fell for?

Keiller was gay? I asked Martin. My grandfather was gay? Even though he was with my grandmother?

Another of his gusty sighs. You don't have to be gay to sleep with men, apparently. Or be straight to marry. Well, excuse me, I knew that, but Martin seemed to have some other agenda he was pursuing. Finally I heard a woman's voice in the background saying, *For Chrissake give it a rest, Martin*, and he suddenly shut up and said we'd talk when he was next in Avebury. That could be weeks away.

A blast of wind rattles the window. If Davey and Keiller had something going, could Frannie have had any idea? Or maybe there was no affair, unfulfilled yearnings all round. Or maybe none of it was serious, except in an experimental sense. How can you *ever* be sure what really happened? Even if you were there?

I pack the box files away, and shrug on my coat, hoping fresh air will clear my head. It's still raining hard, but that doesn't matter.

It does, of course. The wind keeps whipping my hood off, and the hems of my jeans are wicking water up my legs before I've even gone a couple of hundred yards. Rain lashes into my face. The stone circle is deserted, everyone with any sense being snug under thatch.

My grandfather's ghost seems more elusive than ever. If it was that complicated, maybe I can understand why Fran doesn't talk about it: time wounds all heels, but you don't have to go on limping, as my mother used to say. How much would Fran have told *her*?

The wind buffets me along Green Street, whipping tiny waves into the puddles and pushing me towards the open countryside. We never talked much, either, Mum and me, and now I wonder how much of that was down to the way we are in my family, or to Margaret not wanting to acknowledge her own wrong choices. Married young and regretted it, walked out on her husband, heading into the sunrise with a bunch of musicians she met while working the nightshift in a motorway service-station café. Until I came along to cramp her style, Mum would be on the hippie trail through the Far East, or with Angelfeather, achieving her fifteen minutes of fame as a poster girl when she danced naked on the Stonehenge trilithons, out of her head on acid as the sun rose. For years she was Blu-Tacked on student bed-sit walls, Midsummer Meg next to Che Guevara and Slowhand Clapton.

Whatever she felt about her daughter's behaviour, I never once heard my grandmother utter a word of criticism, even after Midsummer Meg danced right out of my life, and Social Services sent me to live with Frannie in Chippenham. Three, four, five years passed. She's travelling abroad, said Frannie. In Thailand now. Or Australia. Or Africa. Cards came, signed 'Mum', in increasingly shaky writing, on birthdays and at Christmas, parcels too. They always had a Chippenham postmark. All, that is, apart from the last parcel. That came from Goa, where Meg had fallen off the stage and broken her neck. A silver chain with a moonstone pendant, a couple of batik scarves, a silk sari, a copy of *The Road Less Travelled*, a diary that was near enough blank pages, and her passport. Not much to leave your daughter, and I burned the lot, apart from the pendant, which I gave to Oxfam. Wish I hadn't now.

So the last place I saw my mother was . . .

Tolemac. The wind rushes with a noise like floodwater through the branches of the little wood, stripping the blossom from the wild cherries. Beads of pearly water cling to the barbed wire of the fence. Still a few threads from my torn jeans wrapped around it. Don't remember any decision to come here, or any of the walk. The rain's easing off; when I push back my hood, my hair clings to my wet face. There's a glow through the trees. Someone has lit a fire.

Gunmetal cloud, racing above the tossing branches, makes the wood an even gloomier prospect than usual. I should phone Graham, not tackle this myself . . . Only there probably wouldn't be any signal on the mobile, even if I hadn't left it in the car in the staff car park.

Quickly, so I don't have time to change my mind, I hop over the fence, careful not to leave my trouser seat there this time.

The wet leaves on the ground muffle my footsteps. The grey ghost shape of a bender looms between the trees, the polythene rattling and flapping. The fire's the other side, in a clearing. Whoever lit it has found dry kindling: it's a good blaze, whipped up by the wind racing through the branches.

The dog looks up, tilting its head and cocking its ears as if it had been expecting me.

On the other side of the fire, cool eyes with flames dancing in them watch my approach. Now I remember where I saw those eyes before: at the full-moon ceremony, yes, but before that on the Ridgeway, a cold clear afternoon at Imbolc. A trilby jammed over those corkscrew curls, and a perfect arse, side-stepping down the hillside.

'Go on,' he says. 'It's May Eve. Jump.'

So I grin at him, and take a flying leap over the fire.

CHAPTER 27

1940–1941

Seize the day, Frances, my dad used to say, when I visited them in Devizes. Enjoy yourself while you can, it's later than you think.

Only way to be in wartime. That first winter of the war, seemed like time was at a standstill though everything was changing. Village school became an air-raid shelter. Land girls at Manor Farm; evacuees in the Manor house – kept well out of Mr Keiller's way, needless to say. The whole country was on the move, people crammed into buses and trains, silent, morose, bored, shunting through stations with no names, through landscapes where the signposts had all been took down. The weather froze, great festoons of ice hanging from the telegraph wires, inches thick, bowing the lines almost to the ground. One of the men who'd raised the Barber Surgeon's stone died of pneumonia. The sound of trees cracking was like gunshots. Mr Keiller was now a police inspector with the Special Constabulary, and Miss Chapman – Mrs Keiller, I should say, still couldn't get used to that – went to London to be a nurse. Mr Piggott was in the army, to everyone's surprise. 'Thought he was a blinking pacifist,' said Mr Keiller. 'I used to tell him he'd be the first to be shot.' There was next to nothing going on by way of excavation, though Inspector Keiller was first on the scene, measuring the craters and poking round in the mess, when Jerry ditched a bomb on the East Kennet long barrow.

A room came free in the attic of the Lodge, in the heart of the village. So I give up my place down the road in the draughty old house in Winterbourne Monkton, that I'd found after Mam and Dad went to Devizes, and moved in sharpish before it could be requisitioned for unhappy Londoners. That was the day the thaw started. Spring came. From my window I watched the evacuees learning to maypole dance, somebody's damn fool idea of making them feel at home. They kept getting the ribbons tangled, and picked fights with the village children for laughing. Eventually they were all moved back home.

Every morning I caught the early bus to Swindon, to work at the hospital. My war was fought on a sea of paperwork, chitties for this, dockets for that. I did the rounds of the wards, handing out chocolate and cigarettes to the wounded men, and I don't mind saying that the odd square made its way into my mouth. Thought I'd grown up before the war, that afternoon in the terraced house across from the cemetery, but I never, not until I met those sad boys with their burned skin shiny as cellophane. They and their friends asked me out dancing plenty of times, but it didn't seem fair to say yes when I knew I wouldn't so much as hold hands at the end of the evening.

But Davey – Davey and I had come to an understanding, like.

By the start of 1941 he was stationed at Wroughton airfield, not far out of Swindon. Wroughton was a maintenance unit, preparing planes from the factories to be sent all over the country: easy work for a good mechanic like Davey. He used to wait for me outside the hospital gates on a Friday or a Saturday night to take me dancing. He seemed happy enough with that. He never kissed me, we never held hands. If he told his pals at the airbase I was his girl, I didn't mind. It stopped any other fellow trying to cut in while we were dancing.

You had to go dancing. What else could you do? I'd bring my dance dress with me on the bus and change at the hospital, in the room with bunks that we used when we were on fire watch. One of the other girls would kneel behind me and draw a line of black pencil down the back of each bare leg while I put on my lipstick in the mirror. Then I'd do the same for her.

Sometimes the air-raid warning went while we were in the hall, siren playing a duet with the trumpets from the dance band, but we'd step on while the wardens tried to shoo us out down to the shelter. 'If your number's on the bomb, your number's up,' one of the girls at the hospital used to say, fatalistical, and she was right because she died when her dad's Anderson shelter took a direct hit.

Davey had a car, an old Baby Austin he'd bought with money Mr Keiller had given him when he left Avebury. He kept it in a lock-up garage in town, over by the railway yards. One night the garage was bombed, and a piece of masonry went through the tin roof of Davey's car, so he salvaged a sheet of steel from the railwaymen and welded it onto the top. Wouldn't have won any races after that, and the welds leaked when it rained, but he could drive me home after the dance.

Some nights I was on fire-watching duty at the hospital, up on a cold rooftop waiting for the bombers' drone. Rest of the time, if the bus wasn't cancelled because of an air raid, I went home to Avebury. As the blacked-out bus lumbered out of the town, its shaded head-lamps casting only a faint gleam on the road ahead, sometimes there'd be lights on the hills.

Davey knew what was up there. Hush-hush, mum's the word. One of his mates at the airbase had helped build a dummy town on the top of the Downs near Barbury, a burning ghost to fool the bombers and lure them away from Swindon and the railway yards. There were other decoys on the hills around: fake airfields called Q-sites, runways with goose-necked flares that no plane ever took off from.

Sometimes, when he was driving me home, we parked up under Hackpen Hill, near the White Horse that the grass'd been allowed to grow over, to stop the bombers using him as a landmark. Along the ridge in the moonlight were the chalk ramparts of the old hillfort at Barbury Castle. Funny to think it'd been built thousands of years ago, by men with spears and bows and arrows; now it held an anti-aircraft battery.

'I'm going away,' said Davey. 'I'm being transferred to Scotland. Training for air crew.' It was the spring of '41, awful dark in the car, but the moon was up, showing he'd taken off his forage cap and was twisting it in his hands. He never tried to kiss me now. I felt sorry for him; I should have let him be, so he could find another girl who would love him back properly, but he seemed happy enough to be with me.

'What for?' I said stupidly. Obvious, really: the Battle of Britain had been won, by the skin of Mr Churchill's teeth, but a lot of young men had gone with it. The RAF needed new flyers. 'You promised me you wouldn't be a pilot.' There were tears pricking my eyes. Didn't usually get sentimental, but there'd been a bowl of cider punch at the dance and I'd had a few glasses.

'Fed up of being an erk. I'm going to be a navigator.'

'I'm surprised they're letting you,' I said. His eyes gleamed in the moonlight as he whipped round and glared. 'That come out wrong. Meant to say, you're too good a mechanic to lose.'

'They're training *girls* to be mechanics now. Bleedin' heck, one turned up in the Air Transport Auxiliaries the other day – pilot trained. She's going to be flying planes across country to deliver to the bases. Can't have them flying missions, though, can they? Men still the only ones can do that. Anyway, the brass seem to think I have an *aptitude*.' He laughed. 'An aptitude for altitude.'

'Yes, but . . . what'd you know about navigation?'

'That's why I'm learning.'

'Star charts and dead reckoning?'

'It's cleverer than that these days. There's a thing they call AI – airborne interception – shouldn't tell you, because it's hush-hush, but that's what I'm off to learn in Scotland. I already did a radio direction-finding course at Yatesbury.'

He'd kept mighty quiet about that. Yatesbury, where I'd sat in the churchyard with Mr Cromley, specialized in training for wireless and signals. It was so close to Avebury that some of the officers stationed there had made their living quarters on a caravan site behind Rawlins's garage. The bar of the Red Lion was stuffy with their pipe smoke and beer fumes.

A navigator. Davey had always been a clever boy, good with maps, good with the size and shape and lay of things. But clever boys still got killed. Not much that brains could do to stop a line of tracer coming through the skin of a Wellington or a Beaufighter and splatting them.

Wasn't much I could do, was there? If I'd begged, wouldn't have stopped him.

'You got a death wish,' I said. 'Or worse. You any idea what I see on the wards every day? Air crew without faces. Bald and shiny as babies, their pretty ears and noses burned away, eyes gummy slits. Want to end up like that?'

'Ninety-six out of every hundred planes come back safe. Chances are . . .'

'That's what the body-snatchers at Bomber Command tell the lambs. You can work all sorts of fakery with numbers. Chances are *terrible*. Average plane lasts seventeen ops. You know that – you send the bloody things out factory fresh and get 'em back in bits. Like I get the airmen.' Now all he showed me was the back of his head, every prickle on his close-barbered neck sulking.

'When are you going?' I asked.

'Monday.'

'Monday? *This* Monday?'

'Tonight's goodbye.'

It was my turn to look out of the window; couldn't think of anything to say. The hedges on either side of the car were dripping with may blossom. He pressed the starter button and the engine caught. Made a sound like the end of the world, that car, with the heavy vibrating piece of steel on the roof shattering the peace of the night. He rammed it into gear, and it bumped forward on the pocked road surface. A bit up the lane was a gateway where he usually turned the car round.

'Hold on,' I said. 'I don't want to go home yet.'

He put his foot on the brake, and the car came to a juddering halt.

'Fran. You know they got a word for girls like you?'

'That's not what I mean,' I said. 'Take me up to where your city of lights is.'

The car bounced along the ruts of the Ridgeway towards Barbury, its steel roof creaking and groaning. It hadn't rained for a while and the track was solid, though winter had been wet and cold. Below us lay the airfield at Wroughton, a great dark hidden thing, no lights showing from its camouflaged hangars where planes slept in their maintenance cradles. Davey stopped at the bottom of the slope leading up to Barbury.

'Are we there?'

'It's a bit further. Have to walk the rest – don't want anyone to hear us coming or we might be shot as spies.'

'You joking?' The cooling engine ticked in the silence. 'Love-a-duck, you're *not*.'

'Still keen to see it?'

'Try and stop me.'

He looked at me doubtfully. 'Path'll be hobbledy-gobbledy.'

'I can manage.' I was in dance shoes, ankle straps and platform soles, but if I had to I'd go barefoot on the grass.

'Don't blame me if you break a leg.'

I opened the car door and got out. It was a warm spring night, hardly a breeze, half a moon. 'Where is it? Can't see any lights.'

'They won't be lit unless there's a raid on the way. This way.' He set off, a faint stocky moon shadow trailing his back. We climbed the path; I kept my eyes on the ground, watching where I placed my feet, pretending I was a hind picking her delicate way across tussocked ground.

A shadow loomed out of the darkness: a Nissen hut.

'Are we there?'

'Sssh. That's where the crew will be.'

'There are people up here? In't that dangerous? Don't they get bombed?'

'Course they get bombed. But somebody has to be here to start the fires. There's an underground bunker beneath; protects them from anything other than a direct hit. But you're right, it in't the most popular duty.'

'Did you ever have to do it?'

'Still do, some nights.' No wonder he wasn't scared to be a navigator.

The ground had levelled out. Davey put a finger to his lips. We came round the end of a bank of earth, and there it was.

It was the bones of a city, in the moonlight, stretching half a mile or more across the Downs. No buildings, apart from the Nissen hut we'd passed; only spindly frames of pipework, a giant Meccano set. Every so often, a taller scaffolding tower rose twenty feet into the air, supporting pairs of square tanks. The place was utterly silent.

'Welcome to the Starfish.'

'Starfish?'

'No idea. That's what they call the decoy towns. Maybe starfish glow in the dark.'

'I don't understand how the Germans don't know it's here. They must fly over it in the day sometimes.'

'If you saw it from above, it'd look like chicken sheds or farm buildings.'

And from down here? Set me in mind of Mr Cromley's soul traps.

'Mind where you're putting your feet,' said Davey. 'Don't want to trip over they feed troughs.'

They did look like feed troughs – long shallow iron baskets filled with something dark.

'What's in them?'

'Coke and coal. Wood chippings, sawdust, brushwood underneath, soaked in oil.'

'What are the tanks for?'

'That's the clever bit. One's full of oil, the other of water. When the fire baskets are alight, the men in the bunker can trigger the tanks to flush – a bit like a WC cistern. The flames go up to thirty foot.' He sounded so proud you'd have thought he'd designed it himself.

'And the water puts them out again?'

'No, no. The opposite. It *explodes*. You seen a fire in a chip pan? Try putting that out with water. *Whoomph*. Steam, flames shooting to high heaven everywhere. Makes Jerry think one of his pals has just dropped a bomb, so in he comes for his own bombing run. With luck the blokes on the anti-aircraft battery pick him off, but doesn't matter anyway, see, 'cause he's dumping his bombs on a bit of nowhere.'

Everything was so quiet; hard to imagine this silent place lit by fire and explosions. In the distance, a ewe called to its lamb. I stepped cautiously over one of the long troughs.

'Hey, hang on, Fran,' said Davey. 'That'd warm your knickers. I shouldn't—'

'I want to explore.'

'It isn't a good idea. You don't know what might be over the horizon.'

'Come on. It's late, only a bit of old moon. There won't be a raid.'

'I don't know. These days, bombers don't need a full moon to find their way. And if they come, remember, it's all remote control. There's electric detonators in those troughs, wired back to the bunker. The blokes in the hut can't see us – and, anyway, they wouldn't hold off if they could.'

I felt reckless. On Monday Davey would be gone, my protection against the world; all I'd have left would be the airmen without faces. 'Come on,' I repeated. He shook his head.

''Tisn' safe, Fran.'

'Thought you was going to be a bold brave airman.'

'I mean not safe for you. Look at those daft shoes you're wearing.'

'Not so daft I can't run in them.' I jumped over the next fire basket, off like one of the racehorses Davey used to ride out on when he worked at the stables.

'Fran . . .' I could hear him following, feet thudding on the chalky ground. One of the scaffold towers with its square tank loomed above me. I ducked under it. Hide and seek. Heard him run past. I ran out and across the middle of the ghost city, playing hopscotch over the fire baskets. The troughs and pipes seemed to spread all over the top of the Downs and I ran up a little rise to see if it continued beyond, where the ridge of chalk ran on northwards . . .

There was a glow. Flames on the skyline.

'Davey!' I could hear the panic in my own voice. 'Davey, looks like Swindon . . .'

His voice was a way off. 'What was that?'

'Swindon's getting it.'

'Don't be soft. We'd have heard the bombers go over. You're confused, must be Bristol getting it again . . .'

Bristol was to the west. I was looking north. Or—

The chalk fell away to the north, down to the plain. I must be facing eastwards then. Not Swindon. Not Bristol. So what was burning?

The night was still silent, apart from us. Faintly, at some distance, I heard a telephone ring.

'FRAN! Move it. Get out, get away from the fire baskets . . .'

Where was Davey? I couldn't see him. All around me, a vast grid of troughs and pipes and tanks. The telephone still ringing. Then it stopped.

Paralysed, didn't know which way to go.

'Those fires are Liddington, Fran. It's the next Starfish along. Bombers must be coming from the east.' Davey was somewhere a long way off to my right, a shadow among shadows. 'MOVE. They'll be igniting the fires any minute.'

I started running, hoping it was back the way I'd come, hoping that was the quickest way out of this maze, trying to dodge away from the fire baskets, though if they lit them and flushed the oil and water so the flames exploded I'd be incinerated anyway, a black charred thing like I'd once seen an airman's hand when they brought him in, with deep pink oozing cracks in it. They couldn't give those boys enough morphine. They screamed themselves to sleep, the nurses said.

Had to get a grip. If I thought about burning I'd have to give up, sink down where I stood . . . MOVE it, I told my feet in them silly shoes. Take them off? No time. Had to run. It was no good, the place was a maze, if I tried running round the fire baskets it'd take all night – I had to jump over them . . .

Couldn't do it. Came to a halt, teetering. What if I jumped just as the detonator went off? All I could think was what Davey'd said when I first set off into the Starfish – *That'll warm your knickers.* I could feel a long, tight scream building up inside me. Had to do it, had to jump. Couldn't, couldn't.

Then RUN. I ran along the length of the fire basket, round the end of it, down the length of another one looking for the next gap. My ankle went over, I was on hands and knees with my nose an inch from the ironwork. I could smell the sawdust, the creosote and the oil on top. If it went up now I'd be a candle, a flaming head on a melting body, my eyes running down my cheeks as they seared and split . . .

I screamed, screamed again, and it was such a tiny sound in the immensity of the darkness. Had to get up. Had to get AWAY . . . I was clawing myself backwards away from the trough like an upended spider, legs tangling, and oh, God, the pain in my ankle, a deep sick-making pain but nothing, nothing like the pain of burning up would be.

There were arms under my arms, lifting me up. God, lift me up so I could float away, a flake of ash on the smoky wind spiralling upwards.

A red light flashed about fifty feet away.

'Sweet Jesus, what's that?'

'Railway signal light.' Davey's voice, close by my ear.

'Where did you come from?' Oh, the relief. Not to be alone.

'Never you mind. Can you put your weight on your ankle?'

'What's a railway signal light doing up here? Don't tell me I'm going to be made mincemeat by a train next?' I tried a step forward. Still sick-making, but possible, at a lurch. One shoe had come off, the strap torn on a piece of flint when I'd tried to crawl away from the trough. My leg was scraped and bleeding.

'Don't joke.' He knelt down, and his fingers fumbled with the ankle strap on my other shoe. 'Have to be quick. Now they've started switching on the decoy lights, fires'll be next.' Another light came on a few feet away. It looked for all the world like a carelessly blacked-out window, lamplight leaking through a gap in the curtains. All around us lights were winking out of the darkness. The ghost city was coming to life. Still not bright, had to be a city under blackout – but could easily have been Swindon railway yards.

'How do they do that? It's so real.'

257

'Film people designed it.' On his feet again, he yanked my arm. 'You got about fifty yards to go. Come on, run. No, you got to jump the troughs. No time to run the length.' He was pulling me towards the next fire basket.

'I can't.'

'You have to. Fifty yards, that's all.'

He was lying, I knew. Now the lights had come on I could see the extent of the ghost city. Had to be a couple of hundred yards at least, and four or five of the black iron troughs. We'd never do it in time . . .

We jumped the first. I ran fast as I could across the open space towards the next, him pounding beside me.

WHUMP.

A line of orange brightness in the dark over to our left.

'Oh, Jesus.' Davey's voice breathless, scared. 'They've started igniting the troughs. Come on, Frannie, run like you never run in your bleedin' life. Won't all go up at once, but won't be long.'

WHUMP. Another. Somebody was sobbing no no no. It was me. I jumped the next fire basket. Maybe three to go. There were lines of fire all over the site now. It looked like the ground was cracking open and letting loose the pit of hell.

WHOOMPH. One of the tanks had let go a gush of oil: flames shot up into the sky, no more than a hundred feet away. I could feel the heat on the side of my face like sunburn. Any second now the water would fall onto the blazing troughs too, and the night would explode.

'Jump.' Over the next. Then a bang, and brightness half blinding me. The next trough ahead had ignited. I stopped, looking desperately left and right for the easiest way through.

'You – still got to – jump it, Frannie.' Oily black smoke was drifting across the site, making it harder and harder to breathe. 'We're – all right till they start flushing more tanks.'

'We'll get burned.'

'Better – burned than fried. Don't – think – jump.' He took my hand. 'High – as you can.'

I soared. Ran. Soared. Terrible spitting crack split the night, a great shower of sparks, billowing clouds, a rain of smuts. One of the water towers had let go. As I ran on, somewhere in all this dreadful blatter, a different note, a low bass humming. The bombers were on their way. But we was out of the ghost city, beyond the reach of its starfish arms of fire.

'Davey?'

''S OK. My trouser leg caught fire.' He was limping across the grass, backlit by the flames, bending to rub at his calf. 'Stings like billy-o. You all right?'

'I'm *fine*.' I was too. Could hardly breathe, heart up high in my throat and revving like Mr Keiller's motorbike, but I was better than I ever been, before or since. I was *alive*.

As he came up to me, I took his hand again. 'Davey, boy, you're a bloomin' hero.'

'I'm an effing idiot, is what. Don't know that you deserve rescuing.'

Never worth pushing your luck. There were Germans in the sky. I ran ahead past the Nissen hut and down the path, hardly feeling its sharp stones under my bare feet. Didn't stop till I was in the car.

Seconds later Davey was in. Then we were off, bouncing and jolting. No time for three-point turns; better to go on ahead. The track twisted sharp downhill, under the ramparts of Barbury hillfort. Behind us the ack-ack started up. A searchlight beam swept the sky.

'Where does this go?'

'Quick way back to Wroughton.' The track was plunging steeply down. 'Levels out in a mo', then we're almost back where we started.' Farm buildings ahead on the left; a plantation of trees to the right.

'Stop. Please stop.'

'Not again.' All the same, he slowed.

'You wasn't anywhere near me when we saw Liddington burning, were you?'

He didn't say anything.

'You weren't in the Starfish at all, then, were you? You came back in to fetch me.'

'I was in the Starfish. Over the other side, though.'

'Liar. You wouldn't have been able to see it was Liddington if you had been. You'd gone right through the Starfish and out, and you was safe, but you ran all the way back through it to find me.'

'Think that if it makes you happy.'

I put a hand on the steering-wheel. 'I said, stop the car.' We drew to a halt at the end of the little wood, the steel on the roof clanking away. 'You're a damn bloody fool, Davey Fergusson. And you're off to kill yourself on Monday. Give us a kiss.'

A bit later he says: 'You sure about this, Fran?'

'Wouldn't be here if I wasn't.'

'Only . . .' He lets out a long, juddering sigh. 'You don't . . . have to.' Clear from the way he's breathing there's not much longer it'll be a choice. 'Oh, *God.*'

Then, a bit after that, he says, with his face in my hair, 'You're my first, you know. My first girl.'

I don't tell him he's not my first. That everything I know about what we're doing was taught me by Donald Cromley and his twisted uncle.

CHAPTER 28

'You look – different,' says Ed. 'And make it a latte.' He wanders off
to look at the cakes. If he's trying to make a point, I don't know what
it is. I'm not going to forgive him that easily.

Corey nudges me in the ribs. 'He only comes in on the days you're
here,' she hisses.

'Rubbish.'

'He's mad for you. Can't keep his eyes off you.'

Nonsense. Ed's eyes are undressing an organic flapjack. His hand
wavers over the biscuits. He makes a decision, and pushes his tray
back towards the till. 'You were blonde last week,' he says accusingly.

'Copper.'

'Well, different. This is . . . um. Need time to adjust to you dark.'
He counts out some coins, yawning. 'Sorry. Graham and I were out
first thing – and I mean first thing – dealing with a group of witches
from Bristol who wanted to dance skyclad on Silbury Hill for May
Day morning. Caught up with them as they were trying to climb over
the fence.' Ed's getting the hang of Avebury. 'Oh, and there's a bender
again in Tolemac. No sign of the occupant. We'll try again this evening,
and move him on politely.' He looks dubiously at his coffee, and digs
in his pocket for change. 'And if politely doesn't work . . .'

—*a windscreen exploding into crystals of glass*—

'Isn't much else you can do, is there?' I say nastily.

'Graham says politely will work,' says Ed, looking worried.

The bender's occupant comes to Avebury to worship the Goddess. He's
here for every one of the eight festivals, takes time off work and hitches

261

down from Cheshire. Man of few words, mind, so it took about half an hour to glean that much. Mostly we sat in companionable silence. I felt surprisingly easy with him.

'Saw you at the full-moon ritual,' he said, when I landed on his side of the fire. 'Which Path do you follow?'

'Um ...' I was mesmerized by his bare feet in the firelight. The ground was squelching, but they were astonishingly clean. 'Sort of ... eclectic, me. No special path. Bit of this, bit of that.' Thumbing in my memory through *The Bluffer's Guide to Paganism*.

'The Lady's my Path,' he said. 'Brid. I feel her here more than anywhere else.'

'Here at Avebury?'

'In this wood. And at her spring. You know where I mean?'

'Um ...'

'The Swallowhead. You ever been there?' I shook my head. 'I'll take you.'

He offered to roll a spliff. I shook my head again.

'You don't smoke?'

'No.' I hated seeing my mother stoned: that stupid giggling. When we camped in Tolemac, her laugh bounced off the trees at night as she and John sat at the campfire after I had been sent to my bunk in the van.

'It's good sleeping close to the stones,' he said. 'You feel how the Goddess uses the circle for healing.'

'Oh, no, it's a place of the dead.' Goddess knows why I felt bound to correct him. 'I've a friend who's an archaeologist. He says it's where people came to be with the ancestors. That's what the stones represent.' I felt no shame in embellishing Martin's tentative conclusions about the function of Avebury. 'A woman's skeleton was found in the ditch, laid in a ring of sarsen. Like she was the guardian of the place. Possibly a sacrifice.'

He shook his head in wonder. 'Didn't know that.'

We sat side by side, not saying much, the last of the rain dripping off the trees, his brown fleece hanging on a branch to dry in the gusty wind, his hair in damp ringlets. His skin glowed in the firelight. Eventually I stood up, stepped over the fire again and went home, not sure what had happened between us.

After clearing up in the café, I set off again for Tolemac, to warn Bryn he's about to be evicted from the wood. At least, my guess is he's the mysterious Bryn Kirkwood, whose signature was scrawled in a book on Gurdjieff: the bender is in the same place under the trees as the one there at equinox. Names never entered yesterday's conversation. Generous with information about the Goddess, he was sparing with what he revealed about himself. All I know is that he works on building sites, off and on, as a carpenter. Age, parentage, significant others: all a mystery. Not much small-talk, rather intense.

The bender's still there, its sheeting scattered with wild white cherry blossom. No sign of Bryn. He has secured it by weighting down the front flap with a row of stones, as if to say 'Private', the fire banked with turves, emitting a thin trickle of smoke. He told me he spends most days walking with the dog, looking for crop circles; never becomes tired because the energy they give off is *amazing*.

I hesitate, unsure what to do. Sometimes the pagans abandon tents for no clear reason. Graham would have no scruples about dismantling the bender and dumping Bryn's belongings in the skip.

. . . *a handful of withered wild flowers on damp leaf-mould, a smell of burning, clothing scattered, a pair of torn jeans hanging off the bough of a birch tree, like the aftermath of an air crash* . . .

At Greenham, the children screamed when the bailiffs came to evict the women camping there. Frannie threw our backpacks into someone's car just in time, but we lost Margaret's tent and the sleeping-bags.

Nothing I can do. I shouldn't get involved. I jog through the wood to the lane and climb back over the barbed wire. In the distance, someone is on the chalk track coming down from the Ridgeway, a dog racing ahead.

Then the dog's tangling with my legs, jumping up to plant muddy paws on my jacket.

'Hey, hey – what's his name?'

'Conan,' says Bryn, arriving in time to save me from being licked to death. The late-afternoon sun picks out golden lights in his caramel-coloured curls.

'The Barbarian?'

'No.' Not a flicker of amusement. 'Spelt C-y-n-o-n. Celtic name, means Divine Hound.'

'Right.' Spattered with mud and burrs, nose jammed in my crotch, Conan/Cynon looks about as divine as my left buttock. 'Glad I caught you. I came to warn you you're about to be evicted. The National Trust wardens are on their way.'

'Are they now?' He doesn't ask how I know this. 'Movin' on tomorrow, anyway. Goin' home to see my boy.'

'Your boy?'

'His mother and I aren't together. If I don't turn up for his birthday, day after tomorrow, she'll try and stop me seein' him altogether. Got my solicitor workin' on it, though. I could look after him better than her. She's all over the place.' He snaps his fingers to call Cynon, who is quivering ecstatically as he sniffs a pile of horse droppings, and starts strolling towards the wood. 'There's an amazin' crop circle appeared below Barbury. Like – spheres, with interlocking zigzags. Met a feller along the Ridgeway said it represented the diatonic scale of musical notes because that's the way aliens can communicate with us.'

'Wasn't that the plot of *Close Encounters*?'

Bryn looks blank. 'That the one set in the railway station? My foster-mother had it on video – made her cry every time.' He hooks two fingers into the dog's collar, to hold him safely as a vehicle comes trundling up the lane. 'Hey, said I'd take you to the Goddess's spring, didn't I? We could go now.'

The vehicle is a National Trust Land Rover.

'That's not such a good idea,' I say, as it parks on the verge by Tolemac. 'I think you're about to be evicted.'

'Dawn, then? Best time. It's *amazing*.'

I've no memory of agreeing to any such expedition. 'Hurry up. The wardens will pull down the bender.'

'I'll wait for you at the lay-by on the A4. Half past five, sunrise.'

He lopes off down the lane. Ed, on his own, climbs down from the Land Rover. Instead of following Bryn into the wood, he strides towards me. 'Who the fuck was that?'

'He's the one who's camping in the wood.'

'I'd worked that out. You never said you knew him. You could have mentioned it this morning, saved me the bother of coming out.' The lines by his mouth are chiselled more deeply than usual into his cheeks.

'Hardly your business who I know, is it?' I say, then regret it.

'No,' he says, turning and starting to walk back down the lane. 'You're right. None of my fucking business.'

I watch him climb over the fence into Tolemac to remonstrate with Bryn. As arses go, I'd say it's level pegging.

On the way home, I remember Frannie's social worker was calling in this afternoon. Frannie's watching television. There's a note on the hall table.

Ring me on my mobile. I think we should have your grandmother
at the Geriatric Psychiatric Day Centre for assessment.

Frannie looks up from *Neighbours*.
'How are you feeling?' I ask her.
'Fine.'
'What about Adele's visit?'
'Nosy.'
'What do you mean?'
'Kept wanting to know who the prime minister was. I told her, Smarm Bucket Blair, much good have he done us pensioners. And she must've asked three times what day of the week it was.'

'What did you tell her?' Holding my breath.

'Told her to look on the calendar in the kitchen.'

'She was playing with you,' I tell Adele on the phone. 'Being deliberately obstructive.'

'Well, I could see on the calendar that she marks off the days. So she clearly has some difficulty with short-term memory.'

'Maybe *I* mark off the calendar. OK, I admit, she does keep track so she knows she's taken her pills, but I have difficulty remembering which day it is, and I'm twenty-five.'

'India, you have to accept your grandmother finds it harder to cope than she used to. I did a couple of standard cognitive-function tests on her. Not a perfect diagnostic tool, but it gives us a yardstick. She did significantly worse today than she did six months ago. It's time we had a proper assessment done. I've booked her in for the first appointment I can get.'

Behind me, Fran calls from the lounge: 'Ind! Forgot to tell you, those buggerin' lights were there again last night, up on the hill.'

The sun hasn't yet lifted over Waden Hill as I make my way down the river path, wondering what on earth to do about Frannie. It's impossible to see *any* hill from her bedroom downstairs. Whatever she sees is in her dreams, which suggests she has trouble sorting what's real and what's not.

The early-morning light is pearly, and a white skirt of mist clings to Silbury. Cobwebs beaded with dew are strung across the path. Yesterday, May Day, there would have been people around, but this morning there's no one on the path, and hardly any early commuters on the A4. No sign of him in the lay-by. I wait a few minutes, scanning the road from Avebury, until I look behind me over the hedge and spot him making his way across the field, Cynon the dog racing ahead.

'I was expecting you from the other direction,' I say, going through the gate to meet them. 'What were you doing up that way?'

'Spent the night in the Long Barrow.' He tips back his battered trilby, and brushes ragged curls out of his eyes.

'That must have been spooky.' A five-thousand-year-old tomb isn't my idea of a cosy campsite.

He looks at me as if he doesn't understand what I'm talking about. 'It's beautiful there at night. So quiet.'

'So dark.'

'Not with candles. Come on, let's get to the spring before the world wakes up.' He sets out confidently across the field. 'We'll take the long way – less muddy.'

The sun has risen, and our shadows stretch ahead like long peg dolls. Bryn leads towards a plantation of trees clinging to the hillside below the Long Barrow. We skirt the top of the wood, then drop down into the trees, following what can barely be described as a path. He reaches out a hand to help me over a fallen branch. His fingers are dry and warm; he doesn't let go. It seems perfectly natural, like children holding hands.

'There she is,' he whispers.

'Who?' I peer through the tree-trunks for an animal: a deer, perhaps.

'The Goddess.'

There's a flash of blue, something winking in the sunlight. As we step out of the trees I see her, sitting under a willow by the sparkling water, legs tucked to one side, head slightly bent. She's the river-daughter, the naiad, the water nymph, iridescent as a dragonfly's wings, silver-haired, scaly-skinned. A shiver goes through me: she's beautiful and terrible, and watching me out of the corner of her eye.

A step further and she resolves into humbler parts: a shop dummy, with huge painted eyes, mosaic pieces of china and coloured glass glued all over her like fish scales, a tinsel wig stuck to her bald head. Something so urban ought to be grotesque, here in the middle of a wood with tiny green leaves unfurling overhead, and dog's mercury and celandines pushing through the leaf-mould at her feet, but instead the effect is graceful, magical. The tree above her is threaded with coloured ribbons.

'She's lovely,' I say. 'You didn't make her, did you?'

He shakes his head. 'Wish I had. It's a healing place, this.' Beyond the Goddess, a shallow brown pool trickles away in two streams, sunbeams striking dancing lights on the surface.

I'm still holding his hand. Embarrassed, I slip my fingers out of his grasp, sensing his reluctance to let go. 'Thank you,' I say.

'What for?'

'Bringing me here.'

'Are you going to make an offering?' Bryn digs in his pocket and brings out a scrap of silky blue material, perhaps part of a woman's scarf, and ties it round a willow branch. It's the kind of thing my mother would have done. When the fabric rots and falls away from the bough, so will sickness and hurt fall away too . . .

How Ed would scoff.

'For you,' Bryn says. 'Blue's your colour. Like hers.' He nods towards the Goddess.

'And for your boy?'

The smile lights up his whole face.

I stand on the stepping-stones that jut out into the pool, watching strands of weed ripple in the current. Coins glint in the water, half buried in silt. 'What's he called?'

'Fergus. Means "best warrior".'

'How old?'

'Five.' He bends to pick a celandine from the bank, and drops it onto the stream before joining me on the stepping-stones. It swirls lazily away in the direction of Silbury. 'I'm going to bring him here in the summer. We'll hitch down together, come for Solstice.'

'Won't he still be in school?'

'I'll bring him out. Educational, I reckon, to come to a place like this.'

'My mother brought me to Avebury when I was small,' I say. There are tiny fish in the water, hardly visible against the muddy bottom. Cynon is nosing around the edge of the wood, hoping for rabbits. I hunt for a twig to play Pooh sticks.

'Will you come for Solstice?' Bryn asks, unaware that I live here.

I shrug my shoulders and throw my twig into the stream before walking back across the stones to the bank. There are empty tea-light cases scattered around the Goddess's feet, and I automatically begin to pick them up, my hair as usual coming loose from its pins as I stoop to reach them.

'Hey, you shouldn't do that.' Bryn, from behind me.

'I was only tidying . . .'

'They're *offerings*. Leave them.'

'But they're finished.'

'Doesn't matter.' Not angry, but determined to get his way. He takes them out of my hand, and places them carefully back on the ground. Straightening up, he turns to face me. His eyes are clear blue, long-lashed. He brushes the hair off my face with careful fingers, and a thrill goes through me. 'You have lovely hair. Like chocolate.'

The Goddess is watching us, with calm, indifferent eyes. We're inches apart. What would that soft, sulky mouth taste like? But no, it would be like kissing a damaged flower.

'Thank you,' I say again, turning to the path that leads through the wood.

We part on the track to the Long Barrow.

'Have to get my stuff,' he says, jerking a thumb in the direction of the barrow. The megaliths ranked at one end jut up on the skyline, making it look like a sleeping dinosaur. He keeps looking steadily at me until I understand, too late, I'm meant to respond to an invitation.

'I'd better head . . . um, back where I'm staying,' I say. 'So . . . er, goodbye. Have a nice time with Fergus.'

'Goodbye,' he says. 'Goddess go with you.' He holds me with his eyes a moment longer, like he's memorizing the look of me, then sets off briskly up the hill, the dog at his heels. I walk back to the gate, and watch them until they eventually disappear between the tall stones guarding the entrance to the barrow, wondering what it is about him that still feels so hauntingly familiar.

PART FIVE

Earth Magic

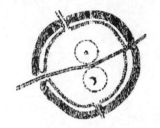

One of the ideas about ancient religion that gained currency in the 1930s was that of the Great Goddess, a female deity believed to be common to all primitive cultures, the embodiment of fertility so essential in agricultural societies, and the prototype for later divinities such as Demeter or Isis, or the triple goddesses of Celtic folklore – Maiden, Mother, Hag. Archaeologists produced as evidence big-bellied and breasted figurines from digs in the Near East; Margaret Murray's claims about witch cults and Robert Graves's book *The White Goddess* seemed to add body and blood to the theory.

Alas, like most simple and pleasing theories that claim to explain everything, it turned out to be wrong or, at least, unproven and unprovable. (Keiller was one of the first, incidentally, to debunk Murray's research into witch trials and prove that she had twisted the evidence to fit her thesis.) The big-bellied figurines may or may not have been goddesses. But the idea of the Goddess had caught the popular imagination, and has since proved difficult to shift, particularly among modern pagans.

Dr Martin Ekwall,
A Turning Circle: The Ritual Year at Avebury,
Hackpen Press

CHAPTER 29

1941

Mam was terrible thin when I went to see her and Dad in Devizes. I'd taken her eggs from the hens at the Lodge, and a bit of extra butter I'd laid hands on.

'You shouldn't have,' she said, with a weak smile. 'Keep 'em for yourself – you're a growing girl, Frances, you need 'em more 'n me.'

'I *should* have,' I said. 'Look at you, Mam. I swear there's less of you every time I come. Dad working you too hard, is he?'

'It's only the Change,' she said. 'Some women get fat, some thin down. I'm one of the scrawny old birds.'

She was barely thirty-nine. But I didn't understand then – or didn't want to know – how young that was for the menopause. It was a relief to have something to explain the way she looked.

'How's Davey?' she asked. 'And the village?' We'd finished Saturday tea and I was at the kitchen table while Mam dried the crocks. She wouldn't let me help, said I was a guest now, not a skivvy.

'Oh, Davey's doing fine,' I said. Letters came regular from Scotland, where he was in the thick of his navigation training. 'But I don't see much of anyone in Avebury. I'm hardly there, working long hours at the hospital. I'm thinking maybe I should find a room in Swindon. It'd be easier all round.' Especially now Davey was gone. There was no one to drive me home if I missed the last bus.

'Oh, don't do that,' said Mam. Her hand slipped, and a couple of spoons dropped with a clatter on the draining-board. 'I'd worry terrible about you in the air raids.'

'Swindon hasn't had much. I'd be safe as . . .' Well, no one could say houses were safe any more. But there'd been hardly any bombing there. Bristol was getting it bad night after night, and we all knew what was happening to London, but there was probably as much chance of a bomb landing on me in Avebury as there was in Swindon. More, maybe – the base at Yatesbury was only a mile or two off, and the countryside was full of dozens of little out-of-the-way airfields, as well as Starfish and Q-sites begging the bombers to dump on them. Still, I wasn't going to explain that to Mam: she worried enough as it was. I took out my cigarettes and looked round for an ashtray.

Mam wrinkled her nose. 'You want to do that, you go out and join your dad in the garden.' She peered out of the window at Dad, pink and perspiring, digging over the trench ready to sow his runner beans. The sky was full of massing grey clouds. She hung the tea-towel on the back of a chair and sat down with a sigh. 'I could do with closing my eyes for five minutes anyway. Have to put up with it in the shop, I suppose, but the smoke makes me sick as a dog, these days.'

Garden was hardly the word for the miserable sunless patch that lay behind the tobacconist's shop. Dad had done his best and dug up the lawn for a few rows of veg and some raspberry canes but, what with his tool shed and the Anderson shelter, there wasn't room for much. All the same, he spent what time he could out there, trying to coax green treasure out of the exhausted soil.

'Needs a bag or two of manure from the Manor,' he said, straightening up as I came out with my cigarette in my mouth like Bette Davis. 'Couldn't get your Mr K to drop some off, could you?'

The idea of Mr Keiller loading sacks of manure onto the back seat of his posh car was absurd enough to make me laugh, which was what Dad intended. 'No horses at the Manor now,' I said. 'If Davey was still here, I bet he could wheedle some from the stables where he used to work.'

'You heard from him yet?' asked Dad.

He'd sent me a poem, yesterday. A letter the day before that. And his photo, in his new air-crew uniform, lit like a glamour boy off the films: must've had it taken special. He'd been gone hardly a fortnight.

'He's a bit homesick,' I said. 'Scotland's a long way . . .'

Dad gave me one of those looks. He never said much, Dad, but he could convey paragraphs in a look. This look said: *Careful what you're doing, girl.* He'd heard what I hadn't said: *Scotland's a long way, but not far enough.* I knew I shouldn't have given Davey encouragement, that night after the Starfish, but I couldn't bring myself to write and dash his hopes all over again. All I could hope was that he would find himself a nice Scottish girl. I wanted Davey to be happy, but I wasn't the one to make him that way, and I didn't know how to tell him so. When he said he'd be looking for a posting south as soon as he was trained, I wrote back telling him that would be lovely, couldn't wait. Thinking to myself, the real action was along the east coast. That's where they'd send him, wouldn't they? And so he might be killed, and wouldn't it be better for him to die thinking I loved him back?

'I was lucky with your mother,' was all Dad said.

Waiting at the bus stop, it started to pour. I'd forgotten my umbrella. While I was struggling to hold my coat over my head, a black car came hushing through the puddles. It stopped twenty or so feet beyond me, and came reversing back.

'Get in before you drown.' Mr Keiller leaned across to open the passenger door.

He was in his police uniform. I sank into the leather seat, relishing the smell of cigarettes and hair oil.

'Where've you been hiding yourself, Heartbreaker?' he said. 'Haven't seen you for months.'

'The hospital keeps me busy, sir.'

'Not at weekends, surely. Come over to the Manor tomorrow afternoon. I've invited some chaps from the convalescent home. Delightful young men, all Scottish, pining for the sight of a pretty face.' No 'would you like' or 'please' about it. Mr Keiller always assumed everyone would fall in with his ideas. 'Put on a nice frock and turn up about half past three. Damn . . .'

Ahead, a soldier had stepped out into the road and was waving us to stop, to let a convoy of trucks out of the army barracks on the outskirts of town. Mr Keiller slowed the car and took out his battered old cigarette case. He could've afforded a brand new solid silver one but he always kept his Russian cigarettes in that old tin with the engraving worn right off. 'Smoke, Heartbreaker? We'll be crawling behind them for miles. Tell you what, let's take the pretty way.' He dropped the case in my lap, swung the wheel into a U-turn and we roared back the way we'd come, then branched off past the sports ground. It was a good straight road and Mr Keiller took it fast, but I felt completely safe as I lit cigarettes for both of us. Flat fields showing the green of young barley flashed past. We crossed the canal, speeding through tiny hamlets with the steep scarp of the Downs rising to our left, past isolated airfields, hangars turfed like long barrows, planes hidden under camouflage. There used to be a white horse carved into the chalk up there but, like the one at Hackpen, he'd been allowed to grow over in case the bombers used him as a landmark.

I sneaked a glance at Mr Keiller. His profile was as clean carved as ever, but his eyes, fixed on the road spooling out under our wheels, looked tired. I wanted to tell him how sorry I was for being young, that sometimes you behaved a certain way because you didn't know better, or thought it was expected of you.

Perhaps he sensed me looking; he turned his head and grinned. 'Speed doesn't bother you, Miss Robinson?'

'The faster the better,' I said. Ahead of us, a plane was banking to make its approach to the airfield at Alton Barnes.

'Training flight, I expect,' said Mr Keiller. 'Yes, it's an Avro. I took one of those up, in 'thirty-six. He's coming in a bit low.' The plane was dipping towards the field at right angles to the road. Mr Keiller pressed the accelerator down hard and the car leaped forward. 'We'll give him a run for his money.' We raced along the road on what seemed a collision course with the little biplane. Even I could tell it was far lower than it should have been. There was a smile on Mr Keiller's lips as he gunned the car along the road. 'Fast enough, Heartbreaker?'

I could hear the plane, an angry wasp. It was wobbling as it made its approach, the wings dipping and lifting as the pilot fought to keep it on line. Perhaps this was his first solo. Surely Mr Keiller would ease off the accelerator – the plane was low enough to catch the car with its undercarriage. But, no, he pushed the throttle even harder. The plane was huge now, bearing down on the car from our left. The wheels seemed level with my window. Raindrops streamed off the cockpit glass. I could see the pilot behind it, his goggles insect eyes under his leather helmet. Impossible to see an expression but I could sense panic in the movements of his head as he wrestled with the controls. I closed my eyes. The buzzing turned to thunder.

And then the thunder rolled away. I opened my eyes, let out my breath, and turned in my seat in time to see the plane cross the road behind us, wings swaying. He came down in the field on the other side of the road, his wheels bouncing right off the ground and the wings tilting alarmingly, a flock of sheep scattering before him, but somehow he brought the plane to a halt safely. There were at least two hedges between him and the airstrip.

'That'll teach him to keep his nose up,' said Mr Keiller, easing off the accelerator. 'And much as I'm enjoying it, you can let go my arm now, Heartbreaker.'

I wanted to impress him the next afternoon so I put on my favourite frock, the one I went dancing in, red polka dots on a cream background. Was it too formal for tea? But I didn't want to wear blouse and skirt, or either of my flowery summer dresses. The horse-chestnut candles were like gnawed corncobs now, and June not far off, but the sky hadn't got the message: the grey clouds were as heavy-bellied as fat ewes in February. So I put on the red polka dots – it was the Manor, after all, where they dressed like film stars – and a pair of red shoes I'd bought off one of the nurses at the hospital, to replace the ones I'd lost at the Starfish, then set out with my umbrella.

The tea party was held in the Great Hall, the biggest room in the Manor. Seven or eight young men in RAF uniform, their faces white and fragile, were sitting uneasily on sofas and dining chairs; a couple of crutches were propped against the wall. Mr Keiller was standing by the vast fireplace, china cup and saucer in his hand, holding forth about the visit of Queen Anne who'd had her dinner there hundreds of years ago. The young men were trying to look fascinated. There was no sign of Mrs Keiller.

'Heartbreaker! A sight for sore eyes,' said Mr K, as I came in. 'You've put your glad rags on. I'm sure these young chaps will appreciate it. Help yourself to a scone.' There was a teapot and crockery laid out on the dining-table, and two platters of scones, with dishes of jam. I filled a cup and plate for myself and sat down on the edge of one of the settees next to a young man who was biting his lip nervously.

'Aren't you having a scone?' I said cheerfully to him. He shook his head. I glanced down, and saw metal gleaming below his trouser turn-up: an artificial foot. 'Let me bring you one. They're delicious.'

'Honest, I don't want one,' he said, in a Glaswegian accent. He was a tall, solid lad, with strong features and thick dark hair swept back from a widow's peak. 'But you could fetch one for my pal.' Beyond him sat a blond boy with bandaged hands. He leaned forward and smiled at me.

'Jam?' I asked, putting my cup down on the side table – the tea was almost cold anyway.

'Just a bit o' marg.'

It was butter, of course, from one of the local farms. I halved two scones and spread a good thick layer on them. The dark-haired Glaswegian mouthed *knife*, and mimed cutting something up with a knife and fork, so I divided each of the halves again and took them back to the boys on the sofa. The Glaswegian fed his friend, a mouthful at a time, while the blond boy raised his eyebrows and winked at me. My own scone sat unfinished on the plate. Something in my throat was choking me, and I couldn't have swallowed to save my life. I could have asked what had happened to them, but their stories would have been like the others I heard on the wards: hands burned trying to heave a friend from a blazing cockpit, legs lost when the impact of a crash landing shunted a red-hot engine onto a lap.

The door swung open under its massive carved pediment. The latecomer sauntered into the room, another young man in air-force blue, this one the picture of health, wearing a pilot officer's chevrons.

It was Mr Cromley.

He caught up with me in the passage when I went to ask for another pot of tea. 'Hello, Heartbreaker.'

'I can manage,' I said. 'No need . . .'

'Every need.' He was laughing at me again. 'You were playing lady of the Manor so nicely. Doing good works. But you haven't quite the hang of it, have you? You shouldn't go yourself to tell Cook to put the kettle on.'

'I don't see what business . . .'

'Oh, and another thing. That dress. Lovely, I admit, but not the thing for tea-time.' Before I could stop him he'd run a finger over the curve of my breast. 'Nor the shoes.'

'Take your hands off me.' I was trembling.

'Don't be too proud, Heartbreaker. You might be grateful one of these days for what I can do for you.'

'Fuck off.' The men on the wards sometimes forgot themselves and used it, but I'd never said that word before.

'Well, well,' said Mr Cromley. 'Aren't you spirited, these days, Fran? But remember who and what made you that way.'

I was too angry to speak. I turned and clacked on my second-hand platforms down the passageway, tears leaking from my eyes. Mr Cromley didn't follow, and I told Cook it was the young men, so brave, poor things, so hurt, that made me cry.

What was he doing in Avebury? Last I'd heard he was in Kent, on a fighter base. I spent the rest of the afternoon talking as brightly as I could to the boy with burned hands and his pal, avoiding Mr Cromley's eye. But he was watching, all right. I could feel it in the prickle of my skin.

I wanted to leave, but he might follow, so I was determined to stick it out. I heard every story those boys could tell; I laughed at every one that needed a laugh; I touched their arms when they told me how they'd been hurt. They were bomber crew, both of them, one a gunner, the other a wireless op. I told them my feller was training in navigation, up in Scotland; maybe one day he'd be posted to their squadron. Did they have sweethearts? The blond boy shook his head, and raised an eyebrow hopefully. The tall tin-footed lad blushed, and said he missed his special girl back home.

Mr Cromley was bored. He was fidgeting next to Mr K on the other side of the room, like his faithful dog, but where Mr K was all gracious-ness and easy chat – he loved planes, and he could talk flying for hours – Mr Cromley was sullen and superior. I used to think of him as charming, but now I could see through that front. He left after about three-quarters of an hour.

Mr Keiller was about to move on to the next group of airmen, so I made my excuses to the boys, stood up and put my hand on his arm. 'You didn't tell me Mr Cromley was coming.'

'Didn't I? I meant to. Awfully good news he's back, isn't it? I've always liked young Donald. I was worried he'd be killed – a terrible loss to archaeology. Odds aren't good for the fighter boys, but he's done his tour of duty and lived, and won a DFC – his squadron shot down thirty-seven Hun in a single day during the Battle of Britain – so they've given him a cushy posting as a rest.'

'Where's he stationed?'

'Didn't he tell you? He's flying trainee wireless ops at Yatesbury before he rejoins his squadron. If I were five years younger . . .' Mr K grinned ruefully. 'Well, maybe ten. He's living in the caravan park behind Rawlins's garage with a lot of other chaps from the base.'

I sat through another half-hour, jaw aching with my clenched smile, then made my excuses and left. The clouds were blowing away and there was blue in the sky as I walked down the Manor drive, the breeze wrapping my silly silky dress round my legs, scared half to death he'd be waiting for me. But he wasn't. He was a lot cleverer than that.

CHAPTER 30

Avebury has become an Ed-free zone. There is no sign of him for most of May, and the start of June.

'What did you do to him?' asks Corey, adding another layer of shine to the countertop. 'He's not been in for coffee for weeks.'

'I don't know.'

Don't like to admit it, but I miss the clunk of those stupid cowboy boots on the cobbles outside the café. I'm regretting the way I blanked him after our argument. Perhaps what he was asking wasn't so very terrible after all. Or, at least, it's understandable he'd want to do anything to avoid losing his pilot's licence. When I catch sight of Graham, unloading bin-bags from the back of the Land Rover, I ask him what's happened to Ed.

He taps the side of his nose mysteriously. 'Personal business, I guess.'

'He's working on his dissertation for the MA,' says Michael, *en route* to the museum. 'On archaeology from the air. He's been helping with a Lidar survey of Savernake Forest.'

'Wow,' I say, little the wiser. Later, I look it up – laser photography that penetrates tree cover and can detect earthworks.

Meanwhile, with the academic year almost over, the film crew are back and Martin has taken up residence again in the cottage the Trust have lent him. He seems quieter and more distant, disappearing at frequent intervals to Bath. Permission has at last been granted to raise a stone. Although Martin's favoured option was to lift the Bonking Stone, local opinion was against the idea, and instead the excavation will focus on a buried one, in the untouched northern part of the circle. Nobody seems to remember that it was my idea.

By mid-June Martin's archaeology students have finished exams and arrive, pale and slightly twitching, to start the dig. The men whip off their shirts to make up for lost tanning time. The girls are all thinner than me and wear shorts to display sleek thighs. Graham decides it's an opportune moment to repair the pathway and starts to spend most of his time on the henge banks, trundling barrowloads of gleaming chalk, with his shirt off too. Two days later, Ed's with him.

'You've spent at least as much time watching him prowl the banks as you have filming,' says Martin, coming up to stand beside me at the lip of the deepening trench. He's lost weight; under the beard, his cheeks have hollowed. 'Don't play games, petal. If you like him, let him know. Life's too short.'

'I don't mean it to be games,' I say. 'But how do you tell, Martin? Suppose you *never* have dreams about a Brushwood Boy. Maybe all you're feeling is . . . just about shagging.'

Martin's face has that closed-down look again. 'No point asking me. I'm one of the bloody dreamers.'

The team has been excavating for a couple of days now, Harry and I wielding cameras. First, the skin of turf has been peeled away over an area the size of a small living room. Now the students are chipping away layer by layer at the soil. They're a metre down, and still haven't reached the stone. One of the men – rangy, bearded, bright red sunburn – holds up a fragment of something. Martin leans down and takes it from him. 'Clay pipe,' he says. 'Seventeenth century, I'd say. Bag it, Reuben.'

'Boring, then,' I suggest.

'*No.*' Martin brightens as soon as the subject is archaeology. He pretends to tear out handfuls of hair. 'Why can't television people ever get it into their thick heads that the past isn't about frozen moments, it's about layers and continuities? That was Keiller's mistake. He was only interested in prehistoric Avebury, so it didn't strike him as vandalism to wipe out the later settlement that grew up within the circle. How's your grandmother, by the way?'

'Fine,' I say, watching Ed set down the wheelbarrow on the bank and strip off his shirt. 'Look, he's flaunting himself.'

Martin sighs. 'Petal, he's hot.'

'I know.'

'And stop being jealous of the students. One of them's engaged to Reuben, and the other two are lesbians.'

'He'd think of that as a challenge,' I say gloomily. 'When are they going to uncover the stone?'

'Patience,' says Martin. 'Serious archaeology cannot be rushed.'

'It has to be when it's Solstice next week.'

Michael has insisted that all digging be suspended for the Solstice period, when the campsite and the village fill with pagans. He arrives on site shortly after Martin's friend Kit, who is some kind of engineer, to discuss how the stone can be lifted.

The upper surface has been revealed. It's massive, nearly three metres long, diamond-shaped, buried in a pit cut exactly to fit its shape.

'Like . . . a coffin,' says Ibby. 'Like it was alive, but now it's dead.'

'Or sleeping,' says Martin. 'One line of thinking is that the stones represent the ancestors. More than represent, perhaps – they're the physical embodiment of them. They have to be enclosed within the earthen banks of the circle to prevent their ghosts wandering. So when the later inhabitants of the village at Avebury start to bury stones, are they making sure the spirits sleep even more soundly?'

'Interesting,' says Michael. 'How long will it take to lift?'

Kit shrugs her shoulders. She's a petite woman, in her late thirties or early forties, with dark hair in a spiky cut. 'We're aiming to use the same techniques as the people who first put it here,' she says. 'So no modern ropes or pulleys. The students will plait hawsers from honeysuckle, which is the kind of material they might have used. Could take a few more days to finish that and wedge it upright in its original socket. Afterwards we'll bring in modern gear and mix up a nice safe concrete base to hold it in place. No wandering ghosts, I promise.'

'You have until Friday,' says Michael. 'Then you have to be off site.

Solstice is the middle of next week, but people start arriving at the weekend. If you haven't finished that afternoon, you'll have to make the area safe and cordon it off. Ed and Graham will help.'

'We'll be done by then,' says Kit, confidently. 'Promise.'

CHAPTER 31

On Thursday morning, Adele and the social worker from the Geriatric Psychiatric Unit turn up at nine sharp to collect Frannie. The new social worker is called Bob. He's in shorts. Frannie catches one glimpse of his thick white legs, covered with gingerish fur, and takes against him.

'Okey-dokey, Frances,' he says, in the jolly tone that men of his age – not much older than me, that is – reserve for elderly ladies.

'I think she'd prefer to be called Mrs Robinson,' says Adele.

'I would have called you that but I was afraid you'd have the pants off a young chap like me.'

Adele's eyes roll heavenwards. As Bob helps Frannie into the back seat of the car, she jabs a finger towards her mouth and mimes retching.

'Mrs Robinson, you know?' Bob continues, oblivious. 'Like in the film with Dustin Hoffman?'

'No need to be fresh,' says Frannie. 'Thought all you social-work boys were poufs anyway. Where are we going?' she asks, under Bob's helping arm, as she sinks arthritically onto the back seat.

'You're going to the day centre,' says Adele. 'Remember? We did discuss it.'

'What for?'

'To make new friends,' says Bob, brightly.

'Got plenty of friends here,' mutters Frannie. 'Nancy-boy.'

Adele, a small dark woman whose eyebrows meet in the middle, clamps writhing lips shut to prevent a giggle escaping. Bob's jovial expression has not shifted one millimetre. Perhaps it rolls off him, though he shuts the door with a little more force than necessary.

Click: like a police car, the rear seat of his is fitted with childproof locks. Frannie's imploring eyes meet mine.

'Have a nice time,' I say helplessly.

The stone should have been raised today, but an emergency in the underground quarries where Kit usually works has called her away. Instead the morning is spent filming students plaiting yet more ropes from strands of tough, woody honeysuckle, and cutting timber props with bronze axes.

'Can't we lift the stone without her?' asks Ibby. 'Don't get me wrong, what you're doing is art, Martin, but if I see one more shot of a honeysuckle rope I'm going to strangle someone with it. Or brain them with a bronze axehead.'

'Sorry.' Martin is unrepentant. 'Can't be done, unless you want to film squashed students. Wouldn't trust myself to supervise without Kit around.'

By late morning, there is still no Kit. The students are given a half-day off, and the film crew set up outside the Manor instead, on the paved pathway between two beds of fragrant lavender. Martin is explaining to camera that Keiller lived under this historic roof, when my phone rings.

Ibby shoots me a withering look.

'Sorry, sorry,' I say. 'Forgot to turn it off. Wasn't expecting it to work here.'

Martin tries to pretend he doesn't care, but such is the perversity of mobiles at Avebury that I've wrecked what would have been a perfect take.

'You might as well answer it now,' says Ibby. 'Harry, you ready for a tape change?'

I retrieve the phone from my jeans pocket.

'I've been trying you for ages,' complains Michael. 'Is Martin with you? Something I want him to take a look at.'

Martin's doing his actor bit, striding up and down waving his hands and repeating the lines of the piece to camera to fix them in his head. His face goes still and blank as he puts the phone to his ear. 'Right,' he says, after a minute. 'Yes, I'd be delighted.' There's a twinkle in his eye.

'Martin!' Ibby and Harry have finished conferring. 'We need to crack on.'

'OK,' says Martin. 'We'll head up there when we're done.' He peers at my phone, ostentatiously turns it off, and slides it closed.

'What was all that about?' I ask.

'Tell you in a minute.' He grins. 'My favourite kind of archaeology. Poking around in mysterious holes.'

The afternoon sky has turned grey by the time we set out for Windmill Hill, and a sprinkle of rain dampens the air. Ed drives us in the Land Rover, parking at the top of the track. Martin unfolds a natty little rambler's stick.

Ibby was singularly unimpressed when we explained what Michael wanted.

'So all we're talking about basically is a hole in the ground? And not a terribly big one?'

'With animal bone and flints,' said Martin.

Ibby's face showed what she thought of that.

'Think I'll stick to Plan A,' she said dismissively. 'The crew and I will take the Steadi-cam to the Avenue. India can take the smaller camera and film anything . . . interesting in this hole.'

The gate onto the hilltop is padlocked. Ed climbs over, then notices me struggling with the camera bag. This afternoon is the first time we've been in talking distance since his return to Avebury. 'You want a hand with that, India?'

'I can manage.'

'Wasn't implying you couldn't.' He takes the bag, then offers his arm to help me down. His hand is warm and dry, the palm roughened by his weeks as a warden. Outdoor life suits him: today he looks better than I've seen him since last summer. The cowboy boots have gone, replaced by a pair of hiking boots, his skin is tanned, and he seems relaxed. He gives me a smile and I feel suddenly shy, wishing I were as lithe and confident as the golden-limbed students in shorts.

'You know where we're going?' asks Martin, jumping down after me.

'Somewhere near the top end of the wood.' As Ed turns to point the direction, the light reveals faint lines of strain around his eyes. Not so relaxed, after all. 'This morning a woman walking her dog found recent digging under the trees and rang the estate office. She was vague about the exact spot.'

'*Is* it exciting?' I ask.

'Possibly.' Martin adjusts the strap of his leather satchel across his body. As we stride across the open hilltop, the first of the round barrows dotting its crown pops into view like a green pimple. 'See, those are Bronze Age, but the occupation of Windmill Hill goes back much further, even before the stone circle. All the lower humps and bumps aren't natural features: they're older banks and ditches, forming what archaeologists call a causewayed enclosure. Probably a meeting place with ritual use.' He waves at some shallow undulations in the field. 'It shows up better from the air. This was where Keiller found Charlie's skeleton, in one of the ditches, on his first dig in the Avebury area in the 1920s – the Marconi Company wanted to put a radio mast on the hill, and he led a campaign to prevent it. But he didn't excavate the slope on the far side so we've no idea what's under the trees.'

'Of course,' says Ed, 'you have to ask yourself how the hole the dogwalker found got there. That's what's bothering Michael.'

'What do you mean?'

'Nighthawks.'

'Sorry?'

'Metal detectorists,' says Martin. 'The illegal sort. Meaning they don't bother to ask the landowner's permission, and they don't declare what they find. They'd be interested in Bronze Age barrows: chieftains, grave goods, swords, jewellery, maybe gold.'

'There's treasure up here?'

'Well, probably not. The barrows were excavated long ago: gentleman archaeologists and nineteenth century vicars plundered the lot. But nighthawks'll still scavenge for anything that might have been missed.' Martin glowers. 'I spotted a hole in the side of one of the Hedgehogs last week.'

'Meaning someone found something?'

'Meaning someone dug a hole in the side of a scheduled ancient monument. If they did lift anything valuable out of it, it'll be on eBay by now. Bloody *thieves*.'

'You really don't like them, do you?'

'"Nighthawks" makes them sound far too sexy,' says Martin. 'Dung beetles would be better.' He spreads a molehill with his foot and crouches to peer at the soil.

'Um . . .' says Ed.

'That's different. The mole did the digging and, anyway, I'm a professional.' He peers at the earth, picks up a flint pebble and sighs, drops it back, then straightens up, looking towards the trees. 'I'm always hopeful I'll find an arrowhead Keiller missed.'

John says you don't find arrowheads, they find you. He has half a dozen or more at his cottage. But I don't mention this in case Martin says they ought to be handed over to a museum.

'How are we going to tackle it?' says Ed, as we reach the trees. 'You take the bottom while India and I work our way along the top?'

Martin scrambles down the hillside, and Ed and I walk slowly along the top edge of the wood. The stone circle and Big Avebury, a mile away, are hidden among foliage, but the church tower lifts above the green canopy and, further on, I can make out the houses at Trusloe.

Lights, buggerin' lights

'If there were metal detectorists here at night, they'd be using torches, right?' I ask, wondering if that was what Frannie saw from her bedroom window.

'I suppose so.' Ed steps carefully over a dead crow. 'For Chrissake, don't tell Martin, but I used to own a metal detector.'

'Ed. Is there no end to your iniquities?'

'I was still at school. My proudest find was a Civil War musket ball.

At least, that's what I told people it was. For all I knew then, it could have been a modern ball-bearing.' When he flashes that conspiratorial bad-boy smile, he's almost unbearably sexy.

'Ed! Indy!'

Martin has come to a halt below us.

'You found something?' shouts Ed.

'Looks like it.'

Ed waits for me to clamber over the wire fence, then follows me down the slope through the trees towards Martin's red anorak. He's at the bottom of a steep bank, a metre or so high, using his stick to probe between the gnarled roots of an old beech.

'*Not* nighthawks, then?' I sling the camera bag over a bush, and jump down to join him.

'Careful, petal. Don't want to cause any more damage.'

The hole is impressive. Or, rather, holes, plural – I almost fell into another. Two burrow sideways into the crumbling soil of the slope: the largest, framed by tree roots, is wide enough to admit an Alsatian. A third cavity, smaller, is sunk into the plateau near the lip of the bank. All three have disgorged spoil heaps of fresh earth, mixed with dead bracken and grass.

'That's a relief,' says Martin. 'Definitely not nighthawks. Badgers, bless 'em – too big for rabbits. My guess is this will be the work of a young male who's been kicked out of the main sett, striking out on his own. There was probably an entrance to an abandoned outlier here, stopped up years ago by foxhunters. But the soil's soft, and this lad's dug it out again to reoccupy it.' He pulls a trowel out of his satchel, and scrapes at the bank further along. 'Very soft, in fact. Badgers are lazy buggers. They prefer places where something or someone has already done the hard work. Could be only the tree roots that have loosened the soil, but I'm inclined to think there was some sort of earthwork here.'

'Lend us your trowel, will you?' says Ed, looking at the nearest spoil heap. 'Ind, why don't you do the honours? There . . .'

He passes the trowel to me. Delicately, I flip over a clump of dried-out bracken. Under it, shining greyish-white in the dull light filtering through the trees, is a perfect, leaf-shaped flint arrowhead.

Magic.

By the time Ed's phone rings, we've amassed a small pile of finds.

'Did you locate it?' comes Michael's voice, loud enough for us all to hear. 'What've you got?'

'Loads of stuff,' says Ed. 'I'll pass you over to Martin.'

'Animal bone, mostly,' Martin tells him. 'Probably pig, but I'm no expert. There's even a couple of tiddly bits that *could* be human, small bones, finger or foot, but this really isn't my field. Some of the bone's charred, but not all. Worked flint, including a pretty little arrowhead that's definitely Neolithic. At the least I reckon there could be a hearth site. Needs a proper dig because what we've picked up is a real jumble, obviously, having come out of a badger sett, but—'

Michael's 'What?' explodes out of the phone.

Martin winces, holding the handset away from his ear. 'Well, what did you think it was going to be?' he asks, when he can get a word in. 'Come on, Michael, you can't be serious nighthawks would've been preferable . . . OK. Right . . . No, we only touched the spoil heap. We'll leave it and come back.'

'What's the problem?' asks Ed, as he hands back the phone.

Martin sighs. 'I never paid enough attention to law. Michael has reminded me the badger is one of the most protected species in the British Isles. It's illegal to damage any part of a badger sett that's in current use. *Might* be possible to get a licence to dig, on the basis that it's so close to a scheduled ancient monument, but Michael isn't sure. He thinks it's probably too far down the hill.'

Before we leave, I borrow Martin's torch to lie flat on my belly and peer into the hole under the tree roots.

'And before you ask, no, I won't let you have the stick to poke about inside,' he says. 'We've probably earned ourselves about four hundred years apiece in prison just for shining a torch up there.'

Ed pats my bottom. 'Come on up. There's nothing else we can do today.'

'So what *are* you going to do?' I ask, clambering to my feet and brushing bits of bracken off my trousers.

'Well, Michael will want to get the curator involved, and English Heritage, and God knows who else,' says Martin. 'But I'll make the point we should apply for a licence to dig, and soon, though almost certainly too late to be part of Ibby's TV programme . . . What's the matter, petal?'

'Oh, God.' I scramble up the slope to where I left the camera bag. 'I didn't film *any* of it.'

When I return home, John's battered pickup is parked outside the house. The front door opens before I'm halfway up the path. 'It's OK,' he says. 'I wanted to reassure you she—'

'Reassure me about *what*?'

'Sssh. She's asleep.'

It's a quarter past four. 'How long's she been home? She shouldn't have been back until five. And why are you here?'

'Come into the kitchen. Adele did try to reach you but your phone was off.'

'I was filming, most of the day.' I follow him through the hallway past Frannie's closed door. 'Why didn't she leave a message? What's been going on?'

John shuts the kitchen door behind us. There's a bottle of wine open on the table. He pours us both a glass.

'She was . . . difficult at the day centre. They called me to fetch her home.'

'What do you mean?' It sounds like the title of a song – Geriatric Punk, 'Difficult At The Day Centre'. But in all fairness, I could see the portents this morning through the car window.

'Someone seems to have thought it was a good idea to get her to cut out paper tulips. Frannie couldn't see the point.'

'Frankly, neither can I.'

'According to the wally I met, it's a normal part of the assessment procedure.'

'Assessing *what*, for Christ's sake? She's arthritic in her right wrist, it's almost impossible for her to use scissors with any degree of dexterity—'

'Indy, don't get angry with me. Sit down.'

'I'm not angry with you, I—' I am angry with myself, though, for letting them take her to the day centre and allow her to be humiliated. I glare out of the window, over a pile of breakfast plates, still in the sink. Feel like I betrayed her. The garden's a mess too. There are more molehills. Ought to have mown the lawn weeks ago.

'She told them she wanted to go home. They said there was no one free to take her. Then they left her to her own devices while they were getting ready to serve lunch, and she wandered off. Somehow they lost track of her until she started screaming the place down, according to the wally. Not sure I entirely believe his version. She seemed perfectly calm when I got there.'

Hysteria isn't Frannie's style. 'I'm going to ring Adele,' I say.

'She'll have gone home by now.' Having worked briefly in social care, John doesn't have a high opinion of the system; according to my watch, it's only twenty-five past four. The pipes start to rumble as the downstairs loo flushes.

'Uh-oh,' says John. 'Frannie's up and about. Maybe you should ask for her version first.'

'Didn't she tell you anything on the way home?'

'Not a word, apart from how buggerin' stupid it was having to cut out paper tulips.'

I open the kitchen door at the same time as the cloakroom door opens. Frannie spots me, tries to retreat.

'Hey,' I say, before she can. 'What've *you* been up to?'

'Forgot to pull the chain.'

'You didn't – I heard the flush go. What happened at the day centre?'

'Buggerin' tulips. Like we was at nursery school. What's the point of that? I'm not a basket case.'

'Was that it?'

'In't that enough?'

'I thought something else must have upset you. They told John you were screaming.'

'Social workers are bloody liars. Might've got a bit heated, tellin' em to take me home. Didn't scream, as such.'

'And that was it, then? You wanted to go home because of the tulips?'

'Nothin' there for me. All *old* people. Load of old men with dribble down their jumpers playing cards, old women staring into space. Not even a decent newspaper to read, only the *Star*, and somebody'd filled in the quick crossword with a load of gobbledegook words.' Her eyes are sliding away from mine towards the half-open bedroom door. 'I'm tired, India. Let me go back to bed.' There's a plaintive crack in her voice.

'Go on, then.'

I watch her shuffle into her room. Before she closes the door, she peers out and gives me an apologetic smile. For a moment her face is lit with the ghost of the old Frannie. 'Lysol, cabbage and pee,' she says. She watches my face for a reaction. Clearly this is supposed to mean something, but I haven't a clue what. 'Sorry,' she adds, looking disappointed. 'Don't mean to be a trouble.' Her refrain.

There's a choking feeling in my chest. The tap thunders in the kitchen sink as John tackles the washing-up. The letter from Social Services, with Adele's telephone number, must be somewhere . . . It's on the dining-table along with the gas bill, which I've forgotten to pay.

The switchboard answers immediately, but Adele is not in her office. While I'm waiting for them to track her down, I plug the mini-DV camera into the television so I can play back the film shot this afternoon, belatedly, of the badger sett on Windmill Hill. Martin refused to dig into the spoil heap again – 'Sorry, petal, not even in the interests of reconstructive telly' – so I made do with wide shots, and a piece to camera as he crouched by the side of a yawning hole under the tree roots.

John sticks his head round the door. 'I'm off . . . sorry, didn't realize you were on the phone.'

'It's OK. Thanks for everything.'

'Would stop, but I've a client due in twenty minutes . . .'

'Adele Kostunic,' comes a voice in my ear. I wave goodbye to John, who is backing out of the room.

'I thought you'd phone,' Adele says, when I tell her who's calling.

'So what happened?' I ask.

'Can't get to the bottom of it – I wasn't there at the time. I gather Frannie took against—'

'I know about the tulips.' On the television screen, a close-up of the mouth of the badger sett wavers in and out of focus. 'But was there anything else that upset her?'

'I don't know,' says Adele. 'Bob reckons she'd wandered off into the other room. Which is fine – we encourage them to amuse themselves. Then suddenly she's screaming her head off.'

'Shouldn't Bob should have been keeping more of an eye on her? Wasn't assessment the whole *point* of today? Besides, she says she didn't scream.'

'Well, I know for a fact she did because I heard it. I was in an office down the corridor – it was that loud.'

On the rushes, Martin begins his piece to camera. 'What did happen at Avebury, five thousand years ago?' I grope for the remote to turn down the volume. 'This badger sett, on the slopes of Windmill Hill, could hold some of the answers . . . no, dammit, start again—'

'Frannie isn't a screamer,' I say into the phone. 'She'd become angry and shout, perhaps – though she's far too polite to do that among strangers. But she'd never scream. Not unless something really bad happened. Have you asked the other old people what they saw?'

'It's a geriatric psychiatric centre. Most of them are confused.'

'She says there were old men in there playing cards. They can't be that doo-lally . . .'

'"Doo-lally",' says Adele, sternly, 'is not a term we use.'

'So how did people live here in the past?' The piece to camera blares out again.

'Sorry,' I say. 'Need to turn the telly down . . .'

'This badger sett, on the slopes of Windmill Hill, is about to give up some of its secrets . . .'

There's a strange noise on the tape: a thin, high, breathy keening sound.

'India, have you considered the possibility that your grandmother has been concealing from you how disturbed she is . . .'

'In the spoil heap, dug out by a young badger searching for somewhere to live, ancient flint and bone . . .'

'Sorry, what did you say?'

A movement reflected on the TV screen, a white flicker like a ghost, makes me glance over my shoulder. Frannie is standing in the doorway, transfixed by the picture on the screen, tears running down her cheeks. If there was more breath behind the sound she's making, you'd call it screaming. Screaming that comes out like a whisper.

CHAPTER 32

1941

Lysol, cabbage and pee: the hospital always has the same smell, winter or summer. In the almoner's office we giggle about it, tell each other if we had a music-hall act that's what we'd call ourselves. After a bit, the names get transferred to three of the young housemen, who we reckon are a bit bumptious even for junior doctors. Lysol's tall and dark, with arched eyebrows and flaring nostrils and a posh voice. Cabbage is round and jolly, a Scouser, but turns nasty if the nurses don't jump to it. Scholarship boy, they sneer behind his back, like they can't forgive him for being poor and clever. And Pee is what my dad would have called a long streak of dripping, skinny and stoop-shouldered with glasses, pockmarked skin like he never ate a fresh vegetable in his life.

It was Cabbage I saw in the day centre, his skin all loose and folding now like wet cheesecloth, but no mistaking that stocky barrel chest and whiny, sneering Liverpool voice. He was clutching his cards like someone was going to snatch them off him, and his glasses were held together with a piece of grubby sticking plaster. But it was Cabbage all right, Cabbage who could maybe take a guess at what those buggerin' lights are looking for on the hill, if he put his confused old mind to it.

He was always kind to me, but still I'm blowed if I want him to see me, here, now, and start reminiscing about what's past and done. Never know but what he might turn poison, writing letters like that old bitch from Berwick Bassett that used to be the housemaid at the Manor, spying on me the night Mr Cromley made me go masked into the garden. I backs out of the room slow and careful, like. Then I'm standing in the corridor with its shiny green lino, and the smell of gravy floating down it from the dining room, and I think, Was it Cabbage, really? Or is it only the smell makes me think of him?

That makes me feel all panicky and sick, because suddenly I'm in that place where I don't know any longer when it is, where all the pathways of time meet and cross and twist round on each other, like the moonlit gravel paths between the box hedges in the Manor garden, and I think of Mr Keiller holding the chalky white thing aloft, and the Barber Surgeon's bones smashed to smithereens in the Blitz but somehow whole again, and my torn drawing of him uncrumpling itself, and his eyeless sockets looking up at me from where he'd been hidden all them centuries under the big stone. I thinks, The truth will out in the end. What lies under stone don't lie there for ever.

And then I realize my hands are over my eyes and my mouth is wide open and my throat hurts, and that gay-boy social worker is trying to shush me. I in't having none of it. Maybe if I shout loud enough, nobody'll hear what Cabbage has to say. Because it's rubbish, in't it? It's all old rubbish. Rubbish that has to be hid away where no one can see it. La la la. I can't hear you, no one can hear you. None of it happened, after all. If I go far enough back I'll lose meself and none of it will happen. La la la. Someone grabs my shoulders and starts to shake me, la la la, so my teeth clash together and I'm afraid my plate will fall out, then there's footsteps down the corridor and Adele, the one thinks I don't remember her name but I do, is saying:

'What the *hell* do you think you're doing, Bob?'

CHAPTER 33

'I can't do this,' I tell John. 'I'm not capable – or qualified, for God's sake. I don't understand what's happening to her . . .'

'I'll come over,' he says. 'I'll get rid of my client—'

'Oh, sorry, I'd forgotten. Shouldn't have rung you. Why didn't you let it go to answering machine?'

'Call it shaman's instinct.'

'Don't cancel your client. Frannie's back in bed, anyway.' The bedroom door is firmly closed. I feel like putting a bolt on the outside of it, but I know that's not the answer.

'You're filming again tomorrow, aren't you? I'll be over first thing. Leave it to me to ring Adele and sort this.'

'I can manage, really . . .'

'No, Indy, you can't. Not on your own—' He breaks off. There's a silence.

'Oh, bollocks,' I say. 'I can't let her be put into a home, John. She'd turn her face to the wall and die.'

In the night it rains again. I hear it lashing the windows, imagine it running in hissing rivulets down the slope where we found the badgers' sett, eroding the spoil heaps and washing away the bone and flint. Undermining the sett itself until it crumbles, melts down the bank and there's nothing there.

I climb out of bed and peer through the streaming glass. Lights flash on the hill, bobbing and weaving to and fro. Nighthawks, searching for treasure under cover of the rain? The ghosts of Neolithic farmers?

299

Or was that part a dream?

At any rate, it was a disturbed night, lying awake mithering, as John would call it. Worrying what to do about Frannie. I'm afraid she's becoming too confused to look after herself, but it's no exaggeration to say putting her in a home would kill her. *Old folks wither in them places like rows of dead runner beans*, she says. *Rot from the inside.* I couldn't do that to her.

Mithering, too, about other stuff, Ed and piles of paper that keep growing, letters that come in bank envelopes and tell me I owe thousands of pounds, bank statements that are endless columns of numbers, changing faster and faster until they become a flickering blur, streams of numbers running down the windowpane, streams of numbers bubbling down a hillside, pouring into stone pits in the circle, dark holes under the trees, mud slides of numbers, fragments of paper and bone, the dark thud of helicopter vanes overhead, whirlwinds of letters that make no sense, old photographs that fade and grow unfocused, Alexander Keiller smiling like a Cheshire cat at the camera, the water dissolving his face into a mask of carved bone, nothing left of his essence but the grin, a grin that wavers and becomes a ripple on water, water making everything sodden and unreadable, water that explodes into fragments of glass and fire under the trees . . .

Then I'm awake again and a miserable damp Friday dawn is bleaching the curtains.

In spite of Kit's promise to finish before Solstice, this is the last day we can work before the masses start to arrive, and it's clear to everyone the stone won't be cemented in place by the end of the afternoon. The megalith is fully uncovered, lying in its pit under a heavy sky, but at two o'clock the students still haven't finished trussing the sarsen with honeysuckle ropes to Kit's satisfaction.

'Look at the size of him,' says Ibby, admiringly, as Harry pans along the side of the stone where a brawny lad in shorts is tugging away on the Neolithic equivalent of a reef knot.

'Her,' says Martin. 'Assuming you mean the stone. This would be what Keiller categorized as a Type B, lozenge-shaped rather than a straight-sided pillar, therefore symbolically female.'

'A Goddess stone, in another words?' suggests Ibby, ignoring Martin's pained expression.

'You're not going to attempt to raise it, now, are you?' says Martin, to Kit. 'Maybe we should hold on, till after Solstice.'

'Martin,' says Ibby. 'Stop fussing.'

'There won't be time to cement it in place. I cancelled the delivery.'

'We can still make it safe,' says Kit. 'Chalk blocks, that's all the original circle-builders needed. But if you want to leave raising it until the week after next . . .'

'No,' says Ibby fiercely. 'I don't have a crew to film it the week after next. Now or never, Martin. Leave Kit to it. You and India go and do a piece to camera about stone types.' She squats down by the portable monitor again and concentrates on the screen.

'Yeah, go on, piss off,' says Kit. 'We'll be faster without you.'

'No problem.' Martin picks up his satchel, huffily extracts a Mars Bar and strides away. 'I'm only the bloody archaeologist, after all.'

Carrying the mini-DVC and a lightweight tripod, I follow, scanning the bank, hoping that Ed might appear. As a result, I almost trip over Martin, who has squatted to examine something on the ground. 'Hey, India. It's a modern offering.'

At his boots is a newly turned mound of earth, easily mistaken for a molehill if it weren't for the wildflowers strewn on top, and the protruding corner of a glossy photograph. Martin starts to scrape off the dark brown soil, mixed with pellets of chalk.

'Hold on,' I say, kicking open the legs of the tripod. 'This would be good to film.'

'You want me to talk?'

'Of course. Describe what you've found. I'm shooting over your shoulder.' I focus the camera close-up on his big hairy fingers. 'Speed. In your own time.' The fingers brush away the final layer of dirt, revealing a family snapshot, a fair-haired boy holding a pink and green plush-furred dinosaur up to the camera and peeping from behind it.

'Oh.' The camera catches only a glimpse, before Martin's fingers go into reverse and start sweeping earth back quickly to cover it. 'I don't think I want to describe this after all,' he says.

Someone was standing next to the boy, probably his mother, her arm round him – but all that shows is her hand and a few strands of blond hair. Her face has been fiercely scribbled over with black biro, so heavily that the glossy surface is pitted and scored, and part of the photo has been torn away, the jagged edge bisecting her breast. There are ashy flakes mixed with the soil.

'Sorry,' says Martin. 'It seems – sort of private. And creepy, too. I think he's burned the rest of the picture.'

'You don't know it's a he.'

'Take my word for it, it's a he.' Martin has completely covered the photo. 'Let's leave it, OK?'

I turn off the camera. 'Sorry.'

'No, I'm sorry. Stuff like that – well, it makes me feel a bit sick. Kind of black magicky. Not that I believe in that twaddle, but I am the son of a vicar. Dad was always having to clear up peculiar things from the churchyard. Let's go talk girl stones and boy stones.'

He strides off briskly. I fold the tripod and follow, with a faint sense of unease.

At three o'clock, Kit pronounces herself satisfied with the ropes and prehistoric-style pulleys, and assembles three teams of students and onlookers to haul on them, as well as a fourth team (mostly girls) to dart around slotting timber props into place as the stone starts to come upright.

'Can we do the whole thing twice?' asks Ibby. 'It'd be easier to film.'

'No,' says Kit. 'And keep your people well out of the way. This is dangerous. Remember what happened to the Barber Surgeon?'

Ed and Graham have been co-opted to help. There are beads of perspiration sparkling in Graham's blond beard as his team takes the strain, and the stone judders an inch or two above the lip of its pit.

'Get a prop under there,' shouts Kit. 'Reuben, your team mustn't slacken off.'

Ed's navy T-shirt is dark with sweat, his arms as corded as the honeysuckle rope. A blonde student in shorts and a bikini top darts under the hawser to jab a prop into place.

'She's coming up,' calls Martin. 'Steady . . .'

Ed clenches his jaw and grunts, catches sight of me filming, and mouths something that will have to be pixillated.

'Don't let her twist!' yells Kit.

Rain starts to fall as, slowly, inch by inch, the stone is levered from its bed. We've gathered quite a crowd, standing under umbrellas on the henge banks for a grandstand view. There's scattered applause at the moment when the huge diamond finally comes upright.

'You can't relax,' shouts Kit. 'Hold her there while we check the props.'

Chalk blocks are packed into the stone hole. Eventually Kit announces she's satisfied the megalith is secure. The teams release the ropes, which are attached to stakes in the ground. Kit tests every one.

Martin is still looking worried. 'I'd have liked to cement her in. And backfill the trench.'

'It'd take an earthquake to shift her. Even without the ropes, the blocks would hold her. We'll come back and finish the job when Solstice is over.'

'Well, on your head be it.'

'Or yours,' she says, punching him lightly on the arm.

I miss the rest of the conversation because I've caught sight of Ed, chaining together metal barriers to keep the public away from the trench containing the trussed stone. The blonde girl in shorts is leaning on one, helping steady it while he loops the padlock through. He bends his head towards her and says something; she grins and laughs.

Rather than go straight home, I walk down to John's. Frannie woke this morning before I left the house, entirely lucid, though without any memory of having caused so much fuss. John has been with her most of the day, leaving mid-afternoon for a couple of reflexology appointments.

By the time I reach his cottage, the weather has done one of those conjuring tricks it likes to pull in June and unexpectedly hauled out a steamy sun. Raindrops are sparkling on the summer jasmine outside the door.

He looks tired: he's wearing his old glasses, instead of contact lenses.

'So, did Adele have anything useful to suggest about Frannie?' I ask, as he makes tea for us.

'Yes.' His voice through the kitchen door is unusually wary.

'And Frannie was OK when you left?'

'Not too bad.' He comes back in carrying two mugs. I'd swear that's guilt on his face.

'You said on the phone she was fine.'

'Yes, of course, that's what I meant.' His eyes slide away towards the brick hearth. 'Sorry, fire's a bit miserable. It's been so damp today I thought it worth getting one going. I'll stick a log on.'

'So she seems OK now?'

'Well . . .' He throws some kindling onto the embers, then kneels to hold a sheet of newspaper across the fireplace to improve the draw. 'You know what she's like. Weather conditions variable on Planet Fran.' He seems to be spending an inordinate amount of time building an elaborate pyramid of coal and repositioning the newspaper.

'John. What's going on? Did you find out something else about what happened yesterday?'

'What?' The newspaper catches fire. 'Ouch.' He lets the flame take it up the chimney in a roar of sparks, and finally turns to face me. 'What do you mean?'

'I've never seen you this tense.'

'Sorry.' Getting to his feet, he wipes a hand across his face, leaving a black smudge on one cheek. 'This is a bit difficult.'

My heart's thundering. 'What is?'

'I told Adele I thought you needed help. That it's too much to ask you to cope with Frannie by yourself. I told her about the helicopter crash, and how badly it affected you . . .'

The bastard. How dare he?

I storm straight out of his cottage, leaving the tea undrunk, slamming the front door so hard the window panes rattle. The door opens again behind me before I'm more than a couple of yards down the path. 'Don't flounce off with your arse in your hand,' roars John. 'This isn't about you, it's about what's best for Frannie.' The front porch frames him with pink sprays of summer jasmine, like a parody of an old-fashioned Valentine card.

'I was managing fine until you and sodding Social Services stuck their oar in.' I lash out at a molehill on the lawn, which disintegrates in a shower of damp earth. The garden gate has warped in the rain, and I have to struggle to open it.

'Indy.' He's holding out a sprig of jasmine. 'Peace offering? I agree, we shouldn't have let them take her to the day centre. But . . .'

'There is no but,' I say. 'I *have* to look after her because she took me on after . . . after . . .' The words are sticking in my throat. 'When Mum didn't want me any more.'

His hand tightens on the framework of the porch. 'Life's not a series of emotional IOUs,' he says. 'Frannie'd hate you to crucify yourself on her behalf. Besides, it wasn't that way, you know it wasn't. Jesus, I've been stupid. I should never have suggested you came back to Avebury after the crash. Didn't take into account this place has other memories for you. I should've understood that's unfinished business too.'

'Yeah, yeah, time wounds all heels, et cetera,' I say, with pressure building up in my chest. 'But I was eight. I got over it. Gone, done, forgotten.'

'Forgotten?' He throws the piece of jasmine onto the damp Tarmac of the path. 'If you're not limping, ask yourself why you hit the bottle every night. Why you can't convince yourself you weren't responsible for that lad dying in the chopper, why you still see his eyes every night when you go to sleep . . .'

'How do you know about the eyes?'

'. . . why you won't let anyone talk about what happened in Tolemac to Mick Feather.'

My throat closes up completely. 'I don't *know* what happened to Mick Feather,' comes out as a croak. 'I don't. Want. To hear.' I turn and run down the path, and my eyes are so blurry I can hardly find the catch on the gate.

CHAPTER 34

On the Ridgeway, the air is thick and still, thunder on the way. My T-shirt is clinging to my back, and my head is pounding. *Gone, done, forgotten.*

I'm walking fast, punishing the ground with the impact of my heels, away from Avebury. But it doesn't matter which direction I take. I can't escape the vortex: I'm still going round in circles. This was the path we took in 1989, the night I first watched John make a crop circle: guiding the mothership in.

Mick Feather, Keir's dad, was with us that night, though Keir stayed with Mum at the van in Tolemac, in case his hayfever flared up. Mick, with skin that always looked grimy like a coalman's, irrespective of how often he washed. I was afraid of Mick. There was something forbidding about him, with those heavy black eyebrows and muddy skin. Keir said he was fun when they did things together. Much of the time Keir was with us, though, in our house, and then in our van under the trees at Tolemac.

Keir and I were almost the same age, best friends because he spent so much time at our place. Mick and the others had nowhere else to be apart from the pub, or the smelly vans and crash pads they inhabited after their wives and girlfriends had kicked them out. Mum wasn't just saddled with me to look after, she had a tribe of dysfunctional kids who'd never grown up. No wonder she wanted rid of us and ran away.

I can picture her, face hard as sarsen, cheeks the same dirty, stained white as the chalk scars on the hillside. She grabbed hold of me by the shoulders, her hands trembling with anger, and shook me like a beanbag. 'You stupid little cow. Who did you tell?'

I didn't know what she meant. There was the sound of a helicopter overhead, and the air smelled of burned plastic.

'Don't you realize what you've done?'

I've lost track of time and place, under a lid of thick grey cloud, clamped over the Downs like the headache that's screwed itself onto my skull. The sun is hidden, but it must be close to setting. Somewhere around here we made the crop circle. I've watched the Barley Collective, friends of John's from Bristol, make crop circles half a dozen times since, but that summer was the first and most vivid. The western sky still on fire, though it was past ten o'clock at night, May bugs dive-bombing the flashlights. No one to see us, a mile at least from the nearest farmhouse, sculpting a field of ripening barley hidden in the folds of the downland. The little fellow with hair like a black man's, the one who came into the church – what was his name? Rizla? – moving in a huge arc with the string and the pegs to mark out the design to John's orders. 'Callin' in the mothership, babe,' the little guy kept shouting. 'Lovin' the alien and callin' in the fakkin' mothership.' Afterwards, he hoisted me onto his shoulders, and said: 'Back to the mothership.' Back to Margaret's camper van.

I sit on a stile, with a view of the fields below. A creature is moving through the young grain, too distant to identify in the fading light. The night we trampled out the crop circle, a hare danced across our path, long-eared and leggy. John spotted it first, grabbed my shoulders and turned me so I saw it run across the field. When he became a shaman, he took a hare for his power animal.

In 1989, the landscape seemed touched with promise, under a rising moon near the full, made enormous and golden by dust in the atmosphere. Tonight the same fields are tired and colourless, sticky grey air thickening to twilight.

Across the valley, a long cigar shape looms on the misty downland. That night, it seemed between worlds, drenched in moonlight. I sat cross-legged in the barley, gazing up at it on the ridge, while John and his friends called out instructions and song titles to each other, all their old favourites, Pink Floyd, Hendrix, Echo and the Bunnymen, Angelfeather. 'Set The Controls For The Heart Of The Sun'. 'Hot Summer Night'. 'Killing Moon'. 'Callin' In The Mothership'.

The other mothership. Watching us. Tall stones like teeth.

The Long Barrow.

The path climbs the downland towards the barrow. A pulse throbs in my temple. Panting in the claggy air, I can't stop myself glancing uneasily over my shoulder, sensing someone or something behind, shadowing my footsteps. *Like one who on a lonesome road, doth walk in fear and dread . . .* But when I turn the whole narrow valley is laid out below me, empty.

And having once turned round, walks on, and turns no more his head . . .

The ground levels out towards the barrow, sinister in the fading light, with its massive stones guarding the forecourt.

Because he knows a frightful fiend doth close behind him tread.

Pressure builds up in my ears, my heart kicks, pumping ice-water and adrenalin and superstitious terror. The fiend isn't behind, but ahead: a shape wrapped in darkness, on the mown grass in front of the barrow. Twilight has wiped blank its face. Wearing a cloak emblazoned with mystic symbols, motionless, cross-legged, stiff-armed, head tipped back, it stares at a starless sky. Behind it, an unearthly light seeps out of the barrow between the megaliths.

Not cool to run, but on this occasion . . .

Too late: I've been seen. The shape moves its head. A grey shadow slips from its side.

CHAPTER 35

'I knew you were coming,' says Bryn.

Cynon the Barbarian, giving up the struggle to masquerade as Hell Hound, is as pleased as ever to see me, leaping up and trying to land flying licks on my face, dancing away, then coming back for another slobbery go.

Bryn's wrapped in a dark, fleecy blanket, beaded with dew, whose mystic symbols turn out to be the crest of Newcastle United Football Club. The unearthly glow between the megaliths is a small campfire in the mouth of the barrow.

His rucksack is open beside him, by his bare feet an enamel mug and a half-empty tin of baked beans with a plastic fork sticking out of it.

'Your boy around too?' I ask. 'Weren't you going to bring him with you for Solstice?'

'Didn't work out.' He reaches for the beans. The blanket slips from one shoulder, revealing he's bare-chested beneath it. 'None of it: home, boy, lady. Goddess told me I'd be better off alone.' He rummages in the rucksack and produces a plastic cap that fits exactly over the can's rim. Waste not, want not. 'Tomorrow's breakfast,' he says apologetically.

'You haven't got a paracetamol in there, have you?' I ask. My head is still thumping.

'Got something better.' He pulls up a Velcro flap on a pocket of the rucksack, with a tearing sound that sets my teeth on edge. 'Try one of these. Tramadol. It'll take the edge off anything. Headache?'

'That's it.'

He nods. 'Give it ten and it'll be gone.' He pops the pill out of its blister pack and proffers it on a grubby palm. 'Sorry. No washing facilities up here. There's bottled water to wash it down, though. Have two – that'll magic away the pain.'

I take a long swig of water with the pills – headache probably dehydration as much as anything – and settle myself on the ground. 'What—'

'Sssh,' he says. 'Give it time to work. Breathe steady.' We sit in companionable silence, gazing upwards, looking for stars coming out, but the cloud's too thick. The air's still, the quietness occasionally broken by the far-away hum of traffic on the A4. The ache in my temples eases. With it, the huge over-inflated stress-zeppelin that is Frannie, the row with John, dead Steve, live Ed, television that may or may not be about my grandfather, seems to shrink and float away into the distance. A sense of well-being steals over me.

Eventually Bryn shifts his position and smiles.

I smile back. 'Better already.'

'Good.' Quiet confidence in his voice; he'd known it would work. 'I were thinkin' of walkin' up to the Wansdyke, spend the night watchin' for crop circles. If you're there when one forms . . . amazin'. Sun comes up and there she is, grown like a mushroom in the dark. But now . . .' He pats Cynon, snuggled against the Newcastle blanket. 'Have to wait for your walk till mornin', boy.'

'Are you camping in Tolemac?' I ask, massaging crampy calves.

'No, no. Sleepin' here, in the womb of the Goddess.'

I'm used to John chucking the odd mysticism into conversation, but how seriously does Bryn take this Goddess stuff? He strikes me as a lost soul, casting about for a philosophy to make sense of his life. Last year it was Newcastle United, this month the Goddess. Next week he could move on to bodybuilding, computer gaming or creative writing.

But there's something lovely about his devotion to simplicity. He pulls the blanket closer, not ashamed of his bare skin but sensitive to what I might think. 'Washed a couple of T-shirts at the spring, didn't dry quickly as I thought.' He does the nature-boy bit well, knows how to look after himself, builds a neat fire.

He's looking at me hopefully, an invitation in his eyes.

'Cynon and me are well set-up here,' he says. 'Come and see.'

'Bit spooky for me.' I'm reluctant to go into the barrow. 'At Tolemac, you're not far from people. This . . . well, it's a tomb.'

'Told you, it's beautiful,' he says, clambering to his feet, and holding out his hand.

We step over the small fire that dances in the forecourt of the Long Barrow. Perhaps this is how it looked five, six thousand years ago. Fragments of what I've read, or Martin's told me, come back. The stones guarding the entrance are later additions: someone decided that what happened in the forecourt and the tomb should be secret, hidden from uninitiated eyes. Both Bryn and I have to stoop beneath the massive stone lintel to enter the narrow passageway. Not all of it is constructed of sarsen. Some of the drystone walling between came from as far away as Bristol. They built the barrow of stones that meant something to them, stones they brought with them from their original distant home, or familiar stones used for generations to polish flint tools and axes.

To left and right are dark, empty chambers, two on each side. When Stuart Piggott opened the barrow, in the 1950s, he found the skeletal remains of more than forty individuals, children as well as adults. Many skulls and jawbones were missing, probably removed for use in rituals, and in some chambers the long bones of legs and arms had been neatly stacked together against the walls.

Piggott rebuilt the barrow, placing a porthole of thick glass in the roof of the passageway to let daylight in. Tonight the stone passage is illuminated by small flickering flames. On every ledge, in every cranny, Bryn has put tea-lights: Neolithic Fairyland. In the end chamber, glittering with candles, a black plastic groundsheet is spread over the muddy floor. On top he's laid a worn Indian bedspread like a carpet, and unrolled a straw beach mat under his sleeping-bag to insulate it from the chill of the tomb's earthen floor. The Gurdjieff book from the bender is open, face down, on the sleeping-bag.

He's looking at me for a reaction, nervous pride in his eyes.

The light from the candles winks and shifts, as if the earth around us is breathing. The barrow insulates us from all notions of the real world outside: it's another space, another time, a parallel universe, between worlds. The mothership, maybe. So when he touches my breast, it seems . . .

. . . natural.

CHAPTER 36

Shit, shit, shit. I come awake with a start, hoping to see the familiar walls of my room at Frannie's, a sliver of charcoal sky through the curtains.

Instead there's a star overhead, misty and wavering like it's reflected in water. I'm lying on my back, looking up at Stuart Piggott's glass porthole in the roof of the Long Barrow. Something underneath is digging uncomfortably into my shoulder.

The tea-lights are still burning, but Fairyland has lost its glamour. The chill of damp earth strikes up through the groundsheet. The air inside the tomb is cold, but thick and unpleasant, musty with baked-bean farts and the spillage of male seed. While my back is clammy against cold plastic, my hip and thigh are unpleasantly hot. Something warm and rough-haired is snuggled against me. It twitches, emits a low dreaming whimper. Cynon, who smells very doggy indeed, up close and personal.

Across the chamber, Bryn is curled in a foetal shape, caramel curls over his eyes, his buttery skin smooth and perfect in the flickering candlelight. He's breathing softly, slowly, like a child, clutching a corner of his Newcastle United blanket bunched up to his mouth. His jeans are concertinaed at his feet.

Oh, no. How could I have done that?

I'd known it was a terrible mistake less than five minutes in. His fingers tangling in my hair (grubby fingers, how had I forgotten?), his soft, damp mouth exploring my face and neck like he wanted to suck me in; the somehow rubbery feel of that smooth skin against mine as he butted for entrance.

But by then it was too late to draw back and make apologies.

314

What followed was . . . awful.

Tears spring into my eyes, tears of shame, disgust, anger with myself for letting it happen. Poor bastard, it wasn't his fault. I should never have followed him into the tomb. Should have retreated the moment he touched my breast. There was nothing gross about his approach: his fingers were delicate, hesitant, and I—

—behaved like a slut. Forgot how to say no.

I roll over, careful not to disturb the sleeping dog. I'm even embarrassed about the dog being there. It feels sordid, like parents who make love in the same room as their children are sleeping. He tried, he really tried. None of it worked for me. Not a quiver. Everything getting more and more sore. Easiest to fake it, and let him finish.

Then, right at the end, I thought of Ed, and felt the blood gather and my breath starting to quicken but it was too late.

After it was over he wiped himself. 'She said you'd come.'

'Who?'

'The Goddess. She told me you'd be here with me.'

That was all I needed. I fucked a fruitcake. Feel sick to think of it.

The hard object under my shoulder turns out to be Bryn's Gurdjieff book. In the wavering light it's hard to read my watch, but— *Oh, my God*. Frannie. On her own all evening, no idea where I am, probably frantic with worry.

Mustn't wake him. I crawl off the ground sheet, dragging my clothes into the muddy passageway, not caring how filthy they get, hauling them on any old how . . . Bryn hasn't stirred. One last look into the chamber – *no. I don't believe it*. On a ledge in the corner, so high I'd missed it before, watching me, mocking. It's one of the figurines you can buy in the village gift shop, a resin copy of a stone carving, in primitive style: bulging eyes, big-breasted, big-bellied, a crude slit between its legs. The Goddess. We shagged in front of the Goddess. That's somehow . . . even sicker.

Cynon trembles all over, as dogs do when they're dreaming, and I back slowly out of the chamber.

*   *   *

315

It's nearly eleven o'clock when I limp into Trusloe. John's pickup is parked outside the house. The front door swings open as I come up the path; he's been looking out for me. 'Where the hell have you been?'

I lift my shoulders in a weary shrug. 'Walking. Lost track.'

'Frannie's been worried sick. *I* wasn't, mind. Knew you'd gone off with your arse in your hand. No convincing her, though, that you weren't lying with your throat cut under the stars.'

'Can I come in now?'

He stands back to let me step into the hallway, under the light. 'Jesus, you're a mess. You been rolling in mud?'

Frannie comes out of her room, and utters a shriek. 'India, you bin digging. What you bin digging, this time of night?' There's panic in her eyes. 'You *mustn't* dig.'

She's still fully dressed, probably refused to go to bed until I was home safe. My heart twists, my eyes start watering again. I can't bear having made her suffer. 'Sorry, Frannie, I – I fell over. No digging, I promise.'

'What were you doin', then? You all right, darlin'?' She reaches up and strokes my cheek. Her hand is icy.

'Honestly, I was walking on the Downs and went too far south, lost my way.'

A tear spills onto her seamed cheek. 'It's me, isn't it? I don't want to be a trouble.' She turns her head away, her purplish lips trembling. 'Wouldn't blame you for going. Did a bad thing, didn' I?'

CHAPTER 37

1941

'I knew you'd turn up eventually, Heartbreaker,' said Mr Cromley.

Pilot Officer Cromley, DFC, now, and billeted at the caravan site behind Rawlins's garage. Would have to happen I'd bump into him eventual in the village. Every night I had to get off the bus at the stop by the Red Lion, where the airmen drank outside under the tree on summer evenings. He stepped out from a group of men in RAF grey-blue, an unlit cigarette cupped in his hand. The uniform made his shoulders seem broader. 'Come and join us. They're not a bad lot – Poles, mostly.'

'No, thanks.'

'Suit yourself.' He smiled, stuck the cigarette into his mouth and strolled back to the others. I heard the fizz of a match as he lit it, and began talking to his chums, glancing back over his shoulder at me. The Lodge, where I had my room in the attic, was close by the pub. Instead of turning in through the gate, I walked down the high street and sat in the church, praying they'd have left the Red Lion by the time I came out, wiping angry tears from my eyes.

Told myself I wasn't frightened of him. That the war had taken away my fear because there was so much fear all around you; when boys were getting shot to pieces in the sky, there wasn't room in the world for any more. But I was still afraid of what he could tell.

What you begged to do, as I recall

I changed my ways. Every evening I jumped off the bus at the stop before Avebury, or the stop after, and walked into the village by a route that avoided the pub. Staring out of my attic window, I could see the grey-blue uniforms below on the pub forecourt and hear the men's chatter as it grew dark. Sometimes Mr Cromley was among them, striking a match on the bark of the tree, the flame showing me his face. I thought about finding a room in Swindon instead, close to work, but that would've been double the journey to visit Mam and Dad, and more of a worry to them. And what was I to tell Mr Keiller? That I couldn't come to any more of his tea parties because I was afraid of meeting Mr Cromley there? The summer was passing fast, and I'd already turned down two invitations.

No, I was not the sixteen-year-old girl who had cowered at the end-of-season party three years ago. I wouldn't be driven out of my home. The next time Mr Keiller had one of his tea parties, I dressed in the better of my two summer frocks and tottered up the path between the lavender beds on my highest, bravest heels.

This time the staff had set two long trestle tables in the garden, and there were deckchairs on the lawn. Mr Cromley was not there. My legs went rubbery with relief. I sat with a couple of friendly boys from Aberdeen, with accents I could barely follow, until I saw the dark-haired Glaswegian with the tin foot arrive, limping, dot-and-carry-one.

There was no sign of the boy with bandaged hands.

'Where's your blond friend?' I asked, joining him at the table to pour myself another cup of tea.

Saddest smile I ever saw.

'The grafts didn't take. Became infected. They took his hands off on Friday.'

I wanted to kick the table leg. Wasn't fair. Why did it always happen to the nice ones?

'You're a kind girl for asking,' said the Glaswegian. 'You remind me of my girl back home.'

'The chap your friend pulled out of the plane,' I said. 'Did he make it?'

He shook his head. All for nothing, then. I sometimes despaired of God. What was He doing up there? Having a bloody tea break, while the world tore itself to pieces? My own hands were trembling, the cup and saucer playing a clinky little trio with the teaspoon so I had to put them down.

On the other side of the lawn, Mr Keiller was talking to Mr Piggott, in his brown army uniform, on leave for the weekend and spending it with his wife in Marlborough. I wanted to say hello, so I patted the Glaswegian's arm and promised him I'd be back in a tick.

'Don't make such a thing of it, Stuart,' Mr Keiller was saying, in a low voice. It struck me how sad his eyes were. Mrs Keiller was in London, nursing, and though she was supposed to come home to the Manor alternate weekends, there were whispers she hadn't turned up for weeks. 'Whatever you've heard is greatly exaggerated, I assure you. Doris and I are travelling up to Scotland in September for a few weeks.'

So there were no more tea parties until October, and that was when Mr Cromley snared me again.

Mr Keiller was in a black mood the Sunday afternoon after his return from Scotland. 'That's it,' he said, to Mrs Sorel-Taylour. The flames from the fire in the huge grate made his face ruddy. I should have been talking to the airmen – I could see that boy with the artificial foot, again, trying to attract my attention, the rubber tip of his walking-stick squeaking on the oak floorboards – but instead I was hanging on the edge of their conversation, sick to hear Mr K so depressed. 'I can't carry on at Avebury. The house in Scotland is falling to pieces under the tender mercies of His Majesty's Army, and I haven't the money to keep on both establishments. I've told Young I'm closing the museum in November. We'll stow the finds safely in the out-buildings, but the sooner I persuade a buyer to take the Manor off my hands, the better.'

'You know what this is about, don't you, Miss Robinson?' said Mr Cromley, sauntering over from the tea table, with a cigarette between his fingers. Even though I'd braced myself for him to be there, I could feel my nerves tighten as he came up to us, his plate piled high with egg-and-cress sandwiches. The Manor hens must have been on overtime. 'The poor old Barber Surgeon. It's taken the heart out of him. Tell them, Alec.'

'The Royal College of Surgeons took a direct hit, earlier in the summer,' said Mr K. 'Frightful mess, and the least of their priorities was what had happened to our bones, but it looks definite now that the Barber Surgeon's skeleton was destroyed in the fire. They can't locate him anywhere.'

'You know what I think?' said Mr Cromley. 'We should hold a requiem for the poor chap. All Hallow's Eve next week, Alec. Samhain. The night of the dead. Let's hold another of your jolly ceremonies in the garden. Dinner, cocktails, good company, and we'll raise a glass or two to your statue of Pan.'

'Pandemonium,' said Mr Keiller, gloomily, looking out of the window where yellow leaves drifted across the lawns and piled against the box hedges. 'The principle of Chaos governs the world, now.'

'Ah, the trick is to control your demons,' said Mr Cromley. 'It'll be fun. Miss Robinson will assist, won't you, Heartbreaker?'

'Count me out,' I said, quick, not wanting to be part of anything Mr Cromley had his fingers in. 'I'll be . . . on fire watch that night.'

'Nonsense,' said Mr Keiller. He had brightened. 'Of course you'll be there, Heartbreaker. Join us for dinner. It won't be quite the sort of fare we used to enjoy, but we can dress in our finest and laugh in Mr Hitler's face. We'll assemble for cocktails at eight.'

I couldn't suppress a shiver of excitement. I'd never been invited to a proper dinner before. The thought of being among a procession like the one I'd watched in the Manor garden, all that time ago with Davey, filled me with joy. This, after all, was what I'd wanted, the magic of being part of that crowd.

'Donald, I leave you to be Master of Ceremonies. Bring one or two young chaps from the base, if you like. Let's give those demons a run for their money.'

I felt uneasy then, but what could go wrong at the Manor? This wasn't some hole-and-corner ritual in Swindon with Mr Cromley and his creepy uncle; wasn't a ritual so much as a party. Mr Keiller would be there, and plenty of others, and I'd be safe. But as I left the Manor, Mr Cromley caught up with me by the gate.

'You *will* be there, Heartbreaker,' he said. 'By command of the Marmalade King. And if you're not . . .' He shook his head. 'Amazing how far the sound of a single whisper carries at Avebury.'

I stood in the topiary garden at the Manor House on Hallowe'en night, shivering in my thin evening dress, ill-wishing Mr Cromley hard as I could. Moonlight glimmered on the pool between the box hedges behind the Library Wing. He'd made me leave the dinner inside to stand outside in the cold dressed as Isis or Diana, some old moon goddess anyway, in a long glittery white cloak, a black mask hiding my face. Another of Donald's carnivals, all smoke and mirrors and a cheat from arse to tip.

I wouldn't have gone along with it, but I was afraid of his threat. Any hint of what I'd done would've killed Mam. She was proper ill, now: some days she couldn't keep any food down at all. The doctor had told Dad it was nerves, lot of women suffered the same with the war, and Dad believed him, but I didn't. Mr Cromley's poison would eat away what was left of her.

He was drunk tonight and so more dangerous still. He was the only one, for a start, who understood what I was doing there, for it had been plain from the moment I arrived that I was out of place. Mr Keiller, with his usual expansive generosity, had invited me on the spur of the moment, and he probably never meant it serious. Even Mrs Sorel-Taylour's eyebrows rose a little when she saw me in my borrowed pale blue crêpe. The dress belonged to one of the nurses at the hospital. It was too big for me and gaped at the bosom, for all I'd tried to pin it to my brassière, and there was a stain near the side seam, which wouldn't come out though I'd soaked it over and over in cold water. I'd hoped it would be dark enough in the Manor for no one to notice, but every electric light was blazing away behind the blackout like there was no war on, and I had to pull my woollen wrap lopsided to hide the mark.

Donald Cromley must have known how it would be, but he had let me make a fool of myself because it suited him. There had been about twenty people at the party when I arrived. Mrs Sorel-Taylour's was the only friendly face so I made my way across the room towards her, passing two slick-haired airmen I'd never seen before. One of them was with a girlfriend, lovely in a red silk evening frock, but smelling of Chanel and pig muck.

'Marvellous to have an excuse to slip into something pretty,' she was saying, in a cut-glass accent. 'Being a land girl's terrific fun, of course, you meet such interesting types . . .' She tossed back her waterfall of hair, like Veronica Lake's, and eyed my dress. 'A great leveller, war, isn't it?'

'Cocktail, Heartbreaker?' said Mr Cromley, blocking my path and holding out a tall glass with something oily and amber swirling in its depths. 'Ready to dance for your dinner later?' His eyes flicked to the tunnel between my breasts. He was flushed, and seemed to find it hard to focus.

'Frances,' said Mrs Sorel-Taylour, behind him, 'how lovely to see you.' There was an edge to her voice. She took my arm and steered me away from Mr Cromley and his golden glass. 'There's fruit punch over here.' She leaned over to whisper: 'Donald is already the worse for wear, I'm afraid, and would like everyone else to be that way too.'

I wanted that drink. It might have given me courage. Why had I been so stupid to think I was one of these people? But I let Mrs Sorel-Taylour find me a soft drink, still whispering: 'He and Mr K have had an argument. Donald took it upon himself to invite his uncle: so discourteous to Alec, without as much as a by-your-leave. When Mr Keiller found out, this afternoon, he made Donald telephone his uncle and cancel the invitation. Stood over him in the office while he did it.'

I felt myself go hot and cold with the mention of Mr Cromley's uncle. Thank God Mr Keiller had forbidden it. He was by the fireplace, talking to a tall lady in violet satin. She was looking at him in a way I didn't like.

'Mrs Keiller was hoping to be here, but telephoned this morning to say she would be needed in London after all,' added Mrs Sorel-Taylour, and frowned in the direction of the violet lady. Mr Keiller looked up and saw me. He seemed puzzled for a moment, then gave me a brisk nod. He'd forgotten he'd invited me, I could tell.

The drinking went on far too long; it was quarter to ten before we sat down at the table. Mrs Sorel-Taylour saved me from the humiliation of standing ignored at the edge of conversations by introducing me to the other airman, the one without a girl. From his accent – the vowels too flat, the gs a little too carefully pronounced – I could tell he was a fish out of water too, and he stuck to me gratefully for most of the evening, while Mrs Sorel-Taylour left us and clamped herself to Mr Keiller's side like a watchful chaperone. The airman turned out to be a wireless operator from Mr Cromley's old squadron, on leave for the week from their base in Kent, and he was the worse for drink too.

'You know why old Donald's so het up, don't you?' he said. 'He's not happy flying circuits round Yatesbury – too tame. But there's a question mark over whether they'll allow him back when the squadron moves to Colerne.'

'Why?' I asked, but he ignored me.

'Not looking forward to Colerne, myself. Have to learn a whole new set of gubbins when we fly the de Havilland Mosquito.'

'Should you be telling me that?' I said. 'My fellow usually keeps mum about what he flies.' Davey had passed his exams in the summer, top of his class, and had been posted to a night-fighter squadron in East Anglia. His tight-lipped letters gave little away about his job, though I gathered he was kept busy patrolling the coast and chasing German bombers. But they revealed far too much about his feelings for me, and his longing for a transfer back to Wiltshire.

'Pilot or wireless op?' asked the airman. He wasn't interested enough to wait for my reply. 'Anyway, Don shouldn't fret. He'll be operational before Christmas, I bet – too good a pilot to waste in training, though I hope to Christ Yatesbury will have calmed him down.'

'What d'you mean?'

'Silly bastard was taking too many risks. Final straw was when he chased a bomber all the way to France, against orders I might add, and was shot up so badly he only just made it home on one engine. It looked touch and go, and he told his wireless op to bale out. Don brought the plane down safely, but Tony landed in the drink, and washed ashore dead. After that, word went round the squadron he was bad luck. No one wanted to fly with him.'

Donald was very drunk by now, sitting close to Mr Keiller near the middle of the table and doing his best to compete for the attention of the woman in the violet dress. For all my fear of him, I could pity him that night. He'd always been a good-looking boy. When you caught him unguarded, there could be gentleness in his face, but he seemed to want to slough off that side of himself. And I knew, because I'd seen it in the house in Swindon, that he was terrible frightened of his uncle. I wouldn't have liked to be the one to tell him he shouldn't come to the party.

The clock chimed the quarter hour. Forty-five minutes to midnight. The dessert plates were being cleared. Mr Keiller looked at Mr Cromley. Mr Cromley lurched to his feet, banging his cake fork against his glass, leaving a yellow smear of custard. 'Ladies and gentlemen,' he slurred, 'when you have finished your coffee and brandy, please assemble in the Library to prepare for our sss-solemn ritual in honour of the late Barber Surgeon of Avebury.' On cue the door of the dining room swung open, and the surly housemaid came in, carrying two tall coffee pots. She scowled when Mr Cromley beckoned to me and I stood up, full of dread, aware of curious eyes on me all around the table.

In the Library, I was shaking as he dressed me in the hooded white cloak and the black domino mask. I had known for several days what would be expected of me: he had come knocking, bold as brass, at the door of the Lodge one evening and made me go with him to the Red Lion where he bought me a port and lemon and explained the ritual. Hadn't seemed so much, then, just more silly games like I'd seen them play in the Manor garden with the white chalk pizzle.

But now, after the humiliation of the evening, with midnight approaching and the mask on my face, for two pins I'd have run away if it weren't for the power of his whisper to harm Mam.

He stood back, eyes narrowed, then reached to adjust the set of the cloak on my shoulders. 'One more detail.' He took from his breast pocket a five-pointed silver star on a chain and hung it round my neck. A trace of white powder was caught in his moustache. 'There.' His fingers brushed my collarbone, and I flinched. 'Ready to draw down the moon. They won't be long. You remember what I told you?'

I nodded. 'Where'll I find—'

'Where I told you. I'll leave it on the path behind the hedge; you pick it up before you enter the Half-Moon Garden. We'll show them something,' he said, his eyes glittering.

So now I waited in the cold, under a fat moon a few days off the full. They'd surely be out any minute. I thought I'd seen a chink of light as someone lifted the edge of a blackout curtain, though that might have been the staff watching, curious as Davey and I had been once. My instructions were to bow, lift my arms to the sky and disappear as fast as I could down the hidden path between the hedges and the curved wall. Mr Cromley and Mr Keiller would lead the guests into the Half-Moon Garden, and I would then reappear, emerging between the horns of the tall yew hedges in the centre.

The door from the Library swung open, a dark yawning mouth because no one dared show a light in the blackout. But it was only Mr Cromley, who ran down the steps with something white in his hands. 'They'll be out any second,' he hissed. 'Careful with it, mind, or Alec will murder me.' He pressed the white thing into my hands, and dashed back to the steps, at the same moment as Mr Keiller appeared in the doorway at the top. He had a brandy glass in one hand, and was looking back over his shoulder to talk to the lady in the violet dress.

Something was amiss. It was all happening too fast. This object was to be part of the ritual later: I should have been empty-handed when

I saluted the moon in the topiary garden. But I did what I'd been told. As they came out, I dipped my head, then rose as tall as I could, lifting high under the moon the thing he had given me. It was cold in my cold hands, yellow-white under the yellow-white moon. Only when I lifted it did I understand what it was: not one of the plaster skulls, not a fake as Donald had told me it would be.

It was Charlie's, bulbous and misshapen.

Moonlight poured ice-water through my blood, running down my arms, like the relic was channelling it from the white orb in the sky to my heart. I near dropped the child's skull with the shock, because this felt wrong, there was something cruel bad about it, a horrible parody. Charlie was only a little boy: he deserved to be left in peace.

Mr Keiller knew it was Charlie too. He swung round looking for Donald, his face furious, bellowing. The brandy glass hit the bottom of the steps with a gurt smash, where Mr Cromley had been a second before. I didn't stop to see any more. Mr K'd never forgive me.

Didn't know what else to do, so I slipped between the tall bushes and sped along the hidden path by the curved wall, clasping Charlie's skull. In summer this path was scented with catmint and honeysuckle, but tonight there was a dank, rotting smell behind the yew hedges, like I was carrying death with me. Had some idea if I ran fast and far enough, I might be able to hide from them all, so I kicked off my shoes and pelted past the gap in the hedge that led into the Half-Moon Garden, on to the end of the path, near tripping on the hem of my long dress as I turned the corner into the Italian walk bordering the ha-ha at the Manor boundary.

He caught me there, stepping out onto the paved walk in front of me so I had to slow.

'Give it to me, Heartbreaker,' he said, holding out his hands for the skull. 'Poor old lad's lasted five thousand years – I'd hate for him to be smashed now.'

'I'm sorry, Mr Keiller,' I said, cowering, expecting his temper would flare as soon as he had the skull safe. 'I didn't think it would be a real skull, I swear.'

'I know,' he said gently. 'Donald overstepped the mark, I think.' He put his free arm round my shivering shoulders, and walked me into the orchard. The night sky was enormous over us, a mass of white pinpricks, and there was a sparkle of frost on the grass.

'What about everybody else?' I asked.

'I have no doubt Mrs S-T has everything in hand. Waters will be serving another round of brandy in the Library.' He led me to a bench under one of the apple trees. There were still windfalls underfoot, slippery against my bare feet. 'Sit down. Remove that ridiculous mask and pentacle Donald's made you wear. I take it you won't want to go back in for the moment?'

I shook my head, shivering violently, tucking my frozen feet under me as I sat. He set Charlie's skull down carefully on the end of the bench, and stripped off his dinner jacket to wrap round my shoulders over the white cloak.

'You'll catch your death,' I said.

'Nonsense.' He gave an elaborate, theatrical shiver under his starched white shirt, and sat down next to me on the bench. 'If Donald's sensible, he'll have fled to his billet in the caravan park. I'd have half killed the little sh– if he'd been near enough. As it was, seemed to me saving the find was more important. I was afraid you'd trip. Now, snuggle up because you're absolutely right. I'm cold as charity.' He put his arm round me, and hugged me against him. 'We'll give it five minutes for Cromley to exit the premises, then I'll ask Waters to walk you home. You're at the Lodge, aren't you?'

I curled against him in the moonlight, wanting to be part of him. The Manor was a dark shadow against the sky, blacked-out and blank-eyed. For a second I thought I saw a gleam again from one of the upper windows, but perhaps I was mistaken, and there was no watcher.

'Why did he do it?' I asked.

'He's lost, Heartbreaker,' said Mr Keiller. 'First his damned uncle ruined him, now it's the war. And Cocaine Bill.' He began to sing into my hair, a jazz song I'd heard before at a dance in Swindon.

'Cocaine Bill, and Morphine Sue
Strolling down the avenue.
Honey, have a sniff, have a sniff on me,
Won't you have a sniff on me.'

He pulled away, and looked down at me. Then his mouth touched mine, only for a moment, so quick I wondered after had it happened at all, and he pulled me to my feet. 'Go and find your shoes,' he said. 'Time you were leaving, before I do something I'll regret.'

I bent to pick up my evening shoes, lying on the path where I'd kicked them off, between the yew hedges. My lips were tingling, like there was electric in them. In the orchard, Mr Keiller was still singing as he strolled towards the house to put Charlie's skull back safely in his study, and call for the butler.

'All o' you cokies is gonna be dead
If you don't stop a-sniffin' that stuff in your head.
Now where they went no one can tell
It might have been heaven or . . .'

I felt the lightest of pressures against the small of my back, no more than a pinprick, tracing a figure of eight against my kidneys. My knees locked and I could hear my breath coming in little snorts, like an animal's when it's dragged into the butcher's pen. A hand snaked over my hip and under my belly.

'So you finally made him kiss you,' he whispered. 'Though you don't really understand the power you have, do you?'

'You're . . . sick,' I said, straightening up slowly. 'I don't understand why he doesn't see that. He always forgives you.'

Mr Cromley took hold of my arms, and turned me to face him, walking me back until I was against the curved wall. He slipped a hand under the hem of my dress and lifted it until I could feel woody stems of clematis prickling the backs of my knees. Then he let the hem of my dress fall back. He had that little bronze dagger in his hand.

'What's that for?' I said.

'You know what it's for.'

'I know it's harder than what's in your trousers.'

'You're very brave all of a sudden,' he said. 'Alec's gone indoors.'

'You wouldn't dare hurt me,' I said. 'Because it matters to you that he forgives you, doesn't it? You're only trying to frighten me again.'

He used the dagger to push back my hair from my forehead. Then he ran it across my lips, cold and rough, where Alec had kissed me. 'Don't fool yourself,' he said. 'You see, this little knife goes with me wherever I go. Earthbound, or in the air, it's my charm. And that's how I shall be for you. Your special charm. I'm never going to leave you, Heartbreaker. Wherever you go, you take me with you. And I take a piece of you.'

The dagger was sharper than I'd thought. He had lopped off a curl from my temple and was gone.

When Davey wrote to say he had leave due, I replied saying I'd be sorry not to see him, but better not to waste it on me because I was with Mam every minute I could get away to Devizes. She was becoming sicker. Even Dad had to admit now that there was something wrong. Her skin was the colour of a pub ceiling, like it had been smoked, and a pain in her side woke her nights.

Davey wrote back that it didn't matter, he'd be seeing me soon enough. His transfer had come through at last, and though he'd flown enough missions to choose a quieter posting, instead he'd asked to go to a night-fighter squadron in Kent. He'd be right in the thick of the action, he said, and the best news of all was that some time in the new year, they'd be moving to an airfield in Wiltshire.

He was joining Mr Cromley's old squadron.

CHAPTER 38

'Let me go over it again,' says Martin. He stirs his cappuccino thought-fully, and gives a Monday-morning yawn. 'Sorry, petal, hard weekend caving. It's difficult keeping track of your love life. I go off for a couple of days, and when I come back everything's changed. So, there's your ex living on his ownsome in a caravan—'

'Not really my ex,' I butt in.

'Now I am confused. You're still carrying on with him as well?'

'*No*. I meant there wasn't a proper relationship in the first place.'

'Fine. Leave him aside for the moment. Then you happen across some Goddess-worshipping nutcase at the Long Barrow, and you leap into bed, or rather onto plastic ground sheet, with him—'

'Keep your voice down.' Corey is wiping tables, working her way down the café towards us, ears flapping. 'I wasn't myself. I had a headache—'

'That's usually a reason *not* to sleep with someone, rather than the other way round.'

'You seem to find this funny.'

'Petal, it's the only way to look at these things. Otherwise I'd've slit my wrists years ago.'

Whenever Martin discusses relationships, he slips back into camp banter. Even if I wasn't at loggerheads with John, Bryn isn't someone I'd want to discuss with my spirit-father: he'd be far more judge-mental. Martin never confides what his own relationships are like, but he seems to understand the principle of lurching from one sexual disaster to the next.

He's looking thoughtful. 'The more worrying aspect is that you

330

accepted a couple of Tramadol from this gentleman. You do know what Tramadol is?'

'I thought it was like Anadin.'

'In the same way a chainsaw resembles a pair of scissors. It's one of the more powerful painkillers, prescription only. Induces a pleasant euphoria, though it has also been known to give people hallucinations. You can buy it on the Internet from dodgy Mexican pharmacies. We might ask ourselves where your friend obtained it.'

'Perhaps it was prescribed?'

'Not unless he's had major surgery recently. Still, let's look on the bright side. At least it wasn't Rohypnol.'

'What, date-rape stuff?' I can't imagine Bryn doing anything so underhand. All the same, I find myself asking hopefully, 'Don't suppose it *could* have been Rohypnol rather than Tramadol?'

'Most unlikely, given that you seem to have total recall of every sordid detail. Rohypnol victims tend to wake up with a sense of unease, but remembering very little. Sorry, petal, that ain't your get-out-of-jail-free card.'

'What about you?' I ask, anxious to change the subject, because this is starting to prick my conscience as effectively as any conversation with John. 'How *was* your weekend in Bath?'

Martin looks away. 'Not exactly marvellous . . .' he begins, but then Ibby walks into the café.

'There you are, Martin. Shift your fat arse. I've a couple of old codgers waiting to be interviewed in the Manor garden, and I don't want them to expire before you get there. You're not with us this week, India, are you?'

Reluctantly I wrap my apron round my hips again. Much as I'd rather be filming, the television company has not paid me so far. Corey catches my eye and waves J-cloth and disinfectant spray. To be translated as: coffee break over, tables to clear, toilets to clean.

Martin hangs back as Ibby strides out of the door. 'Mind, there's the other worrying question too,' he whispers.

'What's that?'

'What your ex has done with his wife. I can tell you for a fact he isn't going home at weekends.'

'How do you know?'

'Spotted him in the cinema in Bath, on his own, on Saturday night.'

I could walk up to the Long Barrow, and tell Bryn: sorry, big mistake. Or – I could do nothing. Doing nothing is as good a way as any of ending a relationship. Though this isn't exactly a relationship, is it?

So what *does* constitute a relationship in your book, Indy? That's what John would say. Everything has significance. Under Wyrd, the web of fate, all things are connected: a smile as you pass a stranger is a bond.

Bond meaning tie. Obligation.

Walking back to Trusloe at the end of the day, that prickling feeling between the shoulder blades hits me again, as if I'm being followed. I remind myself Bryn knows nothing about me, not where I live, not even my name. In a few days, once Solstice is over, he'll be gone again. But who am I kidding? I shagged a man who sleeps with a plastic replica of a Celtic mother goddess looking down on him. No telling what that might have unleashed. And this isn't London. It's hard to hide in a place the size of Avebury.

I knew you'd come

The feeling grows on me again that I've been walking widdershins since the helicopter crash. So, when I let myself into the house, it isn't exactly a surprise to find a letter on the hall table from the Wiltshire coroner's office. Steve's inquest is scheduled for the end of July.

He opens the caravan door before I've even knocked, like he knew I was coming.

'Oh,' I say. 'You've had a letter too?'

A weary nod. 'Want a drink? A proper one?' Behind him, on the fold-down table, there's a bottle of Waitrose Sauvignon Blanc, three-quarters empty. 'I'll open another.'

'I'd rather have something soft. No, bugger it, pour me a smidge of the Sauvignon. I'll see how that goes down.'

Ed uncorks the bottle and fills a straight-sided tumbler. 'Ooh dear, better open another after all.'

'You're not trying to get drunk again, I hope? That won't solve anything.' Listen to me, the Queen of the Solpadeine. Never let a crisis pass without a crippling hangover.

'You ever get to the point where you drink and nothing happens?' he asks. 'You don't get drunk, you don't feel better, and the more you drink the more sober you get? I'd love to get smashed, but I don't think it would work tonight. Actually, I haven't had so much as a sip yet. That bottle's been on the go since Saturday.'

'Sorry.' I take a gulp of the wine. 'Euughh, yes. It's vinegary.'

'Hence the need to open another. If there is one.' He checks the cupboards. 'Sorry, it'll be warm. Unless . . . Ah.' Triumphantly he produces a bottle of red. 'Chuck that battery acid out of the door. So – you going to the inquest?'

'Have I a choice?'

'I certainly haven't.' He runs a hand through his dark hair. 'I somehow thought it'd never happen. It's been nearly a year since the crash. Dumb, of course, but I let myself imagine that if I could ignore it, the inquest would be postponed indefinitely. I'm going to lose my licence, Indy.' A muscle's jumping under his eye. 'You any idea what that means to a pilot? I mean, it's not just my livelihood, it's my whole fucking way of life. Sorry, didn't mean to drown you in self-pity.'

He looks so unhappy I put a hand on his arm. I can't think of anything to say that will make it better.

Then somehow his mouth ends up on mine, and it's the full works, tongues and pushing and hands all over the place, and really not very much room in a caravan at all.

The sun's sunk out of sight below window level, and the caravan's interior is crepuscular. Nothing has been achieved, as yet, apart from some energetic snogging that makes my face sore from his stubble, when he suddenly pulls away and says, 'Hang on.'

'I'm on the pill.'

'That wasn't what I meant. Shut up a moment. No, be really quiet. Don't move – the caravan creaks.'

I even hold my breath. Silence. Faintly, in the distance, a dog is barking.

'There's n—'

'Sssh.'

The barking goes on, louder. Something else too: an engine, way off. Ed disentangles a hand from my T-shirt and slides carefully off the bench seat onto the floor. He puts a finger to his lips. The engine is coming closer. 'Bingo,' he whispers.

'Wh—'

'Alan's dog. Best doorbell a bloke can have.'

Oh. That was how he knew I was coming.

The caravan door is still open. Through it, the trees look much darker than when I arrived. I glance at my watch. Nearly ten o'clock. Ed shuffles carefully across the floor on his stomach, and comes to rest a few inches short of the half-open door so he can peer out. The sound of the engine is much louder. He leans as far forward as he can, then grabs the corner of the door to pull it closed.

'Thing is,' he says, propping himself against the side of the sink unit, 'I really wouldn't have liked us to be interrupted by my wife.'

'Your— Shit! That's your *wife*?'

'No, no. Keep your voice down – they'll go away in a minute, I hope. It's probably someone who's lost, but in case they're looking for me . . .'

'You're sure it's not your wife?'

'Definitely. She drives one of those bite-sized hairdressers' 4×4s. Wouldn't be caught dead in a white Transit van. Don't think it's likely to be creditors either, but you never know. Sometimes these things can get heavy.' He levers himself carefully to his feet, and leans over me to look out of the window. There's the scent of woodsmoke on his skin, and a clean tarry smell that makes me want to grab him and push my face into the fuzz of black hair revealed by his open shirt.

'Yes, they've stopped. Looks like they're studying the map. Let's not attract their attention, anyway.'

'You haven't really got debt collectors after you, have you?'

'There was a bit of fuss after a card game . . .'

'Ed!'

'Only joking. But it's late for a drive in the country. Might be someone looking for me, I suppose, and to be honest, I'd rather spend the evening with you.'

'Oh, *God*,' I say, in a whisper.

'What is it?'

'I said I wasn't going to do this. You're *married*, Ed. I mean, I fancy the arse off you, you make me laugh, you smell right to me, even when you haven't washed—'

'I *have*, this time.'

'—but I don't do married men. It's pointless. I don't mean I want to marry *you* or anything, God forbid – sorry, I'm making a terrible mess of this. But someone always ends up hurt with a married man. You, me, her, doesn't matter who, one or both or probably all of us are going to regret it. This is the *second* time.'

'Hold on. I'm not married. She threw me out.'

'You called her your *wife*.'

'Technically, she still is. Shut up a minute, though.' He's staring out of the window again. I start to scramble upright, but he makes a flapping motion with his hand. 'Keep down. They're still there.'

'The van? What are they doing?'

'Sitting. Bugger. Maybe they've come to nick something. I might have to leap into action.'

'You can't tell me they're going to load a helicopter into the back of a Transit.' Pulling my T-shirt down to look more respectable, I wriggle under his arm until my eyes are above the bottom of the window.

The mud-splashed white van is parked by the gates to the yard, near the notice on the chainlink fence warning of Bingo the would-be Alsatian. Its lights are off. A cigarette glows behind the half-open window on the driver's side.

'They're not doing anything,' I whisper. The whole thing seems less a joke, now, more sinister.

'There is another explanation,' says Ed. 'They might be here to do what we were doing until about five minutes ago.'

The glowing end of the cigarette flies out of the window in an elegant arc. The driver's door opens. A man gets out, dressed in army-style camouflage combats and a khaki jacket. On the other side a door slams, and another man, dressed all in black, eyes invisible under a broad-brimmed hat, comes into view round the snub-nosed bonnet of the van.

'Oh, *shite*,' says Ed. 'They've either come for rough sex in the open air, or they're going to steal something. I knew it. I'm going to have to be a hero.'

'Ring the police.'

'Mobile's out of battery. If I could get a signal.'

'Well, write down the numberplate, and let's pretend we're not here. There are two of them and they're—'

'Rather big. I can see. It is mostly lard, though,' he concludes hopefully.

'In which case they'll *fry* you. You don't stand a chance, Ed.'

'Unfortunately it's my job to be beaten up by burglars.'

The man in the camouflage combats goes to the back of the van and opens the doors. One bears a sticker: a luminous triangle with *Stargate Earth Project* inscribed underneath. The other man, in black, flicks on a powerful torch, strolls a few paces under the trees, bends down and picks something up off the ground. When he straightens, the torchbeam flares and almost blinds me as it finds Ed's grey-green caravan, which until then would have been invisible in the semi-darkness. The beam dips and the man in black stares – can he see us watching? – then calls, 'Not here, Karl.' He throws down whatever he picked up and starts back to the Transit, a circle of torchlight bobbing ahead of him and illuminating Karl's puzzled face. He is mid-way through hauling something out of the back of the van. His friend in black swings the torchbeam to show him the caravan.

'Oh, *crikey,*' says Karl.

'Crikey?' mutters Ed in my ear. 'What kind of self-respecting villain says crikey?' He drops down under the window, his shoulders shaking. Giggles are welling in both of us. I stuff a corner of the Thomas the Tank Engine curtain in my mouth, then remember how grubby it is, which makes it all the harder not to laugh.

The torchbeam gleams on shiny black plastic as it catches the long, awkward object Karl is shoving hastily back into the Transit. The van doors slam. Karl trots back and hauls himself into the driver's seat. The engine fires, the Transit executes a hasty three-point turn, and lurches up the pot-holed perimeter road away from us. A few moments later, Bingo's high-pitched yap starts up again.

Ed erupts into snorts of laughter. 'Crikey!' he splutters. 'I say, *crikey!*' Then he spots me zipping up my jeans. 'Indy, don't go. I'm serious – Jeanine left me right after the crash. We communicate mostly through her solicitor.'

'I'm not going.' I fasten my belt, and cast around for my fleece. 'Or, rather, you need to come along with me. I arrived on foot. Where are your car keys?'

'What are you on about?'

'Didn't you see what those guys had in the back of the Transit?'

'I was laughing too much.'

'That was a metal detector. They're *nighthawks*. Bet you a tenner they're off to dig up barrows on Windmill Hill.'

The Transit's rear lights, bouncing slowly over the rutted perimeter road, are still visible as we race out of the caravan to Ed's Land Rover, parked by the hangars. Bingo, a white blur dancing back and forth across the road in the semi-darkness, is barking his stout little heart out. As the white van reaches him he makes a dash and tries to bite one of the wheels. I avert my eyes, but when I open them again, Bingo is still in one piece, his tiny frame quivering with indignation as he yaps a 'good riddance' after the Transit. Then he hears us driving along the track, jumps round joyfully and starts up all over again. Somehow we avoid flattening him – not an easy job without headlights – and swing out of the turning in time to see the Transit's rear lights disappear up the lane that leads to Yatesbury village.

'D'you suppose they know we're following?' I ask.

'Possibly. The driver might not have spotted us if he isn't looking in his rear-view mirror.'

Ahead, the van's lights are crawling along the lane.

'They must be lost,' I say. 'Seems unlikely you'd go looking for treasure round the perimeter of an airfield – the soil has to be full of old nuts and bolts and all sorts of junk. Must play havoc with the settings.'

'Why are you so sure they're heading for Windmill Hill, though? Plenty of other sites round here you could pick up Bronze Age finds. Roman stuff too.'

'Because my grandmother's seen them, I'm sure, late at night.' *Lights, buggerin' lights.* 'And there's a farm track that takes you from Yatesbury to Windmill Hill, avoiding all the cottages. The ideal route, if you're up to no good.'

'Oh, come on. You heard what Martin said. All those barrows were dug years ago. Victorian vicars took the lot.'

'He also said that wouldn't stop them trying—'

The Transit, about fifty metres ahead, stops. Ed jams on the brakes and pulls into a farm gateway. But the van's already moving again, at walking pace, eventually disappearing up a side road towards the church.

'There you are. He *is* lost,' I say triumphantly, as Ed crunches into gear ready to follow. Before he can do so, headlights appear, coming back towards us. The Transit bowls past.

'Must've turned,' says Ed, executing a three-point turn in the narrow lane. By the time we catch the van's taillights again, it's almost at the junction with the A4.

'I still think he's looking for Windmill Hill,' I say, confident the van will now take the main road and turn off at the Beckhampton roundabout.

But he doesn't. After circling the roundabout twice, the Transit lurches onto the Devizes road.

'He's going home,' says Ed. 'And so should we.'

'No.' I'm reluctant to give up, so close to confirming there's a rational explanation for Fran's mysterious lights. 'Like you say, plenty of other sites nearby. Do you have a map in the car?'

'Indy, what exactly do you have in mind once we catch up with him? There's an Ordnance Survey in the glove compartment.'

'Can I put the overhead light on?'

'Then he *will* see us.'

We're bowling along an A road at maybe fifty, sixty miles an hour. 'Actually, Ed, I think I might feel safer if you turned the headlights on now.'

Ed switches the main beam on, with a disappointed grunt. 'I was enjoying that.'

'It was dangerous.'

'So are most things that are fun. I could see perfectly well. People drove without lights in the blackout. And you didn't answer my question. What are we supposed to do if we catch them digging up a barrow?'

'We don't have to do anything. I'm curious, that's all. My grandmother's been going on about lights on Windmill Hill, and until now I've assumed they weren't real.'

Ed grunts and puts his foot down, until our headlights pick out the *Stargate Earth Project* sticker on the Transit's rear door. Almost immediately, the van's taillights glow a brighter red, forcing us to brake again.

'Either he's sussed us or you're right, he's lost . . .' We sail past the Transit as it pulls into a recessed gateway.

'Can we sit and wait for him round the next bend?'

'You're in charge of the effing map. But, as far as I can see, there is no bend.' Ed is grinding his teeth in frustration. 'This is straight enough to be a bloody Roman road.'

A quarter of a mile on, another field gate appears, and Ed bumps the Land Rover onto the verge. I flip on the map light. 'Damn. We've lost him. Those are barns, where he stopped – he must've turned there.'

Ed peers over my shoulder. 'Oh, you can drive up that track.'

'It's marked as a bridlepath.'

'Well, I've driven it with Graham. Twists and turns along the escarpment – fabulous views of the Wansdyke, and plenty of barrows.' He backs into the gateway.

The absurdity of chasing nighthawks into the middle of nowhere hits me like a bucket of cold water. Beyond the barns, no other buildings are marked on the map for miles. 'Sorry, Ed. Might as well go home. Should we call the police?'

'You think they'd be arsed to leave the comfort of Devizes nick to chase a van that might be evil treasure-seekers but alternatively could be two gay gentlemen seeking outdoor fun? No.' He swings the wheel and accelerates into the road, back towards the barns. 'We've come this far, might as well see it through. We'll get the van numberplate and report them in the morning.'

My feet are chilling by the second. 'OK.' Not my most confident, assertive OK. 'Umm – keeping well out of sight?'

'Yes, indeed,' says Ed, sounding far too enthusiastic for my liking. 'I'll do the full commando bit and sneak up on them to take a photo with your phone.'

'I didn't bring it.'

'And mine's out of battery, so we'd never have been able to phone the police anyway, would we? Hold on, this is where we go off-road.'

How the white Transit negotiated the rutted track is beyond me. I'm amazed we haven't yet come across its ripped-off exhaust. The Land Rover bounces and jolts, throwing me against Ed. He's turned off the lights again: darkness has fallen now, but a bright three-quarter moon has lifted over the horizon, making it easy to see where we're going. The track runs straight across a sloping field, then climbs steeply before skirting the summit of the hill.

'I'm pretty sure there's a barrow up there,' says Ed. 'Might not be the one they're after, of course.'

I'm studying the map, with a slender Maglite from the glove compartment. 'Barrows all over the place. D'you have to go so fast? We'll catch them up if we're not careful.'

We top the crest and begin the descent into a valley. On the other side, the headlights of the Transit are crawling up another rise. Ed slows to a standstill, and switches off the engine while I check the map again.

'That's Easton Down. A long barrow's marked, and a couple of tumuli.'

Across the valley, the lights of the Transit wink out.

'Where are they?' I say uneasily. No sound reaches us from the other side of the valley.

'They've stopped. I know exactly where they are – pilot instinct. Give 'em a few minutes to sort themselves out, then we can risk creeping closer . . .' Towards the top of the rise, torchbeams bob and weave, too far away to make any sense of what's happening. Several minutes pass. Then the torches disappear over the starlit brow of the hill.

'Right.' Ed turns the key in the ignition. 'We'll take the Land Rover to the bottom, then walk from there.' He edges the vehicle down the track and across the valley floor. 'Maybe we *could* risk driving a little further . . .' He revs as the slope suddenly steepens. 'How the hell did they get that old heap up this?' We shoot forward as the track levels. 'I'll park before we get too close – oops.'

The white Transit looms out of the darkness in front, a matter of metres away.

'I thought you said you knew exactly where it was.'

'Sorry. I'm better at this in the air.' He turns off the engine. The sudden silence beats at our eardrums. The same thought strikes both of us simultaneously.

'How far away do you think they are?' I ask, in a low voice. 'Within hearing distance?'

'Only one way to find out.' He opens the driver's door and the overhead light comes on. 'Shit. Not very good at this, are we? Still, with luck, they'll be—'

The clang on the side of the Land Rover makes me jump. Ed, halfway out of the door, suddenly folds up. A furious Bristolian voice snarls, 'What the fuck you think yur doin', my cocker?'

Oh, Lord.

My door is wrenched open, and somebody grabs my sleeve and hauls me out. A torchbeam blinds me.

'Bugrit, Pete.' The occasion calls for something stronger than *crikey*. 'Issa girl.' White-hot scars of light burn themselves into my retina as he waves the torch across my face, and drags me round the bonnet. When my vision clears, Ed's on the ground in front of me, hands clasped to his midriff. Pete, the Man In Black, is standing over him, hefting a metal detector with both hands.

'Doggers, probable.' Pete waves the metal detector menacingly over Ed. Christ, he didn't hit him with that, did he? He'll have cracked a rib at least. 'Durrty doggers. Followed us thinking they was followin' a courtin' couple they could spy on. Be disappointed tonight.' He kicks Ed in the leg an inch or two above the knee, and Ed lets out a tight, hissy little noise. My heart's pounding: this ought to have been funny, but these guys aren't amusing at all: up close, they're pathetic but scary at the same time.

Pete's drawing back his leg for another kick, aiming higher up the thigh.

'*No*,' I say. 'Can't you stop him, Karl?'

'Eh?' Karl releases my arm in surprise. 'Pete, she *knows our names*.'

Pete stares, foot drawn back for the next kick and something dangerous in his piggy eyes. I've probably made the situation a million times worse.

There's a flurry of movement, a shout, and suddenly it's Pete on the ground, clutching his shoulder and grunting through clenched teeth. 'You tosser, you've dislocated my fuckin'—'

Ed's getting to his feet, using the metal detector he's pulled out of Pete's hands as a kind of crutch. '*Crikey*,' he says, making the word grate. 'My heart bleeds. You, you bastard, were about to kick me in the balls – what d'you think I'm going to do, lie back and wait for you to get on with it? Indy, get in the Land Rover. No, driver's side.'

Karl backs away towards the Transit, hands in the air. Ed waves the metal detector threateningly at him. I climb into the Land Rover.

'Key in the ignition,' says Ed. 'Turn it. Headlights on.' The engine throbs and the scene springs to dramatic life, Karl flattening himself against the Transit doors, terrified, the other man still on the ground, trying to push himself one-handed onto his knees. 'Now put her in reverse. Let the clutch out – no, *not yet*, wait till I say go, then straight backwards, if you please.'

In the wing mirror, I watch him walk round the back, carrying the metal detector. He emerges on the other side, his hands empty.

'OK, Indy.' He grins at me through the windscreen. 'Your turn. *Go.*'

I grasp the gear stick, hesitate, then shove it back into neutral, turning off the engine. I don't want to be the one to do this.

'I'm sorry,' I say. 'I . . . can't.' I hand him the keys through the open window. Impossible to explain my reluctance, and the sudden queasiness that has swept over me.

Ed gives me a puzzled stare, lets me climb out, then gets into the driver's seat. Karl shrinks away as I approach the white van, eyes like a spooked horse's. He really isn't very bright, I realize – possibly even has learning difficulties.

'Is that *your* metal detector?' I ask him. 'Not his?'

Karl nods nervously. 'Pete's is still in the van.'

'Hang on,' I call to Ed. 'Don't . . .'

But he doesn't hear me because the engine catches. The Land Rover moves backwards, and the back wheels crunch on something solid. Then the vehicle comes forward again, with another sick-making splintering crunch. Ed turns off the engine, climbs down, and walks to the back to look. 'Don't think the Man In Black will be detecting much Bronze Age treasure with that.'

'What the fuck you on about?' says Pete, clambering awkwardly to his feet, still clutching his damaged shoulder. 'That's criminal fucking damage. Could sue you. We got rights.'

'Not to dig up ancient monuments.'

'Ancient monuments?' says Karl, next to me.

Ed pulls a phone out of his pocket – the phone that has no charge. 'And don't pretend this is innocent because I took a photo when you stopped at Yatesbury. Any more aggro and it's going straight to English Heritage and the landowner, van numberplate, the lot.'

'We didn' touch a thing at Yatesbury,' says Pete. He limps towards the passenger door of the Transit, rubbing his shoulder. 'Never even had the detectors out. 'Sides, what were *you* doin' at Yatesbury if you aren't after same as us?'

'You wouldn't have found much there.' My legs are trembling. 'It's an airfield. The ground's full of old metal so you'd never've been able to pinpoint antiquities.' I touch Karl's arm and whisper, 'Sorry.'

In the headlights, Pete gives me a withering glare.

'Who said anything about antiquities? Course it's a fucking airfield, you daft cow, that's what we were fucking there for. We're into aviation archaeology.'

'You're shivering,' says Ed, as the white Transit turns awkwardly and bumps down the track, taking Pete and Karl back to Bristol, probably via the nearest A and E. 'Jump in the Land Rover, and start the heater. It's the one thing that does work efficiently in this vehicle.'

I haul myself into the driver's seat and turn on the engine. Hot air blasts out of the vents. 'I wish we hadn't done that. They were harmless.'

'Harmless? He hit me with a metal detector, for God's sake. They deserved it.'

'Karl didn't. He was just some poor slow-witted kid, and it was his metal detector you crushed. It didn't belong to the bloke who hit you.'

'Hmm.' Ed turns and gazes at the retreating taillights. 'Well, I'm sorry about that. Though if everything was so sweet and innocent, why are they doing it in the dark?' He leans in and rubs my thigh absent-mindedly. 'And the Man In Black was remarkably easily pacified, wasn't he? Shouted a bit, but pissed off exceeding quick. Threw everything in the back of the Transit and fled. They were twitchy at Yatesbury too.'

'You think they're the ones responsible for Frannie's lights on Windmill Hill, after all?'

'No, no. The aviation-archaeology line had the ring of truth. Only ... no airfield up here on Easton Down that I've ever heard of. And I know all the Wiltshire airfields. Even the ones that closed down years ago. So what were they looking for?' He pokes me in the ribs. 'If you've warmed up a bit, you going to move out of that seat and let me drive?'

'We'd be far safer with me driving.'

'Bollocks. Get out.'

Obediently, I step down to walk round the bonnet, where insects dance in the headlight beams.

Ed stands in my way. 'I've had a better thought.' His fingers wander down the side of my face, across my lips, under my chin, hook themselves into the V-neck of my T-shirt and tug gently. 'How about rough sex in the open air?'

Funny, the same thought was going through my mind.

CHAPTER 39

1941–2

Although, as the airman at the dinner predicted, Donald Cromley had been posted back to his squadron in early November, all that autumn and winter I couldn't rid myself of the notion he was following me. I knew the squadron was still in Kent, because Davey was with them now, his letters frequent as ever, full of his hopes for the eventual move to Colerne, which kept being postponed. But sometimes when I walked on the Ridgeway, I'd be sure I'd heard another step. I'd whip round to see the track empty behind me, a long white tongue licking the darkening Downs. The beech leaves reddened, crisped, fell, and turned to a brown sludge. Frost hardened the ruts. The journey home to Avebury each night seemed longer and longer. This year, if there was an air-raid warning and I missed the bus, or if I was fire-watching, there was no Davey along the road at Wroughton to run me home in his steel-roofed Baby Austin. More than once, I made a nest of blankets borrowed from the nurses and slept on the floor at the hospital.

If Mr Cromley hadn't forced me out of Avebury, that winter would. January '42 was a black, icy month. So was the beginning of February. One of the nurses was getting married, and giving up her room in Swindon Old Town to go and live with her fiancé's parents. I had a couple of hours to spare between the end of work and the start of my fire watch, and I agreed to meet Nell when her shift finished, to walk back to her lodgings and be introduced to the landlady. I was still reluctant to move into town, but I knew it was the sensible thing to do.

Everyone else in the almoner's office had left for the evening. I'd already put on my coat and turned out the light when I realized

I'd forgotten to deliver some discharge papers to the sister on Orthopaedics. It was bright enough by the moonlight pouring through the sash windows to see them on the desk; I picked them up with a little shiver, thinking I'd been lucky so far on fire watch but that tonight was what they used to call a bomber's moon. Bombers were flying all weathers by then, no reason to think they'd be more likely tonight than any other, but that moon filled me with superstitious dread.

My shoes squeaked on the polished lino as I walked down the empty corridor. The hospital was never asleep, but some nights, like tonight, it seemed to be holding its breath. Swindon, with its railway yards and the Vickers aircraft works at South Marston, was bound to get it bad eventual, and maybe this would be the time. Not long ago there'd been a raid on Kembrey Street, where the Plessey factory was, only Jerry had missed that and blown a row of houses to bits instead.

Ahead of me, the thump of double doors announced I wasn't the only person left in the building. A telephone rang unanswered in an office somewhere; on a side corridor a door opened, and a burst of laughter escaped, cut off a moment later as it closed again. Footsteps receded in the other direction, and I glanced down the passage to see if it was anyone I knew, catching only a glimpse of a flapping white coat. When my eyes returned to the corridor ahead, a blue uniform was approaching from the direction of Orthopaedics.

He was more surprised than I, but recovered himself quickly.

'Visiting the sick, Heartbreaker?'

I'd have liked to pretend, but I was carrying a folder full of bumph. 'I work here,' I said curtly. 'Hadn't you figured that out?'

Mr Cromley's eyes slid to the buff folder, and my varnished nails digging into its flank. 'Not a nurse, then,' he said slowly. 'But hospital clerk seems a bit tame for you. Had you down for a factory girl, stuffing high explosive into bomb casings and sending them on their way to Mr Hitler with your very best wishes.'

'What are *you* doing here?' I transferred the folder to the other arm, eyeing my escape route through the doors leading to the ward at the end of the corridor.

'Hasn't your boyfriend told you? Half the squadron transferred to Colerne last weekend. The rest will be following shortly, including Davey.'

Davey's letter must have been delayed, or he hadn't got round to writing yet, though I doubted that. Worried me more that he'd been boasting to Mr Cromley I was his girl.

'I meant, what are you doing in the hospital?'

'Dispensing cheer. One of our Polish pilots broke his leg making his escape through a window after a visit to the WAAF quarters at Wroughton. He doesn't speak much English, so I drove over to bring him cigarettes and condolences in case he was lonely.' Mr Cromley smiled, his old charming self, like Hallowe'en night had never happened. 'Entirely unnecessary, it turned out. He seems to have made friends with all the nurses. So I felt a bit of a spare part. Can I buy you a drink? The Goddard Arms is comfortable. I can give you a lift home after.'

'I'm on fire watch tonight,' I said. Did he still carry that little dagger of his? 'And I'm meeting a friend first.'

'Bring her along,' he said. 'Two's company, three's even more fun—'

The double doors banged again, and Nell came through them, hauling her cape over her shoulders.

'We've other plans.' I caught Nell by the arm. 'Have to deliver these,' I said to her, brandishing the folder. 'I know the boys are waiting for us, but I promised Sister . . .'

Nell's eyebrows lifted a fraction. She allowed herself to be wheeled round and marched back through the double doors.

'Goodbye,' I called over my shoulder to Mr Cromley. 'I should get your skates on back to Colerne, if I were you. Likely be a raid tonight.'

'I don't know what you're playing at,' said Nell. '*Boys*, my foot. But if I wasn't a respectable engaged woman, I'd gladly take him off your hands. He's a bobby dazzler.'

'Don't be dazzled,' I said. 'He's a sorcerer.'

By the time we came back through the double doors Mr Cromley had gone. We left the hospital, making for Drove Road through the blacked-out Old Town. The moonlight silvered the metal hoops of the unlit lampposts; there was hardly anyone about.

'We've time for a quick one at the Victoria,' said Nell. More our sort of pub than the ivy-clad Goddard Arms.

'Not tonight,' I said. 'I don't want to be late for fire watch. Mervyn's on.' He was one of the older ARP wardens, a retired porter with a pitted nose like the burr on an oak tree, and a stickler about time-keeping – though also such a gent he usually tried to persuade me to kip down for the duration. He thought fire watch was no place for a woman, but was always glad, he said, when it was my turn because he reckoned I brought good luck: never a raid when you'm on duty, he used to say.

'You'll stop and have something to eat, though?' asked Nell. 'Probably bloody Woolton pie again, but better than dripping toast in the hospital.'

'I like dripping toast.'

'Reminds me of engine oil.'

We grumbled amiably about food all the way up Cricklade Street. I was bringing a half-dozen eggs from my Avebury landlady for hers, each one wrapped careful in tissue paper and nested in the shoulder bag that was meant to hold my gas mask – which I'd stopped bothering to haul around with me months ago. The ARP wardens would have fined me if they'd caught me without it, but the carry-case came in useful for all manner of cargo.

On the right, the dark pinnacle of Christchurch spire pierced the silver sky: the Old Lady on the Hill, the locals call it. Behind the churchyard lay the overgrown gardens of the Lawn, a crumbling mansion house where the Goddard family used to live. It had been empty for years, though there was a rumour it was to be requisitioned to billet troops. I turned round and checked behind us. A couple of soldier boys were disappearing round the corner a long way off, but no one else was around as we took the fork that was Drove Road.

Nell's lodgings were about halfway up. Her landlady made a fuss of me, wanted to know all about my family. Devizes, eh: full of soldiers now, was it? Was my young man one of them?

Every time someone asked me if I had a young man, I felt a sense of dread. It was as if denying Davey would be condemning him to death. And here he was, arriving in Wiltshire any day now, and no doubt planning to drive over to see me, soon as he could find petrol for his car. How was I going to explain to him that the night after the Starfish had been a mistake and could never be repeated?

No, I said. He's not a soldier, he's in the RAF. A navigator.

Though she's got a pilot officer after her too, said Nell, with a wink.

The landlady's husband came in from his shift, tired, not saying much. He worked on the railways, and went to get washed while the landlady and Nell took me upstairs to show me the room. The land-lady was especial proud of the alarm clock, Canadian made, same as they'd issued to all the railwaymen: you'd have it, she said, he sleeps so light, these days, neither him nor me needs it. The room was comfortable, spacious, with a double wardrobe and a bay window, but I knew immediately I wouldn't take it.

They asked me to stop for supper, and I looked at my watch and said, no, I'd better be going, old Mervyn was a Tartar for punctuality.

On the way back down Drove Road I was cursing myself for all kinds of fool, because it had been a good room, better than my little attic in Avebury. I could still take it. I hadn't told them I wouldn't. But after bumping into Mr Cromley earlier I'd been sure, against all sense, if I'd pulled back the blackout material on that window, instead of their vegetable patch and an Anderson shelter at the end of the garden there'd be a row of tombstones. I couldn't shake the sickening memory of the bay-windowed house with the cemetery behind, and a voice that said, *Spit. Lick my finger.*

I was nearly at the end of the road when the siren started up. Could've gone back to Nell's landlady's house easy, and asked to crowd with them into their damp little shelter. They'd be expecting me to dash back, Nell's hospitable landlady hovering uneasily at the kitchen door while her husband urged her to hurry up, the bombers weren't going to wait for them to stroll at their leisure to the bottom of the garden.

But if I went back I'd be late for fire watch.

Mervyn wouldn't mind. He'd have worried, but he'd be happy on his own. He'd enjoy pressing one of the medical students into service.

I hesitated, almost turned. But, no, it'd be letting him down. It wasn't that far. If I ran, I'd be at the hospital in a jiff.

I started to leg it down the road, hoping I wouldn't see the shape of a Heinkel or a Junkers crossing the silvery sky towards the spire of Christchurch. The carry-case for my gas mask was banging against my hip, and I realized I'd forgotten to give Nell's landlady the eggs in it. Probably scrambled by now. I wasn't scared. I knew I could make it back easy. The street was familiar, and empty: there was only me, and the banshee wail of the siren, no thunder yet of engines in the sky, no oil-saturated wood shavings ready to burst into flames, like that mad night at the Starfish. If I met an ARP warden, he'd only tell me to get a wiggle on back to the hospital.

The slope was gentle but I was flagging as I came up to the low wall that bounded the churchyard, its iron railings spared from being melted down for Spitfires. A breeze rattled the leafless branches of the pollarded trees edging the path to the porch. A shadow came at me from the gateway, a hand caught the cloth of my coat, and fingers dug cruelly into my arm, jerking me almost off my feet.

It was all slow and dim, like I was watching myself then, the shadow tugging me through the gate, its other arm snaking round my neck, a knee in the small of my back forcing me up the steps and onto the churchyard path. He said something, but I couldn't make it out, because the voice was distorted, and I'd caught enough of a glimpse to know why. It was like looking into the empty stare of a black skull instead of a face. He was wearing a gas mask. For a moment, stupid, I thought it was the ARP warden. He'd tell me there was a gas attack tonight, to put on my own mask, and then he'd have to fine me because he'd discover that I had a mess of raw egg in my carry-case instead.

'I'm sorry . . .' I tried to say, but then my brain started working again. The ARP warden wouldn't have his arm round my throat, nor stink so powerful of beer.

I heard the sound of the bombers then, coming from the south like fat blowflies homing in on raw meat. He half pushed, half dragged me up the path, and now I reckoned I understood what he'd been saying, because when I struggled the arm tightened across my windpipe, cutting off my air. Time stopped and started, came and went. Between the trunks of the trees I glimpsed Victorian gravestones, an angel leaning at a drunken angle on a pedestal. The night was swirling with lights, searchlight beams, sparks behind my eyes, the white moon, the thunder of the raid starting, streams of tracer and the pulsing glow of incendiaries as he hauled me round the side of the church and leaned against the wall, panting, his arm still crooked tight on my throat. The Old Lady on the Hill spread before us a grandstand view of hell, where a bomb must've landed on the railway yards. Behind us the old tangled shrubberies of the Lawn were black and empty. No one courting there tonight. No one to hear me, if his arm slackened and freed my throat enough to scream.

Then suddenly he swings me round so our positions are reversed, and it's me against the wall, the weight of him pushing my face against the rough stone, and his unmistakable intention pressed into the small of my back like a horrible parody of the night with Davey, watching the procession in the Manor garden.

'Fucking in a boneyard,' he whispers. 'You owe me, Heartbreaker.' His nail rakes across the side of my face and he tears out my earring: he's opened a vein, because I feel the slow drip of blood trickling down my neck. Then I realize it in't his nail, it's the ragged point of his old bronze dagger; I can see it out of the corner of my eye. More magic, then, the dirty sort that's only about power.

He releases my throat but his hand's like a claw on my shoulder. This time I hear him loud and clear. 'You can turn round,' he says. 'Don't be afraid.'

I told myself I wouldn't be afraid anyway. I'd decide how I'd be, not let him decide for me. I turned round.

Eyes like a fly. The Insect King.

'Don't be afraid,' he repeats. 'It's only a mask. And you know about masks, don't you, Heartbreaker?'

PART SIX

The Sun Stands Still

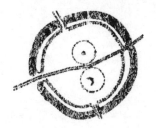

Without a doubt Solstice – from the Latin *solstitium*, the sun at a stand-still – would have been an important occasion for our ancestors who gathered at Avebury. Unlike at Stonehenge, where the midsummer sun rises over the Heel Stone, there seems to be no obvious solar align-ment; but for all agricultural societies, it is a critical point in the year. On 21 June, the sun rises at its most north-easterly degree. Morning after morning, as the days have lengthened, its point of appearance has crept in an arc around the world, only to pause before changing course and completely reversing its motion.

Dr Martin Ekwall,
A Turning Circle: The Ritual Year at Avebury,
Hackpen Press

CHAPTER 40

1942

'I've found a nice room in Swindon, Mam,' I said, 'and you've no need to worry because there hasn't been a raid for more than a couple of months.' I was holding her hand; she was too exhausted even to sit up in bed. There were only a couple of other patients in the side ward in the cottage hospital at Marlborough. Mr Keiller had fixed it, bless him; he seemed to know all the right strings to pull.

I hadn't had to offend Nell's landlady by turning down the room with the bay window because Nell was still living there. Her fiancé was missing in action, so the wedding and her plans to move in with his parents had been postponed. Her landlady recommended me to a woman further along the road, and now I was in lodgings hardly bigger than a boxroom. It had a narrow single bed, a chest of drawers, and instead of a wardrobe, a hook on the back of the door. Her husband worked at the railway yards too, and she had a job at the Plessey factory at the far end of Drove Road; it wasn't so much the money she wanted but the extra ration book in the house. I rarely saw them, except at mealtimes, and spent all the time I could at the hospital. There was more than enough work to keep me busy.

My mother blinked slowly, and sighed. After a while I realized she was trying to raise her head from the pillow.

'I got eyes in my head, Frances,' she whispered. 'Don't think you can fool me, like you can your father.' She paused for an effortful breath. 'I won't tell him, though. It would kill him. I know I can trust you to do the right thing.' Her fingers tightened on mine.

* * *

There wasn't a soul I could have told what had happened that night. When Mr Cromley buttoned up his air-force-blue trousers and left me in the churchyard, he knew he was safe. War hero: DSO, DFC. Reckon I wasn't the only girl in the blackout who knew she wouldn't be believed if she cried rape.

God knows how Mam could tell I'd fallen pregnant, and she was the only one, because I was still thin as a stick. She thought the baby was Davey's, and she wanted me to shame him into marrying me. But he wasn't some country simpleton who couldn't add up. Even if he had been, wouldn't have been fair on him.

He trundled over in the Baby Austin from the base whenever he could, which was mercifully not often. Colerne was a long way from Swindon, almost to Bath, and flying night-fighters could be cruel tiring, so he was busy nights while I worked days. Easy to fob him off, too, with the excuse that visiting Mam took up all my spare moments. I'd managed to avoid being alone with him much by insisting he brought a pal along so poor unhappy Nell could come out with us, to cheer her up. Davey was so good-hearted he didn't mind, or if he did, he didn't show it, so long as I allowed him a kiss at the end of the evening. Nell gave me some odd glances when I fended off her attempts to give us time on our own, but I told her afterwards Davey was always pressing me to go too far. The strange thing was, he wasn't. Something had changed in him, and sometimes I had the feeling it was him keeping me at arm's length, rather than the other way round.

I walked out of the hospital doors and onto the sunny forecourt. The Baby Austin was waiting, Davey in the back seat, head back with his forage cap pulled down over his eyes. He woke as soon as I rattled the door handle. 'You're tired out,' I said, opening the passenger door. 'They must be keeping you busy. Tell you what, drive me straight home and you go back to base for some proper shuteye.'

Davey climbed into the driver's seat. 'Don't fuss. I'm fine.' He yawned as he fired the engine. 'Well, all right. I wouldn't mind grabbing an hour or two before we take off tonight. But let's stop on the way back, shall we? The afternoon's too beautiful to waste.'

We drove up to the common overlooking the town, and Davey reversed the car a little way up a track. We sat in silence, looking down across the roofs of Marlborough.

So here it was, then, the moment I'd been dreading. Any minute now he'd lean across and start to kiss me. Then, unless I stopped him, a hand would sneak between the buttons of my dress. What was I to do? How could I explain? And what if I did tell him it was over between us, and tonight was the night he never came back from patrol over the dark Channel coast?

Davey didn't move. He was staring out of the windscreen, his eyes ringed with fatigue.

'You're done in,' I said. 'Start the car, take us back after all.'

'No,' he said, still not making a move. 'I don't want to go back yet.'

There was something in his voice. 'You hate it, don't you?' I said. 'You should've stayed an erk after all.'

He shook his head. 'No, that's not it. I'd rather be doing this.' He opened his mouth, then closed it again.

'There's a but missed off the end of that sentence.'

'It's . . . hard sometimes, that's all.' He was twisting his cap between his hands.

'Hard?'

'Hard to explain. Just . . . you have to push yourself.'

His face was all screwed up with tension and he couldn't meet my eyes.

'Is it frightening, going out at night?' I asked.

He started to shake his head, then nodded instead. 'But not like I thought. I'm never afraid when we take off. It's coming back.' He tried for a laugh. 'Nobody really talks about it, except they call it the Twitch. Some have it more obvious than others. Some never seem to have it at all. But if you do, you keep it to yourself.' He couldn't look me in the eye, afraid I was going to condemn him. 'Same as . . . I used to care when we shot a bomber down. Used to watch out to see if they'd managed to bale out, used to hope the poor buggers had. And then I stopped caring. Same time I started thinking about whether or not I'd be coming back.'

So that was it, the reason he'd been awkward with me.

'You're burned out,' I said. 'They were on at you to take an easier posting. You shouldn't have joined that squadron. Tell them, Davey. You can't go on this way.'

He ignored me because he'd unstoppered himself, and it all had to come pouring out now. 'Something keeps you going for the first hour or so after takeoff. Looking for trade, we say, waiting for the controller to give you a vector to steer onto on a bomber's tail. And when you do make contact, you're too busy staying alive, too busy reading off the AI screen, looking at them blips, working out is he above you or below you, how far before your pilot can shoot the bastard out of the sky, will the gunner at the back of the bomber wake up and see us first. But afterwards . . . I think, dear God, how did we make it? Why did You pick us to come home, and not those poor sods in the flamer we shot down?' He stared down between his knees, and began picking at a loose thread in the fabric of his cap. 'Ought to feel glad on the way home, but I never do. Keep looking over my shoulder or listening to the note of the engine and thinking, any minute, God'll change His mind, and we're going to fall out of the sky. And you know what's the worst? Nights there's no contact, when we fly all over the sky searching for the buggers and they never show up. When the order comes to head for home, I think, that's torn it. Soon as our backs are turned, there'll be a Messerschmitt sneaking out from the dark side of the moon and sitting on our tail.'

He twisted in his seat to face me, with a rueful grin on his face. 'You know what I do then? I start saying what I call the Navigator's Prayer. The Lord is my shepherd, he leadeth me up the Bristol Channel, above safe waters. Over Bridgwater Bay, he hideth me in clouds, to turn east at Avonmouth. Yea, though we fly through the valley of the shadow of death, if we follow the rivers, watch for the moon on the water, we'll come home at last. I think about you, coming home to you, and I keep repeating to myself, watch for the moon shining on water. Helps push down the panic, when we're leaking fuel and the pilot's depending on me to find the quickest way back to base. And when we see the Kennet and Avon, I know we're nearly there. Only a few miles, and I'll be flying near above where you are. I tell the pilot to sit above the canal and it's a straight road. I never feel safe till then. Same on the nights we cut across country from the south, I still look for the canal to know I'm coming home.'

'Davey . . .' I said.

He shook his head quickly. 'Don't say anything, Fran. Don't say a word.' He jabbed the starter with a trembling finger, and the car rolled down the bumpy track towards the main road.

Right now, with Mam so ill, I couldn't afford to be sick, so I told myself there was plenty of time to make up my mind what to do. Working in a hospital, I knew there were ways to solve my problem – risky ways. We'd had enough girls in with blood down their legs, trying to persuade the doctor it was nothing but a heavy period.

Lucky I wasn't the other kind of sick, like some women are in the early months. There was only one thing did it to me and that was the smell of wine. Found that out one morning in church, at communion. The vicar wiped the chalice, I tottered unsteady to my feet, ran up the aisle and out the door. I made it into the fresh air just in time, and lost my breakfast over some old worthy's tombstone. This wasn't Christchurch, of course. The devil had settled in that churchyard. Like he'd settled in me.

But wine was easy avoided: there weren't much about in the war. Only trouble was, tonic wine was popular with the young doctors. God knows where they got hold of it. Cabbage was the worst of them; the nurses said he held parties in his room, tonic wine and pure ethanol in the punch.

Must've been the day after one of his famous parties I came across him on one of the wards. He looked terrible, even by junior-doctor standards: curly hair rumpled, purple bags under his eyes, and the eyeballs all veined a watery red.

The sister on Men's Surgical was a terror. Didn't matter you weren't one of her nurses, she'd still dragoon you into doing her bidding.

'Miss Robinson!' she said. 'Dr Prentice being somewhat the worse for wear this morning, perhaps you'd make him a cup of tea. Otherwise we shall never get these dressings done.' The nurse with her rolled her eyes. I'd only come in to drop off the cigarette rations.

While I was in the sluice waiting for the tea to brew – the nurses always made it from the hot-water cylinder there – Cabbage came in. Hadn't realized his name was Dr Prentice; to us, he was only ever Cabbage, with his stocky frame and fleshy, flattened nose.

'I gorra terrible head,' he said. He leaned over the sink, arms slightly bent. 'No, won't come up, more's the pity.' He belched. 'Beg pardon. That's better.' In his Scouse voice, the word became *berra*.

The smell was coming off him in waves, cheap sickly red wine, like it had drifted up from the communion cup. He was blocking my way to the door. I tried to hold it back, but the belch was what did it. I elbowed him out of the way and threw up in the sink.

When I came up for air, he was leaning back against the wall with his eyes closed.

'Know how you feel,' he said. 'But not for the same reason, maybe.' He opened one eye and winked. 'Earned my best marks on Obs and Gynae. You need birra medical advice, you let me know.' Written across his hangover pallor was kindness, and genuine concern.

I wiped my mouth on my hankie and muttered something about the Spam fritters in the canteen. Then I stumbled out, leaving him to pour his own tea. In the corridor, the thought of Cabbage's meaty little hands poking me about almost brought the sickness on again. But at least I knew now who to ask for help.

CHAPTER 41

Solstice

The sky starts to lighten at about three in the morning. I lie there for nearly an hour, watching the curtains turn paler and paler, lying first on one side, then the other in the hope of fooling my body back into sleep. Eventually, when the bedside clock shows four, I unwrap the tangled sheets from my legs, get up and stare out of the window. Nothing moving on the street apart from next door's cat, dark coat glistening in the drizzle. In the distance, the breeze occasionally blows the sound of drumming towards Trusloe. Solstice: the pagans are welcoming sunrise – not that there's any sun to see through the low cloud – in the stone circle. Bryn will be there.

I pull on my jeans, quickly, not wanting to give myself a chance to change my mind.

There are two police cars at the junction where the Trusloe lane meets the main road, making sure no pagans park where they shouldn't. I walk down the road towards Avebury, but cut off across the field opposite the public car park. Two more patrol cars at the entrance, and the barrier's closed, a man leaning out of the window of a people-carrier, shouting at the coppers who won't let him in. A short queue of cars waits hopefully behind. Nobody, apart from residents, is allowed to stop anywhere near the village this morning. There are cones across every lay-by and farm gateway, the narrow country lanes patrolled by more police vehicles. If the idea was to keep people out of Avebury, it hasn't worked. Several woebegone pilgrims are behind me on the main road, in walking boots and cagoules beaded with rain, hiking from cars parked miles away, too late for sunrise. As I clamber over the stile onto the field path, a flaming paper lantern rises high into the sky above the circle.

The water ripples quietly over the long weeds on the streambed. I was afraid there might be people here. But no one is at the spring except the Goddess, with her winking mosaic skin of broken mirror tiles and china. She averts her eyes, staring into the brown water, while I tie the offering to the branch above her head.

This time I came prepared. A scrap of an old blue cotton shirt – one of Frannie's dusting rags. *Blue's your colour . . .* I've stapled an envelope to it: BRYN, in bold letters. It took three attempts to settle on words that might finish the matter, with reasonable grace:

Thank you for a lovely moment. The Goddess smiled on us, once and once only. Goodbye.

There didn't seem much point in signing it, since we've never exchanged names. All the same, I scrawled *India* at the bottom, out of habit.

When I came here before, in May, this place seemed beautiful, magic. Now it makes me want to cringe. The rags hanging from the tree seem tawdry and pathetic. The Goddess – only a bald shop dummy, after all – is spattered with mud, and her plastic foot cracked. The note I'm leaving seems embarrassingly twee . . .

Something – bird or rat – stirs in the hedge. Spooked, I lose my balance, fumble the knot and tear the staple from the material. The note drifts down like a dead leaf into the mud at the Goddess's feet. A twig cracks behind me as I'm bending to pick it up.

'Hello.' Soft northern voice that's almost a whisper.

I hadn't heard him coming. The note's in my hand, the envelope smeared with mud. Straightening up, my eyes meet Bryn's wild blue ones. If he says, 'I knew you'd be here,' I'll scream.

'Thought you'd be at the stone circle,' I say. His eyes are bloodshot and scratchy-looking, the lids red and puffy.

'Nah.' He glances round like priest-in-residence of the grove. 'Spent the night in a vigil at Adam's Grave, lookin' out over Alton Barnes. Walked back to make my offerings here.'

'That's *miles*.'

'Doesn't worry me.' He seems exalted from lack of sleep. 'A crop circle appeared in the East Field, overnight. Flashing lights. Whole landscape lit up.'

'Sheet lightning?'

'Nah. Pulses of energy. That's what makes the crop circle. Not everyone can see it. There were some guys watching with night-vision scopes along the ridge, said they never saw a thing till the sky started to brighten, and there was the circle, out of nowhere.' His lips part in the small, superior smile of one the gods favour. 'The military were there already, before dawn. Great black helicopter hovering over the field. And men in black combats in an unmarked van. I went down, and there was grey dust around the circle. Guy with the night-vision scope came with me, said it was radioactive because his Geiger counter was kicking off. The men in combats told us to keep away. See, that's what happens, the pulses of energy register on secret detectors, and the military send a team out to investigate. They don't tell us what's going on because it would scare people too much.'

'Right,' I say, with my own thoughts about men in unmarked vans. 'Probably wise to keep away.'

'Didn't get close, but it gave me a headache and my legs are aching. They say all that kind of stuff – nausea, cramps – can hit you if the circle's on a leyline, and the flow of energy's been reversed.' He rubs his eyes. 'You come to make an offerin' too?'

He'll have seen me, through the trees. But did he see the note fluttering to the ground?

I could hand it to him to read now. Or – I could come back later.

With the other hand, the one not holding the note, I point into the tree. 'That's mine, the blue one.'

'Your colour.' He smiles at me, and a poisonous little voice in my head tells me I'll never wear blue again. 'I'll hang mine on the tree, then we—'

'I should be getting back. Have to be at work.' I glance down at my watch, which isn't there because I forgot to put it on. 'Busy week.'

Bryn gives me the unconvinced look of one who doesn't understand the concept of 'at work' or why anyone should be 'busy'. He steps under the tree, fumbling in his pocket, then reaches up to hang a red fabric dog collar on a branch that bends over the water. A fleeting gleam of sun makes shadows of the leaves fall across his tanned face: he's frowning with concentration and breathing heavily through his mouth, like a child, as he fastens the clasp.

'Where's Cynon?' I hadn't noticed until now that the dog wasn't with us.

'Back at the Long Barrow.'

For a moment I'd been worried something had happened to the animal. 'You camping there again? Anyway, I should go. Sorry. I'll leave you to it.'

Coward, whispers my conscience.

'We can walk back together,' says Bryn. 'I'm near finished here.' He faces the Goddess, his face reflected over and over in the broken mirror tiles. His lips move, but I can't make out what he's saying. I edge backwards towards the conifers. Before I can make my escape, he's turning to me again, his eyes alight with something I can't, and don't want, to read. All through the wood I can feel his eyes boring into my back, making my legs clumsy and awkward on the slippery path.

'Right,' I say, as we arrive at the track leading to the Long Barrow. 'Er – see you around.'

'Mebbe not for a bit,' he says, and sneezes. 'Sorry, hayfever. Leavin' tomorrow, I think. Decided I'm goin' back for Fergus.'

Relief washes over me. 'Great. I mean, well, goodbye, then.'

'I'll be back.' His eyes lock with mine. 'It's still early . . .' He gestures vaguely in the direction of the Long Barrow.

'Sorry,' I say, with an enormous effort not to let my eyes slide guiltily away. 'Have to make breakfast for my gran.' The most I've told Bryn about myself, and already I wish I hadn't let it slip. I don't want to let him into any part of my life. He's nodding as if he understands.

'Goddess go with you.' His hand touches mine, and he leans forward but before he can kiss me I've stepped back. His eyes flinch, like a lost child who expects nothing better from life than disappointment. He gives me a tight little smile and starts up the hillside track towards the sleeping dragon on the skyline. I'm half expecting to see Cynon race out of the barrow to greet him, but there's no sign of him.

I plod down the hill, turning my head every so often to check. The minute he's disappeared between the stones guarding the barrow, I cut back into the wood again to the spring.

Without the staple to fasten it, I have to untie the blue cloth, and wrap it round the envelope. He's bound to come back before he leaves tomorrow . . . The faded red dog collar trembles as I pull down the branch. Something doesn't feel right about it. I re-knot my blue rag, making sure the name on the envelope shows, glancing uneasily over my shoulder, imagination setting eyes into the trees.

No one there. But when I glance towards the water, the eyes of the shop-dummy Goddess are fixed on my treacherous face.

CHAPTER 42

1942

So there was no way to tell Davey I couldn't be his girl. He still didn't touch me, apart from a chaste kiss at the end of our evenings. I pretended there was fervour in the way I kissed him back, though it was a relief he didn't seem to want anything more. I wondered if he was afraid of failing and appearing less than a man. But I'd come to dread hearing the unmistakable misfire of the Baby Austin as it turned the corner into Drove Road – he somehow kept that car alive, but it wasn't a well machine. I couldn't bear the hope in his eyes when he climbed out of it and waved to me.

You made your own bed, Frances Robinson, now you get down and lie on it. That's what Mam would have said, though now she was too tired even for talking. When I visited, she lay watching me with dark eyes that were wells of pain. The doctors – and Dad – talked breezily in front of her of an operation, when she'd found her strength again, but anyone could see that would never happen.

Davey turned up at Drove Road one Saturday morning in June. I was more than four months gone, now, still skinny, with a funny little tum on me, like a peapod that hasn't yet filled out proper. I'd my set of excuses – hospital food, all stodge, can't keep the weight off – but I never had to use them. People were too polite or too blind to ask. No forgetting, though: the babba was going to be a kicker, already beginning to flutter its tiny heels against my belly wall five or six times a day. It felt like butterfly wings beating inside me.

'Too lovely to stay in,' Davey said. 'Brought us a picnic. Swapped some cigs for a tin of ham.'

'I can't,' I said, hating myself for killing that hope. 'You know I see Mam Saturday afternoons.'

His face was near exploding with eagerness. 'I know. I'll drive you again. We'll stop on the way.'

So this time we wound up sitting on one of the barrows on Windmill Hill, eating ham sandwiches made with no butter. The wind was rustling the grasses, fat seeds bending their nodding heads. There were flowers all over, blue scabious, pink-veined orchids like stretched skin, trefoils the colour of spilt egg yolk, the edges tinged red. High clouds raced each other across a blue sky.

I reached for another ham sandwich. Lord, I was hungry these days. Davey yawned.

'Keeping you up again, am I?' I asked.

'Have a heart, Fran,' he said. 'Night op. Saw sunrise over the Mendips as we came back up the Bristol Channel. Thank God.'

'You not applied for a transfer yet?' I said. 'Davey, I told you, you can't go on . . .'

He turned on me with a flash of anger in his eyes. First time he'd ever been so sharp with me. 'Forget what I told you. You can't understand.'

'I understand burned out,' I said. 'Don't think you're the only one. I see it all the time with they lads on the ward, pushing themselves to go back to operations and crying at night when they think no one hears. It's no disgrace, Davey.'

He wouldn't meet my eyes again, and started ripping up roots of grass, one by one, and I knew what it was. He was looking away towards the stone circle and the Manor at Avebury, hidden in the trees. Poor old Davey. Always trying to live up to something, or someone.

'Last week we lost two crews,' he said. 'One came too close behind the bomber they were stalking, and when it blew up, they blew up too. The other crew caught it coming home over Weston-super-Mare. Still dark, moon set, and the bloody ack-ack mistook them for a German fighter. No bale-outs, no survivors.' He looked down at the blood streaking his fingers where the blades of grass had cut him. There were tears in his eyes.

They was brave boys, the ones like Davey. The ones with imagination and brains, who could work out the odds, and picture the end, and still they made themselves climb into those fragile wooden planes night after night. Poor sod. I remembered the sunny day four years ago when I sat up here with my sketchbook, seeing him carefree and driving the motorbike with Mr Keiller on the back, bouncing over the hilltop, before I'd known about Mam being ill, before . . .

Davey put his hand on my leg.

Time twisted round on itself. Couldn't help it, I flinched.

Everything pulled itself out then, into a long moment. *Heartbreaker* . . . The wind picked at the seed heads and the hem of my dress. Davey was frozen, his hand an inch away from my knee.

'I'm sorry,' I said. 'It's . . . Mam, you know . . .'

But he heard the lie in the pause. 'You met someone.'

'No. Yes—' Too late again, I tried to grasp the excuse.

'I've been stupid,' he said. He put his chin on his hand and looked away, trying to hide the wetness in his eyes. 'I've always been stupid about you, Fran. I let myself think you'd come round, eventual, I only had to be patient. And I was, wasn't I? I thought you had come round, that night at the Starfish – and these last months, I've fooled myself into believing the only problem was with me, and one day if I was patient we'd be over that too. But it's like that sodding car, innit? I coax the bugger into starting, but she in't ever going to run sweet, is she?'

'No,' I said. It was a relief to tell the truth, though I could hear the tearing grief in his voice. 'There in't – what there needs to be. I do love you, you're my friend, but I can't love you the way you want me to.'

'So who is he?'

'There in't anyone.' Then, bugger it, I was crying. Couldn't stop myself. Was in that place where you cry so hard feels like the earth under you ought to be washed away. Face down on the barrow, grasses prickling my arms and chest, cheeks scalding. There was a moment I felt Davey touch my back, very light, but I tensed and he drew his hand away.

Don't know how long I cried. Sun went on beating down on us, a plane droning in the distance, one of the training craft at Yatesbury, probably. Imagined Mr Cromley in it, flying circuits, looking down like a god and laughing his socks off. But he wasn't at Yatesbury now. Davey saw him every day at Colerne, bless him, and Davey didn't know.

After a while I realized Davey was talking, his voice low, like an embarrassed man mumbling prayers, the wind whipping the words out of his mouth and scattering them.

'. . . Look for the moon shining on water . . . Kennet and Avon running east–west, a straight road home and lock onto the signal . . .'

'Davey.' My voice was all claggy with tears, but it still worked.

I heard the rustle of grasses. I rolled over, and there he was, good couple of yards off, sitting at the edge of the barrow's pudding top, back to me but his head turned to look over his shoulder. 'You all right, Fran?'

'What in buggeration you on about?'

He shuffled his body round to face me, his hands still wrapped tight about his knees. 'Navigator's Prayer. Reminding myself we always do come home in the end. Dun't matter who he is, I want you to be happy. Best friends, eh? We still best friends?' Then he saw my face. 'Dun't he make you happy? What's wrong, Fran?'

I was a godforsaken fool. Could have told him then, everything, every blessed detail. But I was afraid of the strength of what he felt for me. If he'd known about the baby that was on the way, he'd have made me see it through and keep it. He'd have married me, like Mam wanted; it wouldn't have been love, or not the kind I was after, but it would have been family. And I nearly did tell him about the baby. But I knew that baby was a curse; it was Mr Cromley's bastard, and I'd be getting rid of it. And we were on Windmill Hill, where I'd lain in the grass daydreaming about Mr Keiller. I wasn't yet the age where you see more than one shade of green.

I told him everything else, though. What happened in the churchyard. What Mr Cromley made me do. All the way back to the sick
little ritual, the two of them, spilling my blood and taking my virginity
in the house by the cemetery because I'd begged them to do it.

CHAPTER 43

1942

After I'd told him about Mr Cromley and the house backing onto the cemetery, Davey said nothing. The wind shivered the flowers and the long grasses on top of the barrow; a skylark was singing somewhere overhead.

'So now you know,' I said, to break the silence.

'You should've told me before.' He was tearing up grasses by their roots again. 'I'd've—'

'Lost your job, if you'd done anything. Or lost me mine.' I put a hand on his arm. 'Leave them grasses alone. They done you no harm.'

He shook my hand off. His face was knotted and bright red.

'You do believe me?' I asked.

'I don't know what to think.'

'I went with him willing, the first time, but you do understand why?'

He shook his head. 'Don't know if I understand anything 'bout you any more, Fran.' There was defeat in his voice. He wouldn't look at me. I'd been too truthful.

'Dear Christ, I'd do anything for it not to have happened. I wish a bloody bomb *had* landed on us. If I'd been stronger, I'd have fought him off and killed him with my bare hands. Why don't he fall out of the sky, when so many good lads are never coming back?' The baby gave two feeble kicks, like it was knocking shyly to come out. A lark was twittering high above. Davey slowly tortured a grass head. 'You think I asked for it, don't you?'

'You should've stayed at Nell's.'

'The air raid didn't start till after I'd left.' I was angry with him now, too, for blaming me. 'I wasn't looking for a poke, Davey. I was trying to get back to the hospital for fire watch.'

'Poke's a vulgar word.'

'Well, what word'm I supposed to use, then?'

He looked at his watch. 'Time I took you to see your mam. Visiting hours'll be over if we don't get a move on.'

And that was that. We walked in silence across the hillside back to the top of the track where we'd left the Baby Austin, me thinking maybe I *had* asked for it, maybe it *was* all my fault. Then I'd think, no, it wasn't, and who was Davey to judge? I could've wished him in a place where he'd understand how powerless a woman is when a man wants his way. But that kind of thinking in't no good. You only get it back yourself, threefold, like they say.

Outside the cottage hospital, I'd climbed out of the Austin and was almost at the entrance when I heard behind me the squeak of the car window being wound down.

'Fran?'

I stopped and looked back. Yards of forecourt between us, as well as the concealed peapod of my belly.

'Give me time, OK?' he said. 'It's . . . not easy to understand, you know?' There were tears in his eyes. 'Feels like you've taken everything away. There never was any hope for me, was there? That night we were together wun't no more than pity, was it?'

'Gratitude,' I said. 'You saved my life.' Then wished it unsaid: it made what we'd done sound like a ten-bob note pushed into a beggar's hand.

His jaw tightened. 'I'd still do anything for you, Fran. But I can't think about what you did without getting angry.'

'Be angry with him,' I said. 'Not me.' I turned my back and pushed through the double doors.

Mam was frailer than ever, more yellow, skin like old newspaper with dark bruises along the veins of her arm.

'What they doing to you, Mam?' I asked, trying to keep the cheerfulness from leaking out of my voice.

'Always sticking needles in me,' she said. 'I tell 'em, it won't do no good.' How defeated she sounded.

'Davey's outside,' I said, and felt a wrench as relief lit up her face. 'He'll . . . do the right thing.' Didn't know what I meant by that, but it was a lie to comfort myself as much as her.

'Good girl,' she said. 'I can go easy now.'

'Don't talk about going anywhere,' I said. But she was drifting to sleep already, poor tired thing. I sat by her, stroking her hand, seeing a smile ease the corners of her mouth when I did so, but she didn't open her eyes. After a while her breathing deepened and I knew she was no longer aware of me. I stood up, wondering how long I should stay. I went to the window to wave to Davey, to tell him I was ready to leave, but the Baby Austin was gone.

Mam died less than a week later. The telephone call came while I was on fire watch. Dad didn't have a phone at the shop; he was calling from his neighbour's. I could hear the clink of cups in the background, the meaningless chatter that begins when someone dies and never stops for weeks and weeks. I thought I made out someone saying, 'A blessed release.' Dad could hardly speak: his voice was raspy with unshed tears. 'Harold,' called another voice halfway through. 'Your tea's getting cold.' Dad, lost without Mam to give him the cue how to behave, said 'I'd better go,' and hung up.

I went up to the hospital roof again and sat waiting. A bomb would have been a relief. But the bombers had missed us: the glow to the west showed it was Bristol's turn again.

Then there was so much to sort out because Dad wasn't capable of sorting anything. The hospital gave me time off and I went to Devizes, sleeping for the first time in the boxroom that smelt of cigars. I tried to persuade Dad to open the shop, but he couldn't function. If anyone came in he stared, unable to work out what they were there for.

The funeral was held in Avebury at St James's, the church packed, sandwiches and beer after at the Red Lion. I'd hoped Mr Keiller would come, but Mrs Sorel-Taylour said he was away, in London. Perhaps he was patching things up with Mrs Keiller again. I'd wanted to ask if there was any chance of a cottage for Dad because it seemed to me my poor lost father would never manage the shop without Mam. Mrs Sorel-Taylour shook her head.

'I very much doubt there's anywhere suitable,' she said. 'The new houses at Trusloe, if there'd been time to build them, one of those would have been ideal.'

'I thought maybe the cottage in Manor Drive?'

'Mr Keiller has other plans for that.' The twist of her mouth suggested she disapproved of those plans, whatever they might be. 'Can't he manage for the time being where he is?'

'Avebury was his home,' I said. 'And now Mam's here, he should be too.'

'Well, there's a war on. People have to make do.' Her face softened. 'I'm sorry, Frances.'

Afterwards Dad and I went back to the flat over the shop. He'd been drinking whisky in the pub; it had befuddled him. I put the kettle on for tea. When I carried the cups through into the sitting room, he was staring into space, his face drained of all hope.

'We need to talk,' I said. 'What'll you do when I go?'

'Go?' He turned bewildered eyes on me. 'What do you mean? Aren't you staying?'

'I have to get back to the hospital.'

'But she's dead.'

I didn't understand for a moment, then realized he was away with the fairies again. 'Not *that* hospital, Dad. I work at another hospital. War work. They need me there.'

'I need you.' His eyes pleaded. 'Thought you'd stay. Not sure I can cope on my own.'

'I'll stay another week,' I said.

I stayed for three. I wrote to some cousins, who lived in Yorkshire;

they hadn't come to the funeral, because it was unpatriotic to travel, but they'd sent a letter of condolence. I asked if Dad could stay with them – 'He needs a holiday,' I wrote untruthfully. He needed more than a holiday, he needed a home, but I hoped they'd offer without me having to beg. They replied that he'd be welcome. 'Stay as long as he likes.' Probably had weeks rather than months in mind, but I told myself getting him there was half the battle. Part of me didn't want him to go, but I knew it was for the best, especially now my skirts were so tight that elastic in the waistbands didn't help, and I had to let panels of material into the side seams.

I saw him off at Swindon station. My legs ached as I waited on the platform for the packed train to leave, my shoes pinching. The baby drummed its heels on my belly wall, savage blows now instead of polite taps. Dad stood in the corridor with his little suitcase at his feet, waving at me through the window as the carriage pulled away. He looked so lost I hoped a soldier with a seat would take pity on him. Then I took my throbbing feet straight to the hospital.

I found Cabbage smoking with one of the nurses in the sluice.

'Can I have a word?' I asked him. 'Private, like.'

The nurse gave me a hoity-toity look but stubbed out her cigarette in the sink and left.

'How many weeks?' he asked. I counted back and told him. He seemed astonished. 'You sure? You don't look that far gone.'

'It was the beginning of February,' I said. 'I can be certain.'

'Some women hardly show the first time,' he mused. 'There was a girl when I was doing my training, hadn't a clue, thought it was belly-ache. Had the junior doctor in Casualty fooled: he was looking for appendicitis until the nurse pointed out she could see the baby's head crowning. Patient tried to claim it was a virgin birth, but that's bog Irish for you.' The casual contempt in his voice made me wince. I'd thought of him as kind, but perhaps I was no more to him than that Irish girl – another chance to show off his cleverness. 'So, what do you want me to do? I can get you into a place I know in Liverpool, a midwife runs it, very discreet, she'll find a home for the baby afterwards . . .'

'I want rid of it,' I said. 'You know what I mean. You can do it, can't you? I can't go on with this.'

'Can't be done,' he said. 'You're too late, sweetheart. Too risky now – we could kill you as well as the baby. Should've come to me a month or more ago, if that's what you were after.'

I closed the door of the little room in the house on Drove Road, kicked off my spiteful shoes and hung my coat on the hook, on top of the hanger with my best polka-dot dress. I'd not be going dancing for a while. I wondered what people did, faced with this. I'd been so sure Cabbage, or someone like him, would help. There was the place in Liverpool, and no doubt somewhere like it closer. But what was I to tell people? They'd guess, wouldn't they? And how soon would it be obvious if I didn't vanish? Despair near sank me. Outside, everyday life on Drove Road continued, men bicycling home from work at the railway yards, women walking back from the aircraft factory. The early August heat was killing. The scent of gravy made with browning stole through the house as my landlady prepared another meatless supper. Grief for Mam, pushed so deep down, swelled up and burst like a great bubble in my chest. I lay face down on the bed, the scratchy cotton prickling my hot face, clawing at handfuls of the material to keep the tears inside, and the baby too, wishing these things could be swallowed back into the body and never let out to shame me.

A knock at the door. 'Frances? You in there? Tea's nearly done.'

I wiped my eyes on the maroon bedspread. 'Having a lie-down.'

'Thought I heard you come in. Did you see the letter on the hall table?'

'Be down in a jiff after I've had a wash.'

Maybe the letter was from Davey. There'd been nothing since the picnic at Windmill Hill. I'd tried ringing the base after Mam died, but the phone was answered by a man who told me Davey's squadron were 'operational': he'd leave a message. He'd sounded drunk, slurring his words, but maybe that was because he was posh. Colerne wasn't that far and even if Davey couldn't wangle a pass surely he could've sent a note. I felt angry with him. He'd took it hard, I knew, but he'd come through, wouldn't he? Like you had to?

Didn't understand how thin Davey'd been stretched already.

I stood up, my legs tingling when my feet hit the floor. My feet were puffy; now my shoes wouldn't go back on. I forced on slippers and padded downstairs.

It wasn't from Davey. The address on the envelope was typed, on a machine I'd used often enough to recognize its crooked *R*s and squashed-up *d*s. I ripped it open eagerly.

My dearest Heartbreaker,
Damnably late to be saying this, but I have
been away in London and Sorel-Taylour has only
just informed me of your sad bereavement. It is
thirty-five years since the death of my own
mother (and nearly forty-five since my father
died) but I feel her loss as keenly today as I
ever did. I am sorry to hear of your mother's
death; though I did not know her well, she must
have been a fine woman to instil in her
daughter the truth and talent and feeling that
is yours.

I regret I cannot help with the matter of a
home for your father. The cottage in Manor
Drive is promised to a friend. But please do
call in at the Manor when you are next passing
by. I am hoping to resume my entertainments for
airmen, and you would be a welcome adornment to
our tea parties.

Sincerely,

A.K.

PS: Talking of the Brylcreem Brigade, I hear

I turned the page with disappointment, glad he'd taken the trouble, but wishing there'd been more. The rest of the postscript overleaf almost stopped my heart:

```
our Brushwood Boy and Cromley are partnered!
Donald's navigator apparently broke his leg
falling off his bicycle after revels in the
NAAFI, but young Davey stepped into the breach.
Cromley's lucky to have such a steady chap
flying with him. You should have married the
Boy, Heartbreaker — I never understood why the
pair of you didn't tie the knot long ago.
```

For once, the kicker in my belly remained still. It must have understood the shapeless fear in my heart.

CHAPTER 44

The drizzle has hardly let up, but nearly four hours after Solstice sunrise Avebury's still clogged with footsore pilgrims. Despite gritty eyes and a mouth like the bottom of a birdcage, I'm too wired to sleep after the visit to the spring. I woke a surprised Frannie for breakfast at six thirty, then set out an hour later for the stone circle. Drumming pulses from the campsite; I half expect to see John, but there's no sign of him.

A black 4×4 lurches off the main road with squealing tyres and pulls up at the top of the high street, dance music blasting combatively, going head to head with the pagan bongos. The window on the driver's side glides down and Ibby pokes her head out. 'India! You might have told us.'

'Told you what?'

'That there wouldn't be anywhere to park. Got up at the crack and drove here from Bristol to film sunrise – bastard police wouldn't let us stop. We've been cruising the lanes for hours – missed the whole bloody thing apart from a couple of wobbly shots out of the car window, and footage of crusties' vans parked on the Ridgeway.'

'I thought you knew.'

'How could we know? You're supposed to be the sodding researcher.'

Not worth the row to say that since I've not so far been paid I don't see why I should nanny the film crew through every minute of their day.

'I told Martin.'

'Well, he didn't pass it on. Probably has his head up his arse again about that married man he pines for in Bath.'

'What married man?' And how come Ibby knows about this and I don't?

She ignores the question. 'And if you read your callsheet, you'd remember he isn't joining us until early afternoon, for filming at the Long Barrow. Don't forget you said you'd help cart the equipment up there when you finished at the café. We haven't a soundman today, so I can't manage without you. Two o'clock. Don't be late.'

Harry, in the passenger seat, mouths, 'PMT,' careful not to let Ibby see him.

She slams the vehicle into gear again. 'We're off to breakfast in Marlborough.'

The window slides back up with a clunk, the 4×4 executes a neat turn and squeals away.

There's still an hour before my shift starts at the café – in the kitchen, for a change, so I can leave in time to help the film crew this afternoon. Corey hasn't yet arrived, and I don't have a key, so I wander over to the Trust offices in the hope of finding one. Ed's beaten me to it. His jacket and boots are in the lobby.

He wanders into the kitchenette, looking rumpled, as I'm filling the kettle.

'What are you doing here?' I ask. 'I thought Graham was covering the overnight Solstice watch.' It comes out sharper than I intended, perhaps because my encounter with Bryn at the spring is making me feel guilty, as if I betrayed Ed in some way.

He doesn't seem to notice, but yawns dramatically, playing for sympathy. 'Couldn't sleep.'

'What kept you awake?'

'Oh, this and that.' He hoists himself onto the countertop a couple of feet away, long legs kicking the cupboard door. 'If you're making a cuppa, I'll have one. Want to come out with me to pick up litter round the Long Barrow this morning? I have strictest instructions it has to be pristine for your film crew.'

'Sorry. I'm sandwich-making in the café as soon as Corey opens up.'

'I'll manage.' His eyes follow me as I open the cupboard looking for coffee and sugar. 'Knowing Graham, he'll probably turn up to help, in spite of being up all night chasing pagans off the verges. Sad bastard can't seem to keep away from this place.' He jumps down, puts his hands on my shoulders and bends his mouth to my ear. 'Neither can I. Do you think there's time for a quick snog before Michael arrives?'

The drizzle stops and the day brightens, so on my mid-morning break I make myself a sandwich and take it to eat at one of the tables under the trees by the museum, like a tourist, waving smugly at Corey when she comes out to clear crockery. It's been an easy morning in the café so far. Solstice celebrations put off the more staid National Trust members, and the pagans favour bring-your-own-tofu-burger barbecues on the campsite.

'Keeping you busy enough?' I ask.

She makes a face. 'Why does it knacker you more when it's quiet? We've more than enough sandwiches, I reckon, so you can piss off early if you want.'

The Trust's Land Rover drives into the staff car park, the back loaded with black plastic bin bags full of rubbish. Ed and Graham climb out: Graham must have turned up, as predicted, after a short kip. They begin to unload them into the skips.

'That Ed's stronger than he looks,' said Corey, with a sly glance. 'Want a bet he'll be over this way for a free cup of coffee when he's done?'

'He'll be lucky.'

Ed reaches for the last black bag; Graham lays a hand on his arm and stops him. A conversation starts, too low to hear.

'Anyway, better crack on,' says Corey. 'You finished with that plate?'

Graham climbs into the driver's seat and slams the door. The engine coughs, and the Land Rover heads off up the drive, the single black bin-bag jolting sluggishly in the open back.

As Corey threads her way through the tables with the loaded tray, Ed comes out of the car park heading for the café, changing direction when he catches sight of me. He sits down heavily at my table. 'Hi.'

'You look like you've had a good morning,' I say. The circles under his eyes are, if anything, darker.

'Marvellous,' he says. 'Utterly marvellous. Litter all over the place. Hundreds of bloody tea-lights in the Long Barrow. Soot marks on the stone, which Graham and I had to scrub off. And, to cap it all, a dead dog.'

John has been washing T-shirts when I reach his cottage, hanging them on the line in the front garden.

'You idiot,' he says, when we're nursing mugs of Brummie-strength tea in the living room. 'You know what the Long Barrow is, Indy? It's an entrance to the Lower World. The place I start when I'm making the Journey. Why the hell didn't you tell me that's where you went that night?'

There is absolutely no way I believe John goes anywhere beyond this room when he does his shamanic thing, the drums and the trance and all that, but all the same it gives me a chill to think of him sitting here bare-chested, chanting, picturing himself slipping between the big stones flanking the Long Barrow's doorway and passing through its dark chambers into an alternative reality.

'You ought to have more respect,' he continues, 'or at least understand that what you do there can have . . . repercussions. Sex is one of the most powerful elements of some magics. Under a waning moon, too. Not good Wyrd.'

I shiver, deciding I'd prefer not to know why a waning moon is bad, exactly, and wishing the fire were lit. The brick hearth holds a basket of pine cones around a dried-flower arrangement donated by one of his lovely ladies.

'Why's he killed his dog?'

John shakes his head. 'You're jumping to conclusions. Maybe it was hit by a car. Your . . . friend could have left it at the barrow as a burial. Or maybe it wasn't his dog, someone else dumped it. He's probably harmless, but from all you've said . . .' He looks dubiously into the hearth, stretches forward to lift a pine cone out of the fire basket, and tosses it from one hand to the other. 'I sometimes think the pagan

movement is an alternative Care in the Community. And if I were
you, I'd retrieve that note from the Swallowhead springs.'

Outside the window, grey cloud has muffled the sun again. John's
newly laundered T-shirts flap in the wind that has risen. One is black,
fluttering next to a pair of dark, faded combat trousers.

'What were *you* up to last night? Were you and your friends out
near Alton Barnes, by any chance? Wearing black combats?'

'All sorts of ways to celebrate Solstice,' he says, standing up to light
the candle on the mantelpiece, to ward off the gloom. 'But let's concentrate on the problem in hand.' He stares into the cold fireplace. 'You
are such a pillock, know that? Why do you keep behaving like this?
It's like you have no respect for yourself.'

'I—' I can't come up with an answer that sounds credible even to
myself.

'I'd like nothing better than to see you in a relationship. But you
don't do relationships. You do dysfunctional shags. Usually associated
with an excessive consumption of alcohol, far as I can make out.'

'Not this time.'

'Tramadol, for God's sake. Were you born yesterday? Thought I'd
brought you up with a healthy respect for drugs.'

'You're not my father, John.'

He winces. 'No. Maybe I should have behaved more like one.' He
starts tossing the pine cone again. It's starting to remind me of a live
grenade. 'But my own dear dad wasn't the finest role model. I've always
tried to look out for you, though, haven't I?'

'Sorry.' I take a sip of tea. It tastes awful, because I keep thinking
of poor old Cynon, head crushed, according to Ed, and . . .

Get in the van, Indy

'John,' I say.

He puts the pine cone carefully down on the arm of the chair.

'I think I need to talk about what happened to Mick Feather.'

CHAPTER 45

'Once saw a film,' John says, bringing two more mugs of tea from the kitchen, 'in which someone had their memory wiped by a sinister corporation, and they keep getting inexplicable flashbacks and go round trying to get their memory back. Made me laugh like a drain.' He sits down again next to me on the sofa and puts a fatherly arm round my shoulders, squeezing tight. 'You don't need a sinister corporation. People wipe their own memories clean, happens every day. You think I really remember what happened when I shot that Argie? It's like in another life, someone else's . . .'

The memories are there, locked into the crystals. All you have to do to release them is turn them the right way, towards the light. First come the sounds—

The sound of the wind in the trees over Tolemac. Lying in the van at night hearing it, hearing . . .

Keir's breathing. Heavy, for a kid. His nose was always a bit blocked up. Not snores, baby snorts and sighs. He kicked in his sleep. He was a couple of inches shorter than me, and a few months younger. His father had fought for custody of him – his mother had a drug habit, but the courts still found against Mick. He stole Keir back, kidnapped him, and Keir's mother never once came to look for him, though Keir was certain she would when she was better.

The sound of the wind across the fields and . . .

Who are we?

We're the Barley Collective.

Calling in the fakkin' Mothership. Riz, the bloke with the curls, the one who caught Keir and me in the church. I rode on Riz's shoulders as we walked home along the Ridgeway under the bright moon, my legs either side of his neck, his hands clasped across my thighs to keep me steady. At the bottom of the hill, by the padlocked gate into Tolemac, he bent to let me slide off his shoulders. Then I felt his lips against my ear.

'You goin' to the party, Ind?'

'What party?'

'The one where your mum's dancin'.'

'Don't know about that.'

'Where is it?'

'What?'

He patted my bottom, and I scrambled over the gate and ran towards the van under the trees. The back door opened. Mum stood there, in her jeans and a sloppy T-shirt. She smiled at me, but her eyes were like Keir's when the grass was cut, puffy and red.

My eyes focus on John, the other side of the hearth.

'Riz,' I say. 'Short for Rizla? Funny little bloke. Mixed race? We made the crop circle with him.'

'Little *shit*,' says John. 'And not Rizla, Rissole, we called him, because somebody said his curly hair was like a plate of rissoles. He was a leech, clung on to whoever'd let him cling. Story was he'd been a Jehovah's Witness for a while, then for a joke some chick invited him in, served him a hash brownie, turned him pagan and he never looked back. Don't believe it, personally – Riz *always* looked back, because he'd be scared there was someone he owed money to on his tail.'

'Why were we there?' I ask. 'Why *did* we go to Avebury that year, not Stonehenge?'

John sighs. 'Because of a party. Your mother wanted to be there, nothing I could do to talk her out of it, or out of taking you along: she was being paid to dance, first time ever, by the people organizing it. Two little creeps from Clifton College she'd met in the pub in

Montpelier, who had that poster of her dancing the sun up at Stonehenge on their study wall.'

'Louis?' I have to dredge the name out of the sludge at the bottom of the crystal. 'And . . .'

'Patrick. Eighteen, hardly left school, spotted a business opportunity. Summer of Love? Summer of Money. They were running huge outdoor parties. People were paying to go, driving miles in convoys of cars from London, Bristol, dancing the whole weekend.'

Louis and Patrick were camping in a derelict farmworker's cottage half a mile off the Ridgeway. Mum took me with her when she went to see them, soon after we arrived at Tolemac. The house was almost hidden among trees and scrub, the only sign of occupation a black VW Golf GTi parked outside, at the end of a valley littered with sarsen stones like dead sheep. The boys were sitting in what had once been the garden, on folding picnic chairs that were absurdly low for their long legs. On a table stood tall, misted glasses and a bottle of Pimms – they had mint leaves and cucumber and slices of lemon, and *ice*, for God's sake: how did they produce ice in a tumbledown cottage that had no electricity? They must have had a generator because inside it was crammed with eighties hi-tech: boom boxes, an Amstrad computer with a green screen, and mobile phones hefty enough to make your arm ache when you held them to your ear. Mum left me in the garden while Louis showed her round inside. By the time they came out of the cottage again Patrick, wearing Walkman earphones, was asleep on his picnic chair, his T-shirt rucked up exposing a hairy stomach.

'Meg,' Louis was saying, 'you think we're being paranoid. But we could be stuffed if anyone finds out the location in advance.'

'Your mother didn't take it seriously,' says John. 'She didn't understand this was the end for the free festivals, where people used to trade skills – half an hour of *reiki* in exchange for a bundle of perfumed candles, or servicing the engine of your van. Heroin dealers' cars used to get burned out at the free parties. Now they were hanging round the back of the sound systems offering free samples and nobody gave a shit. Angelfeather had broken up by 1989 – poor old Dan Angell was already in a mental home. But Meg thought she could go on dancing for ever, and she'd already told someone about Louis and Patrick's rave: Mick Feather, who turned up Solstice Eve with his band of hangers-on, including Riz and a zoned-out dickhead called Biro. Mick'd taken Keir to Stonehenge, but they couldn't get near the stones – been chased all over Salisbury Plain by police helicopters.'

Tried to break through the exclusion zone on foot, said Mick. *Fuckin' pig helicopter spotted us, pinned us down in a fuckin' bush, couldn't move for the fuckin' downwind, and the pig cavalry came steamin' over the fuckin' horizon, fuckin' pitched battle. Wasn't anythin' to do but fuckin' run . . .*

'I thought it was idiotic to take a kid,' says John. 'There'd been violence the year before, anarchists from Class War hurling beer bottles at the police until they got fed up and baton-charged the crowd. But Mick thought if the Establishment was getting heavy, maybe this was Keir's last chance to experience Solstice at the stones, could be a memory that'd shape his whole life. When they couldn't reach Stonehenge, they turned round and headed for Avebury.'

Can Keir kip down in your van? Mick asked Mum. *Little bastard kicks in his sleep.*

'We've only two bunks—'

'He can go in with Indy.'

'He can go on the floor.'

Keir's arrival meant I had someone to roam with over the Downs. His hair was turning white gold in the sun. He wore stupid cut-off shorts that had once been a pair of my jeans and were way too big for his skinny hips, though Mum had gathered the waistband and sewn in elastic so they didn't fall down. He was into dens that year. He'd made one for us in Bristol that Mum didn't know about, in the allotments beyond the railway embankment. But the Downs were miles better. Up at the Hedgehogs we had a mound each, under the beech trees, our castles where we laid siege to each other and fought shrieking battles with pretend swords made out of twigs. I'd already found my own secret den before Keir and Mick arrived, one I shared with some scabby-looking sheep, among scrubby bushes in a valley full of sleeping sarsens. I wanted to keep that one to myself, and I wouldn't take him there. Keir was furious, and shouted he'd go off to find his own. He disappeared for a whole afternoon and never came back until after tea, by which time Mum was panicking and about to send John off to search for him. Mick said Keir could look after himself, and what was to harm him in the countryside? Mum's lips went thin and I could see her picturing Keir squashed like a rabbit on the verge of the A4, or impaled on rusty old farm machinery in the corner of a field.

So it was this wonderful golden afternoon with a breeze ruffling Keir's white-gold hair, and we're walking along beating twigs against the side of our legs, for no reason, really, except that's what you do when you're eight, and Keir says, Why won't you show me your den? and I go, Because it's *mine*, stupid, it's *secret*. Then I thought of how I could get him off my back, and I said: 'Can show you something else, though.'

We went through the hunting gate and down the track that crossed the Gallops. ('What's this?' asked Keir, and I said, 'It's for training race-horses, pus brain.') After Mum had brought me, I'd often come here alone, not right up to the cottage because I was scared of the two young men, but I'd scrambled through the wood into the overgrown garden, where the grass was so long you could wriggle unseen close enough to watch the comings and goings.

Today the black car wasn't parked by the gate outside the cottage. So we walked down the track in the open, bold as buggery, as Frannie would say.

'Fu-hu-huck!' said Keir – his dad's favourite word – when he saw the cottage. 'That's a den? It's someone's house, innit?'

'No way. It's a wreck, but someone's camping there. With computers.'

I took him past the rusty folding chairs and the table littered with beer cans – Keir picked several up and shook them, hoping there were dregs left, but the only one that still held any lager also held a dead wasp and that stopped him in his tracks. We went up the steps – I was certain there was no one in – and I rapped at the front door self-importantly as if I was an expected guest. To my surprise, it gave, and I half fell into the hallway, almost wetting myself in terror. Keir was by now at the other end of the garden.

I picked myself up, expecting the sound of a chair scraping on the kitchen floor, or footsteps on the narrow stairs as someone came to investigate. Silence.

Nobody home. I'd been right all along. They'd left the front door unlocked because this wasn't Bristol: this was a tumbledown old hovel in the middle of nowhere that you'd never find unless you knew it was there and, anyway, they were probably stoned when they'd left. I knew the difference between ordinary cigarettes and the lumpy ones that made people giggle, and I knew which ones Louis and his posh friend had been smoking when Mum and I came to the cottage.

Keir was back already, hovering on the doorstep, trying to make out he hadn't run off like a scaredy-cat.

'Where's the computers?' he said. Just like a boy.

'In here,' I said, pushing on the door in the hallway without the slightest idea whether I was right, but thinking I should look like I knew. It wouldn't budge, to Keir's disappointment – maybe Louis and his mate weren't so stupid and had locked it, or maybe the wood was warped and the door was stuck. We went upstairs – camp bed in one room, double sleeping-bag on the floor of the other, clothes in untidy piles spilling out of expensive leather grips. The bathroom was disgusting; the toilet bowl was nearly black. When we came back downstairs, Keir gave the stuck door a good kick, but it didn't shift, and then we had to go into the kitchen to find a cloth because his sandal had left a mark on the peeling paintwork.

Keir went for a pee in the garden while I cleaned the door; he said he couldn't possibly use the toilet upstairs. As I took the smelly dishcloth back – it stank of old onions – I heard him call. 'Indy! Car coming.'

I dropped the dishcloth and ran, only remembering just in time to pull the front door closed after me. Keir was diving into the bushes at the end of the garden. I followed him, wriggling under cover between overgrown raspberry canes. A bramble scored a line of blood-beads down my leg. I came to rest a couple of feet away from where Keir lay on his stomach, behind a clump of low, spiny bushes through which tall, bleached grasses grew. He pulled a fat gooseberry off one and passed it to me.

We heard the car engine cut. Two doors opened, then slammed, one after the other. The gate's rusted hinges made a fingers-on-a-blackboard screech, then Louis and the posh one were coming through the long grass towards the house. They passed within kicking distance of us, but we held our breath, and anyway they were lads: children were invisible to them. If it had been Mum, she'd have smelt us at thirty paces.

'You tit,' said the posh one. 'You left the door unlocked.'

'You were last out.'

'Was I bollocks.' They disappeared inside, emerging a minute later with cans of beer. The *psssh* of the ring pulls made me thirsty. I popped the gooseberry into my mouth for moisture, then screwed up my face at its sour, metallic taste. I spat it out. Keir kicked me.

'That was a wasted trip,' said Louis, sinking onto one of the picnic chairs.

'Worth a try.'

'They were slappers.'

'Come on. We need more stage dancers. And they were better than that old slag you're obsessed with.'

'I'm not obsessed,' said Louis. 'She's iconic. Like that poster of the tennis player scratching her bum.'

'She's geriatric.'

'She's pretty fit for her age.'

'Don't tell me you've had her. Jesus, you have. You sad git.'

'I have *not*.'

'I can tell when a boy's lost his virginity and become a man.' A clunk, as the empty beer can Louis threw at his friend missed and hit the side of the house. 'When did you manage to slip her the laughing carrot, then?'

'Wash your mouth. She's a goddess.' Louis was grinning.

'It was that time you took her off in the car to show her the party field, wasn't it? Fucking hell, man. You are really twisted. I wouldn't stuff her with a cold chip.'

'What the fuck you on about? Of course I haven't shagged her. She's old enough to be my mum.'

'Word is, Townsend, that wouldn't stop you.' There was another liquid *psssh*, a screech, guffaws. They were having a play fight, drenching each other with beer. Keir rolled his eyes. We wriggled silently backwards on our stomachs, through the raspberry canes, past a crabby old apple tree and into the birdsong of the scrubby wood.

'What was Stonehenge like?' I asked him on the way back to Tolemac.

'Mick let me drive the van,' said Keir, proudly. 'Round the field. I sat on his lap and he did the pedals but I steered.'

'What about the helicopter chasing you through the stones and all that?'

'Dunno. They left me in the van.' Keir screwed up his face to think. 'There were black helicopters flying low all night, making that horrible noise, like giant pterodactyls. I had a bad dream about one picking up the van in its claws and flying away with me. But I don't think there was much of a chase, because Mick's legs weren't working when they came back. He kept flopping about and Riz did all the driving after that.'

On thy belly thou shalt go

'Mick liked ketamine,' says John. 'You know what they used to call it, don't you? Going to Mr Softeeland. It's a horse tranquillizer, and your legs go rubbery. Not numb – you know they're there, they just won't obey instructions to move. Ketamine wasn't illegal. People used to bring it back from India in pop bottles, pour it onto a baking tray and stick it in a warm oven until it turned to crystals and you could snort it. Delivered to the festivals on what used to be called the Special K Coach. By 1989, people were doing K and Es together. Lying there all night under the stars, loved up but limp as a wilted dandelion.' He shakes his head. 'Pointless bloody drug.'

'I don't understand why the location had to be so secret, though,' I say.

'The mystique of those parties was that you didn't know where you were going until you got there. Map references left on answering machines, messages passed via mobile phones – relatively rare, then – convoys of cars driving round the M25 or up and down the M4. But that wasn't the problem, so much as all the people who would have turned up if Meg had let slip exactly where the party was being held – people who had no concept of paying for anything. The Brew Crew would have insisted on their right to go in free, Louis's security men would have beaten the crap out of them – there'd have been a riot. So now, far too late, Meg was being careful not to say anything about where or when in the hope Mick and his friends would get fed up and go away eventually.'

I always knew when someone was moving in the van at night because the floor creaked and you could feel the bunks move. I came awake suddenly, thinking it must be Keir going for a pee. Mum wasn't in bed yet; I knew because I'd curled up in her bed instead of my own top bunk. But Keir's regular, snorty breathing from his sleeping-bag on the blow-up mattress hadn't altered. Must be Mum then, though that was odd because I thought I could still hear her laugh among the voices outside the van, where she'd been sitting with John and Mick and the others. They'd built the fire far enough away not to keep us awake, but the mutter of voices was a soothing reminder that Keir and I weren't alone under the trees.

Someone sat down on the end of the bunk. I knew it wasn't Mum:

wrong smell, sour and oily and spoilt-meatish, the smell of someone who hadn't washed for several days.

'I know you're awake,' said Rissole, very quiet. I'd made the mistake of inching my legs away from the weight pushing down the side of the bed. His fingers stroked my hair, and he leaned down to breathe softly in my ear, 'Shoulda mentioned it at the time. Seein' as how I saved you from the Bad Guy in the church.' His breath smelled garlicky, and the oily stench poured off his tight curls. 'Wouldn' look too good now, if you said anythin' to anyone about me hangin' round that ol' church, nor the black fella you might have passed in the porch. Don't want your mum thinkin' I took you in there 'cos then your pal Riz really would be up the fakkin' creek. So seein' as we're mates, thought I'd pop in and remind you. No tellin'. You tell that to Keir, too.' I could hear something rustling, something he was doing with his other hand. 'Got a little reminder for you. You put out your hand now.'

'Riz . . .' I was scared, and not so innocent I couldn't imagine what he might want me to touch.

'Oh, come on, Indy, whatchoo take me for? We're mates, right? Here, I'll tuck it under the blanket.' He lifted the corner of the coverlet and something crumpled and scratchy brushed my arm. 'There. Nothin' to worry 'bout. But you keep your mouth shut, darlin', or there might be. The Bad Guy with the long white beard don't like people knowin' he let a pagan escape.' He patted my hair, and his weight lifted from the bed, but his mouth came down to my ear again. '*On thy belly thou shalt go.* 'Magine that, Ind, no legs.' The van floor creaked again, and he was gone.

The scratchy thing was against my flat little chest. I knew what it was now. The crumpled page Riz had torn out of the Bible in the church.

And the Lord God said unto the woman, What is this that thou hast done?

My mouth's unbearably dry. On the footstool, my mug of tea has gone cold; it tastes vile.

John lights another cigarette, and I'm amazed to see his hands are trembling. 'Trouble is, the dead wrap their arms round your neck and cling on. You got to prise their dead fingers off you. Whose eyes do you think I see at night, Indy? He's waiting for me in the Lower World, every time, first thing I have to step over a poor bastard in Argentinian uniform, lying in the mud of that God-forsaken place, the wind tugging the photo of his wife and his two kids that's clutched in his hand. And sometimes he has Mick Feather's eyes.'

'I'm not ready after all,' I say. 'Let's . . . not talk about it, John. Please, not now.'

'Riz was the problem,' says John, implacable. 'Riz owed money to a dealer. Somewhere further up the food chain, someone was interested in finding out where the party was being held, and who was organizing it. Louis and Patrick thought they were so clever, but they didn't have a clue. They saw themselves as hip young businessmen cashing in on a new idea, but they had no idea how much of a business opportunity those parties were for the people who controlled the Es and whiz that kept people loved up and dancing all night. So Riz found out somehow where Louis and Patrick were hanging out and, armed with that information, he did a deal.

'Few days before the party was to be held, Louis and Patrick had a visit from some heavy gentlemen. They brought a contract for the boys to sign: a partnership opportunity, was the way they put it. To help them understand the advantages of this new business arrangement, they smashed the computers and set fire to the garden. Then the same gentlemen, for reasons that remain obscure, possibly for no more than fun, turned their attention to the hippies camped in Tolemac.'

Keir and I were sitting under the trees by the side of Mick's van, taking turns on an Etch-A-Sketch Mick had picked up cheap at Eastville market. Mum and John were over by the fire, talking. Mick was . . .

'Mick was sprawled on the ground at the back of his van with one of his mates, both of them about six light years out of it because they'd been doing K and Es together.' John rubs his face. 'Is it me, Indy, or has it gone cold? Riz was nowhere around – maybe somebody slipped him the word to make himself scarce. First we knew of it was revving engines, then this bloody great crash that was the gate, smashed to matchsticks.

'Two Range Rovers came slewing across the grass into the wood, one doing a handbrake turn so he was pointing the right way to make a getaway when they'd done what they came for. The doors flew open and these guys – don't ask me how many, could only have been four or five at most but it looked like a frigging army – came piling out with sledgehammers and, Christ albloodymighty, a couple of shotguns. Had no notion who they were, what they wanted, or what the hell to do. I still had the insane idea they were only pissed-off locals and I'd be able to talk them out of it, until I saw that the one at the back was a huge black guy with a sawn-off, and you don't get many of those to the pound in rural Wiltshire.'

Keir and I looked up, and saw Mum rising to her feet, flapping her arms at us and screaming: 'Get in the van!'

It felt like one of those dreams where you see danger coming but you can't move. Keir was round-eyed. I tugged on the back of his T-shirt, but Mum had to shout again before we scrambled to our feet and jumped into Mick's van through the open passenger door.

'The *wrong* van,' says John. 'Meg meant you to run for hers – she probably had some notion she'd follow you and drive you out of there to safety, though it was too late for that: the second Range Rover was parked across the gateway. I've no idea if the guys with sledgehammers even saw you because they were already going for Biro's ridiculous little Citroën van, the nearest and easiest target. The sides crumpled like paper. I started yelling, but the black guy with the sawn-off shotgun stood in front of me, making it crystal that discussion was not an option. You think this can't be happening – middle of the afternoon, hardly a quarter of a mile from houses, cars, buses, visitors, telephones. Someone had to be walking round the stone circle; someone had to hear the noise. But it all happened so fast. The other shotgun was pointing at Mick and Biro, who were not laughing now, lying on the ground with their mouths open wondering if they'd dropped acid by mistake.'

'They set fire to Mum's van, didn't they?' I ask.

John nods. 'Meg tried to go over there but I grabbed her arm and wouldn't let go. The doors were open. I could see the bunks, pillows still dented, covers half pulled up, your old Ted lying on the quilt next to a pair of your shorts. The guy jumped out of the back of the van, a metal can in his hand. He tossed a lighted rag inside and everything caught at once with a whoosh. Then the guys with the sledgehammers got fed up of battering Biro's Citroën into scrap metal and went for Mick's van, where you were.'

Keir, first in, had wriggled along the bench seat towards the steering-wheel, and I threw myself face down on the cracked brown plastic upholstery. *On thy belly*... The van was parked with its nose towards the woodland, away from the clearing. We couldn't see what was happening, but from all the shouting I knew it was something bad. There was a crash, glass breaking. Maybe this was what Rissole meant, about Christians hating pagans.

'Indy,' said Keir, his face all crumpled. 'Where's Dad?' He never called him Dad, always Mick, so he had to have been frightened.

'John's with him,' I said. 'John's been a soldier. He's got a power animal.'

'Better be a fucking tiger, then,' said Keir, trying for brave. He was clutching my hand, his fingernails digging into my palm.

'Course it's a fucking tiger.' Better not let on it was only a big rabbit. 'But, anyway, I'm going to lock the doors.' I sat up, and risked a look out of the side window. Mum and John were standing by the fire. Someone else was there, in front of them, and I couldn't see what was happening. 'I can see your dad,' I lied. 'He's with John and Mum.' I pushed down the button to lock the door, then squirmed back along the seat and locked my side too. 'Maybe we should stay down. Mum wants us to hide.'

Keir slid down, almost under the steering-wheel. I lay along the bench seat, my nose full of the sweaty, farty smell of the cracked plastic. There was a flat *whump*, like someone had kicked a soggy football, and the glass on the passenger side shone with orange light, tipping Keir's blond hair with red-gold.

'What's happening?' Not being able to see was really frightening. I couldn't remember the Battle of the Beanfield, when the police had attacked the Peace Convoy, but Mum had told me about helicopters overhead and policemen with shields and sticks, and John punching one of them and ending up flat on the ground with three of them kicking him.

Keir shuffled upright to peer out of the side window. The glow from outside reflected his face onto the windscreen, a crumpled autumn leaf, golden brown and orange. I thought he was probably crying.

Then the windscreen exploded.

'When the guy with the sledgehammer went for Mick's van, your mother and I forgot we were looking down the barrels of a shotgun. Soon as I moved, I got the rifle butt in my face, but Meg managed to duck under his arm, and was at the van before anyone could stop her, pulling on the door handle and screaming her head off that there were kids in there.'

'We'd locked the doors,' I say. 'I thought that was what she wanted us to do.'

'She was terrified the pyromaniac bastard was chucking petrol in the back already, though he was nowhere near. The bloke with the sledgehammer was in a trance – couldn't work out how this fury had got past the shotgun, which right then was being jabbed handle end into my stomach. At the back of the van, the other shotgun's screaming *On yer feet*, at Mick and Biro. *Get up, you cunts*. Then Keir's little face appears over the lip of the windscreen, tears rolling down his face and shouting for his dad . . .'

* * *

Mum's yelling and there's glass all over the place, can feel it in my hair, it's on the seat and when I try to push myself up a piece jabs into my hand and there's red blood on the brown plastic. Thunder overhead, too much noise.

Keir's going, *Dad!* And *What shall I do, Indy?* and Mum's shouting, *Get out of there, fast as you can,* and peering in through what's left of the windscreen is this man with thick red lips, and a tattoo on his neck, blue curling flames licking out of the top of his black T-shirt. Then Keir's reaching for the key that Mick's left in the ignition and I don't know if this is a good idea or a bad idea but I know we have to get away somehow. Never occurs to me that Keir can't drive the van, his feet don't reach the pedals.

Keir turns the key and the engine coughs but the van doesn't go forwards. It jumps backwards, and the wheels bump down hard. Something screams like air coming out through a tiny hole, a thin sharp needle of sound skewering through the thunder overhead, transmitted from the heart of the memory crystal.

And the Lord God said unto the woman, What is this that thou hast done?

'The other guy with the shotgun had been telling him to get up, and he couldn't,' says John. 'When Mick took ketamine, his legs went. Mr Softeeland. He was at the back of the van, trying to remember what his feet were for when Keir started the engine. The van'd been left in reverse. It leaped back and stalled. Mick's legs were under the back wheels. You didn't see this, of course.'

'I heard him,' I say. 'Oh, God, I heard him.'

'The bastards had done what they came for, and more. They were already piling into one of the cars because the column of smoke from the burning van had attracted the attention of a military helicopter that was on exercise over the Marlborough Downs.'

The memory crystals are releasing more pictures. Billowing black smoke, leaves crinkling, trees on fire. Helicopter rotors fanning the flames. Sirens, men in dark blue jackets and yellow trousers and helmets, hissing snakes of water, the acrid stink of wet, charred plastic.

Keir, white and terrified, clinging to my hand, thinking the dinosaur bird was coming for us. Mum's face through the passenger window, shaking her head, her face hard.

She wouldn't let us out until the helicopter had taken off again.

John rubs his hand over his face. 'Meg lost it. She was out of her mind that she'd come so close to losing you, and she started yelling at you like it was your fault, the way people get angry when they're frightened. You don't remember that, I hope?'

What have you done, Indy? Who did you tell?

I shake my head. 'Not a thing.'

'The military chopper airlifted Mick to hospital, which saved his life – for the time being. Both legs were amputated, he couldn't adapt to life in a chair, and managed, after a couple of wretched years, to overdose himself. I'd like to believe in cosmic justice, and tidy endings, and that, years later, the bastards who torched Meg's van died in a fireball crash on the M4, or had *their* legs shot to blazes by a fourteen-year-old crack-addict, but I doubt it. Wyrd never works that way. The police didn't catch them, but instead they had us, a group of good-for-nothing travellers, and a pile of drugs from the back of Mick's van. When they realized there were two children involved, Social Services stepped in.'

'Did Mum even try to get me back?' I ask.

John stands up to light another cigarette from the Solstice candle. To my amazement, his hands are shaking. 'Meg was never lucky,' he says. 'Her lawyer was useless, Frannie was furious with her for putting you in danger, and she was beating herself up so badly about what a crap mother she'd been to let it happen that all she wanted to do was run away. Took me long enough to crawl back into your grandmother's good graces. Only reason I managed it was that I'd backed Frannie when she tried to talk Meg out of taking you to Tolemac that summer.'

My eyes meet John's. 'This is why I needed to come back to Avebury after the helicopter crash, isn't it? Whoever my grandfather may have been isn't the point, is it? I've been digging up the wrong past, chasing the wrong ghosts.'

He nods, slowly, as if he's not entirely convinced. 'Nothing's over till it's over. You have to let Wyrd work itself out – all the inter-connections.'

'What happened to Keir after his dad died?' I ask.

He shrugs. 'No idea, except that Social Services swooped on him too.'

The dinosaur bird caught him in the end, then.

CHAPTER 46

'See, Frannie's a great woman,' says John, 'but she doesn't believe in looking back. That's why, whatever the truth about your grandfather, you won't necessarily hear it from her lips. And after Tolemac – well, as far as Frannie was concerned, there was nothing to discuss. The pair of you had to carry on living life as it was, not chewing over stuff that would upset you. Bet you never saw her cry when Meg died, did you?'

'Not really.' The scent of the bonfire on which I burned everything that was left of my mother is in my nostrils. I'm not willing yet to tell John that I never cried either – because I thought you weren't supposed to.

The phone is painfully loud, startling me so I kick the stool, spilling cold tea from my forgotten mug. A brown stain spreads across the pale carpet. In the confusion, I fail to recognize my own ring tone, so by the time I find the mobile in my jacket pocket it's gone silent. Half a minute later, voicemail pings.

'Where the hell are you?' barks Ibby. 'You were supposed to meet us in the lay-by on the A4. Well, too effing late. I've called Ed and he'll lend a hand carrying the gear. But if you care to honour us with your presence, I need someone who knows one end of a radio mic from the other. I'll be hands full directing the presenter – when *he* deigns to show himself.'

John is on hands and knees with a J-cloth and a bowl of cold water, blotting the tea-soaked floor.

'Sorry,' I say. 'I should be doing that.'

'Don't worry. You'd better run.' He looks up at me, with a worried expression. 'Or ring them back and tell them something's come up . . .'

'No,' I say firmly. 'I'm fine. But do me a favour? I hauled Frannie out of bed so early she probably thinks it's teatime already. The more tired she is, the more confused she becomes.'

'I'll ring her to make sure she's OK,' he says. 'I've . . . a client due in half an hour, but I'll ask Fran if she'd like me to go over and make tea for her later, if you want.'

'No need. Filming should be over by five, latest.'

'Stop mithering,' says John. 'And . . . I'll come over tonight anyway.' He has a remote look in his faded eyes, thinking through something else. 'We should finish what we were talking about.'

I'm out of the front door and halfway to the A4 before I start wondering whether he means Tolemac or the uncompleted conversation about Bryn and the dead dog.

At the lay-by, Ed's Land Rover is parked behind the Overview crew car. A distant figure is toiling up the slope to the Long Barrow, the occasional gleam of sun flashing off silvery lighting boxes. Ibby is at the side of the Range Rover with a phone to her ear.

There is only one other vehicle in the lay-by, at the far end. A dirty white van.

Ibby acknowledges me by lifting her fingers, and turns her attention back to the phone.

There's mud splattered over the rear doors of the white van, half obscuring the *Stargate Earth Project* sticker. Wyrd is giving me the chance to put one thing right at least. I walk round to look through the windscreen, rooting in my backpack for my purse.

Karl's in the front, eating a cold pasty. There's no sign of Pete. Instead a black-and-white collie raises its head from the passenger seat.

'Here,' I say, shoving the two twenties and a ten through the window at him. 'All I have on me. It'll help buy another metal detector.'

He stares at me, mouth open and full of pasty, with no sign of recognition, but takes the notes, folding them and zipping them into the breast pocket of a fleece emblazoned with a logo saying 'A2B

Drains'. Then he raises the pasty in a gesture that I hope means 'thank you'. I walk back to Ibby at the Range Rover.

'Fine,' she's saying, the politeness conveying that whoever is on the other end of the phone is dead meat, 'you do that. Make it quick as you can. We'll be setting up.' She folds up the phone and catches sight of me. 'Thank Christ for small mercies. Bloody Martin's still looking for the ring road round Chippenham. Apparently he was staying with his old chum in Bath last night and she's about to leave her boyfriend. *Couldn't very well dash off, could I?* he says.' She kicks the side of the car. 'What kind of an outfit does he think we are? We're television professionals. We don't fucking *do* relationships.'

'Is the tailgate unlocked?' I ask. 'I'll sort out the sound gear.'

'Ed has it.' She runs a hand through her heavy fringe, then pinches the bridge of her nose. 'Take up some more batteries if you want to be useful. Sorry. I'm being an old cow today. Hormones. And getting up at three a.m. for nothing. Oh, for some real sunshine.' She kicks the car again. 'If not today, for the aerials, now we've arranged the chopper hire.'

'Aerials?' I say uneasily.

'Of course. Your mate Ed's going to help.'

'He doesn't have a helicopter.' I can't believe Ed would do this, with the inquest imminent. It's asking for trouble.

'Told you, we're hiring one.'

'When?'

'Soon as the weather improves.'

'You OK?' asks Ed, taking an armful of camera batteries from me at the top of the hill. 'That dog seemed to upset you, this morning.'

'I'm more upset by the idea of you filming aerials.' Under a cloudy sky, the entrance to the Long Barrow looms over us, huge stone snaggle teeth hiding its dark throat. The entrance to the Lower World. 'Ibby doesn't know you were involved in the Alton Barnes crash. You think she'd be happy about letting her crew fly with you if she did?'

'I need the money.'

Harry the cameraman appears from behind the stones masking the entrance to the barrow and, without a word, picks up a new battery, clipping it to the back of the camera.

'Sell the bloody house and barns,' I hiss.

'They belonged to my wife,' he says, so quietly I have to lean forward to make out the words. 'I owe more than a hundred thou. Told you. I'm fucked unless I keep flying.'

Ibby arrives, face flushed from the climb. 'Martin's here. Saw him parking as I came up the hill.' She goes to confer with Harry, handing him a PAG light to attach to the camera.

I kneel and open one of the silvery boxes to find the radio mic. Ed hasn't moved.

'Go on, piss off,' I tell him. 'I'm working. And while you're about it, don't suppose you noticed the white van in the lay-by?'

'You're kidding.'

'Aviation-archaeologist Karl on his lunch break.' I check the mic's power pack and start unwinding its lead. 'I gave him fifty quid to replace his metal detector. Broke as you are, you might like to stump up a tenner too, if he's still there.'

Ed snorts. 'Christ, Indy, you can be so naïve. Aviation archaeologist, my arse. They were nighthawks, all right. Vultures. And it *is* against the law. I looked up a couple of metal detectorist sites.'

'What's so illegal about hunting down old airfields?'

'That's not what they're after. They're looking for crashed planes – Second World War, usually, and that *is* against the law, regardless of whether they have the landowner's permission, because it might be a war grave. If the plane burned, the bodies weren't always recoverable. Sometimes the site was simply covered with earth. And if it was a German plane, there's a thriving market for Nazi memorabilia. Anyway, now you know what your fifty quid's going towards. Excuse me if I don't contribute.' He throws the last battery onto the ground and walks off.

I stare at the microphone in my hand, thinking of what Frannie said about Davey Fergusson. *He in't buried. He's with what was left of his aeroplane, ashes, mostly*

Where?

'Sorry to hear about your friend,' I tell Martin, as I pin the tiny radio mic to his lapel.

Martin, for once not making his usual flirtatious comments when I'm fiddling with his clothing, grunts.

'And . . . your married man. I didn't know. You let me blether on about all my romantic entanglements and . . .'

Martin's cold stare dries the words in my mouth. 'If you weren't so bloody self-absorbed, India,' he says, 'you might have picked up the clues.' He wrests the mic from my fumbling fingers. 'Leave it. I'll fix this.'

'Sorry,' I mumble, as he stalks off towards the camera at the barrow entrance.

'Pub, India?' asks Ibby, at the end of the afternoon. Martin has already left, without another word to me. 'Celebrate our last day of filming, apart from the aerials? Unless you can have another go at your grand-mother to be interviewed?'

'I don't think she'll do it.'

'Pity. Well, come and have a drink.'

'Sorry. Something else I should do while I'm here.'

Why did I leave that note for Bryn? Stupid idea. With luck, it'll have disintegrated already in the rain. As the crew car pulls away, I set out across the meadow towards the spring to make sure.

Goddess, water, willow. A late-afternoon gleam of sunlight on the broken mirror tiles, and I could swear the Goddess winked. On the branch that overhangs the water, Cynon's red fabric collar shivers as I stand on tiptoe to pull down the branch with my scrap of blue cotton.

It's looped loosely round the bough. I was in such a rush this morning, can't have tied it properly, the note's fallen out. On the ground, into the stream?

But deep inside (the place where, in all of us, the entrance to the Lower World yawns) I know that however hard I look I won't find it. Someone took it.

John's pickup passes as I'm waiting to cross the A4 to the stile onto the field path home. The brakelights go on, he pulls over and reverses to the lay-by. As he walks back to meet me, I can tell he's making an immense effort to keep a smile on his face. My heart contracts.

'You been home yet?' he asks. Too casual.

'Is she all right?'

'Phoned a couple of times. Thought she must be sleeping – you said you'd woken her early. Didn't want to disturb her, and my client was due. But afterwards . . . Anyway, still can't raise her on the phone so I'm on my way over. I'm sure she's napping, that's all . . .'

He's trying to keep it light, but there's something he isn't telling me.

'What's the matter?'

'Nothing,' he says. I take him by the shoulders and stare into his eyes. His pupils are tiny black pinpricks.

'There was no client, was there? You went into a trance.' I've started to shake, with anger or fear or both. 'For Chrissake, did you see something about Frannie?'

PART SEVEN

Killing Moon

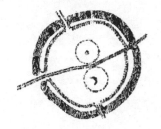

Avebury was a place where the living walked with the dead. The landscape was dotted with earthworks, tumuli, stone settings, and palisaded mortuary enclosures where corpses were laid out for excarnation – what Tibetans call 'sky burial' – before the defleshed bones were put into long barrows or used in rituals at the henge. People gathered in the circle year after year, to remember the ancestors and petition for their help and protection in an uncertain future.

Was ritual murder a part of the proceedings? There is no hard evidence. The skeleton of a woman, buried in the ditch near the southern entrance and surrounded by a ring of small sarsens, may have been a sacrifice, or she may have been an important person in the clan, entitled to burial in sacred ground. Charlie, the child burial found in the ditch of the enclosure at Windmill Hill, may have been killed deliberately, or died of a congenital condition that caused the distortion of the skull. Some would even like to claim that the Barber Surgeon, pinioned under his stone in the fourteenth century, was the victim of ritual murder.

But that is the way of archaeology. We dig down through the layers of history, and often as not, instead of answers, expose more questions.

Dr Martin Ekwall,
A Turning Circle: The Ritual Year at Avebury,
Hackpen Press

CHAPTER 47

29 August 1942

Hurts like buggery. But I'm good at keeping quiet when it hurts. If I try to lift my head, even an inch off the ground, everything goes woozy. Be all right if I lie still a moment; I'll get up in a bit, if I could remember how I ended up on the floor. Cold as charity lying here. Aches summat terrible down below, and I'm sick as a bloody dog. Head thumping, and a mad bird in my chest trying to flap its way out. Need to lie quiet a bit, gather meself...

29 August 1942. Don't want to remember but, with the ache in my back, can't help it.

When I woke at six, there was already a steamy feel to the day, though the bedroom window had been wide all night. I lay for a bit, trying to will myself out of bed, hearing morning sounds, milk cart, cat moaning on next door's porch, my landlady moving about downstairs, her man scraping the razor over his chin in the bathroom. Usual thing was to eat breakfast with the pair of them, but this morning when the call came, I shouted back I wasn't feeling so good.

At last the front door slammed as they left for the aircraft factory and the railway yards. I dragged my body out of bed. This morning it didn't feel like it was mine. I'd been transplanted into someone else's clumsy lump of flesh. There was a low, griping pain in the small of my back, as if I'd lain awkward in the night, and my feet were puffy again. I hobbled into the bathroom and tried to wake up.

Tiredness sandbagged me in the kitchen. The smell of singed toast hung in the air; I'd no appetite, but I was thirsty. There was lukewarm tea in the pot and I poured a cup and swallowed it, then had to make another dash for the loo. That was nothing new. Last week or so, it'd felt like tiny hands wringing my kidneys all the time. Near seven months, now, but still my belly hardly showed.

The oak-cased clock in the hall chimed: eight flat bongs. In response my belly vibrated eight times. Could it hear in there? Lie *quiet*, I told it. A shiver went through me. That was the first time I'd spoken aloud to it.

Had to get a wiggle on or I *would* be late for work. I hauled on a cardigan, then took it off again and tied it round my waist. My ankles were bulging over the tops of my white socks. Catching a glimpse of myself in the hall mirror, I looked a fright, hair sticking out at all angles because I'd forgotten to pincurl it last night. Too late to sort it, too tired to care. I opened the front door and stepped out into the sweltering heat.

The sky was blue, but yellowish white round the edges, like a sickly eyeball. Sullen clouds with dark bellies had puffed up on the southern horizon, loitering with intent on the edge of the Downs, but there was no wind to carry them closer. My legs were two heavy logs as I started the walk to work at the hospital. I was late. Drove Road was deserted, apart from two little girls playing hopscotch on the pavement. Where did they find the energy?

Today I'd look for Cabbage at the hospital. I'd ask him for the address of that place in Liverpool. Then I'd go to the almoner and tell her my dad was ill, and the cousins couldn't cope, so I had to go north to nurse him. A lie, of course: he was settled comfortably with them now.

When the baby was born, I'd have it adopted. There, I said under my breath, that's made you lie still, you little kicker. Maybe it was as exhausted as I felt. I pictured it rolling gently in the waves made by my walking, a sea creature on a stalk, opening and closing its tiny mouth in warm water. Were its eyes open in there? *No.* Tried to stop thinking about it as a live being. It was the devil's tadpole.

The leaves hung limp on the pollarded trees that laced over the churchyard path where Mr Cromley had dragged me, near seven month ago. I counted back. Cabbage had worked out my due date for me, but I'd pushed it out of mind, hadn't wanted to believe it would ever come. I'd no appetite since Mam died, but I kept growing fatter. How big was it? Did it have hair and toes and fingernails?

Overhead, the thunder of a plane shook the jelly air. I couldn't help flinching, though the siren hadn't sounded. A long way off, over the Downs, I thought I saw a trail of smoke, maybe a crippled night-fighter limping back to the nearest base. When I looked down again, I found my hands clasped protectively over my belly.

It grew hotter and stickier as the morning passed, the day tightening and whitening like the head of a boil. There seemed to be no end of forms to fill in. The typing pool in which I sat was airless, stinking of sweat and cheap scent, though every tall window was open. My lower back ached insistently.

I found an excuse to slip away to the wards, to look for Cabbage. No sign of him on Men's Surgical, but Lysol's tall back stalked the corridor ahead of me. He would know if Cabbage was on duty. I tried to run to catch him up, but my feet could get no grip on the shiny green lino and the ache in my back began to burn like I'd torn something. Breathless, I had to stop at the junction of two corridors. Which way had Lysol gone? My head felt heavy and dull. I closed my eyes and could feel myself swaying where I stood, wheezing like an old woman.

Someone cannoned into me with a muttered 'Sorry.' It was Pee, the youngest of the three housemen, head down, white coat flapping, bony lantern jaw sunk onto his hollow chest. He stopped a few yards along the corridor.

'Miss Er . . .?' He could never remember any of the girls' names. 'Are you all right? You're very pale.' He started to walk back towards me. His eyes were fixed on my feet.

I followed his gaze down. There was a tiny puddle, hardly more than a couple of teaspoons of fluid, on the lino between my legs. I baked in shame. I'd wet myself, dear Lord, without even noticing. I'd have to pretend it hadn't happened, was nothing to do with me. Puddle, Dr Matthews? Some careless nurse must've slopped a bedpan.

'Hot,' I said. 'Sticky day. Didn't sleep.' Waving my hand all airy, fanning my face, anything to take his eyes off my soggy shoes. 'You seen Cab– Dr Prentice?'

'Dr Prentice is off duty,' said Pee, like it was mothballs in his mouth.

'When'll—'

'Clever Dr Prentice has the Almighty on his side. His next shift isn't until tomorrow.' There were bruised bags under his eyes, a crêpey look to his pale, pockmarked skin. I'd heard the girls in the office this morning talking about a car crash in the blackout last night, and remembered that Pee had been called out with the ambulance. He'd had to cut off a girl's leg to free her from the wreckage of the passenger seat. The firemen kept their torches trained on the girl's feet so Pee wouldn't have to see the boyfriend's severed head watching him from the back. He was young, in his mid-twenties, but today he looked like a grey ghost of an old man.

He wiped a hand across dry lips before carrying on: 'But they'll probably call him in later. All hands to the pump when the casualties arrive.'

'What casualties?' My heart started thudding.

'There's been a big raid on Bristol. The infirmary there can't cope, and they're talking about sending the overspill to us.'

'They can't . . .' My head was spinning with the thought of it. 'We're full – I was doing a requisition to move some of the convalescents out.'

'Full or not, they're already on their way,' said Pee. 'Are you running a temperature, Miss Er . . .?'

I was in a muck sweat and dizzy with it. My back ached like blazes. My skin was so tight and tender I flinched when he put his hand on my forehead.

414

'You're more than a bit clammy,' he said. 'That's all we need, some bloody bug rampaging through the staff. Go home.'

'The paperwork,' I said weakly.

He gave a croak of a laugh. 'Bugger the paperwork. What we need today are nurses, not pen-pushers. *Go home.* And while you're about it –' his face grew pink, and his eyes went to my feet again '– you might, er, want to change your sanitary towel.' He turned and went steaming off up the corridor.

I glanced down and saw what I'd missed – a streak of bloody mucus on my white ankle sock. This couldn't be it, could it? What I knew about babies was no more than village gossip and earwigging in the church porch when new mothers whispered the details of epic deliveries to each other. *Waters broke, all of a gush. I were splitting from stem to stern. Hurt summat terrible.* Those women let go at least a gallon apiece: the Red Sea parted, Niagara Falls ran down their legs. Not a pathetic trickle like I'd globbed on the lino. No, this couldn't be it. I had an overwhelming urge to lie down, but any minute now the glass doors would swing open and the corridors echo with trolley wheels and running feet. He was right, I should go home.

The day turned into flashes then, like the lightning that was flickering along the top of the Downs. Outside the hospital the sky was near black, the street lit with a last gleam of sunlight before the darkness swallowed it. The air was like a bath, sweat and electricity running along the nerves in my skin, which felt as tight as a tick. No recollection of asking permission to go home, though I must've stopped off at the office: I had my handbag, but no hat or cardigan. My belly dragged, like the baby inside had turned to a lead brick.

God knows how I got there, but suddenly I was on Drove Road, staggering like a drunk with the weight of my belly threatening to topple me. Still no one about, only the two little girls hopscotching, ignoring the livid sky. There was a blink of bright light, and I started counting, waiting for the thunder. Mam used to say if you went *one a hundred, two a hundred, three a hundred,* you knew how many miles off the storm was. I was up to eight a hundred and still no crack, and if it came after that I never heard because instead there was a cramp in my belly that near split me while I stood on the step fumbling for the key.

Then there's no little girls, only the airless, silent hallway. Must've been stairs too, and bugger me if I know how I climbed 'em, but the next flash comes and I'm on my bed, and counting again, but this time I'm counting the time between the cramps because I know that's what you're supposed to do. No question now but that summat's coming, and I'm cursing myself for not stopping at the hospital where there's doctors and maybe by now Cabbage, Cabbage who understands what's wrong with me, Cabbage with his fat sausage fingers helping me down there, but then I remember there was a raid over Bristol way and they'll all be busy with that, saving lives, doing important things for good people, stitching rips in flesh and straightening mashed bones and mopping up blood—

And there's another flash, and that reminds me I couldn't possibly have stopped at the hospital where people knows me and I can see their faces gawping, mouths open in shock, as they watch me writhing on the corridor floor, the monster wrestling with my body like the devil that was its father the night he caught me in the churchyard—

And now a rumble of thunder much closer and the monster's got his teeth in me, I'm on all fours, panting like a dog, only way to stand the pain, and then comes something so strong and vicious I have to howl, only it isn't me howling at all, it's the Warning, middle of the afternoon, and I can't take it in, there's people out at work and little girls playing in the street and they're sounding the Warning but there's nothing I can do about it; no buggerin' way will the pain let me off the bed to crawl downstairs to the Anderson shelter in the back garden. The bedroom's gone black like it's night, it's one of them August storms that sometimes come near harvest, rolling off the Downs and flattening the corn, and there's the crackle of electricity in the air and a burning smell and the rumble overhead—

And there's another flash, which finally splits me open, and I'm back in the hospital but the lights have all gone out and Cabbage is laughing with his hands plunged up to the elbow in a woman's guts and the nurse is screaming and holding a bucket out for all the blood that's coming—

And then I'm back on the bed in my room on Drove Road, head twisted into the pillow half suffocated, and all the blood comes out of me in a gurt gush, and something else with it, slippery like a lump of greasy rubber—

I washed him in the basin but I knew it weren't no good. When the blood and the sticky stuff came off him, he was no more'n a drowned animal, water making ripples in the fine straggly hair that was all over him like a little monkey. The Germans had hit something nearby and there was an orange glow lighting up the black afternoon, shining through the bathroom window to show me what I had in my hands. Ugly but not ugly: not a monster, after all, but a rubbery doll with a squashed blue face. No telling what colour his eyes would have been. My own eyes were leaking; it wasn't his fault who his father was, poor little dab. Charlie. I'd have called him Charlie.

All the while the sky was splitting, the air-raid siren still howling, thunder in the air and the ground shaking. Ambulance bells drilled into my head, setting off a ringing. Then the water from the tap dried to a trickle and stopped. Bomb must've hit a water main. I stood in the bathroom with blood all down my legs and this lifeless thing lying on the cracked porcelain with *Twyfords Sanitary Ware* writ above him like a religious text, crying because I couldn't finish the job, he was still not washed clean.

Charlie.

I picked him up out of the basin, held him against me, feeling his slithery wetness on my chest and the cold of him between my fingers. *Charlie.* I lifted his crumpled face, smaller than my own fist, to my mouth, and tried puffing into his nostrils like I'd seen Mr Peak-Garland's shepherd do when the sickly lambs didn't breathe on their own.

Next second the walls shook and tossed us on the floor because the house two doors down had been hit.

CHAPTER 48

Before the ambulance arrives, John says, 'I shouldn't have wasted time phoning. I should have driven straight here.'

'You couldn't possibly have known,' I say, then wonder if somehow he did.

The paramedic's staring at his bit of paper, trying to pretend he's not listening. He told us he's almost certain she hasn't had a stroke, not a proper one anyway, though she might have had one of those little ones, a TIA . . .

If it wasn't for the bruising on her face. Red purple, already, eye puffed up and almost closed, a black crusty split in the swollen skin, like a mean mouth.

How long's she been on the floor?

She's still there, in the middle of the hallway, her eyes wide and frightened, drifting in and out, the lids drooping now and then. The grip of her hand on mine loosens. Still with us, though, and no intention of going away, I hope, said the paramedic, cheerily, when he first arrived. Her eyes were closed when we found her, and her breathing seemed dreadfully ragged, but what do I know? John was completely calm, called 999 on the landline, then sat cross-legged by her with his hand on her forehead, willing her to hang on. It seemed to take for ever for the paramedic on the motorbike to arrive, though apparently he made it in less than ten minutes. There's a proper ambulance on its way, too, to take her to the Great Western at Swindon.

Amazing, the gear they carry about with them. The paramedic has already shown us the ECG printout with the extra spike, the blip that says Frannie's heartbeat's doing something peculiar, like a drum out of rhythm. Where everybody else's heart usually goes *b'dum, b'dum, b'dum*, Frannie's is going *b'dm'dum, b'dm'dum*. He said the proper name for it, but I've forgotten already. It might be natural, or a side effect of the blood-pressure tablets she takes – or it might be something much worse. She came to while he was sticking the electrodes on her chest and said, What in buggeration you doing, boy? Perfectly all right, just fell, din' I?

The paramedic smiled, and said, We've a feisty one here, then. What's your name, my love?

Frances Robinson, she said. The end came out like a sigh.

Well, Frances . . .

I think she might prefer not to be called by her first name, I said, remembering over-friendly Bob from the day centre.

Sorry, Mrs Robinson.

Mi . . . Hard to hear her.

What was that, my love? He bent forward.

Miss.

Oh.

But you can call me Fran, if you like.

Contrary old bat, I thought. But she's OK, isn't she? She's winning. Took a tumble, they'll keep her in a couple of days for tests, then . . .

If it wasn't for the bruising. Across her chest, as well, when he loosened her blouse to attach the electrodes. He narrowed his eyes, pursed his lips, felt carefully down her side. She closed her eyes and her face went tight and she made a little puffing sound.

That hurt, my love?

Just a bit.

He fiddled about some more, said something into his radio to Mission Control, then stood up and said: Ambulance'll be here any minute. Can we have a bit of a word, like, in the kitchen?

I'll stay with her, I said. You go with him, John. Sick inside, terrified what the paramedic wanted to say. Maybe she'd had a stroke after all. What if she'd broken her hip falling? Old people die from that, don't they? I clung onto Frannie's hand. She smiled up at me, then closed her eyes. She'll be OK. She's tough. She bounces.

If it weren't for the trace of blood at the corner of her mouth. The yellow-white fragment on the floor I put my hand on, hard like a piece of grit. When I held it up to the light, it turned out to be a broken tooth.

'Oh, no,' I hear John say in the kitchen. 'No, really. She *wouldn't*. She was at work most of the day, then . . .'

I can't hear what the paramedic mutters next, but then John says, with utter incredulity in his voice, 'Where *I* was? You can't seriously think . . .'

I let go Fran's hand and stand up. 'What the hell's going on?'

In the kitchen, the paramedic has his radio in his hand.

'Look, she must have hit her head on the hall table . . .' But he's shaking his head. Shit. *Shit.* He couldn't really be saying that, could he?

Panic chokes off my voice as I stand there staring at them.

And at what they'd both missed, behind them, the glitter on the floor, the back door ajar an inch, and a small ragged circle in the glass next to the handle.

The two police officers, when they finally arrive, fifteen minutes after the ambulance has taken Fran to hospital, are less than thorough. They don't even bother to fingerprint the back door. John's steaming by now.

'Fucksake man, she's in her eighties. We found her on the floor. Could be a fucking murder inquiry, and you're acting like it was kids scrumping apples.' Then he catches sight of my face, and sends me an apologetic look, trying to make out he doesn't really think she's in any danger of dying, he's laying it on thick to get some action out of these two turnips.

'No need for that sort of language, sir,' says the one who's poking his nose round the house. The other one, a woman, is outside, in the police car, talking on the radio. 'The scene-of-crime officers will be along later to fingerprint, if it turns out to be necessary. Any idea if there's anything missing?'

'I'll take a look,' I say. 'He doesn't live here, he wouldn't know.'

I can see the wheels turning, the policeman thinking: What kind of a set-up have we here, then? Bit old to be your boyfriend, isn't he? He gets out a notebook. 'If you wouldn't mind checking, Miss . . .? You *do* live here, then?'

'Robinson,' I say. 'India Robinson. I'm her granddaughter.'

'And she is?'

'Frances Robinson. I haven't seen her handbag.'

But there it is, on the bed, in Frannie's downstairs bedroom. Zipped closed. Inside, purse, pension book, building-society passbook, credit cards. I open the purse. Last week's pension and, by the look of it, the one from the week before too, hardly touched, a fat wad of folded notes.

'Maybe the intruder was interrupted before he found it,' says the policeman, following me in from the hallway.

By what, exactly? Wouldn't a caller have seen her, through the glazed front door, lying in the hallway, and called an ambulance? The policeman is coming to the same conclusion: his mouth pursing, he writes something in his notebook.

'Drugs,' I say. 'Solstice. Lot of strange people wandering about – that'll be what they were after.'

'And where did the old lady keep her . . . drugs?'

'Frannie,' I say. 'Please call her by her name.' The blood-pressure pills and the gastric reflux medicine, the sum total of Fran's pharmacopia, are kept in the kitchen cupboard by the kettle. Broken glass from the back door crunches underfoot. The cupboard contains serried ranks of pill packets, neatly lined up, all full.

'Bathroom?' asks the policeman, still on my heels. Of course, I recognize him now: he's Corey's husband. Only met him once, at the National Trust staff Christmas party, and can't remember his name. Doubt it would do me any good if I could.

Upstairs, the mirrored door of the bathroom cabinet swings open to reveal a bottle of TCP, some out-of-date aspirins, an unopened box of codeine tablets the dentist gave Frannie when she had a root canal filled, and my contraceptive pills.

The policeman peers over my shoulder. 'Anything missing?' I shake my head.

My iPod and stereo are still in my room, as well as my laptop, on the 1940s dressing-table that doubles as a desk. Through the window, I can see the woman police officer getting out of the car, stretching, hitching a bra strap back into place, and starting up the path towards the front door. Another car, a dusty blue Astra, slides round the corner into the cul-de-sac and parks behind the patrol car.

Downstairs John is on the phone. My stomach's full of snakes.

'The hospital?' I mouth.

The paramedic said it would be better not to go in the ambulance, that we should wait for the police and come on later, but now that seems crazy and I wish I'd been more assertive. Fran's scared eyes sought mine when the ambulance men carried her out of the house on a stretcher.

'Where are they taking me?' she said plaintively. 'I'm all right, Ind, I don't want to go to hospital. People die in hospital.'

'You won't die,' I said. 'They're only going to check you over. I'll be along in a bit – look, if I was worried I'd be holding your hand in the back of the ambulance, wouldn't I?'

'Don't need anyone to hold my hand.' She struggled with the blanket wrapped round her and a feeble paw appeared. 'See? I'm waving you bye-bye. Be sure you make them bring me back. I'd ruther be in me own bed.' There was a smile on her lips but her eyes were pleading.

'We'll look after her,' said the first paramedic, handing me a slip of paper with a phone number on it. 'Soon as the police have been, you give the hospital a ring. They'll tell you which ward she's on.' He mounted his bike, and the other paramedics lifted the stretcher into the back of the ambulance. One jumped down, and started to pull the doors closed.

'Hang on,' came Fran's voice from inside. 'Where's the baby? He's all right, isn't he? Is he already at the hospital?'

'She's still in A and E,' says John, putting the phone down.

'Still?'

He shrugs his shoulders helplessly. 'It's Solstice. Not the best day to be carted off to Casualty. Place jammed with kids who celebrated too enthusiastically.'

There's a knock on the front door. Without waiting for a reply, a man in a dull red anorak steps inside, the policewoman a deferential two paces behind him. Under the anorak he's wearing a navy blue suit, the lapels shiny with aeons of dry-cleaning. His face matches the anorak, and his eyebrows are two thick furry tassels set at an angle of perpetual surprise.

'DI Andy Jennings,' he says. 'Hello.'

CHAPTER 49

29 August 1942

I was outside the house on Drove Road and there was glass in my hair and something in my arms, wrapped in a bloody towel. More flashes – lightning or bombs, couldn't tell which, I'd gone deaf when all the windows blew out. The first fat drops of rain were beginning to fall and it was still dark as the Day of Judgment. How did them German pilots see to aim their bombs?

The house next door was a ruined tooth, half shorn away. But where the house beyond it had been – the house where the little girls lived: the hopscotch chalk marks were still on the pavement, blurring in the rain – there was nothing but a hole. Bricks were scattered in the road, dust hung in the air, and a man in a filthy ARP uniform was standing by it shouting. At least, I guessed he was shouting: his mouth was open and he was waving his arms at me, but it was like I was under water, couldn't hear a thing, my arms and legs moving with a current that was pushing me along past him, away from the far end of Drove Road that was all on fire. Up there was the aircraft factory, the Germans would have been aiming for that, but most of the bombs had fallen short and hit houses instead. I kept looking back, wondering if the factory girls had got to the shelters in time, wondering if my landlady was all right, wondering why I was holding a wet, bloody bundle. Another ARP man was clambering over the rubble with something limp and bloody in his arms, too, and there were tears cutting tracks through the dust on his face.

Wouldn't be safe to go west, towards the railway yards, because they was likely being bombed too, and so I began walking down

Drove Road as fast as I could, which wasn't very fast at all, my body one big ache and my knees like jelly. I thought of Pee at the hospital, waiting for the Bristol casualties, now finding he had to sew arms and legs back on Swindon factory girls too. As I came to the end of the road, an ambulance tore past me and stopped by the house that was gone, but anyone who'd seen that hole would've known it was far too late.

I tottered in a daze through the Old Town. My hearing started to come back and I heard a clock strike. Four bongs, that was all. Four o'clock in the afternoon. I'd lost all track of time and it was so dark I thought for a second it must be four in the morning, but the light in the sky was to the west, not the east. The All Clear hadn't sounded and the side streets were empty. The rain started to come down in sheets. When I reached a junction I saw more ambulances clipping along the main road but they couldn't have seen me. I limped on with my bloodied bundle towards the countryside.

A car stopped for me before I'd gone as far as Wroughton village. I was drenched by then, hair in rats' tails, and the bundle in my arms was so small and soaked that the airman behind the wheel could've had no idea what I carried. The rain had washed us clean, Charlie and me.

The airman wound down the window, his face a white blur intersected by the line of a neat blond moustache, and told me to hop in, the buses weren't running because of the raid, he was on his way to Yatesbury and where was I headed? I told him, voice still muffled in my ears, that he could drop me on the main road between Avebury and Winterbourne Monkton. Not if it's raining, he said, what do you take me for, an army oik? I'll deliver you to the door, my darling.

I asked him if I could lie down on the back seat, I was sorry I was so wet, but I was wicked tired with walking in the rain. He turned off the engine and went out into the downpour to find a blanket from the boot for me to lie on, and a coat to put over me, and he held the car door open with the rain turning his blue-grey uniform black on the shoulders.

I fell asleep in the car, Charlie in his towelling shroud on my lap under the RAF greatcoat.

In the end, I persuaded the airman to drop me on the main road after all: told him my mam didn't like me taking lifts, she'd give me what for if she saw me climb out of a strange car. Only a short step home, I said, look, the rain's stopped. But after the airman had driven away, as I struggled up the chalk track to Windmill Hill, Charlie in my arms, the rain started coming down heavy again, the trees tossing. It was one of those storms that prowl round the horizon like a bad-tempered dog, still growling and baring its teeth when you hoped it had backed off. Lightning snapped every now and then, but far away. Couldn't have been later than six, but the clouds pressed down and drowned the light. Rivers of chalky water flooded the path.

By the time I reached the flattened crest of the hill, I was soaked to the skin again, face burning up, a sickly ache in my back and legs, and terrible tired. There were never ceremonies for a stillborn at the hospital. Scraps of flesh like him counted for nothing, waste; they were burned in the incinerator. But I could do something for him, like the first Charlie's mam had done for her child. He'd been laid in the earth with his face turned for the sunrise in the ditch at the top of Windmill Hill. It was near fifteen years since the hill had been excavated, and the archaeologists had hidden the scars of the digging under a skin of turf. The humps of the round barrows pushed out of it like gurt pimples. Charlie and me, we weren't anyone special. We didn't belong in a chieftain's grave. I'd scrabble out a little bed for him in the ditch, if I could find the ditch in the driving rain.

A lightning flash lit the sky, and I wasn't anywhere near it. I'd wandered right off the crown of the hill to the edge of the wood. A yellow seam joined the clouds to the hills in the west, and I knew this, after all, was my Charlie's place, quiet and safe under the trees. I slipped and slithered down the slope a way, knowing I'd find the right spot, and there it was at the foot of a bank under the tree roots, a deep hole like it had been made for us, an entrance to the Lower World that faced not the rising but the setting sun.

I unwrapped him from the towel, a little dark animal with his damp coat of fine hair. I'd thought he'd be cold but he was warm from me holding him, and not stiff yet. I kissed his closed eyes and laid him under the tree roots, well back in the hole but with his tiny face turned to catch the rays of the sinking sun, and scraped soil from the crumbling bank to make it more of a cradle for him. There was old dead bracken mixed in with the chalky earth, but I didn't think this place belonged to any other creature now. They had left it for Charlie.

The rain gradually stopped and the wind died, and soon there was no sound in my ears but the drip of wet leaves. I climbed back up to the crown of the hill, to the edge of the trees. The view from here was like a careless watercolour. Avebury village and the circle were hidden, but the top of the church tower rose above a viridian wash of leaves. To the south and west, there were drenched fields, umbers and ochres and a dash of burnt sienna, under a sky that was heavy Prussian blue and Payne's grey except for that single bright lemon streak. I could see the brown gash at Trusloe where Mr Keiller had given the land for the new houses, and Longstones Field, and the woods that hid the racing stables and Yatesbury. I remembered the watercolour set he had given me, four summers ago, and the thought of it made me warm.

I sat for a while at the wood's margin, waiting for the lemon crack in the sky to fade, and real darkness to fall. When I was as sure as I could be that the sun had set, I went back down the slope, whispered the Lord's Prayer to Charlie, then dug my hands into the soft soil of the crumbling bank, and filled in the entrance to the hole, so that no one would find him.

I didn't turn to look back, once my feet were on the track down the hill, because there was nothing left to see in the gathering night, but I knew he was there, and always would be.

Here's what I think about in the night, though, the nights when I know there are lights up on Windmill Hill: someone looking for

Charlie, maybe that devil come back to search for his son. I think of the moment before the bomb fell on the house two doors away, when I held him to my face and breathed into his tiny nostrils like he was a sick lamb. Did I imagine that his little chest heaved? And, if it did, what happened then? What happened between the bomb and me being outside the house?

CHAPTER 50

Fran looks smaller than usual in the hospital bed. She's asleep, curled on her side, the bruising hidden but a padded dressing on her forehead. An oxygen tube emerges from her nostrils; more plastic tubing snakes from under the bedclothes to a drip stand by the bed.

'Dehydrated,' says the nurse. 'Do you want to sit with her a bit? She'll probably wake. Visiting hours are over, officially, but . . .'

She doesn't wake.

She looks different, now, younger, a woman living in a place I have never been to, inhabiting a set of memories I can't begin to guess. All present time, all will, all *I am* pared away to *I was*, and then even that whittled to nothing at all.

'Stay at my place,' says John, as we walk across the empty car park towards the pickup. It's after eleven, what little light there is left in the sky swamped by the hospital's halogen glare.

'I ought to have stayed here.'

'Don't be silly. She'll wake when she wakes. Nowhere to sleep, anyway.'

'I could stretch out on a couple of chairs—'

'The nurses don't want you around overnight. Better not to antagonize them, believe me.'

'What – patients and their relatives get in the way of the smooth running of the hospital?'

'Something like that.'

We've reached the pay machines. I push the parking ticket into the slot. 'Drop me at Trusloe. I'll be fine.'

430

'No.' The overhead light reveals concern on his tired face as I feed in the coins. 'I've bodged the glass in the back door with a sheet of plywood, ought to hold but . . .'

'Whoever it was isn't coming back. They were so scared, they didn't even stop to nick her purse.'

'Yeah, and where are her door keys, then?'

My knees lock. '*What?*'

'Not on the hall table. Not on the hook by the back door. I checked her handbag while you were in the loo – not there either. I even asked the nurse on the ward if they'd been on her when they undressed her. No keys.'

'Jesus.' I lean against the pay machine, feeling shaky. 'That's creepy. You think they're planning to come back later and clear the house?'

'It's not exactly full of valuable antiques, is it? Could have been another panic thing – saw the keys, grabbed them. They're probably in a hedge by now. All the same, I'd rather you didn't sleep there until the locks are changed.'

He takes the ticket from the machine and walks towards the pickup, his face screwed up in thought. Something else he's not sharing?

'Have you told the police about the keys?' I ask.

'They'd left, hadn't they?'

'You could have phoned them.'

The ponytail quivers; his mouth turns down tightly. 'Don't believe in telling the police everything. Never trust a pig.' He makes it sound like an old country saying rather than a piece of outdated hippie slang.

But what's he concealing from me?

On the way out of Swindon, we both realize we haven't eaten. John swings the truck round and we find a late-night chippy in a row of shops off the ring road. 'What do you want?' he asks.

'What are *you* having?' I'm too tired to make decisions for myself.

'Nothing.'

'John, you haven't eaten all day, have you? Unless you managed a sandwich this afternoon.' His face tells me he didn't. 'Oh, no. Don't tell me you're *fasting*. Not tonight, John. I want to sleep, don't want to be kept awake by your bloody drum.'

'I'll use a CD and wear headphones.'

'Do you have to?'

The trouble is, John's so rational most of the time that I forget he can also be Mr Weird.

'I need to go looking for your grandmother's guardian. After a shock, she could have lost it.' He doesn't need to carry on, to remind me what a shaman believes about the power animal buried in the psyche of each and every one of us, a guardian spirit that protects us.

Without it, you die, sooner or later.

The sheets on the spare bed at John's are chilly, and my legs are restless. He's still moving around downstairs, assembling his stuff for the journey, perhaps stewing a pan of magic mushrooms, though he's so experienced a psychic traveller he doesn't need hallucinogenics. The drumming is enough to take him into a trance and go wherever a shaman goes, through the cave into the Lower World, where everything is . . . different. The same place as the real world, according to John, but altered, like a transparent film that overlies it, or vice versa. You see things there that are magical: magic, that is, in the sense that they represent what is deep down true. So when someone's sick, the way a shaman sees it in the magic world, they've lost their power animal. The shaman has to journey to find it and give it back to them, or they die.

'How do you know it's theirs?' I asked, as we came into the cottage tonight. Silly question.

'It appears four times,' he says. 'That's the sign. Fourth time you grab it. Besides, I'll – know.' He looked at me, unapologetic. 'I realize you have trouble with this, Indy, but think of it as symbolic. Jung's

432

archetypes, that sort of thing. Psychological concepts represented by symbols. Works for me, same way God works for some people.'

Downstairs, the living-room door closes softly. Wherever he's going, he's about to set off to find what my grandmother has lost.

CHAPTER 51

29 August 1942

There was a bird calling, a crazy wet bird in a bush, singing its heart out to the night as I limped down the track from the hill. Avebury was dark in the blackout, the rain keeping people indoors. My legs wouldn't carry me further. I wanted warm water, clean sheets, milk in a tall glass, a hand stroking my limp, knotted hair.

I stumbled through the churchyard, past Mam's grave, still a heap of earth and no headstone. Through the iron kissing gate onto the cobbles of the stableyard, by the museum where I used to work, where the other Charlie lay in his glass coffin. Then up the path between the lavender to the side door of the Manor. The beech trees in the garden rustled anxious, like, telling me to turn back, no good would come of it. No gleam of light between the heavy blackout curtains.

Please, God, let him be here. I knocked. Silence. Put a hand to my forehead, could feel the heat of my skin, the chill of my body where my damp skirt and blouse clung to me. Oh, Lord, he wasn't here, there was nobody, not even Mr Waters the butler, what would I do now?

Better that, maybe, than Mrs Keiller. What was I thinking of? What would I have done then?

The door swung open, light knifing across the lawn.

'Well, I'll be damned,' he said, stepping into the porch. 'Heartbreaker. You poor little mite.' Behind him, pulling together the curtains that hung behind the door to preserve the blackout, was Mrs Sorel-Taylour, shock on her face to see me.

Mr Keiller took hold of my shivering arms. 'You're soaked to the skin. Mrs S-T, could you ask someone to run a bath? She'll catch a fever, if she hasn't already. Did they send a telegram? You poor child, all alone, no wonder you came to us.'

How could he know? The chill in me was so deep I couldn't grasp any of this. In the parlour, Mr Young was standing by the fireplace. He gave me the kindest smile, but pity was etched on his solemn face. Why were they all here? Words buzzing round the room like faulty electric circuits. Someone said, here, give her this, it'll warm her, and Mrs Sorel-Taylour handed me a glass of brandy. But one of those words was already melting my frozen brain, beginning to burn, letters of fire. *Telegram.*

Only one thing a telegram meant in them days, and never good.

CHAPTER 52

Drumbeats in the dark, louder, faster, louder, LOUDER . . .

I come awake to the sound of hammering on the front door, my heart thudding in time, sun hitting my eyes through the thin curtains. My watch on the bedside table says half past nine: full morning.

Shit. Meant to be up hours ago. The knocking starts again. One of John's clients?

I wrap myself in the threadbare towelling dressing-gown John leaves for guests on the back of the spare-room door. Across the landing the door to his room is half open. He's spark out, shirtless but still in his jeans, on the bed. Anyone else, I'd give them a good shake, but John's adamant that people should only ever be roused gently from sleep – another of those moments where, apparently, you can do untold damage by scaring away their power animal. So I draw his door quietly closed and leave him to it, making my way down the narrow uncarpeted stairs on bare feet as the next bout of thunderous knocking begins.

On the doorstep stands DI Jennings. He doesn't look at all surprised to find me at John's. 'Good morning, Miss Robinson. Sorry to be so *early*' – you can tell he doesn't think it's early at all, but we're a pair of slovenly hippies so it would be early to us – 'but I wanted to catch you before you left for the hospital.'

'What's the matter?' Panic shoots up my throat. The police come to tell you when someone's died, don't they? No, that's ridiculous, the hospital would have phoned. Bastard, I bet he knew I'd be freaked. I'm starting to understand why John has a down on the police.

'I was expecting to find you at Trusloe because our scene-of-crime officers arrived at half past eight this morning to take fingerprints.'

'Oh, no.' I close my eyes in frustration. 'I thought the other policeman said . . . Nobody told me. And John's tacked plywood over the back door . . . Sorry. Look, can I get dressed? We were back late from the hospital. Step inside, I'll put the kettle on.'

'I did tell Mr Bolger the SOCOs would arrive this morning. Didn't he pass it on?'

I leave him in the kitchen, assuring me he's perfectly capable of making his own cup of tea. Or, translated, of having a good nose round while I'm upstairs. I throw on jeans and a T-shirt as fast as I can, trying to remember what I should have been doing this morning before the world broke up. Well, ringing Corey to cancel my shift at the café can wait.

'Would you mind . . .' I put my head round the kitchen door to find DI Jennings with his reading glasses on and his fat red face pressed to John's crop-circle calendar. 'Won't be long. I have to call the hospital to find out how my grandmother is.'

DI Jennings's expression conveys surprise that I haven't done so already.

'I was asleep until . . .' For Christ's sake, why am I justifying myself? He's a master of making the innocent feel guilty. 'The nurses don't like people calling too early,' I finish lamely.

It takes three tries on the phone in the living room to reach the ward. Turns out to be doctors' rounds, no one able to tell me much. 'She slept well, though,' says the nurse, brightly.

At the kitchen table, DI Jennings pushes a mug of lukewarm black coffee towards me. 'Didn't know if you took milk.' He proffers the bottle.

'Oh, you found the sugar all right?'

'Just kept opening cupboards.'

I'm sure you did. 'When will the fingerprint people be coming back?' I ask.

'They've finished. Your friend John hadn't done a very good job with the plywood, and he'd forgotten to lock up too. We thought you wouldn't mind if we let ourselves in.' His eyes dare me to disagree. 'We'll need your fingerprints, of course, and Mr Bolger's.'

'Of course.' I try to sound like I'm completely in control. 'I want this bloke caught, Inspector.'

'Well, that's what I'm coming to,' he says. 'You do know your friend John has a conviction for ABH?'

It isn't John. No way. He's the most harmless bloke I know.

'See, Miss Robinson, I've no reason to doubt you're telling the truth when you say you were at work yesterday.' DI Jennings's narrowed eyes suggest he'll be checking carefully nonetheless. 'But Mr Bolger seems to have spent most of the day on his own, apart from the time you were with him.'

'He wouldn't,' I say. 'He loves Frannie . . .' Jennings's furry eyebrows rear. 'I mean, he's an old friend of the family. And he has his own key. Anyway, Frannie would open the door to him. He wouldn't need to break in—' The eyebrows writhe like caterpillars, sceptical. If you wanted to make it *look* like a break-in—

No, for God's sake. The bastard's trying to manipulate me. John wouldn't do anything of the kind, and if you really wanted to make it look like a break-in, you'd take her purse.

'See, half the time these things are family,' says Jennings. 'Granny-bashing's a lot more common than people think. And we talked to your grandmother's social worker.'

'Adele.'

'No, she's on holiday. The other one, at the day centre. Bob. He says your grandmother is disturbed about something. She starts screaming for no apparent reason. Classic. Maybe your friend John didn't mean to hurt her, but she started screaming and it wound him up, terrible noise it can be, red rag to someone with a violent temper—'

'No,' I say, firm. 'He *doesn't have* a violent temper. And if it was him, don't you think she'd have said? She was conscious, in the hallway, the paramedic can tell you, and John was standing right beside her . . .'

'Exactly. Intimidating her. She's frightened to death of him.'

'She's not. You don't know my grandmother.'

'Or she's confused.'

John is still sprawled across the bed, eyes closed. I shake his shoulder roughly.

'Wh—'

'Get up. The police want to talk to you. Jennings has already grilled me.'

His eyes come open, bloodshot faded blue, pinprick pupils. 'Tell them I'll call them back . . .'

'Not on the phone. Jennings is downstairs.' Rotating his teacup thoughtfully, I bet, to read in the swirling tealeaves the secret of whether it was John or me who beat up Fran. 'If you took something last night, I hope to God you didn't leave it lying around.'

John closes his eyes. He looks tired unto death, grizzled stubble furring the seams and gullies of his hollowed cheeks. 'Don't *think* so . . .'

That doesn't bode well. I leave him to dress, and hurtle downstairs before Jennings finds anything, wondering how to make him under-stand the relationship between John, Frannie and me.

On my way to the hospital, I park in Avebury outside the main office to explain why I might not be around for a few days.

Graham, eating a custard cream, strolls out of the kitchen as I walk in. Lilian looks up from her computer screen, with a concerned expres-sion. 'Indy – we weren't expecting to see you today,' she says. News travels in Avebury, it seems. 'How is your poor gran?'

'Not sure. The doctors aren't giving much away, and they've started talking about doing tests, though what for I can't imagine. They must have X-rayed every bone in her body.'

'I heard it was a break-in.' Graham's face is unusually expression-less. Oh, God, don't let gossip about John have started already. Why did it have to be Corey's husband on duty yesterday?

'It was a break-in,' I say firmly.

John's at the police station. Jennings took my fingerprints himself, at the cottage, but he wants John to have DNA taken. There was blood on some of the broken glass on the floor.

Lilian shakes her head. 'They'll never catch anyone. Not unless somebody informs.' She looks me straight in the eyes as she says it. 'Your shifts at the café are being covered. I'll tell the television people as well, just in case. Let us hear when . . . you know anything.'

I nod and walk out of the office, feeling two sets of eyes on my back.

At the hospital, Frannie is asleep again. 'It is sleep, isn't it?' I ask the nurse. 'You're sure?'

'She was awake earlier, when we took her down to X-ray. Groggy, but charming the porters. Tired her out, though. She'll wake if you touch her.'

I lay my hand gently on her forehead. *Be careful how you rouse someone sleeping.* The skin's warm and papery. Her eyes blink open, and gradually focus on mine. A smile spreads across her face. 'Oh, how lovely,' she says. 'What you doin' here, Indy? Come to take me home?'

She's asleep again, only five minutes later. I sit by the bed, back sweaty against the beige plastic upholstery of the visitor's chair, waiting to slip my hand out of hers until I'm sure it won't wake her.

What happened, Fran? I asked her.

Don't recall a bloody thing. Fell over, din' I? Banged me head or summat. Her accent becoming broader, old Wiltshire, a sure sign she's frightened. Not of the person who hurt her – I'm sure she's not faking memory loss this time – but afraid because she can't remember.

The room fills with the thrum of engines, the clatter of rotors.

'Air ambulance coming in. Big excitement of our day,' says a voice, bringing me awake with a jerk. The woman in the next bed nods towards the window with relish. 'Probably a motorway accident.' She's propped up against a pile of pillows, reading *Woman's Weekly*, enormous boobs encased in a black satin négligé with embroidered pink roses. A nicotine-yellow tube snakes from under the sheet into a plastic sac on a stand. 'Why don't you go and have a coffee or summat, my lover? You look wore out. You might want to buy her a nightie in the hospital shop while you're downstairs.'

Fran's bony shoulder is draped in a blue hospital gown, faded with much laundering.

'I never thought. I'll bring one from home tomorrow.'

'Bring her two, dear, one to wash and one to wear. Don't forget her dressing-gown and slippers.' She flaps her magazine at me. 'I'll keep an eye on your nan, don't you worry, and tell her where you're to when she wakes.'

I take the lift down to the lobby. As soon as I turn it on, my phone bleeps with a text. It's from Martin: **So sorry about yr gran, petal. If u need place to stay, my cottage empty tonight. Have to be in Bath, but can leave key**

The air ambulance is leaving, hovering like a nectar-laden bee over the far end of the car park, as I sit down on the smoker's bench to text back that it's a kind thought, but no need.

A second text arrives immediately: **And forgive me for being crass yesterday afternoon**

I buy Fran essentials – nightdress, pants, comb, toothbrush – and a newspaper from the WRVS shop, then go in search of food. John's in the coffee shop, at the till with a laden tray. He doesn't immediately see me. The light from the window behind leaves his face in shadow, hollow cheeks and deep eyes momentarily sinister, until he looks up and his face splits in a smile. 'Indy – want something to eat? I'll pay for it,' he says to the woman at the till.

We sit at a table near the back of the room.

'What's the matter?' he asks immediately.

I play for time. 'How did it go at the police station?'

'How you'd expect. They haven't anything on me, so they took samples, blustered a bit and told me I'd be hearing from them.'

'What's this about an ABH conviction?'

'Oh, for God's sake.' John puts down his fork, his eyes chips of flint. 'Don't tell me you believe I had anything to do—'

'No, of course I don't,' I say. 'Jennings wrong-footed me, that's all. I didn't know what to say.'

'You were there – 1985, Battle of the Beanfield. I gave a policeman a black eye.'

'Oh.' The picture comes back to me, the one in the paper, a startlingly young John being led away by cops with riot shields, blood streaming down his face. 'Sorry. I'd forgotten.'

'Given you were four at the time, that's forgivable. So now you see why I don't rate too highly with the Wiltshire constabulary. Jennings was probably there too, as a sprog copper.' He chews another mouthful of battered fish. 'Anyway, that's irrelevant. He's trying to set us at odds.'

'What do you mean?'

'Jennings put it to me that, at two o'clock, he had only my word for it *you* weren't at Trusloe. That these things are almost always family, and you – young, stressed out by the responsibility of caring for your senile gran – are much more likely than me to have belted her one in a moment of frustration. He good as said *I'm* covering up for *you*. Because, of course, I'm only a drugged up old hippie, aren't I?'

'Oh, my God.' Under the table, my legs have started to shake. 'He can't—'

'Don't panic. He hasn't anything else so he's trying for a reaction from one of us.'

My egg sandwich has become inedible. 'Look, if that's the way they're thinking, it's a bad idea for me to stay with you. I'll go back to Trusloe tonight.'

'You can't. The locks haven't been changed.'

'So? Let's call out a twenty-four-hour locksmith. By the way, Jennings told me you left the back door unlocked last night.'

'I didn't.'

I stare at him. 'You must have. That's how the SOCOs got in to fingerprint this morning.'

'I remember locking it. Come on, you were in the kitchen.'

He's right. I was. I can picture him turning the key. *His* key, of course . . .

'John, you should tell them about those missing keys.'

'You think I'm going to tell them anything voluntarily after this morning?' He glares at me defiantly.

'Anyway, you're right.' I push my chair back and stand up. 'Maybe I shouldn't sleep at Trusloe. But I don't have to go to yours. Martin said I could stay at the cottage the Trust's lent him. The filming's finished but he's not leaving until the stone's cemented in next week and they backfill the trench.'

John seems uneasy. 'You sure?'

'What's the problem?'

'I don't know.' His fingers are drumming on the tabletop, itching for a roll-up. 'Doesn't feel a good idea, that's all.'

'Finish your lunch.' I look around for a bin to chuck my uneaten sandwich. 'I'd like to catch a doctor, and find out what they think about Fran.'

He follows me out of the cafeteria and taps me on the shoulder while I'm waiting for the lift. 'You left your stuff behind.' It's the bag holding the nightdress I bought for Frannie, and my newspaper.

'Thanks.'

'Listen, stay at my place, after all. Don't you think it's better to be together, in case –' He stops abruptly.

'You did . . . find her guardian, didn't you?' I know this stuff is crap, but it feels important that John believes she'll recover.

'Yes, I found it. No mistaking it.' His lips quiver in what is almost, but not quite, a smile. 'It has to come to you four times on the journey, to be certain, but I recognized it immediately. A blackbird.'

That's so much like Fran that I laugh with relief. 'That's all right, then. Thank God one thing is.'

The lift arrives with a ping and the doors open; shiny steel walls reflect our blurred outlines as splashes of colour. He catches my arm before I can walk in. 'No. You don't understand.' His eyes are anxious.

'I found it, but it wouldn't let me near, kept hopping away, head on one side, looking at me. I couldn't catch it to give back to her.'

I feel the smile fall off my face. 'It's *bollocks*, John.' The lift doors are trying to close on me, and I shake his hand off my arm. 'Doesn't work even on a symbolic level. Sorry.' I push into the lift and punch the button for Frannie's floor. The doors begin to shut again, but he's not moved.

'Indy . . .'

'What?' I hit the doors-open button.

'Tonight. I've a bad feeling about us not being in the same place . . .'

'This is spooking me, and none of it's *real*.' I jab the button again, more viciously this time. 'Look, I said I wouldn't go back to Trusloe. I'll be fine at Martin's.'

The doors slide together, cutting off the sight of his worried face.

Fran's awake, though groggy, and chirping merrily as I stow the new nightie in her locker.

'I'm a pickle, in' I?' Head on one side, exactly like a blackbird. 'Look at the shiner I give meself.' She points proudly to her black eye – or what would be her black eye, if she was pointing to the right side of her face. 'Nurse brought me a mirror when she helped me comb my hair, couldn't believe the state of me. And me wrist . . .' She pulls back the covers with her left hand to reveal a cast on the right. 'Plastered up this morning.'

'Doctor been round yet?'

'Ooh, yes. Lovely girl, not much older than you, ever so clever. Nurse said to tell you, if you wanted to talk, go and find her at the desk before the round's finished. Go on, I'll be all right. Might have another little nap. Can you plump up my pillows?'

I help her to shuffle forward, and adjust the backrest. My eyes snag on the whiteboard above the bed, where the nurses write each patient's treatment details.

Nil by mouth.

✳   ✳   ✳

'How long's she been nil by mouth?' I ask the nurse at the desk. 'And *why*? Are they going to operate on the wrist?'

She shrugs. 'You'll have to ask the doctor.'

John's coming up the corridor. I wave at him, and go back to Fran's bedside. Her eyelids are already drooping. 'You go ahead and snooze, love,' I say. 'John's here now. We'll both sit with you, after I've found the doc.' I stoop to give her a kiss on her forehead.

'Love you, darlin'.' Her anxious eyes hold mine. 'You will be taking me home soon?'

The doctor leads me into a side room. She has thin, stooped shoulders and pale hair escaping from a scrunchie, and looks about a year older than me. Probably *is* about a year older than me. In doctor terms, I'd bet she's my equivalent in the food chain at Overview TV.

'You're Mrs Robinson's next-of-kin?' I nod. 'Your grandmother's in no immediate danger, we think, but she is over eighty, and she's had both a shock and a fall. Lucky not to have fractured more than a minor bone in her wrist.'

'Is that what the operation's for?'

'No.' She tugs nervously on the stethoscope slung round her neck. 'The nurses noticed some bleeding today that wasn't apparent last night.'

'That cut on her forehead again?'

'Not her scalp. Down below.'

Beyond the pale doctor's shoulder is a fearsome piece of equipment with an array of lights on the top, looking like something that could reassemble itself any moment into a robot and stomp out of the room to destroy the planet. It's easier staring at it instead of her.

'Down below?' My voice comes from a long, long way off.

'Vaginal bleeding. There are a couple of possible explanations. One would be a gynaecological problem of some sort – anything from fibroids to cancer, I'm afraid. I understand from her she's not been feeling entirely well for several months. We're taking her up for an ultra-sound scan later this afternoon. Don't worry, if there's anything we'll whip her into surgery soonest and have it out; the bleeding's heavy enough to cause a little concern. But we also need to eliminate the other possibility.'

My heart's started to thud with the same stuttering rhythm as Fran's: *b'dm'dum, b'dm'dum.* Reflected in the shiny bulbs of the big lights, the doctor's scrunchie is bobbing in time as she goes on speaking: 'I've notified the police surgeon, and he'll want to do an internal examination as soon as he can get here.'

CHAPTER 53

The other possibility. What kind of sick bastard could hurt an old lady that way?

John and I manage a swift conversation when the tea trolley arrives, while Frannie's arguing with the nurse that surely she could have just a little sip of tea, her mouth's like the bottom of a buggerin' birdcage.

'You go home,' he says. 'You're so tired you're white. Hospital visiting takes it out of you – have to pace yourself. I'll wait around and find out what's happening with the scan, and the police surgeon. Any news, I'll phone.' He ignores my dubious face. 'Go on, you can see how much brighter she seems. I doubt they'd operate tonight, anyway, even if they found something.'

'But what if it's . . .'

. . . the other possibility.

'Let's think about that if and when,' says John.

'She'd have said something, wouldn't she? I know she claims not to remember but . . .'

'If and when, Indy. Have you eaten today at all? Go back and heat up something from my freezer.'

The idea of warm food and bed seems unbearably attractive. 'I still don't think I should stay at your place. What if this doesn't change DI Jennings's mind? It'll probably fuel his sick fantasies that you and I are involved in some conspiracy. I'll go to Trusloe, there's food there.'

'No,' says John. 'Especially not now. If you won't stay at mine, go to Martin's. At least there'll be someone with you there.' As I turn back into the side ward to say goodbye to Fran, he catches hold of my arm. 'Be careful, though, won't you?'

'I'll light a candle to the Goddess,' I tell him.

'Don't be flip.'

As the car takes the bend into the gap between Avebury's massive stone teeth, I remember my return last September, full of hope under a dusty golden harvest moon. Now there's nothing friendly about the stones' smile. Instead, it reminds me of the dead, broken grin of a fleshless jawbone.

Martin will have left the key to his cottage under a stone by the front door. Naturally I didn't tell John that Martin won't be there tonight or he'd have had me behind locks and bars and sitting in a pentagram for good measure at Fortress Bolger. Nor did I mention I'd be going back to Trusloe first to pick up clean clothes.

Bella Vista seems a different place without Frannie. The plywood tacked over the broken glass, the grey dust left by the fingerprint men, a smell of damp, all give it an air of dilapidation. The people who lived here left years ago.

She *will* come back.

I keep seeing things I hadn't noticed yesterday: a saucepan in the sink, encrusted with soup, a bowl and spoon on the table. In the sitting room, there's a cup containing a half-inch of cold tea. I move around the house collecting things Frannie might need in hospital: dressing-gown, slippers, clean underwear, book of crossword puzzles . . . Her reading glasses have slipped down the side of the armchair where I found the anonymous letter months ago. Who it was from, whatever happened to it seem irrelevant now I'm facing the possibility I could lose Fran. From the bathroom, towel, flannel, soap. A flash of white catches my eye—

Glass exploding everywhere, in my hair, trying to push myself down into the upholstery of the passenger seat of Mick's van—

You stupid little cow. Don't you understand what you've done?

Only my reflection in the glass door of the shower. The pink, medical smell of old ointment leaks out of the bathroom cabinet, calming like rescue remedy. I come back to myself, taking deep, heaving breaths. The house is ringing with silence. I kneel down and pick up the toothbrush and the Colgate and the other toiletries scattered on the floor from the sponge bag I dropped.

My phone pings: a text from John. No police surgeon yet, no news, they haven't done the scan. As I lock the front door of the house behind me, I can't help glancing towards Windmill Hill. It's still broad daylight, so what was I expecting to see up there?

I park the car in the lane outside Martin's cottage and sit for a moment, remembering him talking about the strangeness of bedding down for the night in an ancient stone circle. The cottage is set back from the others, the last in the lane, backing directly onto the stones, with a tiny strip of garden to one side. The walls are whitewashed, probably built of sarsen from megaliths broken in the eighteenth century. So, not only sleeping inside the circle: I'll be sleeping inside one of the stones.

Unlocking the door, I realize I'm ever so slightly nervous. Kipping down here reminds me of the woman's skeleton found in the ditch, her body ringed by small sarsens.

Keeping something out, or keeping something in?

There are logs and kindling in a basket by the hearth. Although it's midsummer, I lay a fire and prop myself against the sofa with a glass of wine, watching flames lick the logs, warmth and alcohol making me drowsy.

The rap on the window brings me to with a start, spilling a trickle of wine over my shirt.

'Oh, it's you.'

Ed is peering in.

'I only just heard.' He hovers uneasily on the doorstep when I open the door. 'About your grandmother, I mean. I've been at the airfield all day. Martin rang and said you'd be here. Can I come in?'

I nod, trying to be cool. Truth is, although we parted on less than friendly terms yesterday, I'm unbearably happy to see him. His jeans and T-shirt are so clean they smell of fabric conditioner, as well as the familiar safe Ed-scent.

'I didn't know if you'd eaten,' he says, as he steps into the room, 'but in case you haven't I brought something with me?' The question in his voice suggests he's expecting to be thrown out any minute.

I burst into tears.

'Hey, hey,' he says, stroking my hair, a couple of minutes later. 'I don't normally have this effect on you.'

'I'm sorry,' I say into his chest. He *does* smell safe, and I'd never realized it until now. I'd always thought of him as smelling dangerous. I lift my head cautiously, tracking up the dark stubble until I find his eyes.

'You might be able to tell,' he says, 'that I've suddenly lost interest in supper.'

'Is it going to take a long time?'

'Not if you keep doing that.'

'Supper, I mean.'

'Five minutes in the microwave?'

'That's all right, then.'

Afterwards he makes me sit by the fire while he busies himself in the kitchen.

'Can't stay all evening,' he calls. 'I'm earning decent money for once, flying the R44 to Ascot late tonight. Last-minute booking for a local racehorse trainer and a couple of owners. Right now, lucky bastards are celebrating at the Fat Duck in Bray.' The ping of the microwave interrupts him. 'Of course, nothing as fine as our sumptuous repast...' In plastic containers from Waitrose.

'A triumph, I think you'll find,' he says, bustling in with two steaming plates of lasagne and sniffing the aroma. 'Eat your heart out, Heston Blumenthal.'

'I suppose there are people who would actually cook this from scratch,' I say, propping myself against the sofa and balancing the plate on my lap.

'Like Martin.' Ed pulls an incredulous face. 'I found raw meat and stuff in the fridge, actual ingredients. Though could he better this? Or am I just bloody starving?'

'It's sex,' I say. 'Always makes you hungry. Well, good sex, anyway.'

'Mmm.' He settles himself on the sofa. 'That was outrageously good sex. First time I've shagged in a stone circle, mind.'

'Don't,' I say, with a shiver. 'I mean, don't remind me I'm here by myself tonight. Can't you find someone else to fly your bloody heli-copter?'

'Can't be done,' he says. 'Not if you want me to keep cooking you Mr Waitrose's finest.'

Our eyes meet again.

'That is, if you do want me?' he asks.

He leaves an hour later. The stones are pale in the midsummer dusk, the henge banks dark against the sky, the lights of Swindon already casting a dull red glow on the underside of the clouds. Lamplight spills out onto the tiny front garden as I stand in the doorway to see him go.

'You going to be all right on your own?' he asks. 'I'd come back later, but if it's anything like the usual booking, the clients probably won't even be on the brandy and cigars when I land. Unlikely to be back until two or three in the morning.'

'You'd give me a heart-attack, hammering on the door at that time of night. I'll be fine.'

He glances at the rosy-pink sky over the village. 'Lovely night for flying. Good weather on the way.'

'D'you think?'

'Trust me, I'm a helicopter pilot. I'll give you a wave when I fly over.'

'Are you allowed to over-fly the village this time of night?'

'Of course not. I'm joking.' A few steps down the path, he comes back and gives me another kiss.

'Better hurry,' I tell him. 'Your clients won't be quaffing brandy all night.'

'Oh, God, I hope they haven't had too much. Better check the sick bags are on board.' He lets himself out through the gate onto the lane, where his Land Rover is parked next to my Peugeot.

After washing up, I mount the narrow stairs to the one and only bedroom – just big enough for a brass bedstead – and check my mobile. I'd hoped the cottage would have a landline, but there isn't one. At least I can pick up a faint and intermittent signal upstairs. Slightly puzzled there's no further message from John, though it's nearly half past nine, I send him a text to let him know I'm fine.

Outside, people are still wandering through the stone circle. A torch – or maybe a mobile – flashes between the stones at the back of the cottage. *Lights, buggerin' lights.* It's too early yet to undress and go to bed, but I switch on the bedside lamp, rest my head on the pillows and close my eyes.

I come awake again with a jerk, sweating, heart thudding, thinking I've heard something – phone? Knock on the door? The lamplight makes the bedroom windows seem shiny black, but the hands on my watch have hardly moved at all: a few minutes after ten, not yet full dark. I swing my legs off the bed, but there's no further sound from downstairs, only the creak of the floorboards as I patter across the landing.

In the living room, the fire has died to embers. The short doze has disoriented rather than refreshed me, making everything feel muffled. I switch on the lamp and pull the curtains closed, half afraid I'll see in the window Steve's flat dead stare, or even Mick's stoned pupils, but my ghosts have taken the night off and the only eyes in the glass are mine. I'm irritated with myself for feeling so uneasy alone in the cottage, and try to cheer up by thinking about Ed, thinking about me, on his lonely flight across the darkening countryside.

It doesn't work. Instead I find myself worrying he'll crash again.

I go back upstairs and check the phone. Still no reply from John. The only channel I can tune into on the television is showing a documentary about war casualties in Iraq. Martin's travelling library consists of three academic paperbacks on Neolithic monuments, and a biography of Alexander Keiller. It's the least daunting of the collection, so I brew myself a mug of decaff coffee and flip it open, looking at the pictures as much as the words. Keiller in a kilt, standing by a Bugatti racing car. Keiller driving some extraordinary vehicle with caterpillar tracks across a field. Relaxing on a deckchair, reading a newspaper under the trees, an open picnic basket beside him. Keiller grinning beside a huge pile of excavated chalk. The caption tells me this is on Windmill Hill, in the 1920s. *Lights, buggerin' lights.* Who's up on the hill now? Not Karl and Pete because they weren't nighthawks after Bronze Age treasure. They were looking for . . .

A crashed plane on Easton Down.

Keiller in his wartime police uniform, grim-mouthed, gimlet-eyed. The text recounts that even on duty he couldn't repress his archaeologist's instincts: when a German bomber ditched his load on a nearby barrow, Inspector Keiller was there like a shot, measuring the craters.

Lonely stretches of chalk hills, peppered with barrows . . .

A plane crashed on Easton Down, probably in the Second World War.

And my maybe-grandfather's memorial sits a few miles away in Yatesbury churchyard. *In Loving Memory. David Fergusson, killed 29 August 1942.*

Why Yatesbury? Why not Avebury itself? Or Swindon, or Chippenham, wherever Fran happened to be living during the war? What was the connection with Yatesbury? Could it have been—

Not far from where Davey's plane went down?

If a plane crashed on the hills nearby in wartime, who would know about it, who would be first on the scene? Who would have known Davey Fergusson, because he's mentioned in those letters?

I shove the guard in front of the barely glowing fire, grab my bag and a notebook, and turn out the lamps before heading out of the door.

CHAPTER 54

I lock the cottage door behind me with Martin's key and follow the lane towards the lights of the Red Lion. The moon's well into its last quarter, but the sky is oddly incandescent, streaks of high cirrus glimmering electric blue against indigo.

The lights in one of the thatched cottages wink out as I pass, as if the occupants are giving me the cold shoulder. What made me think I belong? The truth is that people like the Robinsons no longer have any claim to Avebury. Most people who live in the village are blow-ins looking for thatch and roses round the door. Do the incomers ever think about Keiller, and what he did to the place? As the local saying goes, they know more in the churchyard than live here now.

The church tower is black against the glowing clouds, the windows of the Manor blind and expressionless. Perhaps the tenants have fled for Solstice week. The smell of lavender floats from the garden through the warm night. My mobile shows a weak signal, but still no messages; I'm surprised John hasn't responded to my text. I send him another, for good measure, asking if there's any news. Even if the scan's been postponed, surely the police surgeon has arrived by now.

The museum, too, is in darkness, apart from the low-wattage glow of the gallery's nightlight seeping through the windows. I key in the security code at the staff entrance, to turn off the alarm, and let myself in.

There's no need to go into the gallery before heading upstairs, but I have that creepy sense, going into an unoccupied building at night, that it's wise to check every room really is empty. Of course, there is no one, unless you count Charlie sleeping in his glass coffin.

'Hi, Charlie,' I say cheerily, to dispel the shadowy silence. 'Sorry to disturb, come to do a spot of research.' Closing the door on him, I make my way up the narrow stairs.

I've never been into the loft office at night before. The overhead striplight manages to be both harsh and dim at the same time. The curator has left behind a single Anglepoise lamp, but the bulb has blown. There doesn't seem to be a spare.

The letters are in their usual place, in box files along the shelf, next to the photo albums. Further along, in another box file, are photocopies of W.E.V. Young's diaries, meticulous accounts not only of the excavations but of life in wartime Avebury. There's no guarantee Keiller went to an air crash on Easton Down: he might have been away when it took place, or some other officer could have been sent to deal with it. But at least this gives me something to take my mind off Frannie in her hospital bed.

Absorbed in an account of the icy winter of 1940, I almost miss the bleep from my mobile phone: voicemail coming in. Sometimes at night the signal is stronger. The Orange lady tells me the message was received nearly an hour ago, at 9.33 p.m.; my heart starts to sink.

'Indy,' says John's voice. 'Nothing to be alarmed about. Scan's been done, couple of hours ago, though they haven't yet said what the results are, but they don't seem worried. I'm on my way home. Frannie was fine when I left. DI Jennings called. Whatever you do, don't go back to Trusloe because the neighbours reported seeing someone suspicious hanging around this afternoon. I'm driving back that way to check, so if you *are* there, I'll pick you up. Tried the landline a couple of times so I'm fairly confident you're with Martin, but just want to be sure.' He's trying to keep it light, but I can hear the unease in his voice. 'Text me, or something, will you?'

There are still a couple of signal bars showing so I thumb out a message: **Don't worry am fine**. As an afterthought, to keep him happy, I add: **with Ed** and press send.

The phone tinkles to tell me the message is gone. Downstairs, something else tinkles, and my blood freezes.

CHAPTER 55

My first reaction, hearing the unmistakable sound of breaking glass, is: it's OK, all I have to do is keep quiet, the alarm rings through to the police station at Marlborough, they phone the main key holder, who is Michael, and he's even closer at Broad Hinton. He'll be here in five or six minutes to find out why the alarm's going off . . .

Which alarm would that be, Indy? The one you turned off about fifteen minutes ago when you came in through the staff door?

To quote Frances Robinson, *Bugger*.

I'm surprising myself with how calm you can be, alone in an attic with no one in shouting distance except whoever is moving about, quietly but not in absolute silence, downstairs. He or she – or *they* – not bothering to tiptoe, either because they think no one is here (please, God), or because they know that I am, and my only way out is down the stairs.

The phone—

No bloody signal, now, of course. I stare at the screen, willing the satellite to orbit over Wiltshire, praying for a sudden surge of power in the phone masts. The signal bars remain obstinately blank. Rising to my feet as carefully, as silently as possible, I cast around the room: piles of bound periodicals teetering on every surface, old issues of *British Archaeology*, a feather duster, J-cloths, an aerosol of furniture polish with congealed silicon dribbles oozing under its cap, a box of disposable gloves, someone's lost reading glasses . . . but no telephone. Since the attic office is no longer used except for storage, the extension has been taken away. The nearest landline will be in the staff kitchen, downstairs. Down a set of bare-board, creaky stairs.

The alternative is to stay where I am, at least until I hear furtive footsteps creaking upward. I throw one last, despairing glance at the mobile in my hand – *What do you take me for?* radiates its bland, blank face. *Technology that actually improves your life?* – then I edge cautiously round the table towards the door.

Downstairs there's a rattle, a faint screeching sound, and the tinkle of more falling glass. A muffled thud. What the hell is going on? And *do* they know I'm here? The attic office has a single window, in the end wall. If they came through the churchyard, past the Manor, they'd have seen it lit up. But if they approached the museum from the other side, and broke in through the gallery, there's a chance they've no idea there's anyone upstairs . . .

A gentle snick: the sound I've been dreading. Quietly, furtively, downstairs the door from the gallery is opening, somebody stepping through. They only have to take a couple of steps, peer up the stairwell, and they'll see the light's on. Shit, shit, shit. Anywhere to hide?

None of the attic cupboards India-sized. The only place is under the table.

A stair creaks.

I'm under the table so fast I don't remember how, crouched on all fours, back pressed against a strut, heart pounding, trying to control my breathing. I'd like to shuffle into a more comfortable position but there isn't time: already the door is edging open. Two sandalled feet appear, hairy toes, the hem of faded green corduroy trousers.

Then everything goes crazy. A car horn blasts from outside, an engine revs, tyres crunch on gravel. There's a shout downstairs of 'Fuck! Get out', the crash of a door bouncing off a wall, running feet, car doors slamming. The sandals swivel and disappear. I come out from under the table almost as fast as I went in, banging my head on the edge. Feet thunder ahead of me on wooden treads. I reach the landing in time to see a large white blur swooping round the bend in the staircase, grizzled dreadlocks flying. Shouts from outside, then another door crash shakes the building.

'Oh, Jesus motherfuckin' Christ,' says a deep, American voice, followed by one that's unmistakably English:

'I really don't care for blasphemy, you pagan cunt.'

I rocket down the stairs and into the staff kitchen. Michael, blessed, lovely Michael, St Michael, scourge of dragons, is barring the way, his back to me. He's cornered the American Druid who led the Ancient Dead protest at Equinox, holding him at bay with a baseball bat. Looks as if it wouldn't take much to make him use it. Graham strolls in through the other door.

'Police are on their w— Bloody hell, India.'

Michael risks a glance over his shoulder. 'Nobody else upstairs, I hope?' His tone isn't entirely friendly. 'What about the car?'

'Heading for Swindon. Didn't get the numberplate, I'm afraid – they'd smeared mud over it.'

The American smirks.

'Take a look in the gallery, would you?' says Michael. 'The other chap was carrying something in a plastic bin-liner.'

'I'll go . . .' But Michael's face makes the words dry in my mouth.

'I think we'd rather you stayed right here, India.'

'No, hold on.' My chest is so tight with panic I can hardly breathe. 'You've got it wrong – I was upstairs looking at the Keiller archive . . .'

'Hey, man,' says the American, worried I might steal some of his glorious martyrdom. 'Didn' even know she was in the fuckin' building.'

'Nevertheless, India, I'd prefer you to wait with me for the police.'

Graham, avoiding my eyes and careful not to touch me, eases past into the gallery. His feet crunch on glass. The only sound in the kitchen is the American's heavy breathing. There's a look of fierce triumph on his face.

'Well,' says Graham, returning. 'Good news or the bad?'

Michael closes his eyes, composes himself. 'In whichever order.'

'Bad news is that they've stolen a skull.'

The American's lips have parted in a fierce grin. His teeth are perfect, glaringly white, a glimpse of fat red tongue curling between long gleaming canines. 'Not stolen, my friend. Returning it to the ancestors . . .'

'The good news,' says Graham, his face utterly straight, 'is that's all they managed to grab, and it's Charlie's.'

The American's brows knit, puzzled, as Michael and Graham explode into laughter.

'So somebody's busy conducting a Druid funeral for a plaster skull?'

Michael is opening cupboards, looking for a dustpan and brush to sweep up the glass on the gallery floor. Graham's gone to look for plywood to tack over the window where the intruders climbed in. 'Yep, that's about it. Until they hear about their mistake on the news.'

Outside, the door of one of the police cars slams, and an engine starts up. As the car passes under the courtyard light, the back of the American Druid's huge dreadlocked head is bracketed in the rear window between two smaller, helmeted ones. Bet those wolfish teeth aren't on display now.

'That's how I could be sure you weren't involved,' adds Michael, producing a bin-liner from the back of the cupboard. 'Hold that, will you, while I sweep? Anyone who works here would be aware Charlie's skull is a cast. The real thing's temporarily on loan for isotope analysis.'

'Actually, I didn't know.'

'Didn't you? Good grief, maybe it was an inside job after all.' He pats me on the shoulder, to show he's joking. 'Sorry for doubting you.'

'Was my fault, though, wasn't it? If I hadn't turned off the alarm . . .'

'They'd have got clean away. Frankly, this couldn't have been a better result, apart from the mess. We caught one, and they made themselves look bloody silly. The broadsheets will love it – pity it's too late for this morning's papers.' He crouches and starts brushing the glass into a glittering heap. 'If you hadn't been upstairs, the tenants in the Manor wouldn't have phoned me ten minutes *before* the break-in when they noticed the light. I'd never have arrived in time to catch them other-wise. The rest of Charlie would've been long gone.' He scoops the glass into the dustpan and tips it into the bin-liner. 'Not that I want to encourage midnight research. But it was lucky you were here.'

Then the phone in my pocket sounds again, with a sick, stuttering trill, and all the luck runs out.

'Go,' says Michael. 'I'll finish up here with the police, and make things tidy.'

I race up the high street, dashing across the junction without a glance in either direction, breath rasping in my throat and a pain in my chest.

'Get to the hospital fast as you can, Indy,' John's message said. 'The bleeding started up again and they're taking her into theatre tonight, after all.' I tried calling back, but he must have driven to the hospital already, phone turned off as soon as he went inside. I keep thinking of her eyes, scared and pleading. *I don't want to go to hospital. People die in hospital.*

The car is parked in the lane on the verge, but my car keys are inside the cottage. The lamplight through the curtains gives the place a homey glow. The key skids on the lock's faceplate; somehow my shaking hands manage to push it into the keyhole and turn it, shoving open the door. Yellow lamplight washes out onto the path—

I turned the lamps off. I remember switching off all the lights before I left the cottage.

'Ed?'

Can't be Ed. He'd have no way of getting in because I have the door key, the *only* door key as far as I know . . .

'Martin?' He must have a spare.

Hovering uncertainly in the porch, peering over the threshold. No one in the sitting room. The Keiller biography lies open where I left it on the table, my rain jacket hung on the post at the foot of the stairs, my spare cardigan on the back of the sofa. Across the room, on top of the chest, my car keys glint under the lamp, next to my abandoned coffee mug. The fireguard is no longer in place, and flames lick the sides of a fresh log on the fire. A fat white candle is alight on a saucer, on the tiled corner of the hearth. Another candle burns on the window ledge, its flame swaying in the draught from the open door.

It *is* Martin, isn't it? What's he doing here? Is he upstairs? He's supposed to be staying with his friend in Bath.

The log shifts on the fire as a lump of coal collapses, and my heart jumps, but the house is otherwise silent. This feels wrong. But all I need are the car keys, and I can be out of here, *have* to be out of here, whether or not Martin's back, because there's no time to mess around – time's leaking away at the hospital in Swindon. There's no one in the room. Go for it.

I'm halfway to the chair when there's a blur of movement in the corner of my eye. He comes barrelling out of the kitchen and has an arm crooked round my throat before I've had a chance to turn more than my head. My handbag falls off my shoulder, while his other hand closes on the muscle at the top of my arm, forcing a squeak out of me, and the door key drops out of my fingers onto the carpet. Somehow he gets a knee into the small of my back, arching my body and pressing me against the back of the sofa so the air is forced out of my lungs. We must look, absurdly, like some sort of pornographic temple carving.

Then his voice sighs in my ear, 'Indy,' and I understand exactly who this is.

You stupid, stupid girl.

I can't believe I've been so blind. I can feel tears pricking, panic clawing at my lungs making it even harder to breathe than it already is. He has complete control, sliding me down to the floor, my T-shirt rolling up and my exposed abdomen pressed against the rough hessian carpet, the mobile phone in my pocket digging into my hip, his knee pinning me down while his arm is yanking up my chin, making my neck and shoulder muscles scream.

On thy belly thou shalt go

'Indy . . .'

I let myself go as limp as I can.

462

'That's better. Don't fight me.' The pressure on my throat eases fractionally.

'I'm . . . not . . .' He's allowing me only enough airway to force out a whisper.

'No point strugglin.' The arm eases off a fraction more. 'See? I can feel your veins easing. When you strain against me, it's like ropes of lights under your skin, your blood fizzing and sending off sparks.'

Shit. What's he taken? Mushrooms?

'How did you get in?'

'Doesn't matter.'

I can guess: I opened the window in the kitchen to let out the steam while I was washing up, must've forgotten to close it. He'll have climbed in over the sink.

And why? Well, everything goes back to that summer in Tolemac, doesn't it?

He strokes my hair. 'Sssh. No hurry. Your friend isn't comin' back for a while, is he?'

'It *was* you who broke in at Frannie's, wasn't it? How did you come to hurt her, though? Did you knock her down accidentally?' I don't want to believe it could have been anything else. The grip on my throat has eased fractionally. But even if I managed to scream, the nearest neighbour is elderly and takes her hearing aid out when she goes to bed. The loudest pagans drum with impunity behind her cottage.

'She opened the door to me.' There's a high note of surprise in his voice, which suggests it's all unravelling so fast he's amazing himself now. 'The *Hag*.'

He doesn't mean it the way ordinary people would. He means the Goddess.

'She opened the door and said: India's at work. And I was thinkin', Right, yes, I knew that, I suppose, and then she'd closed the door on me again. Realized she didn't like me. Put up with me, when she used to see me, only because of Meg.' The back of my hair lifts with the vibration of him shaking his head – that wonderment again. 'See, it all happens on both planes, doesn't it? The real, and the extra-real?

The Goddess wears three faces: Maiden, Mother, Crone. If you hold the Crone tight, she shifts shape, releases the Maiden again. I went round the back and broke in. She didn't scream: she called me Donald. I told her, my name's not Donald, it's . . .'

This is possibly the longest speech Bryn has ever come out with, in my hearing.

Except it isn't Bryn, is it?

'What the hell happened to you, Keir?' I ask.

CHAPTER 56

29 August 1942

Mr Keiller was in the sitting room, wearing his police uniform, standing with his back to the empty fireplace, the light from the lamps striking a marmalade sheen on his thinning, oiled brown hair, and his inspector's peaked hat laid careful on a side table like he was expecting to have to pick it up again to go out. First time it struck me how much older than me he was: older than Mam, God rest her, near as old as Dad. Tonight all those years were scratched into the skin of his face, his jowls saggy with a kind of defeat, his tense mouth reluctant to let out the words repeating what they'd told him when the call came through about the plane that had crashed on Easton Down that afternoon. Crater. Explosion. Instant. No hope.

'You know, Heartbreaker, I'm sick to death of this bloody war,' he said. 'For two pins I'd . . .' He shook his head. His oiled hair gleamed in the lamplight. 'Why is it the best ones who go, I ask you? Why is it the ones with the brains and the balls? Donald . . .' His voice cracked up. 'Poor old Donald. Such a silly bloody thing to happen.'

Not even the glory of being shot out of the sky by the enemy. And what about Mr Keiller's Brushwood Boy? Was any of that shininess in the corners of his eyes for Davey?

'Did you go to . . . where it happened?' I asked him. 'Were they . . .?'

He shook his head. 'Would have been an irony, wouldn't it? No, a couple of constables from Devizes did the necessary. I'll go up first thing tomorrow.'

'Can I come with you?' Knew immediate he was going to say no.

'I don't think that would be advisable, do you, Mrs S-T? Frances looks like she needs helping to bed, and a good long lie-in tomorrow.'

Maybe I did look bad, hunched like an old woman next to a glowing two-bar electric fire Mr Young had brought from upstairs. I was wrapped in a blanket, hugging a hot-water bottle, one of Mrs S-T's dresses hanging off my shoulders because my clothes had been soaked through, my teeth still chattering.

Mr Keiller picked up his brandy glass, swirled it, stared into it like it could tell him the future. Must've seen rain-drenched grass, mud, sheep, gurt grey stones leaning every which way like crooked teeth. 'It's all over, isn't it?' he said, more to himself than to us. 'Someone else'll have to finish here now. I haven't the heart.'

I didn't need him to describe what happened. Soon as I heard, I knew how it would have been.

They'd been called to scramble that morning. Their squadron flew night-fighters, fragile black-painted wooden Mosquitos that took two men to crew them, pilot and navigator. Donald, and Davey crammed in behind his shoulder, watching the flickering screen of the AI to guide them onto the tail of their target.

'Tired,' said Mr Keiller. 'Poor devils, they'd been out half the night, and the squadron was under strength. Abortive sortie over Weston-super-Mare, chasing a report of some Junkers 88s, coming in to do Bristol some damage. Missed 'em completely. Called back home, landed, as another set of bombers started slinking up from the south – broad daylight by now, mind, but Jerry could count on the weather giving cover that afternoon. Every other airfield within reach had their hands full with the raid on Bristol and, with the forecast so bad, inevitable Donald's squadron of night-fighters would be scrambled again. Donald needn't have gone, but he insisted.'

The little black wooden planes flying down the belly of Britain, out over the Channel towards Normandy, sunlight pinning them against blue sky at first, like night-flying moths caught in daylight. Not long before they were flying into weather, invisible among the massing black clouds. Davey in the navigator's seat, tired, scared. Donald Cromley piloting, cocky, believing he could get away with anything, determined to bag a kill. Relying on the AI, the Airborne Interceptor, what they called radar later on, that Davey had trained on special. Looking for them Nazi bastards, finding bugger all, missed 'em again. They Germans was already blowing holes in Drove Road, aiming for the Plessey factory, but instead hitting houses where little girls had been playing hopscotch on the pavement. Donald insists they keep going, looking for trade as he puts it. Pushing it as usual, flying that bit further than he should have. Out over the Channel, the boys had a skirmish with a couple of Messerschmitts – at least they think they're Messerschmitts, hard to tell in the murk until you're up close. Donald looses off a few rounds, some other bugger fires back, could have been one of them or one of us. Holes in the fuselage, doesn't feel like there's too much damage but all the same it's given them a scare and they've lost the target anyway in the murk. There's a lot of dense cloud around and it's easy playing hide and seek. Weather too bad now, anyway, where Davey and Donald was, and fuel too low to do much more than turn round and set a course for home and hope to God they made it back.

Never afraid when we take off. It's coming back

Poor Davey. Should've stayed an erk.

And you know what's the worst? When there's no contact, and we fly all over the sky looking for the buggers and they never show up. When the order comes over the radio to head for home, I think, That's torn it

Afraid, always, of the luck running out just when they thought they were safe. He sat in the car on Marlborough Common that day, telling me how scared he was of not coming back. Heart pounding, every time they flew, like it must have coming back from France that afternoon. *Listening to the note of the engine and thinking any minute God'll change his mind and we're going to fall out of the sky*

'They were nearly home,' said Mr Keiller. 'Nearly bloody made it. Sorry about the language, ladies. Bit upset.'

Davey reciting the Navigator's Prayer. *When we see the Kennet and Avon canal, I know we're nearly home* . . . If they could see the canal. They're flying through a terrible thunderstorm. Sky black as night.

Rain coming down in sheets. And Donald Cromley, watching his instruments as they fly towards the darkened escarpment of the Marlborough Downs, notices there's something amiss.

'Port engine gave up the ghost, damaged in the skirmish with the German fighters. Colerne says they managed to radio in before the radio packed up too. They were going to try to bring her in at either Alton Barnes or Yatesbury.' Mr Keiller's eyes fixed on the corner of the room, like he can't bear to look at any of us. 'Donald would have favoured Yatesbury, of course, knew it like the back of his hand.'

Thought he did, anyway, cocky bastard. But this is a day like no day he's ever flown before, a day that's not so much like flying through a night as like flying under water. Does that matter? Of course not. Behind him he's got Davey, good old Davey; Davey's an ace navigator, knows his way around Wiltshire, from the air and on the ground. Knows all the roads, all the airfields, knows every fold and wrinkle of the hills. Give us a fix, Davey. Really? Well, you're the numbers wizard. Donald, too tired to argue, believes him.

On the ground it's pitchy black too. The airfields will have to turn on their lights for the boys coming home. Alton Barnes is dark: it's a training base, no novices out flying today. Davey and Cromley are past and gone before the message reaches Alton Barnes to light up the runway.

'Not more than a couple of miles short of Yatesbury field. Simple mistake. Poor bastards weary unto death, flying practically blind, radio not responding, catch a glimpse of what they assume are runway lights.'

Easton Down. Not so fancy as the Starfish at Barbury, but one of the Q-sites Davey's chum helped to build. A fake airfield. Don't tell me Davey forgot it was there. He knew where it was all right.

Easton Down wasn't one of the sophisticated Q-sites. Weren't no Hares and Rabbits, the lighting rigs that made it look like planes were taking off or landing, running across the empty farmland. For Donald Cromley, that was the pity of it, because if he'd seen what looked like a plane taking off he'd have known at once it couldn't have been

Yatesbury, like Alton Barnes a training airfield, so nobody except him and Davey likely to be flying in or out of it that terrible afternoon. Instead Easton Down had gooseneck flares, laid out like runway lights across the bumpy ground. They'd been lit most of the afternoon, since the crew in the pillbox had been alerted there were German bombers in the air, and nobody'd given them the stand-down yet.

There she is, says Davey.

You sure? says Donald, bit of doubt in his voice. Wasn't expecting to be at Yatesbury yet, hasn't seen any of the familiar markers he used flying in and out when he was piloting those trainee wireless operators round the field. But it's a bugger of a day, Satan's own picnic out there; maybe, thinks Donald, he's missed the landmarks in the rain and the gloom.

That's her, for definite. Davey knows exactly where he is, doesn't he? Best sense of direction in the squadron, which is why Donald was so glad to have him volunteer as his navigator when George broke his leg.

And Davey does know exactly where he is.

'Meant to be a fail-safe system,' says Mr Keiller. His eyes are wet, I'd swear, in the lamplight. 'Coded signals, so RAF crews don't mistake them for the real thing. Red light on a pole, flashing the letter K in Morse, supposed to indicate they should back off, it's a dummy field. Poor devils. Such a stupid bloody mistake, but they were tired. I assume Davey must have interpreted it as "carry on". It's happened before.'

No, Davey knows exactly where he is. He's been planning this for weeks, waiting for the right opportunity. What you will shall be.

Wish I could've killed him, I said to Davey, the day of the picnic on Windmill Hill, when I told him what Mr Cromley had done. Shook Davey's world. *Can't think about what you did, Fran, without getting angry.*

Get angry with him, I said. When it came down to it, Davey would do anything for me. Would've married me, if he'd known I was going to have a baby, even though it was Donald Cromley's bastard. But he didn't know. Should've told him.

Donald fingers the old bronze dagger he stows in the pocket of his flying jacket, every mission, his compact with the forces of nature. He swings her round, begins the approach. Does he feel the slightest bit uneasy? Does he see, for a second, the contempt in his uncle's eyes through the leather mask, that afternoon in the house in Swindon when cocky young Donald couldn't get it in, and panicked, and disgraced the rite? Does he hear Mr Keiller's bellow, the night he stole Charlie's skull? Does he hear through his earphones, Davey shouting in triumph, as the fragile wooden Mosquito comes in and bellies, not on a concrete runway but on uneven farmland, the plane slewing and bucking as Donald wrenches the controls to steer away from a stand of trees that shouldn't be in the middle of an airfield? He still thinks he's going to make it, of course, until a wheel hits a sarsen jutting out of the ground and breaks off, the nose tilts, the plane cartwheels and finally ploughs into the side of a Bronze Age barrow.

For a moment, there they are, the fuselage smashing around them like black matchsticks, two young men locked together like driver and pillion passenger on a motorbike bouncing over the hillside. The fuel tank ignites, a slash of orange fire tears apart the unnatural dusk, and thunder rolls across the hills.

CHAPTER 57

'Missed you, Indy,' Keir says, after a bit.

He always could best me at wrestling, even though he was smaller than me when we were kids. And his den, his stupid den on the Downs that he wouldn't show me that summer – that would have been the Long Barrow, wouldn't it?

'You didn't know I was India?' This suddenly seems important. 'Not when I jumped your fire in Tolemac. You'd have said.'

I've been stupid, yes, not realizing Bryn was the boy I played with as a child, but why should we recognize each other? It's seventeen years since we last met: two lifetimes, for eight-year-olds. But I don't want that night in the Long Barrow to have been . . . knowing. Because, looking back, I can understand why it felt so wrong and awful at the time.

'My skin knew,' he says. 'My head didn't. I understood when I read your note. Why didn't you tell me your name before? We'd've been together sooner.'

Didn't tell you my name because *my* skin recognized something: how weird you've become. Another long silence has fallen, giving me time to turn over the full, ridiculous awfulness of it. If only I *had* told him my name, by his campfire on May Eve . . . Well, I thought I was protecting myself.

If only I could see his face . . . But all I have is a view of the carpet, and the soft northern voice, the warm, damp breath on the side of my face. I picture him gazing dreamily over my shoulder into the embers of the fire, seeing his Goddess visions and all the other bonkers stuff he's piled up in his head as his barrier against the world. And, oh, my God, did he—?

'Did you mean to hurt Frannie?' The words are choking me. 'You said the Goddess had to be *held*, didn't you?'

'The Crone shifts shape in your arms,' he says.

My stomach clenches. 'Meaning?'

'Meaning I love the Goddess.'

His voice sounds a million miles away, through the throbbing in my head. I'll kill him, I swear I will. I'll—

His arm tightens on my throat the moment I pitch myself back in an attempt to break his grip. He's as steady as a rock behind me as he whispers: 'And you, Ind.'

Another long, long silence in which that idea turns and spins in the candlelight. My breath scrapes through my constricted wind-pipe, making me more and more panicky. Eventually he slackens his grip enough to allow me a normal breath, still keeping a tight enough hold to remind me that these are carpenter's arms, strong and muscled and capable of snapping a neck as easily as a discarded length of dowel.

'I want us to be together,' he says. 'Here, in the Goddess's place. In the circle.'

'Keir . . .' Better to call him Bryn? Are there two personalities, one rational and the other not? 'Bryn, I mean . . . Was that what your foster-parents called you? You *were* fostered, weren't you?'

'Adopted, eventually. They didn't like Keir, so they called me Dean,' he says. 'Chose Bryn for myself, when I left. More Celtic, like.'

'Thing is, Bryn, we can't be together here. This cottage isn't mine. I don't live here, I live with Frannie, outside the circle.'

'I know that,' he says. 'We can still be together here, though.'

And everything goes distant and breathless again as he shows me the knife.

It's a strange old thing, dull and nibbled by time.

'Bronze Age,' he says.

'Where'd you find that?' I'm trying to push my terror down, keep talking as naturally as I can.

'Walking on Easton Down, with Cynon. He went nosing round the side of an old hump where rabbits'd been diggin'. There it was, half buried in the soil.'

He's allowed me to sit up now, though he's still behind, with an arm across my throat. He turns the dagger in the lamplight, somehow more malevolent than a modern knife would be.

'You give me the idea, Ind,' he says. 'Was you told me about Avebury bein' the place of the dead.'

I try to summon up everything John ever taught me about yoga breathing, meditation, calming the self for whatever purpose, and not one damn bit of it works. Or, rather, it won't come back to me.

'The ancestors,' I say, at least an octave up on my usual pitch. 'Not the dead in any . . . active sense.' Not sure what I mean by this, except it would be good to disabuse him of the notion that people went around committing mass suicide in the Neolithic.

'Thought a lot about the woman in the ditch,' he says.

'What woman in the ditch?' My voice is tiny.

'The one you talked about. Buried in the ring of stones.'

'That was thousands of years ago.' Not that I imagine for a second now that rational discussion will save me. This is a man who believes beings from Sirius make crop circles and the government is trying to stop us finding out about it.

'Do I scare you?' he asks abruptly, like he's reading my mind.

'No,' I say. 'Well, yes, a bit, because it hurts, and you won't let go of me.'

'No.' The pressure of his arm eases slightly, though. 'You have to win my trust back, see?'

The log on the fire has turned to glowing charcoal and collapses with a sigh. A small yellow flame leaps up and dances, as if it wants to partner the candle flame on the hearth, then flickers out.

The candle flame flickers in sympathy, bends . . .

There's a draught. The door. The front door of the cottage is still open.

If I can somehow persuade him to relax more, if I could make a dash for it . . .

'Keir,' I say into the silence. 'I'm really, really sorry about what happened to you. Must've been so *hard* . . .'

'They kept her away from me,' he says. 'My real mother. She'll have tried to fetch me back, but they wouldn't let her.' The same amorphous They, in Keir's mind, who lie about crop circles, who send sinister black helicopters to hover over them and release radiation to poison seekers after truth.

'Yes, probably.' Humour him. If I can make him let go altogether, if I say I need the bathroom, or something? I don't want to think about how the Goddess might have become twisted up in Keir's head with the mother who abandoned him, or for that matter the woman who won't let him see his son, the woman whose face was scribbled out in the photo Martin found buried in the circle, because intuition tells me Bryn was the person who left it there.

It'll only work if I catch him off guard, when he takes his arm from my throat.

'Can I look at you?' I say.

The arm relaxes, in surprise, and I lash out with every iota of energy I possess, driving an elbow into his stomach, twisting out of his grasp, pain tearing across my scalp as he makes a grab at my hair. I arc backwards and drive the top of my skull up under his jaw, hearing the click of his teeth as well as his grunt of pain. Then I'm rolling over and trying to get to my feet, feeling huge and clumsy like in a nightmare, because he's caught my foot and is dragging my leg from under me, so I lash out with the other foot and my heel connects with something hard, maybe the side of his head, sending a shock right up my leg, and pushing another grunt out of him, and I'm shouting, yelling as loud as I can, hoping someone's going to hear, someone's going to come and save me . . .

The point of the old, nibbled knife pricks the underside of my chin.

'Lie *still*,' he snarls, pushing the whole of his weight down on top of me, the way he used to when we played as eight-year-olds, so that the side of my face is squashed against the scratchy hessian carpet. He adjusts his position so he's kneeling on my back, my ribs threatening to crack under the pressure

Then there is no breath left, all I can manage are small, terrified gasps, and the knife plays with the soft skin around my jaw and the side of my neck, while my body's forced so hard into the floor that the pressure seems to turn inside out, and instead of being pushed down I'm dangling, again, floating over an immense void that opens up beneath me, feeling the suck and swirl of the dark greedy vortex . . . A bird is singing somewhere far away, and now I'm leaning right over Steve's face, his eyes huge and black and blank, the oozing blood from his wound giving off a metallic stink that makes my nostrils tingle, then the red rises to drown me as I fall into his eyes . . .

Cold on the back of my neck. My shoulders and arm are chilled too. The smell of chalky earth in my nose, crumbling soil in my mouth, a hard, knobbled surface under me.

Buried alive . . .

Everything spasms and a thin stream of acid pours out of my mouth onto the damp ground. But the unbearable pressure forcing me down has lifted. I can breathe. That's cold air, not cold earth, on my back and shoulders. My eyes open, and instead of pitch darkness, there's light, of a sort, a strange electric-blue rippling.

Somebody is moving around, not far away. I'm lying on my side, legs bent, knees drawn up, in a wide, deep depression. The ditch? No, not that deep, and this is bare soil, not grass. More than bare soil: ground so hard it feels like bedrock. Turning my head cautiously to look upwards, over the lip of the depression I can see the dark, wavy line of the henge banks, some distance off, and above them, curious ripples of light that are like ribbed sand glistening on a beach as the tide retreats. It's a sky like none I've ever seen before, beautiful but chilling because I don't understand what's causing it.

But when I shift my head a fraction of an inch further, at the corner of my eye, the rippling light is cut off abruptly by a huge shadowy bulk.

And now I understand exactly where I am.

In the stone pit.

Above me is the massive megalith the students raised last week. Keir must have taken boltcutters to the padlocks on the metal barriers Ed and Graham put up round the excavation, then carried me into the trench where the stone lay buried. He must be nearby, though I can't see him, because I can hear movement, rustling. It sounds like he's behind the stone, where something is rubbing and creaking and—

The ropes. The hawsers made of twisted honeysuckle. He's trying to saw them apart with that horrible little knife of his. Every muscle tenses, screaming at me to get out of the pit as fast as I can, but something's constricting my arms, something rough and chafing. He's already cut at least one length of rope from the stone to bind me. I try to pull my wrists apart, but the honeysuckle is extraordinarily strong. It doesn't give at all. Are my ankles bound too? No, I can move both feet independently. I stretch one leg gently, and the ball of my foot touches something hard. It's too dark in the pit to see what it could be, but my eyes are gradually acclimatizing to the lack of light. There's a glimmering greyish shape not far from my face . . .

He's laid a ring of stones around my body.

I have to get out of here *right now*, while he's the other side of the stone . . .

But it's too late, he's already moving round this side, sawing away at one of the honeysuckle strands with—

It's not the useless little Bronze Age knife. This is the real McCoy, reflecting the weird light from the rippling sky, a gleaming, wicked, sharp hunting knife about three times the size of the other.

Fuck.

The thin, dry sound of sawing seems to double in volume, the

knife hissing back and forth against the woody fibres. The light from
the sky falls on Keir's face, and now I can see the boy under the skin
of the man, the soft features under the leaner planes, the bruised
eyes that are the same, I remember now, too bloody late, as they
always were, uncertain, trying to stifle panic, a child permanently
on the verge of tears. Now that my eyes have adjusted to the darkness, the honeysuckle trusses stand out against the pale stone as a
set of crisscrossing lines. The note of the sawing becomes harsher,
the knife grating against the stone, and then snap, one of the lines
parts and whips away under the blade. I flinch, expecting to see the
megalith above me topple or at least jerk forward, but the dark bulk
remains steady.

Keir jumps down into the pit beside me, outlined against the silvery
ripples of cloud, a length of honeysuckle in his hand to bind my legs,
leaning over me so I can no longer see the reflection of the sky in
those teary eyes.

But he can see it in mine.

'You awake, Ind?'

I come up so fast he doesn't have time to react, smashing the side
of my head into his nose. Keir goes over backwards, landing with an
oof against the side of the pit in the shadow of the bound megalith,
and I'm glad, hope he's broken his fucking neck, the bastard, for what
he did to Frannie. The knife clatters against stone, somewhere at the
other end where, with luck, I won't have to worry about it. He still
has the bronze dagger on him, but I can't think about that – my
head's ringing, dizzy from the impact with his. Thunder inside my
skull is building and building until I can hardly stand it. A tiny chip
of waning moon slips over the shoulder of the stone, so like a knife
in the blue shivering sky that I instinctively raise my bound hands
to reach for it—

—and she pours out of the sky into me, all glistening power and
thunder so that every nerve in my body jolts at the same moment
and the ripples in the sky run up and down my skin in a tingle that
will never, ever end, scalp to fingertip, toe to groin, my heart

exploding, the blood fizzing along the veins because I am me but I am also the Goddess, this is real, this is what they mean by magic, this is drawing down the moon and taking the vortex and running it in swirls round the boy so he can't move, the thunder pinning him to the ground—

—because the thunder's out of my head and in the air. Felt as much as heard, the beat of wings – no, rotors. Above us is a dark, bulbous shape, two flashing lights, one red, one white. The helicopter arrives overhead so fast it seems it's risen straight up over the henge banks, out of a pit of hell located under the trees of Tolemac – but, no, that must be an illusion created by the strange things a bowl-shaped landscape does to sound.

Keir is cringing as it sweeps over us, so low I instinctively duck and he presses himself against the ground. It's a huge black insectoid beast that has erupted from nowhere, a dark creature that flies over circles in cornfields, attended by men in black and unmarked vans. But it's also Ed, only Ed, on his way home with a payload of tired and emotional racing trainers and owners. The *whump-whump-whump* is making my innards vibrate, shaking pictures from the memory crystals: Frannie on the hall floor, my mother dancing against the sunrise, the windscreen smashing and poor bloody Keir-as-he-was picking glass out of my hair, our van on fire and the smell of all my toys burning, Steve's dead eyes under the red-lipped dent in his head. The sound is destruction. It's the dinosaur bird, overhead, claws unfurled.

'Back off,' I yell, over the cacophony. There's no way Ed could see us, surely, but he seems to know we're underneath, and is holding the helicopter in a tight hover. It's not him I'm shouting at, though.

'Go *away*,' I snarl at Keir, sprawled on the ground. 'I'm not your goddess. I KILLED YOUR DAD.'

You keep your mouth shut, darlin'

I was the one who told where those boys were camping in the derelict farmhouse.

Where's the party, Ind?

Riz, who came to my bunk in the van.

Don't know

You must know. Your mum's shaggin' one of the boys running it. Where're they hidin' out, Ind?

I can't . . .

Want me to tell John what she's up to?

They're the other side of the Ridgeway. A skanky old cottage behind some trees . . .

Mum knew it must have been me. That without me the men with the sledgehammers and shotguns would never have come to Tolemac. I'm bad luck, I'm widdershins, I'm not safe to be near. I'm the destroyer, wrapped in thunder.

On thy belly thou shalt go

The huge force of the helicopter's downdraught blowing around us, somewhere behind the megalith, a half-sawn strand of honeysuckle parts, the stone jerks forward, heaving against its bonds, coming alive, another rope snaps, a peg lifts from the earth, the stone twists and topples and Keir starts to roll across the floor of the pit, panic in his eyes, scrabbling on hands and knees to claw himself out of its way, too late, it's coming for him, he'll never do it . . .

I reach out my bound hands for him to grab and somehow get a grip on his wrist, and heave, pull as strongly as I can, but it's not enough and I'm losing my balance and falling backwards, trying to haul us both out of the path of the stone and someone's shouting (me?) and another voice is screaming (him?) while the thunder rolls over us and the vortex has caught us, spinning, whirling—

Then a terrible ground-shaking impact throws us out into silence.

Above the dark line of the henge bank, the northern sky is still doing that strange electric-blue rippling. Something presses against my hip: the phone in my pocket. Except this is Avebury. No sodding signal, is there?

I'd give anything to see a lantern among the stones: be-antlered Trevor and his beaming wife Michelle, conducting a midsummer ritual.

I wouldn't even mind if they were sky-clad. But there's nothing, not so much as car headlights on the main road.

The sound of helicopter rotors is fading in the distance, almost indistinguishable now from the wind in the trees. Under my hands, a finger trembles.

'Ind?' A croak, so low I can hardly hear it. 'Hurts.'

He's lying full length, in the shadow of the stone, which has toppled halfway into the pit. Too dark to see how much of him is under it.

'Can you move at all?'

His shoulders heave. His other hand is digging into my leg. He makes a noise somewhere between a sob and a scream.

'Fffff . . .'

I can't make out what he's saying.

'Fffffoot . . . caught.'

'Only your foot?'

'Hard to tell. Whole leg's on fire.' His eyes plead. 'Don't leave me.'

'Keir, I have to go for help, OK? I have to leave you. Sorry, can you let go my leg?'

His fingers slacken and I ease upright, wincing at the sharpness of the ground underfoot. For whatever reason, Keir must have removed my shoes before he carried me out of the cottage. I shuffle backwards, looking for the hunting knife. It's landed against one of the small sarsens Keir had arranged in an oval ring round me. I manage to wedge it, blade uppermost, between two of the stones, so I can saw the honeysuckle cord against it. There is one way I could make use of the phone . . . As soon as the strands part, I shake it out of my pocket and flip it open to shed some light, crawling over to Keir and running it along the length of his body. Thank Goddess, only the foot is caught under a corner of the stone, but I catch a glimpse of something jagged and white, and a dark stain is spreading up the leg of his jeans. I shut down the screen quickly, feeling sick.

'I'm going now, right? Back as soon as I can.'

480

No reply. Perhaps he's lost consciousness.

My toe stubs against one of the small sarsens, sending jolts of pain up my jangled nerves. A small, wicked voice tells me I could lift it and smash it down on his head . . . or the knife, the sharp, gleaming . . .

But rage has faded. Whatever possessed me has gone. Someone else will have to deal with the confused, damaged child under the stone.

I heave myself out of the stone pit, and set out across the damp grass, barefoot. Immediately the soles of my feet start to burn: a patch of nettles. I start to jog on rubbery legs towards the back of the houses, which seem an extraordinarily long way off.

'Indy? That you?'

I swing round, then realize the voice is coming from ahead. A shadowy, long-legged figure is clambering over the fence from Green Street, close to Martin's cottage.

'Ed!' I shout. 'Over here!' My knees seem to be folding under me, and I'm shaking so much the stars are juddering.

A light snaps on in one of the houses that back onto the circle, a sash window rattles. Someone yells, 'For Christ's sake, what the hell is going on?' A rich, well-educated voice, like Michael's only much fruitier. 'We've had virtually a whole fucking week of this shit – go back to the campsite so some of us can sleep or I'll call the police.'

But Ed's already reached me, his arm coming under mine to support me.

'How did you get here so *fast*?' I ask.

Everything happening in moments now, pictures in crystal. I must be feverish, because the sky is still pulsing with that strange light.

'Is that real?' I ask Ed, leaning heavily on him as he swings open the gate to the lane.

'Don't see it often. Noctilucent cloud. Summer phenomenon, to do

481

with the sun's rays below the horizon illuminating ice crystals in high cirrus. Even more amazing from the air – rippling right across the northern horizon while I was flying home. Magic.'

It all washes over me. I start gabbling about Bryn, under the stone, losing blood.

Get to the hospital as fast as you can, Indy

'Go,' says Ed, in Martin's cottage, the phone at his ear. 'If you're sure you're OK to drive? The police can come and find you at the hospital. I'll deal with the ambulance – when I raise a signal.'

'Upstairs is better.' Still shaking, I pull his fleece on over my cardigan. 'Could you see us? When you flew over? Where did you land the helicopter?'

'At Yatesbury, of course.' Ed stops halfway up the stairs. 'Why do you keep going on about the helicopter?'

'I must have blacked out, then.'

He shakes his head, punching 999 into the phone again. 'Just go – thank Christ. Ambulance, please, and police – might be an idea to send a fire crew as well . . .'

The car keys are still on the top of the chest, next to my handbag. I snatch them up and run out of the cottage.

Don't let me be too late.

Driving out of the stone circle, my gut tells me I already am. Bad luck, Indy, widdershins. Maybe it happened hours ago. The moonless countryside is alive with light when it shouldn't be. The pale lichens on the huge diamond-shaped Swindon Stone are glimmering under the weird electric-blue ripples of cloud. Feel like I'm driving along one of John's spirit paths, hearing the blackbird's song again, afraid of what my skin is telling me now, wondering if I would recognize the gleam of her spirit as it passed me in the night on its way home.

Everything so huge and complicated, it won't go into words.

At the hospital, the car park is deserted apart from John's pickup. Almost drowned in the glare of light from the glass doors, a small red cinder glows: the tip of a roll-up cigarette.

'Sorry, Indy,' says John. He catches sight of my face, as I slow from a breathless run. 'No, don't panic.' He stands up, drops his rollie and wraps me in a hug. 'It's OK. I meant sorry for calling you back unnecessarily. She's *fine*. They stopped the bleeding: it was a fibroid, a big one, but not cancerous. She came through the op and she's going to be all right.'

PART EIGHT

Sunwise

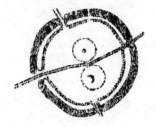

'Life can only be understood backwards. But it must be lived forwards.'

Søren Kierkegaard

CHAPTER 58

Lammas, 2006

'I don't want to do it,' I said. 'Harry would do it better.'

'Harry has bronchitis. I could hire another cameraman, but you've worked on this shoot the whole way through and you know what it's about and you know my style. So . . .'

'Are you going to be there?'

'Not in the helicopter, no. I'm going to be on the ground, filming with the other camera. It'll be you and Ed on your own in the air. I'll *pay* you . . .'

I move the phone away from my head so she won't hear, and take a long swallow of red wine. It tastes vile. They're raising the stone again early next week, pouring concrete round the base this time. No more accidents. No more walking ancestors. The weather forecast's good, and Ibby wants aerial shots.

'So, will you do it?'

'Sorry, Ibby. I don't feel up to it.'

A sigh: Ibby calculating whether it was worth trying to push it any further. She decided not. 'Fine, India. I understand.'

A lot of people having to do a lot of understanding at the moment.

There are not many idle moments in the café now the holiday season has started. When Ed comes in, the queue stretches almost to the door, and Corey and I are red in the face and sharp with one another. He waves and backs out.

Half an hour later things have calmed down, and when Ed reappears, Corey says, 'Take your break now, while it's quiet.'

I pick up a couple of bottles of elderflower pressé and join him at one of the wooden tables outside. The day is sticky hot, under a sun like an over-boiled egg. The duckpond is shrunken, the purple flags flagging, a marshy stink coming off a layer of green scum over the surface. Waitress genes make me pile the dirty crockery onto a tray and take it back to the kitchen before I sit down.

'So what couldn't wait?' I ask, unscrewing the bottle top, and taking a mouthful.

'Ibby said you won't do the aerial filming.'

'No.'

'Care to change your mind?'

'Not really.'

He sighs. People are doing a lot of sighing over me lately. 'You're depressed.'

'That's your expert opinion, is it? Or are you about to suggest I see a psychotherapist?'

'I value my tender parts too much.' Ed smiles hopefully. I glare back. 'And it wasn't an opinion, it was more a question.'

'Well, maybe I am,' I concede. 'Everything is so unresolved.'

A corrosive silence falls.

Drinking my elderflower, moodily staring at the thick green stew of the duckpond, I take a tally of unfinished business. Item one, Bryn, in hospital, outrageously lucky not to have lost his foot – Ed said the paramedics discussed amputating it on the spot, but they managed to lever up the stone and slide him out, though the mashed bones will leave him limping for the rest of his life. He's charged with attempted murder – not mine, as it happens, I only rate an assault charge, but for an attack on Fergus's mother that left her with three broken ribs, a cracked pelvis and a fractured skull. Item two, the inquest on last year's crash – opened day before yesterday, adjourned for another fortnight. Item three, my relationship with Ed – where the hell's that going? He and his wife may have separated, but he's still married to her, and still in his smelly caravan. Item four, my non-existent career – nothing on the horizon, unless I look for a course in Advanced Cappuccino-frothing. Added to all of that, I don't understand what happened in the stone circle: Ed's theory being that adrenalin can do weird things to your head, and John's being something along the lines of advanced chaos magic.

And, finally, Frannie. Out of hospital, but in a convalescent home, for the time being. Unexpectedly loving it, revelling in the attention.

'So?' Ed delicately interrupts my self-absorption.

'So . . . maybe I'm entitled to feel . . . like I'm in a murky, overgrown duckpond. Waterlogged. Weedy. Earthbound.'

'Duckpond, in fact, half empty,' suggests Ed, helpfully.

'Not a duck in sight.'

'Fuck it, you're not *depressed*,' he says. 'You're shit scared of being in that helicopter again.'

So, my legs *are* dangling. My non-existent testicles are dangling. My bum, perched on the edge of the open helicopter door, has gone entirely numb. Below me is a good six or seven hundred feet of nothing. Below that is hard Wiltshire chalk, with a skimpy dressing of barley. The helicopter's shadow races across it, a tiny black insect dwarfed by the bigger shadows of the clouds.

'OK?' says Ed's voice in the headphones.

'OK.' I don't mean it. I'm not OK at all. But there is a dim chance that if I say it, I might start to believe it. This time, thank God and Ibby's budgeting, I'm in the hire company's strongest harness, the camera attached to its most solid mount, my feet on its broadest footrest.

'I could have done this on my own, you know,' says Ed. 'Fixed a remote controlled mini-DVC to the outside, flown the chopper and taken the pictures myself. You're redundant, really, Robinson.'

'And they'd be crap pictures.'

He turns his head and gives me a grin. 'What makes you so sure yours will be any better?'

'Please keep your eyes on the instrument panel.'

'You're enjoying this really.'

'I am not.'

'And you look delicious trussed up in that bondage rig.'

The straps tighten across my body as we bank over the Kennet and Avon canal and turn back northwards, the helicopter's snub nose lifting to take us over the Downs.

'Know what that is down there?' says Ed. 'Easton Down. D'you suppose the nighthawks ever found their crash site?'

'I hope not.'

In spite of my misgivings, the flight is exhilarating, on an afternoon perfect for aerial filming. The helicopter is flying over dusty August fields, Silbury wobbling in the heat haze like a greeny-gold blancmange. Ibby, wielding the other camera, will be darting round the trussed stone, the students hauling on the ropes, timing it for the helicopter to arrive as they lever it finally upright. The invited audience of local dignitaries includes Druids, Wiccans, and anyone connected with the village in the thirties.

'Want me to take her down lower when we fly along the Avenue?' says Ed in my headphones. 'For a better shot?'

'No,' I say. I don't feel ready for that yet. 'I like this helicopter better, you know.'

'Better?'

'It's dinkier. And a lot less sinister-looking than that big black bugger you flew the racing people home in – what did you call it? The R44?'

'This is the R44.'

'But it's not black.'

'Never been black.'

'It looked black, that night.'

Ed banks the helicopter into a turn across the main road. 'Why do I have the feeling this conversation is at cross purposes?' he says. 'Far as I know, you'd never set eyes on the R44 until I strapped you into it half an hour ago.'

'You flew over the circle that night. Really low. With the racing people.'

There's a long, puzzled silence. The tall stones of the Avenue flick past below.

'I didn't,' says Ed, eventually.

'Well, it looked low to me.'

'I mean I didn't take her over the circle. I've told you. Avebury is a PAZ – Permanent Avoidance Zone – unless you clear over-flying it for a special project like the filming today. That was a joke, about flying over the cottage. I wouldn't have risked being caught buzzing the circle late at night with the inquest coming up.'

'Somebody flew over. I . . . heard it. Saw it. The downdraught was what dislodged the stone . . .' My voice trails off into the hiss and crackle of Ed's scepticism over the headphones.

'Is this why you kept asking where I'd landed that night?' Ed banks the helicopter across the A4. 'I'm not going to say you dreamed a helicopter, Indy, but it doesn't sound likely, so late. *Might* have been the military, I suppose, on a night-flying exercise. But definitely, most definitely, not me. Now – I *am* going in low when we clear the brow of the hill. You OK with that? It'll give you much better pictures.'

Before I have time to react, the helicopter is swooping down towards the southern rim of the circle. Ed banks the craft in a slow turn westwards, over the stones Keiller re-erected in 1938, then north towards the high street and the church tower poking through the trees. Avebury is laid out beneath us: museum, dovecote, duckpond, café, another arc of reconstructed stones, then we're turning again, over the Swindon Stone and into the bare north-eastern quadrant, dotted with grubby sheep. We cross Green Street almost at treetop level. Going sunwise. Round, and round again.

Without having to think, I'm adjusting the focus, though we're still too high on the second pass to make out individuals in the crowd gathered around the stone, but I know she's there. She didn't need much persuasion, after all. We come round again, sunwise, lower, and I can pick her out this time, standing a little apart from the rest with John and Martin flanking her.

'Your grandmother's waving,' says Ed.

Completely wrecking the shot, of course. Ibby, with a camera on her shoulder, is making her way across to tell her off about it, gently, since this is her first outing from the convalescent home. Frannie's dressed in her best, the raspberry hat topping a white blouse and custard yellow skirt. From above she looks like a sherry trifle.

The note of the rotors changes, and I can feel myself tightening up in panic, but when I whip round to see what's happening at the controls, Ed's leaning back, relaxed, his hand light on the stick, feet easy on the pedals. We come round the circle again, the camera catching a flare from the late-afternoon sun over the beech trees. The archaeology students are putting tension on the ropes that truss the stone – modern technology's toughest, this time, no more honeysuckle – heaving it upright. I feel something tighten, then release in me. Frannie, bless her, waves again. Weather on Planet Fran occasionally misty, but sun breaking through. She hasn't once talked about the attack, and I'm inclined to think she genuinely doesn't remember: that, and the complicating factor of the operation, being the reason she doesn't figure in the charges against Bryn. The helicopter is turning west again, a slow, circular unwinding, round and round until everything is done. Or undone.

It will be all right, won't it? The inquest, my non-existent career, my stuttering relationship . . . I turn off the camera, and look back, and Frannie's still waving.

In the end, it'll be all right. People find ways through. Or round. Or something. So long as they keep going sunwise.

Ed lands the helicopter on the cricket pitch, which won't please Outraged of Avebury. He lets the rotors settle, then climbs out to undo my harness.

'Not so bad, was it?' he says. 'Or am I going to have to make you pay a valeting charge?'

'Piece of piss,' I say.

'Yep, that's what I was afraid of.'

Martin's approaching over the grass. Ed releases the final strap, and I slide under the camera mount and onto *terra firma*.

'So, did my grandmother agree to be interviewed?'

Martin shakes his head. 'Not even after an afternoon of my boyish charm.'

'I think she might be immune to boyish charm. Though she has taken, unaccountably, to Ed.' Under the trees at the edge of the field, a billow of yellow catches my eye. 'She's here?'

'Sitting on the bench. She's hoping for a helicopter ride, I think. Wanted me to escort her along the path to watch you land.'

Ed laughs. 'Your gran's outrageous.' He unclips the camera from the mount and hands it to me, glancing at his watch. 'Tell her sorry, not today, I promised to have the chopper back by five. I'll fix a trip next week, if she feels up to it. See you in the pub in an hour?'

Martin and I walk across the grass. He starts to say something as we reach the trees, but the noise of the rotors drowns it, the down-draught lashing the heavy green foliage above the bench where Frannie's sitting.

'What did you say?' I have to yell to make myself heard.

'Your grandmother keeps asking me about the badger sett on Windmill Hill. Said she saw me on the telly talking about it.'

'What have you told her?'

'That we have to apply for a licence to dig, not to mention funding, and it's unlikely we'd have either in place until next year or the year after, at the very earliest.'

'I don't know why she's so het up about it.'

'Het up? She seemed curious, that was all. Said something about preferring me to dig there than that devil, by which I assume she means Keiller.'

I glance towards the bench. Frannie waves, a custard yellow blur under the tossing leaves.

'I have to rejoin the crew,' says Martin. 'I'll leave the pair of you to it.'

He disappears through the gate, and I sit down next to Frannie on the bench, as the helicopter rises above the cricket pitch.

She grins at me, the old Frannie peeping through the mask of wrin-kles. We sit for a while, not saying anything, watching the helicopter grow smaller and smaller in the sky as it banks away towards Yatesbury. Then she turns to me as the noise of the rotors finally fades to nothing.

'Met Davey on this field. 1937. I were just turned fifteen.'

'He wasn't my grandfather, was he?' I say.

She shakes her head. There's a long silence. Finally she says, 'Might be time for me to tell you about him.'

CHAPTER 59

January 1945

Life rolls on, dun't it? Either you get on with it or you fall to bits, and I could hear our mam in heaven, whispering to stiffen the spine, Frances. There was bad things happening every day in the war; didn't seem right to dwell on what had happened or what might have been.

In the last winter of the war, a cottage came free and I moved back to Avebury for a while, with Dad. There was no more digging in the circle, no more stones put up. Come the beginning of 1943, Mr Keiller had sold all the land he owned at Avebury to the National Trust, 950 acres, bar the Manor, twelve thousand pounds for the lot. Wasn't much of a return for all the money he'd spent digging. He claimed he'd been planning it since the war started, but something had knocked the heart out of him. Maybe it was financial worries, maybe it was Mrs Keiller carrying on in London, but I thought I knew better. He went on living in the Manor, and the Scottish soldiers and airmen from the con-valescent home still came for tea. The tall Glasgow boy with the tin foot had been given a desk job at Lyneham, and he appeared at the Manor whenever he could, waiting to be allowed back to operations with his squadron up north.

Hadn't been in Avebury a month before I knew coming back had been a bad idea. Getting off the bus at night, by the Red Lion in the blackout, I'd hear the fizz of a match under the trees. No matter how fast I turned, I was always too late to see more than a dying gleam of flame out of the corner of my eye. Sometimes, when I walked alone across the high Downs, I'd hear a splash in a puddle behind me, or a stone rolling along the track like somebody'd kicked it.

See, they never come back, but I think they try sometimes. They in't no more than a set of dreams and yearnings, lifted like ash on the wind, but they follow us, the best they can, hoping someone'll leave a door open for them to slip through, so one day they can come home.

New Year's Eve, I went to a dance at Lyneham with the boy who had the tin foot. He was a lovely lad, minded me of Davey in some ways. He got himself drunk, and in the car park outside the mess he told me how much he missed his girl. As 1945 came in, I held his head and stroked his thick dark hair, then gave him a regretful kiss and told him she was lucky to have someone care for her that much. He was posted north the next week, and I never saw him again, never knew whether he went back to his sweetheart, whether he survived the last months of the war or not.

Next day I walked over to Yatesbury to leave flowers by Davey's headstone. The church door was open. It was a still, icy day, so cold that, kneeling in the front pew, there was mist in the air between me and the altar. I wanted to ask God to help those boys lie quiet, but all I could think of was the emptiness in there, and the chill of the stone floor striking up into my knees. Coming out again, I caught a flicker of movement over by the box tomb. Knew then for definite I'd have to leave, maybe for a few years, maybe for a lifetime, hoping that by the time I came back what was left of them would finally have blown away like fog on the wind.

Hardly more than a couple of weeks after that, the Manor barn caught fire in the night. By morning the stink of burned thatch and charred wood had crept through the whole village, hanging on the frosty air. It was the place Mr Keiller had garaged his cars, where Davey used to polish them to a brilliant gloss, and cover them with tarpaulins to stop the bat droppings spoiling the paintwork.

I left Dad listening to the wireless, where Alvar Liddell was talking about the brave Russians fighting their way inch by inch into Warsaw, and went to see what was left of the barn before I caught the bus to work.

Parts of the building were still smouldering. There were pools of water between the blackened timbers, where they'd tried to put the fire out, but it had sunk its teeth well into the thatch and there wasn't a hope of saving much. Lucky it hadn't spread to the other barns.

'Thank God no one was hurt.'

I hadn't noticed Mr Keiller come up behind me. He looked exhausted, and his hands trembled as he lit himself a cigarette. He offered me one from his battered old cigarette tin, but I shook my head.

'I'm terrible sorry about the cars,' I said. The Mercedes was a blistered shell, pinned under a roof beam.

'Hang the cars.' He took a deep pull on his cigarette, but it made him cough; the stink of the fire scratched the back of your throat. 'Though I do mind about the Caterpillar.' He pointed to a piece of twisted metal. Couldn't hardly recognize it as a section of track. 'Remember the day we picnicked at the Long Barrow? Good times, eh, Heartbreaker?' When I said nothing, he put an arm round my shoulder and tugged me to him, like he wanted to squeeze a yes out of me.

'We were storing cases of finds in there as well,' he went on. 'All damaged beyond recovery, I imagine. Ironic, isn't it? The earth protected them for several thousand years, and we can't keep them safe for more than a decade or so. It's the Barber Surgeon all over again. Maybe we should've let them be.'

'Might not be as bad as you think,' I said, and patted his arm, like I did with Dad when he started coming over upset remembering Mam. Or, worse, when he forgot she was dead, and began walking up the street searching for her and the old guesthouse. 'At least the museum wasn't touched, nor the boxes stored in the dovecote. Anyway, the flints won't have burned.'

'Yes, but the labels will have gone up in smoke. A piece of flint can't tell you much without a record of where it was found.' He coughed again. 'Damn American tobacco. Damn war. None of us has had much luck since it began.'

Mr Young came round the side of the unharmed barn across the yard, followed by a couple of the land girls from Mr Peak-Garland's farm, carrying rakes. He was curator of the museum now, working for the National Trust.

'You'd have married the Brushwood Boy, wouldn't you?' said Mr Keiller, suddenly. 'You had your ups and downs, I know, but it would've worked out in the end, don't you think?' There was summat wistful in his voice, and I wondered if it was for those far-away days when he and Davey rode the motorbike over Windmill Hill.

Barns burn, but hope's like flint. Might not be able to say exact where you found it, but it comes through the fire. He was right, I should've married Davey, but wasn't Davey I was in love with.

Mr Keiller put his hands on my shoulders, and I felt his breath on the top of my head, lifting my hair. There's moments, only moments, that you live for, and know they'll never last, maybe never come again.

And what am I thinking that moment? See, I know that even if I were to stay in Avebury, he won't be with me for ever. Like Mr Cromley said, I'm only a tobacconist's daughter, too young for Alec, ill-educated, with no more than a splash of young-girl prettiness to catch his eye, a little bit of talent with my drawing and that fading through lack of practice. One day, sooner or later, could be next year, could be next month, Mrs Keiller will be back, or there'll be some other woman, a writer or another archaeologist, maybe a sportswoman, athletic, cleverer than me, richer than me, older than me, more beautiful, out of the same social drawer as him, a woman who's meant to be with him: and he'll be with her.

But in the meantime, you can't help who you fall in love with. And who knows, maybe Mr Cromley was right after all, and what you will shall be?

We watched Mr Young and the land girls picking their way through the embers of the ruined barn, looking for what could be saved.

AUTHOR'S NOTE

There are some alternative realities in this novel, so this is for people who like to know what is true, and what is made up. It is also my chance to say thanks to all the people who helped bring the book to print.

Avebury has intrigued me for years. When I commuted between Bristol and London in the 1980s, it was my stopping-off point on the way home. It was always a joy to leave the motorway and drive across the sweep of the chalk downs, turning off the A4 and following the Avenue uphill to the stone circle. But it wasn't until nearly twenty years later, when I made a television programme about Alexander Keiller at Avebury, *Village in the Stones*, broadcast on BBC2, that I came across the real life story that underpins this novel.

In 1938 Avebury had been captured on amateur cine film by Percy Lawes. The television company I worked for, Available Light Productions, really did show the restored footage to villagers at the Red Lion, as Overview TV do in the parallel-universe Avebury invented in the novel. It had not occurred to me until I saw Percy Lawes's film that the stone circle is largely a reconstruction, and that, like an old time squire, Keiller knocked down part of the village to achieve his vision.

For me, the fascination of Keiller is his ambivalence. He was the last of the great amateur archaeologists, funding his own projects, but also one of the first to dig in a scientific manner, his excavations conducted with a scrupulous eye for detail that put many of his contemporaries to shame. For some, as local historian Brian Edwards puts it, he was the serpent entering Eden, destroying their community. Yet he also provided decently paid employment for local men, at a time when agricultural wages were so low that many farm workers could not afford the rents in the council houses built especially for them.

As for his sexual ambivalence, there were indeed four wives and countless mistresses, but some personal glimpses in the letters (those that weren't destroyed by his executors) suggest that he might have been attracted to men as well as women. Homo-eroticism was fashionable in the 1930s, particularly among men of Keiller's class who had been to public school, and possibly more than one of the young archaeologists whom Keiller encouraged was homosexual, though not openly so. Keiller writes of being bowled over and bewitched by a young man he met at a dinner in London – *Sing Ho! for the Brushwood Boy!* – but whether he did anything about it, the letters do not reveal.

This is a novel about what we can't know, as much as what we can. So what's indisputably true, and what isn't? I wanted my story to reflect the ambivalence of Keiller's relationship with the village, so I chose to base it around an almost biblical story of seduction. Frannie is an invented character, and so are her seducer Donald Cromley and her friend Davey Fergusson. But several of the other people who appear in the 1930s/40s strand of the story really lived, including Mrs Sorel-Taylour, Doris Chapman, W.E.V. Young and Stuart Piggott. My regret is that I have had to exclude so many others from the story, or it would have been hopelessly over-populated.

Keiller was a larger-than-life character, and I have tried to be as realistic as possible in my portrayal of him, so that the events Frannie witnesses at the excavation itself (such as the discovery of the Barber Surgeon) are described with some accuracy, though I have taken a few liberties with dates for dramatic purposes. The Barber Surgeon's skeleton was indeed believed destroyed in a bombing raid on the Royal College of Surgeons but, amazingly, was rediscovered in a storeroom at the Natural History Museum nearly sixty years later. A ceremony led by Keiller brandishing a chalk phallus did take place in the Manor garden, witnessed by Mrs Sorel-Taylour – though at Hallowe'en, not Imbolc.

The question of Charlie is more delicate. Keiller removed his (or her) actual skull, and replaced it with a cast, which remained with the skeleton until only a few years ago. But what you see in the museum today is the genuine article: head and torso have been reunited. There is a serious debate about how we should treat human remains uncovered by archaeology: should they be reburied, or kept (on display or on storeroom shelves) as a research resource? I wouldn't presume to have an answer, except to observe that when Keiller dug up Charlie in the 1920s, not even the technique of radiocarbon dating had been invented to release the secrets of organic material. Today ever more sophisticated analysis helps us to understand not only when and perhaps how someone died, but also how and where they lived. Charlie may still have something new to tell us.

Keiller didn't have any direct descendants that we know of. He was a charming, exasperating, obsessive man, both generous and ruthless, who could fly into a rage over almost nothing. He must have been very difficult to live with, and poor Doris Chapman had a hard time. Their marriage limped on, though both she and Keiller had had affairs, until 1947, when she learnt that he had run off to the South of France with Mrs Gabrielle Styles, a professional golfer and heiress. Gabrielle was eventually to become the fourth Mrs Keiller, and stayed with him until he died in 1955 of lung cancer, aged sixty-five. She donated his collection of cow-creamers – there is some dispute, by the way, over whether they numbered 666 or 667 – to a museum in the Potteries.

He certainly had an appetite for sexual experimentation – it was the novelist Antonia White who received the unusual invitation to clamber into a wicker basket. (She dubbed him the Marmalade King in her diaries.) There is also a story, revealed to Keiller's biographer by the son of one of the other participants, that in the 1930s he was one of a group of men who met to engage in ritualized sex with a lady in a South London flat. It is tantalizing to wonder who else was there, and whether the evening's entertainment was merely erotic or intended to have some magical purpose, sandwiched between the activities of Aleister Crowley earlier in the century, and the invention of modern witchcraft by Gerald Gardner a few years later.

The last air raid on Swindon took place on the afternoon of 29 August 1942, as described in the book, under cover of a dramatic thunderstorm. Houses in Drove Road were destroyed, and a number of people killed. However, there was no crash on Easton Down that afternoon (as far as I know), although there was a Q-site there. British planes were occasionally fooled by the lights of Q-sites, with tragic results. The Starfish sites at Barbury Castle and Liddington existed, and there are bomb craters in both hillforts.

In the present-day story, I have taken considerable liberties with the National Trust's organization at Avebury. The job of property administrator, as described in the novel, is not one that exists – the entirely fictional Michael is doing the work of several people. He and Graham are not based on any of those who manage Avebury in the real world, nor will you find Corey working in the café; though you may spot the curator peering at small fragments of Neolithic pot.

Keiller re-erected just over half the stone circle, but most of the ground within the henge remains unexcavated. Every so often there are rumours that someone is planning to put up another stone, but so far it has not happened. But the night of the 22 June 2006 was one of the rare occasions when noctilucent cloud was visible in Wiltshire. Tolemac has recently been cut down and replanted, so looks very different from the woodland described in the novel, and the Goddess, in the form of the tinsel-wigged shop dummy, had sadly been removed from the Swallowhead springs last time I looked. Nothing ever stays quite the same at Avebury. As for the erratic way in which mobile phones pick up a signal in and around the circle, go and see for yourself. It's a godsend for a novelist, but a mild irritation if you happen to be staying there.

So many people gave me help with the book that I am bound to forget some, and a few asked me not to mention their names. Thank you to all, and forgive me if I have misunderstood, or over-embellished, anything we discussed: responsibility for any inaccuracies or mistakes lies firmly at my door. Much of the background for this book came out of the research I had already done on the Avebury TV programme, with the help of Nigel Clark. We interviewed people who grew up in Avebury during the 1930s, including Josie Ovens, the Rawlins brothers (whose father ran the local garage and provided electric power to the village), Heather Peak-Garland, and her sister the late Jane Lees. But I would most particularly like to thank Ros Cleal, the curator of the Alexander Keiller Museum, and her colleagues at the National Trust in Avebury. They put up with my many visits to the Keiller Archive there, and generously shared their experiences of working at the World Heritage Site, as well as their chocolate biscuits. I enjoyed many enlightening conversations on such diverse matters as the sexual dimorphism of aurochs, the law pertaining to the excavation of badger setts, and the politics of keeping human skeletons in museums. Again, everything I have right is down to them, whereas everything wrong (sometimes deliberately so) is my fault alone.

They found me volunteer work so that I could experience at first hand bumping along muddy tracks in a National Trust Land Rover with head estate warden Hilary Makins, and clearing about three hundred spent tea-lights and a muddy ground sheet from the West Kennet Long Barrow. (What *do* people get up to there?) I checked the first-aid kits, sat at the till in the Barn Museum with Chris Penney, and worked behind the counter at the café, so that I can now make a mean cappuccino. Terry the Druid Keeper of the Stones allowed me to join a ceremony to celebrate Imbolc in the Circle, at which he and Gordon Rimes gave me a glimpse of Druid and Wiccan beliefs. The following year I rose excruciatingly early to drive to Avebury for summer solstice sunrise, only to find there was nowhere within miles of the village to park, and no sun. In the strange way that life has of imitating fiction, I picked up my first Neolithic arrowhead, and saw my first hare in the wild, while walking near the village shortly *after* I had written both experiences into the novel. I stayed twice at Fishlocks Cottage, and once at Teachers Cottage, in order to soak up the atmosphere of Avebury after hours, when most of the visitors have gone home. It is truly magical to sit with a glass of wine in the garden at

Fishlocks, watching a September sunset and dodging bats on their way to cruise the ditches.

Thanks to the Alexander Keiller Museum at Avebury for permission to quote from Keiller's letters. (The only fictional quote is the letter of condolence to Frannie.) For further reading on Keiller, I'd recommend *A Zest for Life*, Lynda J. Murray's biography. For the archaeology of Avebury and Neolithic/Bronze Age monuments, Josh Pollard's *Avebury* was immensely useful, as well as Mike Pitts's *Hengeworld*, and Aubrey Burl's *Prehistoric Avebury*. Brian Edwards has written a number of papers on the social history of the village, and Marjorie Rawlins's memoir, *Butcher, Baker, Saddlemaker*, provided details of life in Avebury in the early part of the twentieth century. On pagan belief, historian Ronald Hutton is the author of many erudite books, including *The Triumph of the Moon*. I also found helpful *The Way of the Shaman* by Michael Harner, and *Pagan Paths* by Pete Jennings. Andy Worthington's *Stonehenge: Celebration and Subversion* is a fascinating account of the background to the free festivals of the 1970s and 1980s. I did have a few moments myself in the seventies, but for what it was like to be there in the eighties, Bee Davies was very helpful. The autobiographies of two Second World War night-fighter navigators, Lewis Brandon and Jimmy Rawnsley, provided background for Davey's experiences in the RAF.

My father, Robert Mills, was an RAF navigator, and during the war drove a Baby Austin with a sheet of steel welded to the roof. My mother, Sheila Mills, spent the war years working in the almoner's office of a large hospital, and, during our last conversations, she provided many details of daily life in the 1930s and 1940s. This book was written during a dark and unhappy period for me, as it was conceived at the time of her long illness and eventual death. I miss her immensely, but hear echoes of her voice sometimes in Frannie's, different as their backgrounds and experiences were.

At HarperCollins, Clare Smith and Essie Cousins were patient and inspiring editors. Thanks also to Hazel Orme, whose sharp eye for misplaced commas and anachronisms saved me from several gaffes.

My agent, Judith Murray, made helpful suggestions and kept me going when things seemed bleak. As usual, thanks to friends for bearing with me, and especially to my brother Peter, and his wife, Lynne, for their love and support. Thanks also to my nephew Rob, for his interesting suggestion that I should call the book 'Dead Man Lying in the Stone Circle'. Honestly, Rob, it would have pushed most of the buttons if only it fitted on the cover.

Bristol and Avebury, Autumn 2008

'The true method of knowledge is experiment.'

WILLIAM BLAKE

THE BUSINESS OF CREATION
....

A Word from the Author

PROGRESSION
THROUGH CONTRARIES
....

Things to Think About

IMAGINATION IS THE REAL WORLD
....

Reviews for *Crow Stone*

TRAVELLING TO HEAVEN
....

What to Read Next

BEHIND THE SCENES

THE BUSINESS OF CREATION

··

'I must create a system or be enslaved by another man's; I will not reason and compare: my business is to create.' So wrote William Blake, perfectly capturing the role of the writer. And yet the precise nature of the creative process is a mysterious one. What is it that inspires authors to put pen to paper: curiosity, sympathy, passion, obsession? In her own words, Jenni Mills reveals what inspired her to write *The Buried Circle* . . .

We all like a mystery. It is the inscrutability of the stone circle that draws me back again and again to Avebury. Why was it built? What did people do there? Like Martin, I think it was a place of the dead, and that was the starting point for *The Buried Circle*. Archaeology strikes me as a fine metaphor for the way people dig the human psyche, looking for truth.

Shortly after I began writing it, my mother fell ill. For a while, her memory was affected by one of the drugs she was given, and she found it impossible to follow a narrative because by the time the story ended, she had forgotten how it began. To her immense frustration, she couldn't read a book or understand a television programme. It seemed to me she lived in both a perpetual past and a perpetual present, but the link between the two was broken. I was also aware, as she drew nearer to death, that there were things she and I had never properly discussed: for instance, before I was born, she had a stillborn child. She always dismissed the subject quickly – it happened, no point revisiting how she'd felt.

I found myself writing a novel about what we know and what we forget – sometimes wilfully. It is about the rewriting of history on both large and small scales: about falsehood and fakery, and how some things will always remain unknowable. India's chosen career is no accident. My own background was in television, an industry which specializes in the art of fakery and reconstruction in order to represent what we hope is the truth.

So at the end of the novel, there could be no simple resolution. Whose was the black helicopter? What caused the stone to fall? Was India Keiller's granddaughter? Readers can decide for themselves: not everything can be known or explained.

JENNI MILLS

PROGRESSION THROUGH CONTRARIES

'Without contraries is no progression. Attraction and repulsion, reason and energy, love and hate, are necessary to human existence.'

WILLIAM BLAKE

From Socrates to the salons of pre-Revolutionary France, the great minds of every age have debated the merits of literary offerings alongside questions of politics, social order and morality. Whether you love a book or loathe it, one of the pleasures of reading is the discussion books regularly inspire. Below are a few suggestions for topics of discussion about *The Buried Circle* . . .

▶ How would you describe this book's genre? Is it a thriller, a mystery, a love story?

▶ Jenni Mills sets *The Buried Circle* in the same place – Avebury – but in different time periods. What do you think the author has achieved by doing this? Is this an effective technique?

▶ *The Buried Circle* tells the stories of both Frannie and India. In what ways are these two women similar? In what ways are they different? Did you find either of their stories more compelling and if so, why?

▶ What is your opinion of Alexander Keiller? Do your feelings towards him change as the novel progresses? If so, when and why?

▶ In chapter one, India states that Avebury is a 'state of mind as much as a landscape'. What did you know about Avebury before reading *The Buried Circle* and, having finished the book, to what extent do you agree with this statement?

▶ The search for identity, the uncovering of secrets and the haunting nature of the past are all central to *The Buried Circle*.

In what ways are these themes and ideas tested as the plot unfolds? And, which would you argue, is the most relevant to the novel?

▶ In chapter twenty-three, John tells India, 'Way I see it, all of you in the helicopter that afternoon were in the space between worlds. One of you died in the vortex, the rest came out . . . Nobody's unchanged after an experience like that.' How true, in your view, is this assertion?

▶ How much did you know about Paganism before reading *The Buried Circle*. In what ways has this novel shaped your understanding of Pagan beliefs?

IMAGINATION IS THE REAL WORLD

'Imagination is the real and eternal world of which this vegetable universe is but a faint shadow.'

WILLIAM BLAKE

Praise for *Crow Stone*

'An addictive, high-quality psychological thriller.'

KATE MOSSE, bestselling author of LABYRINTH

'It's ingenious, well-plotted and it really holds the attention. It's a damn good read.'   SUSAN HILL, bestselling author of *The Woman In Black*

'An amazingly accomplished first novel – intricately plotted and with a terrific, engaging protagonist. Anyone who has so much as a hint of claustrophobia or fear of pot holes should read it only in daylight with the windows open.'

JENNI MURRAY

'Slickly told and gripping.'

Independent on Sunday

'This is a remarkably accomplished and well-written first novel.'

Literary Review

'A taut, archaeological thriller [which] keeps the adrenaline flowing high.'

Financial Times

'An intricately designed plot makes this an encouraging read.'

Sunday Herald

TRAVELLING TO HEAVEN

....

'The man who never in his mind and thoughts travel'd to heaven is no artist.'

WILLIAM BLAKE

If you enjoyed *The Buried Circle*, you might be interested in these other titles from Harper Press . . .

The Lace Reader by BRUNONIA BARRY

The Whitney women of Salem, Massachusetts are renowned for reading the future in the patterns of lace. But the future doesn't always bring good news – as Towner Whitney knows all too well. When she was just fifteen her gift sent her whole world crashing to pieces. She predicted – and then witnessed – something so horrific that she vowed never to read lace again, and fled her home and family for good. Salem is a place of ghosts for Towner, and she swore she would never return. Yet family is a powerful tie and fifteen years later, Towner finds herself back in Salem. Her beloved great-aunt Eva has suddenly disappeared – and when you've lived a life like Eva's, that could mean real trouble. But Salem is wreathed in sickly shadows and whispered half-memories. It's fast becoming clear that the ghosts of Towner's fractured past have not been brought fully into the light. And with them comes the threat of terrifying new disaster.

April 2009

The Book of Fires by JANE BORODALE

Brought up in rural Sussex, seventeen-year-old Agnes Trussel is carrying an unwanted child. Taking advantage of the death of her elderly neighbour, Agnes steals her savings and runs away to London. On her way she encounters the intriguing Lettice Talbot who promises to help. But Agnes soon becomes lost in the city, losing contact with Lettice. She ends up at the household of John Blacklock, laconic firework-maker, becoming his first female assistant. The months pass and it becomes increasingly difficult for Agnes to conceal her secret. She meets Cornelius Soul, seller of gunpowder, and hatches a plan which could save her from ruin. Yet why does John Blacklock so vehemently disapprove of Mr Soul? And what exactly is he keeping from her? Could the housekeeper, Mrs Blight, with her thirst for accounts of hangings, suspect her crime or condition?   *June 2009*

Brixton Beach by ROMA TEARNE

Alice Fonseka's idyllic Sri Lankan childhood is blown apart when her mother is deliberately abandoned in labour by her doctor, for racist reasons. Alice's little sister is stillborn and her father leaves Sri Lanka to find a job in England, intending to send for his family later. In the meantime, as the political situation in Sri Lanka worsens and the threat comes ever closer, Alice stays with her grandparents and her mother. When she finally escapes the country, eleven-year-old Alice knows that nothing will ever be the same again.   *June 2009*

Swap by DANIEL CLAY

Angela Kenny wants more from her life. Sure, she's got a loving husband and a sweet teenage son, but she can't help feeling that there should be more. She's tired of going to work and filling in spreadsheets, fed up with cooking the same frozen pizzas every evening, and bored of waking up every morning to do it all over again. Lucas – her husband's best friend – seems to share her dissatisfaction, and over slow summer evenings in their small, settled suburb, their friendship slowly develops into a dangerous affair. When John sees his wife in his best friend's arms, his anguish will have devastating consequences for all of them.

January 2010

Visit www.harpercollins.co.uk for more information.

Also available as an audiobook from

HarperCollinsAudioBooks

www.harpercollins.co.uk

CROW STONE

BY

Jenni Mills

Kit Parry has spent her adult years trying to escape what happened at Crow Stone quarry the long, hot summer she turned fourteen. Growing up in Bath with an absent mother and an angry, unpredictable father is something she prefers to forget, along with the friends who betrayed her. Now a highly regarded engineer, she's back to fill the dangerously unstable quarries beneath the city – with the intention of burying her past for good.

But hers is not the only mystery in the stone mines. And just how long can Kit conceal who she is – especially as she gets closer to Gary, the enigmatic site foreman, who has every reason to remember her? As the past and present begin to collide, the truth threatens to emerge with disastrous effect...

'An addictive, high-quality psychological thriller'
KATE MOSSE, author of *Labyrinth*